C000155380

PRAISE FOR THE H.O.O.K.

"It freaking SLAYED me!"

"I can't believe I loved this even more than The PAN!"

"Fantastic sequel that leaves you breathless!"

"Ultimate swoon..."

"I was on the edge of my seat! Where is my brown
paper bag?"

The H.O.O.K.

Book Two in the Pan Trilogy

JENNY HICKMAN

Midnight Tide
PUBLISHING

Published by Midnight Tide Publishing

www.midnighttidepublishing.com

Cover Design: www.milagraphicartist.com

Interior Formatting by Book Savvy Services

THE HOOK/ *Jenny Hickman. – 1st ed.*

Paperback ISBN- 978-1-953238-07-8

Hardback ISBN- 987-1-953238-19-1

eBook ISBN- 978-1-735614-12-0

For everyone who believed in The P.A.N.

PART ONE

MAY

Vivienne paced from her window overlooking Neverland's Kensington Academy to her bedroom door and back again. The phone in her hands felt heavy and cold. "Pick up. Come on. Pick. Up."

It rang and rang until a woman's monotone voice told her to leave a message.

Then there was a beep.

This was the third time today she'd tried to reach Deacon. While she liked that he wasn't one of those guys who was glued to his phone, it would've been nice if he answered every once in a while. He was better than he used to be. But that wasn't saying much.

"Hey. It's me." *Again.* "I was hoping to talk to you before my meeting with Robert." According to the scribbled note on her desk, Robert needed to speak with her in the lab ASAP. "I guess I'll just talk to you when I'm done. Call me when you can. I *really* miss you."

She pressed the red button and tossed the phone onto her bed.

Deacon had left for a Leadership meeting three days after Vivienne had escaped from HOOK. Then he had dropped the bomb that he needed to stay in London for six months.

At first she had been optimistic, thinking six months would fly by.

She had been wrong.

Vivienne opened the glass door in her apartment and flew across campus to the Hall. The air was humid and heavy; summer was on its way.

Inside the reception area, she located the hidden door in the paneling and descended into the faux-cobweb-lined basement. When she reached the tiny room at the end of the corridor, she pulled the cord on the exposed light bulb, enveloping herself in darkness. A glowing screen emerged from the wall, casting the small space in soft blue light. She bent, allowing the device to scan her eyes. When it finished, there was a cheerful beep, and the left wall disappeared.

Robert waited for her on the other side, his broad shoulders slumped.

"Hey, Robert," she said hesitantly.

The other PAN in the room looked up from their microscopes, computers, and gadgets to gawk at her. She should have been used to it. People were still shocked by her escape and, considering her parents' connection with HOOK, more than a little suspicious. Like she hadn't *really* escaped. Like she had been let go. Like she was some sort of a spy.

The idea was ridiculous.

"Sorry for askin' you down here on such a pretty day." Robert's dark brows lowered apologetically, and the wrinkle between them deepened. "I'm sure you have better things to do."

"It's fine. I didn't have any plans."

Deacon and Max were in London; Emily was on vacation with her parents; classes were on hiatus until autumn.

"Right. I suppose we should get this over with. Follow me." Robert's white lab coat billowed like a cape as he crossed to the wall of frosted windows in the microbiology sector. He scanned his hand, and the door opened with a release of whooshing air.

Four of the pentagon-shaped desks inside were occupied. Behind one was a face Vivienne hadn't seen since January.

Alex McGee stood from his rolling stool and tucked a pen into his lab coat pocket. "Vivienne from Ohio," he said with a smile that didn't reach his eyes. No doubt he had heard she and Deacon were together. "Good to see you again."

Why did things have to feel so awkward between them? They had been friends before she'd made the mistake of kissing him on New Year's. She wanted that back.

So she gave Alex a hug.

At first he was stiff, then his arms came around her, and he sighed into her hair. Whatever cologne he was wearing smelled great.

"When did you get here?" she asked against his *Star Trek* T-shirt. Last she heard, he had been in London.

"A few days ago." When Alex pulled back, he kept his gaze fixed on some microscopes.

This was more than awkwardness. Something was wrong.

"Why does everyone look so serious?" She looked between Robert and Alex, but their somber expressions gave nothing away.

Alex nodded to Robert, who went back to the exit. "Harry, Sadie, and Lucy," Alex called. "Can you give us a minute?"

Everyone filed out of the lab, leaving Vivienne and Alex alone beside blinking machines.

"Seriously, Alex. What's going on? You're freaking me out."

"Sit down, and I'll explain." Alex pushed a rolling stool toward her. He sat on another stool at a desk lined with microscopes. "We need to discuss the results of your blood tests," he said, pulling a piece of paper from an olive-green folder and handing it to her. "Do you remember this?"

It looked like the line chart he had shown her back in November when she had given blood.

"It's a hormone graph," Vivienne said, pointing to the green line. "That's never-growth hormone—the stuff that keeps us young." And when mixed with adrenaline, it gave a PAN the ability to fly.

"You must have had a very good teacher," he teased before clearing his throat and sighing. "Now, the green line indicates normal levels of nGh."

"What's the orange line?" she asked, touching the line above the green one.

"That was the highest level of nGh on record—your mother's."

She licked her dry lips, and her skin started to itch. "And the red line above it?"

"Those are your levels."

"They're really high." When Alex nodded, she asked if that was a good thing.

Alex bit his lip and shook his head, running a hand across his stubbled cheek. "Too much nGh leads to insomnia, nausea, weight loss, and forgetfulness."

"Those are just the possible side effects though, right?"

"The onset tends to be gradual," he said, taking the paper so he could look at her, "but I'm afraid they're inevitable."

Inevitable? That meant . . . "I'm going to get Alzheimer's?" Max's dad had Alzheimer's, even though he was an immortal eighteen-year-old.

"The disease that affects PAN isn't degenerative. Some of us just forget who we are."

This couldn't be happening.

Vivienne wasn't even nineteen years old. She felt perfectly fine. She had a great memory.

For now.

Did that mean she was going to forget everything? Forget every*one*?

Lyle, Emily, Max—

Deacon.

Vivienne could never forget Deacon.

He was etched into the very fabric of her being.

Oh god. Deacon. She needed to talk to Deacon.

Out. She needed to get the heck out of this place. Away from the beeping and blinking lights and bad news.

The stool bounced off the desk when she rocketed to her feet.

"Vivienne, sit back down."

She was at the door before she realized she didn't have access to this part of the lab. "Open the door, Alex."

"Not until you hear what I have to say."

"Open. The. Door."

There was a beep and the door whooshed open. Robert was on the other side, and he jumped back when he saw Vivienne. Tears streamed warm and wet down her face, blurring her vision as she hurtled for the exit.

Alex shouted her name, but she didn't stop. She didn't want to hear anything else he had to say. She didn't want to see Robert's pity.

Vivienne wanted to talk to Deacon.

He would tell her everything was fine. That there was nothing to worry about.

If the workers in the main lab hadn't been gawking before, they certainly were now. Vivienne ignored them as she waited for the main door to open. Alex called for her again, but she was already running up the basement stairs. Her shoes squeaked on the tiles as she sprinted across reception and burst out into the humid day.

The Hall's roof might have been crowded with PAN catching rays; the patio at The Glass House might have been full as well.

5

Vivienne didn't notice anything except the fire burning in her chest as she flew to the glass door outside her apartment. Her hands were shaking so badly, it took three tries to type her PIN into the keypad. When the door finally unlocked, she collapsed onto the cold living room floor.

This wasn't happening. The tests had to be wrong. She felt fine. Completely fine.

From down the hall came a familiar ringtone.

Wiping sweat from her forehead, she pushed to her feet and followed the cheerful noise to her room. Her phone was still on the bed where she had left it.

Deacon.

She needed to calm down. The last thing she wanted was for him to think something was wrong. "Oh, hello. It's nice of you to finally call me back, jerk."

A chuckle. "I miss you too."

His voice. It was meant to be a salve. Meant to make her feel better. But all she could focus on was the laughter and music blaring in the background.

"I can barely hear you." Vivienne was in the middle of a nervous breakdown, and it sounded like Deacon was at a freaking party. "Where are you?"

"Sorry." Deacon mumbled "Excuse me," to someone. A moment later, the noise quieted. "Is this better?"

His voice echoed, but at least she could hear him. "It's fine."

"I got your message. How'd the meeting go?" Why did he sound so chipper? Like he was happy being away?

Vivienne's response lodged in her throat. How the heck was she supposed to tell him the terrible news over the phone? "The meeting was fine." Everything was going to be fine. "When are you coming home?"

"Not this again," Deacon muttered. "I told you, it'll be at least a few more months."

A few more months wasn't going to cut it. She needed to

see him now. "If you can't come back, then maybe I can come there." A trip to London would help take her mind off her current crisis. She and Deacon could figure this out together.

"That would be brilliant. Have you been cleared for air travel?"

"No. But we both know HOOK isn't looking for me anymore." The Humanitarian Organization for Order and Knowledge already had her DNA.

"We can't take the chance."

Deacon refused to come home; she wasn't allowed to leave. There had to be a solution.

Maybe if she told him about her diagnosis, he would jump on the next plane to Massachusetts. But something he had said on their first date niggled at the back of her mind.

I don't see the point in investing in something that's destined to end from the beginning.

Did he still feel that way? There had to be a way to ask him without *actually* asking him. "Okay, so I have a question. It's going to sound weird, but I want you to answer it anyway."

"All right?"

"Would you ever consider marrying an outsider?"

"My girlfriend wouldn't be very impressed if I did."

Vivienne fell back onto her mattress and kicked off her shoes. "It's obviously a hypothetical question, Deacon." If he was ever going to get married, she wanted him to marry her.

"Hypothetical questions lead to very real arguments, *Vivienne*."

"Humor me."

He groaned. "All right. Fine. No. I wouldn't marry your hypothetical outsider."

"Even if she was the most beautiful woman in the world?"

"It wouldn't matter. Outsiders die. They die and leave us

7

to mourn them for eternity. My father passed away over a decade ago and my mother still isn't right. Peter lost Angela fifty years ago. *Fifty.* And he hasn't been with anyone since. Why would I want that for myself?"

Nothing had changed on his end. But everything had changed for Vivienne.

Their relationship was as good as over. When he found out—

"Do you have any more inane questions, or can you tell me why Robert wanted to meet with you?"

"I didn't end up meeting with Robert." Drawing in a deep breath, she curled onto her side, trying to keep the tears at bay. Over. This was over. "Alex wanted to tell me—"

"Wait. *Alex* is there?"

Vivienne closed her eyes against the sun streaming through the blinds. She didn't want to feel its light. She wanted to hide in darkness. "Yeah. He just got back."

"Is that why you're asking me about outsiders?"

"Alex has nothing to do with this."

"Then why did you lie to me and say you were meeting Robert?"

Deacon was the one at a party, refusing to come home. He had no right to be jealous. He had left her for a stupid meeting. "Maybe if you answered your phone every once in a while, you'd know what was happening around here."

"Come on, Vivienne. That's not fair."

"Do you really want to talk about what's *fair*? You're off having the time of your life in London, and I'm not even allowed to leave campus!"

"Don't you think I would be there if I could?"

If he had asked her that question a few weeks ago, she would have known the answer. Now she wasn't so sure. "I don't know anymore, Deacon."

Silence.

Vivienne checked her phone. They were still connected.

"What's that supposed to mean?"

What did it mean?

All she knew was that she was miserable, and had been since the day Deacon left for London. What was the point in trying to hold on? He was going to break up with her the moment he found out anyway. "It means I'm done trying to have a relationship with you over the stupid phone."

"Hold on a minute. Are you breaking up with me?"

There was a knock at the front door.

"I can't do this right now."

"Viv—"

She stabbed the red button and fought the urge to smash the phone against the wall. It rang. She declined the call. It rang again. She put it on silent and shoved it under her pillow.

On her way to the front door, Vivienne checked her reflection. There was nothing to be done about her red-rimmed eyes, but she fixed her lopsided ponytail and straightened her black tank top.

Alex was frowning at her from the hall. His eyes widened. "Why did you run away?"

"Oh, I don't know." She wiped her eyes with the back of her hands, hating the wobble in her voice. "Maybe because someone told me I was going to forget everything." And she was pretty sure she'd broken up with Deacon.

"Maybe you should have let the doctor finish so he could explain your treatment plan."

Treatment plan? Why hadn't he started off saying that? "I thought you said the memory loss was inevitable."

"It is. But you still have options." He brushed a bit of hair from her sticky cheek; his touch was gentle and warm. "Would you like to hear them, or are you going to run away again?"

"I promise not to run if you promise to give me some good news."

His lips tilted upwards. "How about I promise to tell you the truth? And to help you through this? And that, if you run, I'll run after you?"

Run after her? What was that supposed to mean?

"You may come in and redeem yourself," she said, opening the door wider. "Just ignore the mess. I wasn't expecting company."

Her cereal box was still on the counter, the empty milk carton beside it. A damp towel was draped over the back of one of the kitchen chairs, and a basket of dirty laundry sat in plain sight, a pair of pink underwear on top. She hurried over and hid them beneath her tatty Ohio sweatshirt.

Without Emily around to yell at her for being a slob, the place had become a pigsty.

Alex tucked his hands into his lab coat pockets and sank onto the couch. Vivienne sat beside him, toying with the hem of her tank top while she waited.

"We've known about this problem for a while," Alex began, his mouth a tight line. "My great-grandfather was one of the first affected. They're researching potential cures in our Scottish lab. I'm hopeful, but not holding my breath. For now, I suggest treating this the same way I'd treat an overactive thyroid."

Vivienne wiped her sweaty palms against her jean shorts. Potential cure. That sounded positive.

"I'd like to put you on a few rounds of experimental medication to try and inhibit your body's production of nGh."

That made sense. If too much nGh caused memory loss, all they needed to do was decrease her level of the hormone. "Have you tried it before?"

Alex's eyes darted to the blank TV screen. "Yes, I have."

His response was too quick. Too tight.

Vivienne sighed. "But it hasn't worked, has it?"

"It has delayed the symptoms for previous test subjects."

10

He scratched his chin and pressed himself into the cushions at his back. "The only downside is that it could affect your ability to fly."

Forget everything *and* be grounded?

This wasn't fair. She hadn't even been in Neverland for a whole year. Hadn't lived. Hadn't done any of the things she wanted to do.

What did it matter? It wasn't like she would remember any of it in the end.

"What are my other options?"

Alex grimaced and ran his hands through his caramel-colored hair. "There's really only one more." He took a deep breath and met Vivienne's eyes. "HOOK's poison."

"You think I should kill myself?" HOOK's poison would take away everything that made her a PAN—her ability to fly *and* her immortality.

"Of course not." Alex grabbed her hand and squeezed. "But if you were neutralized, your body would cease producing nGh altogether. Your memories would be safe."

Over. This was over. "But I'd get old."

Alex's blue eyes crinkled at the corners when he smiled, and his thumb traced reassuring circles on the back of her hand. "Getting older isn't such a bad thing, is it?"

Vivienne didn't know how to answer that question.

JUNE

(10 missed calls)

V ivienne knew the date by the number of missed calls
she had from Deacon. He had called every day since
their fight. So far that month, there had been ten. Ignoring
him had been torture, and she wasn't sure she could do it
any longer.

Flicking to the top of her contacts, she found Deacon's
name but couldn't bring herself to press the "call" button.

There was no point. It was better this way. Easier.

The phone clicked when she locked it.

At least Vivienne had been able to control something,
even if it was her breakup with the first guy she had ever
really cared about.

Deacon had made it clear that he didn't want a relationship with someone who wasn't immortal. And Vivienne was
destined either to end up in Scotland with the other forgetful
PAN or voluntarily neutralized.

Rain splattered her bedroom window; the droplets raced
toward the sill. According to the weather channel, the
sunshine should be back by noon. Alex had asked her to
meet for lunch, but she had already made plans to go to the
lake with Emily and Max.

It wasn't the first time Alex had asked her out.

Vivienne told herself she wasn't ready to date, but the truth was that she was still clinging to Deacon. Hoping that he wouldn't care about her diagnosis. Praying that he'd rush home and everything would be okay.

But she hadn't really given him the chance to redeem himself or to prove that he cared for her even if her memory —or her immortality—was gone.

Maybe it was time.

Vivienne unlocked her phone, tapped her contacts, and found his name. The call connected before she could talk herself out of it.

"This is Gwen speaking." A girl on the other end giggled. "Dash can't come to the phone at the moment, may I take a message?"

Vivienne jabbed the red button.

Gwen?

As in Deacon's ex-whatever *Gwen?*

Why had she answered his phone?

Oh no. No no *no!*

Vivienne had been pining for Deacon like a love-sick idiot, thinking he was as miserable as she was, and he had been back with his ex the entire time!

Vivienne's phone rang.

She declined the call.

It rang again.

Decline. Decline. Decline.

She finally replied to the texts Deacon had sent over the last few weeks. The last one said that he loved her.

To think she had actually believed him. *We're over,* she typed, tears splattering on her screen. *Don't ever call me again.*

Once the message was delivered, she erased their conversation and deleted his number. Deacon could stay in London for all she cared. He and Gwen could get married and have babies and live happily-forever-after.

And, if she was lucky, Deacon Ashford would be the first person she'd forget.

JULY

48 missed calls

AUGUST

0 missed calls

ONE

J asper Hooke still remembered the first time he saw a human fly. He had been eight years old, and his father had gone on yet another trip to yet another town to help the less fortunate with minor medical issues—pro bono, of course. That left Jasper and his fifteen-year-old brother, Lawrence, with their creepy grandfather in his even creepier house.

Old Edward Hooke never smiled and made no effort to feign concern for his grandsons. Lawrence was his favorite, but that wasn't saying much—Edward seemed to despise them both. While Jasper and his brother were there, his grandfather's housekeeper served as their inattentive guardian. Jasper was used to fending for himself at home, so having very little supervision in his grandfather's cavernous mansion felt normal.

That fateful day, the housekeeper had called in sick.

Knowing better than to leave Jasper in the charge of his

irresponsible brother, Edward brought his youngest grandson with him to the office.

The HOOK facility at that time had been located in a retail unit at the end of an ordinary strip mall on the outskirts of town. The waiting room had dingy white walls, a single poster no one had ever bothered to frame—stuck with peeling masking tape gone brittle from age—and an artificial ficus gathering dust in the corner. A bored-looking receptionist manned the desk behind sliding glass windows. Occasionally, a nurse would come out of the back offices, unlock and rummage through a black filing cabinet, then lock it and disappear again.

Jasper had planned on staying put as his grandfather commanded, but eventually he had to use the bathroom. The receptionist tried his grandfather's office extension, but no one answered. Jasper had danced around the linoleum floor, trying to hold it in.

"Please." His eyes filled with tears from the pain in his stomach. If she didn't let him go, he was going to end up peeing on the floor.

The woman rolled her eyes and let out a disgusted sigh. "Fine. The bathroom is just across the hall. Don't go snooping around, okay?"

"Okay."

And he *had* kept that promise.

It wasn't his fault that, at the exact moment he had emerged from the most satisfying pee of his young life, the door across the corridor burst open. Out ran a wild-eyed young woman, her face as pale as the walls, and her hair plastered to her head like she had been in a swimming pool.

She paused for a moment, undoubtedly shocked by the sight of young Jasper obstructing her path. When a gruff voice shouted for her to stop, she turned toward the red exit sign illuminating the end of the hallway and ran.

Edward Hooke and a man in scrubs came barreling out

of the room after her and quickly closed the distance. She reached the exit first and threw open the door.

She didn't run into the woods at the back of the building or toward the Burger King across the road—but instead shot upward, into the clouds and beyond.

Eventually, Jasper's grandfather noticed him staring out the still open door.

Instead of comforting Jasper and explaining away the confusion, Edward met him with the same unfailing disdain and irritation that defined their relationship. "What the hell are you doing out here?" he snarled, his face contorting with rage. "I told you to stay in the waiting room."

Too shocked by the scene to respond to his grandfather's scolding, Jasper whispered, "That girl. She just . . . "

"Get back to the waiting room!"

"That girl just *flew* away like a bird."

"Yes, she did." Edward knelt to eye-level with Jasper. "But she won't be flying for long."

Twenty-five years later, the small strip-mall office had been replaced by a new state-of-the-art research facility fifteen miles away. Edward Hooke had died the day after its completion. Jasper's father, Dr. Charles Hooke, had concluded that the old man was stubborn enough to keep the Lord from taking him until the building was finished. Jasper wasn't sure the Lord had been the one to take his grandfather, but had mumbled his agreement with the second part of his father's statement.

After Edward's passing, Charles retired from private medical practice to serve as the President of HOOK, although he still volunteered locally one week every month.

Lawrence had a head for business—and his grandfather's ruthlessness to go along with it. He had been voted CEO unanimously by the Board of Directors. Three years after Edward's death, the company's stock had tripled in value, and they were on target for their best year to date.

Meanwhile, Jasper had inherited his father's affinity for science and medicine. Instead of pursuing a career in a hospital, he had chosen to study molecular biology; Jasper had known it would one day be his responsibility to continue the family legacy of scientific innovation and discovery. Only the year before, Jasper had been named Head of Research at HOOK—although the incident this past spring had nearly put an end to his employment there altogether.

Vivienne Dunn had caught him off-guard. Jasper's father had been enraged when Lawrence broke the news of her escape, and had wrongly claimed that his youngest son had been distracted by a pretty face. Unsurprisingly, Lawrence had been blameless in the matter, but Jasper was well used to Lawrence towering over him on his grandfather's pedestal.

Vivienne had convinced Jasper that her NG-1882 had not activated. In the time they had held her at the facility, she hadn't made any attempts to escape . . . until she did.

From his desk drawer, he pulled out an old alarm clock that had been left on top of his car the night Vivienne had gotten away.

"I told you to get rid of that thing," Lawrence growled from the doorway. He stalked over and ripped the clock from Jasper's hands. Then he dropped it onto the tiles with a clang and stomped until it was nothing more than a twisted lump of metal.

"You didn't have to break it." Jasper fell to his knees and swept the broken glass into a pile and—*dammit*. Cut his finger. Lawrence was always breaking his stuff. Like the picture frame of Jasper and his college roommate. And his mini Zen garden. And his Newton's Cradle.

"They've been taunting our family with those clocks for decades. Do you really think it's an appropriate souvenir to remind you how badly you screwed up?"

Of course this was all Jasper's fault. Heaven forbid Lawrence accept any responsibility. Jasper dropped what was left of the clock into the trash can. "What do you want, Lawrence?"

"We got a hit on your girlfriend's whereabouts."

Jasper looked up suddenly. Lawrence had to be talking about Vivienne because Jasper worked way too much for an actual relationship. "Did someone call the tip line?"

"Let's just say we got a lucky break."

Jasper knew better than to ask about this "lucky break." Lawrence probably wouldn't tell him anyway.

"Are you sure your source is credible?" Jasper asked, sinking onto his rolling chair. This was the third time they'd gotten a call about Vivienne, and none had led to anything but dead ends. One woman claimed she'd seen her at a mall in New Jersey. Another at the airport in Arizona. And the last one, a man who had sounded like he was fond of cigarettes, had said Vivienne had been working at his local deli.

Lawrence shoved his phone in Jasper's face. "You tell me."

On the screen was a gritty black-and-white photo of a girl in a convenience store. "I'm not sure that's her." She had the correct body type, slim and petite. Her hair was longer and darker than it had been in April. But her face was turned so that he could only see her profile.

"Your opinion doesn't count."

Jasper's opinion never counted. "Are you going to check it out?" He could use a few Lawrence-free days.

"Dad's out of town this week, so I need to stay here." Lawrence tucked his phone into his breast pocket and leaned across the desk, bracing his hands on either side of Jasper's laptop. "Which means it's *your* job to bring her back."

"We already have her DNA on file," Jasper reminded him for what felt like the millionth time, wrapping his handkerchief around his bloody finger. "What's the point in going through the hassle and expense of traveling to—"

"We need her here, Lab Rat. End of discussion. I'm trusting you to not screw up again."

"Last time was as much your fault as it was mine," Jasper snapped. He was sick and tired of being the scapegoat when things didn't work out.

"I'm in a forgiving mood, so I'm going to let you get away with saying that to me this once." Lawrence kicked the trash can, and the alarm clock let out a final high-pitched chime. "Oh, and one more thing," he said from over his shoulder, "Rhett and Terry will be going along for the ride."

After Vivienne had escaped in April, Lawrence had hired new guards to help with acquiring subjects for the most recent round of testing—or at least that was what his brother claimed. Jasper couldn't help feeling like the two henchmen who followed him like mosquitos buzzing in his ears were there to keep an eye on *him* as much as his subjects.

A few hours later, Jasper climbed into the backseat of a town car and squeezed between his bodyguards.

"Hey, Rhett. How's it going, Terry?" When his greeting was met with silence, he found himself looking forward to seeing the shock on their chiseled, scarred faces the first time they saw one of the PAN fly.

TWO

One Week Earlier

It had nearly been a year since Vivienne had run away from her foster home in Ohio to join her fellow People with Active Nevergenes at Kensington Academy. Entering the Hall still felt as magical as it had that very first night.

Arched windows let in enough light to make the bronze sconces on the wall redundant this early in the afternoon. Two PAN jogged up the sweeping staircase, climbing toward a fountain-shaped chandelier dangling in the center of the coffered ceiling.

"Hey, Julie." Vivienne gave the receptionist a wave as she crossed the black and white checkerboard tiles. "Is Paul around?"

"He left for London yesterday, I'm afraid." Julie frowned back at her computer screen, her red hair sticking out in frizzy spirals around her face. "Give me a sec to check his calendar, and I'll tell you when he's coming back."

Vivienne had been trying all summer to get her foster

brother Lyle allowance to come to Kensington. Paul Mitter, the Head of External Affairs, had promised to let her know the status of her nomination by the end of the week.

"Don't worry about it. I'll just talk to him when I get home from Tennessee."

"If you say so." Julie let go of the mouse and freed a neon pink sticky note from a pile. "Should I leave him a message to call you if he's back before you are?"

"Sure. Thanks."

The door to the underground lab, hidden inside the paneling in reception, opened.

Vivienne smiled at Alex before he caught sight of her. He had forgotten to take off his lab coat again. His sun-streaked hair fell over his forehead. He shoved it out of his eyes and cursed when he realized he was still wearing the white coat.

"Why are you done so early?" Vivienne's greeting echoed off the raised panel walls.

When Alex heard her, his face broke into a wide smile, revealing deep dimples beneath his scruffy beard.

As Neverland's head Endocrinologist, Alex McGee's main job was finding PAN outside of Neverland. When he wasn't visiting hospitals, he was trying to activate dormant Nevergenes like his own. After the news of Vivienne's diagnosis, he had transferred from California to Kensington to oversee her treatment.

"Keep it down," he hissed, pulling his collar up around his face. She giggled at the way he ducked behind a tall potted plant and waved her closer. "I don't want Robert finding out I escaped. I was hoping to convince this pretty girl I know to come to dinner with me in Worcester."

Alex had been asking Vivienne out all summer. When she finally said yes two weeks ago, she was sorry she had waited so long. He was good company, a perfect gentleman, and frighteningly intelligent. But best of all, he was one of the few who knew about her diagnosis. And any time she started going down the rabbit hole of what could happen, he'd drag her back to reality and remind her that she was alive and needed to go on. To make memories while she still could.

And he bought her pie. Lots and *lots* of pie.

"You should ditch her and take me instead." The plant's leaves tickled her bare arms when Vivienne slipped in next to him.

Alex pretended to size her up, tilting his head as he considered. "I suppose I could," he said, pursing his lips. "You're passably attractive."

"Thanks a lot," she snorted, jabbing him in the ribs with her elbow.

"Geez, you don't have to resort to violence. I'll settle for you."

"You're obnoxious. I should turn you down, but I'm starving."

"Lucky me. I'm going to run home for a shower first if that's okay."

She gave him a tentative sniff and wrinkled her nose. "Yeah. Do that. You reek of bleach. But make it quick or else I'll find someone else to take me."

"Don't you dare." Alex poked her in the side, and she nearly fell over the plant trying to escape. "Meet you out front at six?"

Vivienne checked her silver watch. If she hurried, she'd have time to shower and change too. "If you're late, I'm eating without you."

"I'm never late." He grinned before twisting and disappearing out the door.

Vivienne flew across campus to her apartment. The trees around the perimeter were still the green of summer, but it wouldn't be long before they started changing color.

She typed her PIN into the keypad. The silver keys were warm from the sun.

Nothing happened.

She tried a second time, but the door remained locked.

9-2-5-2

Nothing.

That was definitely her PIN. Wasn't it?

She tried once more.

This time, the door unlocked.

She'd have to get someone to come fix the stupid thing. That was the third time this week it had given her trouble. Finally inside, she kicked off her sandals and unzipped her shorts. It wouldn't take her long to get ready, but—

"Geez, girl! Keep your clothes on." Max was sitting at their kitchen table, covering his eyes with his hands.

Vivienne couldn't get the zipper up fast enough. "Don't you ever go home?" she grumbled, fighting a smile.

"Nope. If you had another bedroom, I'd probably just move in." He laughed. "Are you decent?"

"No. I'm stripped naked, dancing around in my birthday suit." Rolling her eyes, she crossed the living room to the kitchen, collecting her sweaty running clothes from where she'd dropped them earlier.

"In that case . . . " Max peeked through his fingers. "Come on. No one likes a liar."

"You're the one who told me to keep my clothes on." Vivienne grabbed a red jelly bean from a bowl in front of him. For some reason, Emily ate all the colors except red. "What're you doing here?"

"Waiting for Emily to get back from the mall for the hundredth time this week." He popped a few candies into his mouth. "Wanna come to The Glass House with us?"

"Can't. Alex and I have dinner plans."

"Again?" Max tapped the spare key Vivienne had given him against the kitchen table. He lived downstairs, but spent most of his free time up here with them. "You remember you have other friends, right? Or are you two more than just friends?"

She ignored the question. Her relationship with Alex was nobody's business. Max and Emily liked to play a game called "Team Alex or Team Deacon" where they picked sides based on different scenarios. They were both "Team Deacon" when it came to dinners because Deacon used to invite them too. Vivienne had given up reminding them there *was* no "Team Deacon." Not anymore.

Before she sat down, she pulled her phone from her back pocket and threw it on the table. "How's your dad?"

"Called him yesterday. Doesn't even remember I was there last week."

Her smile faltered.

Alex and Robert were the only two who knew about Vivienne's diagnosis. Vivienne had tried telling her friends so many times, but hadn't been able to find the right words.

"But he was probably just having a bad morning," Max went on. "Did I tell you that I made him a photo album from some of his old pictures? I was hoping they would jog his memory."

"That's a great idea." Vivienne thought she should take more pictures. They weren't allowed to have any of her fellow PAN in them, but that didn't mean she couldn't capture the memories.

Max's smile was strained. "They're going to find a cure, right? I mean, they have to. If they can make outsiders look young forever, surely they can fix what's wrong with my dad."

"Of course they can," she said, breathing through the tingling that continued plaguing her. Vivienne's friends had already adjusted to the increase in adrenaline and nGh coursing through their veins. But because of Vivienne's crazy high levels, she hadn't been as lucky. "Have you thought any more about moving over?"

Max's original plan had been to transfer to the Harrow Neverland outside of London at the beginning of summer. Then Vivienne had been captured by HOOK.

"I dunno." A shrug. "Maybe after Christmas."

"I hope you're not sticking around because of what happened in Maryland." Vivienne's stomach rumbled. Had she eaten lunch? She couldn't remember. If so, it hadn't been enough. And the candy wasn't filling the void in her belly.

"I'm not," Max chuckled. "But it seems like the Extraction team here sees a lot more action than the one at Harrow."

"And that's a *good* thing?" she asked, dragging bread from the cupboard. Nothing like a few slices of empty carbs to cure hunger.

"I think so. I get bored easily."

Vivienne was the same. She'd been stuck at Kensington since April and had wanted to rip her hair out more times than she could count. "I'm making toast. You want any?"

"Nah. I'll wait for Em."

There was a knock on the glass door.

The two slices of bread in Vivienne's hand dropped to the counter.

The only person who knocked on their glass door had been in London since April.

Max turned toward the noise. "Want me to get that?"

"No, no. I'll get it." Her heart pounded in her ears as she tiptoed through the living room. When she saw who was outside, she nearly collapsed with relief.

Emily grinned at her and nodded toward the handle. There were shopping bags in her hands and dangling from her arms.

"Thank you, thank you, *thank you*. I couldn't face lugging this stuff up the stairs," Emily said once Vivienne let her in. "Sorry for making you wait, Max." She abandoned the bags on the couch. The flowy red dress she had on looked new.

28

Max shrugged and ate more candy. "I'm used to it."

Vivienne poked through the bags on top: a few heavy sweaters, some new black tights, an entire box of makeup. Emily's addiction to retail therapy should have been quenched by her role as one of Kensington's personal shoppers. Instead, it had gotten worse.

"We need to talk." Emily caught Vivienne by the arm and yanked her toward the bedrooms.

"Toast first. Then talk." Vivienne pulled free, inserted the slices of bread into the toaster, and pressed down the lever.

Emily tapped her sparkly blue nail against the stone counter. "Okay, so—"

"One sec." Vivienne pulled down a plate and turned for the fridge. The tapping got louder. "Where's that butter?"

"Ahhhh! You're killing me!" Emily stomped over, dragged the butter from the compartment in the door, and slammed it onto the counter.

"Thanks. Now I need some jelly."

"Forget the stupid jelly!"

Max sniggered.

"Geez. Fine. No jelly." Vivienne stifled her laughter behind her hand. "What'd you want to talk about?"

Emily bounced up and down on her toes, her dark curls swaying behind her. "He's back."

He's back.

Vivienne asked who was back even though she had a fairly good idea.

Emily's glossed lips lifted into a feline smile. "Your sexy buddy *Deaaaacon*."

Oh my gosh. Oh my gosh. Oh my gosh.

"I don't know why you're telling me," Vivienne muttered, pulling a butter knife from the drawer.

"Yeah, okay." Emily's smile widened. "So you don't want to know that the first thing he did was ask me about *youuuuu*?"

Vivienne squeezed the knife's cold hilt. A traitorous rush of adrenaline threatened to lift her off the ground. She didn't care. Not at all.

"He asked me about Vivienne too," Max mumbled, his mouth full of candy.

Vivienne whirled around. "You saw him too?"

"Not here. In Scotland."

"And you never told us?" Emily threw a piece of bread at him. "We need to know these things, Max!"

Smoke wafted from the toaster. Vivienne lunged for the cancel button, but the toast was too charred to salvage—like her stupid heart.

She was over Deacon. It didn't matter if he was in London or in Kensington or in Timbuk-frickin'-tu. She. Didn't. Care.

"It doesn't matter," Vivienne told them, the singed crust disintegrating in her fingers.

Max leaned back in his chair and crossed his arms. "You *don't* want to know what he said?"

"Nope." Vivienne stabbed the toast with the knife and launched it into the trash can before pointing to the pair of them with the dull blade. "And I don't want to talk about him anymore. *Ever.*"

"Too bad." Emily lifted herself onto the counter. "*I* want to hear it."

"Right. Okay." Max propped his elbows on the table and cleared his throat. "So, Dash and Peter were up from Harrow visiting Tootles."

Emily rolled her hand toward him. "*And?*"

"And . . . um . . . he asked me how Vivienne was."

Vivienne swept the crumbs from the counter into the sink and rinsed them down the drain. She hated how interested she was in every syllable leaving Max's mouth.

"Why are guys so useless?" Emily covered her eyes with her hand and shook her head. "We need *details*. How did he look? Did he seem upset? Was he happy? Did he say anything else that we could dissect and over-analyze?"

Max scratched his head. "He looked . . . normal?"

"You're a terrible storyteller," Emily groaned.

Max threw a jelly bean at her. "Like your story was any better."

"You want a good story? Sit back and listen." She slipped back to the floor. "Deacon's hair is longer than it was back in April. He looked even hotter—if that's even possible. He was wearing a navy T-shirt and dark shorts and black shoes, and carrying a dark blue duffle bag. It looked like he was headed to the Leadership House, which means he's probably staying on campus. He smelled *aaamazing* and"—she took a breath—"he seemed absolutely frickin' miserable."

The only detail that Vivienne cared about was the last one. Why did he seem miserable? Did it have something to do with her?

No. That was stupid. They hadn't spoken in months. If Deacon was miserable, it was probably because he and Gwen were having relationship issues.

I promise not to break your heart.

What a liar.

Vivienne's phone buzzed on the kitchen table.

All three of them stared as it vibrated.

"It's him, isn't it?" whispered Emily.

~~*I wish.*~~

I hope not.

Vivienne couldn't bring herself to check.

Max grabbed her phone. "Nope. It's Alex. He's asking where you are."

Alex? Why would he be— "Crap! I completely forgot about Alex!" Dinner. They were supposed to have dinner.

Emily started laughing. "Poor Alex."

Vivienne ran into her bedroom and slid her tired wardrobe from one side of the closet to the other. She didn't

31

have time to shower, but she couldn't go on a date in a sweaty tank top.

The suitcase she had packed for her second mission sat open on her bed. She undressed, sprayed on some of her mother's lilac perfume, swiped on a bit more deodorant, then slipped into one of the folded dresses from the bag.

Why had Deacon bothered asking Emily about her? And Max? What was that about?

Did he honestly think he could show up and everything would go back to the way it was? Or was Deacon just being polite?

His hair was longer? What did that mean, exactly? Was it longer all over or just the top or—

What the heck was she doing? She didn't need to think about Deacon.

She needed to focus on the guy she was dating.

Vivienne needed to focus on Alex.

"Have you thought any more about treatment?" Alex had gone all of dinner without bringing up the tiresome subject. Vivienne should have known better than to think they could go an entire date without talking about her condition. The joys of dating a doctor.

The moon followed them along the empty road back to Kensington. It had been a warm evening, but by the time they'd finished their seafood, there was a definite nip to the air.

"I don't want to make any decisions until we know for certain it's going to happen."

"I've already told you—"

"I know, I know. It's inevitable." Vivienne fiddled with the button for the window, opening it a fraction, then closing it again. "But you also told me that bringing down my levels now won't make much of a difference."

He tapped his thumbs on the steering wheel. Blue light from the dash lit his features in the darkness. "I know you probably don't want to hear this, but you're in denial."

Denial was the only thing getting her out of bed every morning.

"So? Let me enjoy my denial for a few more weeks. I promise I'll make a decision when I get back from Tennessee."

Instead of looking happier, Alex's frown deepened. "You're sure it's safe?"

"As safe as any other mission," she said to the window. HOOK didn't care about her anymore, and her foster mother had made a public statement saying she had been found safe. RISK had cleared her for fieldwork two weeks ago.

His blue eyes flashed to hers. "You're looking forward to it, aren't you?"

It was probably best not to tell him how happy she was about getting out of Kensington in case he took it the wrong way. "I'm looking forward to redeeming myself."

"What's there to redeem?" Alex snorted. "You saved a new recruit *and* managed to escape single-handedly from HOOK's fortress. You're a badass, Vivienne." He pulled his pickup next to the keypad outside Kensington's gates, rolled down the window, and typed in his code.

Vivienne didn't feel like a badass. She felt like a failure. Yes, Megan had made it to Kensington safely, but that had been because of Ethan.

The gates opened, welcoming them back to their safe haven.

Moonlight seeped through the gap in the trees as Alex drove toward Kensington Hall. Seeing the building draped in shadows brought back memories of the first night she had arrived.

Her heart ached when she thought of how much had changed.

"Thanks for tonight." Vivienne rested her hand on the handle, staring out the bug-crusted windshield toward the wrought iron streetlights. "It was just what I needed." *To stop thinking about Deacon-stupid-Ashford.*

Shifting into park, Alex turned toward her. "Thank *you* for finally saying yes." Now that they were stopped, she could hear the alternative rock station whispering through the speakers.

From the corner of her eye, she thought she saw Alex's gaze drop to her mouth. Her lips were so dry, but she had forgotten to bring lip balm.

"Still with me?" Alex waved his hand in front of her face.

Her heart pounded in her chest when she turned fully to face him. "I'm still with you."

"Good. I'd like to keep it that way." The corners of his eyes crinkled when his lips lifted into a hopeful smile. "Would it be okay if I kissed you?"

The muscles in her stomach tightened.

This was it. Did she tell him she wanted to stay friends, or did she let their relationship go to the next level?

Her answer was to close her eyes and lean toward him.

Alex's mouth was warm and inviting—and tasted vaguely like the chocolate cake he'd had for dessert.

She'd always liked chocolate cake.

Vivienne felt for her seatbelt buckle and pressed the button so she could slide closer to him. His facial hair scraped against her skin, but she didn't mind.

The kiss didn't leave her breathless, but it did leave her wanting to do it again.

So she did.

His tongue found hers, slow and patient. She caught the collar of his shirt and pulled him against her, inhaling his cologne. He took his time exploring her mouth, losing his hands in her hair, pressing her into the seat.

This time, when their lips separated, they were both gasping for air.

Alex whispered, "I'm *so* glad you said yes," against her lips, then kissed her again.

When Vivienne finally climbed out of his truck, she pressed her cool fingers against her swollen lips. The skin on her chin felt raw from his stubble.

Emily would never let her live it down if she came home with beard-burn.

From the shadows behind her, someone cleared his throat. She turned slowly, facing a figure standing at the top of the stairs.

No no no.

Not like this . . .

Deacon's teeth flashed in the darkness when he smiled. "How was your date?"

THREE

Two days earlier

Everything was shite. The weather: rainy shite. The news headlines: depressing shite. The eggs Deacon had accidentally burned but eaten anyway: charred shite. The silent mobile he'd discarded on the sofa: smashed shite. The email he'd received last night: utter and complete shite.

"Tell me this isn't true," Deacon snapped, waving the printout in his mother's face. It didn't matter that she had dark circles under her eyes or that she was likely out of her mind with jet lag. He wasn't waiting any longer for an answer.

"Hello, son. I missed you too. My flight was great. Thank you for asking." She took the paper and skimmed the email. "Everything looks correct to me," she said, handing it back to him.

Deacon followed her into the living room of their London flat. "After the disastrous mission in Maryland, I cannot believe you assigned Vivienne another case."

"Vivienne is a recruiter, isn't she?" His mother dropped her suitcase onto the thick oriental carpet and massaged her temples.

"You know what I mean." He helped her out of her damp jacket and jammed it onto the wobbly coat rack by the door. "It's only been five months since her foster family released the video."

"Calm down." His mother pulled off her shoes and set them out of the way before sinking onto the sofa and propping herself up with the cushions. It would be at least three days before she acclimated to this time zone. "We're taking extra precautions."

Extra precautions be damned. Deacon crumpled the paper in his fist and threw it into the unlit fireplace. Empty. Cold. Exactly how he had felt since May. "It's too soon."

"Look, it's been decided that all recruiters must work in teams of two or three, and we simply don't have the numbers for that kind of coverage without her."

Deacon had heard that rumor. Still . . . "Ethan's been recruiting for seven years. He'll be fine on his own."

"This wasn't my decision. It was Peter's."

Leaning against the mantle, Deacon stared at his reflection in the antique mirror. He looked like he hadn't slept all summer—he felt like it too. His mother had ordered weekly blood tests to keep an eye on his nGh levels. For a woman so paranoid about his wellbeing, she didn't seem to give a damn about his girlfriend's.

Ex-girlfriend.

Shite. All of it.

"Vivienne is *not* going to Tennessee."

"Only a few months ago, you were begging to have her put on assignment. And now that she's proven her loyalty, you want her kept on the sidelines?" She exhaled a humorless chuckle. "This is why you'll never serve on Leadership.

37

You're too interested in doing things for your own selfish motives."

"Like I'd have any interest in serving on an antiquated panel stuck in the nineteenth bloody century." A panel that didn't do a damn thing besides point fingers, place blame, and make up rules. A panel he had lost all respect for the moment they said they wouldn't retaliate for HOOK taking Vivienne. Deacon crossed back to the rack to retrieve his jacket.

His mother rose. Her face was flushed, her lips pinched. "Where do you think you're going?"

"To speak to Grandad." Of the two of them, Peter had always been the more reasonable one. Before he could reach for the front door, it opened.

"Where are you off to?" Peter Pan asked, shaking the rain from his damp brown hair. Through the glass panel beside the door, Deacon could see his grandad's old bicycle leaning against the fence. He was soaked through, but that was because he refused to wear a damned jacket.

"To see you, actually," Deacon said, bracing for the inevitable argument.

"That sounds ominous." Peter tilted his head; his brow furrowed. "What do you want?"

"I would like to go back to Kensington."

"Leadership sentenced you to six months' service at Harrow."

"Yes," Deacon said through his teeth. As if he needed the reminder. "But you have the power to suspend my sentence."

"Why would I do that?"

"So I can go on the mission to Tennessee."

"Absolutely not!" his mother shouted from behind them.

Deacon whirled around to find the color drained from her face. "I've done everything you've asked of me for the last five months." And his fledgling relationship with Vivienne had been the price. "Give me this. Please."

Back in April, PAN Leadership had conducted a sham of a trial, holding Deacon accountable for a few missteps and a handful of disregarded rules. He had pleaded guilty to all the charges. How could he not? He had done all the things they had accused him of—and then some.

Slightly had never liked him, and Richard One voted like Slightly's shadow. Curly didn't seem to care either way, which made him easy to persuade to the dark side.

Richard Two always voted for what he thought Peter would do—and since Deacon was Peter's grandson, he voted for leniency. Without fail, Nibs went against Slightly. Maimie was a forgiving woman who preferred not to ruffle feathers—and she had always liked Deacon.

But Alex McGee, serving on the committee in Tootles's stead, had made damn sure Deacon was punished.

Peter closed his eyes and rocked his head from side to side.

For the first time in months, Deacon felt hopeful. "I just want to be there for Vivienne. That's it, I swear."

His mother snorted.

"I'll even come back to Harrow to serve the final four weeks as soon as the mission is over. Mother," he said carefully, hoping to appeal to her softer side, the side he rarely saw, "I promised you I'd finish in the field come December. Give me one last mission. Please. I'm begging you."

With tears shimmering in her green eyes, she nodded.

One down . . .

He turned back to his granddad. "Well?"

Peter squeezed Deacon's arm and said, "Don't make me regret this."

Deacon hugged them both, said thank you a hundred times, and then ran up the stairs to his bedroom. He dragged his suitcase from beneath the four poster bed and transferred his clothes from the dresser to the bag.

Finally. A chance to rectify everything that had happened this summer.

Once he explained, Vivienne would forgive him . . . right?

Of course she would.

She had to.

Because he didn't know what he would do if she didn't.

Where was all the bloody air? Deacon unbuttoned the collar of his shirt and tried again to force oxygen into his lungs, but it wasn't working. Even after his less-than-cordial conversation with Emily that afternoon, he had braved a trip to Vivienne's apartment—only to find out that Vivienne was on a date.

With *Alex.*

Just because Deacon had been living in a hole pining for the last five months didn't mean Vivienne had been doing the same. She was single and free to do what she wanted.

And from the way she was kissing Alex, it was blatantly obvious that she no longer wanted Deacon.

He should have left. Pretended he hadn't been sitting on Kensington Hall's hard stone steps for the last two hours, hoping she'd had a shite time with her bearded boyfriend.

But he had waited five excruciating months to see her. And damn it all if he wasn't going to see her tonight.

"How was your date?" he choked, still struggling to breathe.

Vivienne jumped. He watched as the wide-eyed shock on her suntanned face was replaced by an unreadable mask. Her slight shoulders stiffened beneath her wispy blue dress. She looked thinner than he remembered, more vulnerable.

"I thought you weren't coming back until October," Vivienne clipped, not a hint of warmth in her husky voice.

"They let me go early for good behavior."

"What does that mean?"

He muttered, "Doesn't matter," then jerked his head toward the trail of dust from Alex's truck. "How long have you and Alex been together?"

Her pointed chin jutted forward. "That's none of your business."

"Of course it's my business. You're—"

"I'm *what*, Deacon?" Her sandals crunched in the gravel as she stomped toward the steps, sending lilac-scented air crashing over him.

He snapped his mouth shut. *You're supposed to be with* me.

"I'm not your *girlfriend*," she hissed, "and you made it clear that I wasn't worth coming back for."

How could she say that? How could she *think* that? "You don't know what you're talking about."

Her brown eyes narrowed, sparking with anger. "Says the guy who's been gone for *five months!*"

"Dammit, Vivienne. I didn't have a choice!"

"Everyone has a choice," she spat, jabbing him in the chest with her finger. "You made the wrong one." Another jab. "And now you have the balls to come back and pretend to care that I've moved on."

"Have you, then?" His hands flexed into fists at his sides. "Have you *really* moved on?"

Meeting his gaze with unwavering hostility, Vivienne said, "I'm pretty sure you just saw me making out with Alex in his truck. You. Tell. Me."

In the aftermath of her capture, the last thing she'd needed was to stress out over him. So Deacon had withheld the details of his trial. In hindsight, it wasn't his best move.

He knew Vivienne would be upset. That she'd be hurt. He didn't think she'd be with someone else. "Tennessee

41

should be fun." Scrubbing his hands down his face, he wished he'd stayed in London.

God, he was tired.

He wanted to crawl into bed, pull the duvet over his head, and never come out again.

Vivienne stumbled back, nearly colliding with one of the wrought iron lampposts. "You're coming to Tennessee?"

"Didn't you hear the good news?" he sneered from the darkness. "I've been added to the assignment. I hope that's not going to be a *problem* for you."

"Why should I care?"

Why indeed? Deacon stole one final glance at the girl who had ripped his heart out before stalking toward the forest and shooting into the sky.

FOUR

The windows in Ethan's white bungalow were dark, the blinds had been pulled, and his car wasn't in the driveway. Even though Deacon knew no one was home, he knocked again. He really needed to stop trying to surprise people.

Deacon pulled out his mobile to send Ethan a text. When he saw the date on his cracked screen, he felt like throwing it across the lawn. How was it *still* Thursday? This had to be the longest day in the history of long, shitty days.

Thursday was meeting night, so Ethan was probably at one of Lee Somerfield's rebellious gatherings. Instead of going home, Deacon jumped off the porch and went around back to wait in one of the Adirondack chairs surrounding an ash-filled fire pit.

This was what he should've been doing tonight.

Hanging out with Vivienne and their friends around a crackling fire, smoke being blown toward them by the breeze. She'd be wearing that giant, hole-ridden sweatshirt she always wore when she was relaxing. They'd be enjoying the last bit of heat clinging to the dregs of summer.

Instead, he was staring at a mangled white log while Vivienne was probably dreaming of her new boyfriend.

He drummed his fingers against the chair's plastic arm.

This whole bloody situation was Leadership's fault.

Vivienne had been taken by HOOK, and what had they done? Not a damn thing. They'd been too busy making an example out of Peter Pan's rebellious grandson. If they had focused on what was important, on destroying HOOK, he wouldn't have been kept away for the last five months.

Deacon glanced at his watch.

Leadership had accused him of being a rebel . . . who was he to disappoint?

Ten minutes later, he landed in Lee's back yard. Twenty or so PAN waited outside the basement talking and laughing with one another. He responded to their wide-eyed greetings with a wave and a nod on his way to the concrete stairs. Let them talk. Let them see. Let them tell his mother exactly what he did the moment he came back to Kensington. He didn't care anymore.

The door at the bottom had been propped open by a cinder block, leaving a bit of fresh air to clear some of the mustiness from the unfinished space.

Ethan and Max were already sitting on blocks at the front of a plywood stage. Lee was in the corner speaking to Joel and Ricky.

When Ethan saw him, he did a double take. "*Dash?*" He shot to his feet and rushed over for a hug. "Holy shit, man. When did you get home? Why didn't you call?"

"I texted earlier."

"You did? Sorry. The reception in this dungeon is shit," Ethan said, stepping away. "What're you doing *here* though? Aren't you on parole?"

Parole indeed. The reminder pissed Deacon off even more. "I'm here because I'm in."

Ethan's eyes widened. "Like *in-in?*"

Deacon nodded.

Ethan let out a low whistle. "Lee's not going to believe this."

"Believe what?" Lee had shaved off his beard, making him look ten years younger.

Ethan clapped Deacon on the back and said, "Dash is in."

Lee's eyes narrowed, and he crossed his arms. "How do I know you're not here as Leadership's spy?" He'd never been the most trusting sort, so his skepticism was understandable.

"I assume you heard about my trial." It had been kept off the meeting docket for confidentiality, but Deacon was sure Ethan would've told him.

"Do you honestly expect me to believe that a slap on the wrist was enough to turn you against Peter, your mother, *and* the rest of Leadership?"

"HOOK tried to take someone precious from me, and Leadership was too preoccupied *slapping my wrist* to do anything about it."

Lee's jaw flexed as he considered. Then he held out his hand. "That I do understand. Welcome to the resistance."

Deacon tried not to stare at the black marks HOOK's poison had left on Lee's forearm. Lee had been neutralized almost thirty years earlier. His Nevergene had been deactivated, but the neutralization had killed his brother. Deacon offered his own hand and gave Lee's a firm shake.

Deacon stayed beside Ethan and Max during the meeting, hoping to avoid talking to anyone else. It was short, but charged with an energy he hadn't felt the last time he'd been there. Energy he hoped would bring about much-needed change. The PAN had been doing the same thing for the last hundred years; surely it was time to take a different approach. Time to fight back.

"I wonder where Vivienne was tonight?" Ethan said afterwards. The other PAN were filing out of the basement, but Deacon had hoped to speak to Lee. "She hasn't missed one of these yet."

Vivienne's father, William Dunn, had started the resistance. Lee took over after William left Kensington and moved to Ohio to raise his daughter.

"She's on a—" Max's hand flew to his mouth and his eyes darted to Deacon. "Never mind."

"On a what?" Ethan asked.

Shoving his hands into his pockets, Deacon kicked over the block he'd been sitting on. It clattered onto the cement floor with a satisfying bang. "Didn't you hear the happy news? She's going out with Beardy McGee now."

"*What*! Why is Vivienne going out with—wait." Ethan punched Deacon's shoulder. "You guys broke up and didn't tell me? What the hell, man?"

Max blew out a relieved breath. "Who told you about Alex?"

"Does it matter?" Deacon knowing hadn't made a blind bit of difference to the situation. Ethan asked more questions, and Max kept looking at Deacon with pity in his eyes, and he couldn't stand it anymore.

Deacon left them to their gossip and went to where Lee was sitting on the edge of the makeshift stage. "When are we moving?" he asked. All the energy he'd felt during the meeting needed somewhere to go. A purpose. A plan.

"What do you mean?" Lee frowned at a nail sticking out of the plywood and went to a toolbox in the corner. A moment later, he returned with a hammer.

"You've been waiting for an excuse to go after HOOK. They took Vivienne months ago, but I haven't heard any news of retaliation."

"HOOK." *Bang.* "Didn't." *Bang.* "Do." *Bang.* "Anything." Lee stood up with his hammer.

How could he say that? Lee of all people knew HOOK had every intention of neutralizing Vivienne. Of grounding her. Of taking away her immortality.

"Yes, they kidnapped Vivienne," Lee said with a sigh. "But Leadership sent in Extraction, and she ended up escaping unscathed. It's a bit hard to rally troops without a spark."

Deacon stared at the circle imprinted around the now-flush nail. That's how he'd felt ever since Leadership had brought him to heel—a hammered nail. Forced back into place. "It's only a matter of time before they come at us again." He had an unexplainable feeling in the pit of his stomach that HOOK wasn't finished with Vivienne.

"And when they do," Lee said, turning the hammer over in his hands, "we'll be ready."

The last thing Deacon wanted was to be alone, because then he'd think about Vivienne.

And Alex.

Together.

And then he'd find himself thinking about how satisfying it would be to drive over to Alex's place and break his nose. But that would be a bad idea. Wouldn't it? Yes. Of course it would. He should not punch Vivienne's new doctor boyfriend in his arrogant face.

So he suggested Ethan and Max come over for drinks at his place. Then Ethan had invited Nicola to meet them, which threw Deacon's plans of getting blind drunk right out the window.

"What's she going to say when she finds out you went to another meeting?" Deacon asked, hoping Ethan would call Nicola and cancel.

Ethan shrugged. "She already knows."

"And she's okay with it?" Nicola had hated the meetings almost as much as Deacon used to. What else had changed since he'd been gone?

"Now that you've joined us, she'll definitely get off my back. I mean, if the crown prince of Neverland is on our side, who in their right mind is gonna oppose us?"

Ethan would be surprised.

When Nicola arrived, she didn't bother knocking. She swept right in past Ethan, all long legs and leather, and hugged Deacon. After a chaste peck on the cheek she said, "Welcome home."

Deacon wiggled his eyebrows at her, hoping it'd piss off his mate. "I would've come back sooner if I knew how much you've missed me."

"Hands off, English," Ethan snapped, yanking him back by the neck of his shirt. "She's mine."

"Sure am." Nicola kissed Ethan long enough to leave Max staring at the floorboards and Deacon thinking of Alex's filthy mouth on Vivienne's.

"We stayin' in or going out?" Ethan asked when they finally came up for air. He ended up with more lipstick on his mouth than Nicola.

Max raised his hand, saying, "I vote out."

"Doesn't matter to me either way." Nicola shrugged, still draped around Ethan. Had they moved in together yet? She had mentioned the possibility back in May, but nothing had been said about it since.

"I'm with Max," Ethan murmured, nuzzling Nicola's neck. "Let's go out."

"You sure you two don't want to stay in?" It was hard to be happy for them when he was feeling so sorry for himself.

"And miss your homecoming celebrations? Not a chance." Ethan pulled away from Nicola and rattled his keys. "Come on. I'll drive."

"Only if you promise to leave your car there"—Nicola

handed him a tissue from her handbag—"and Uber home."

The night Ethan had gotten drunk and crashed his car felt like a lifetime ago. Back then, Ethan thought it'd be a good idea to fly away from the scene. Extraction had had a hell of a time cleaning up *that* mess.

Ethan wiped his mouth, tossed the tissue in the bin, and smiled. "I learned my lesson, babe."

Deacon dragged his keys from his pocket to lock up when his mobile buzzed. *Are you home?*

He didn't recognize the number. *Who is this?*

It buzzed again. *Emily.*

Why the hell was Vivienne's best friend texting him at half ten at night? *Just leaving my house now.*

Three dots appeared. Disappeared. Appeared again. *Can you wait for five minutes? I need to talk to you.*

"Dash? You comin'?" Ethan called from the car.

Deacon read the message again, then looked back at the gray Audi. "I'll meet you there in ten." He had to shout to be heard over the pop song blaring through the speakers.

Ethan gave him a thumbs up, rolled up his window, muffling the music, and spun out of the driveway.

For the second time that night, Deacon sat on cold stone steps waiting for a girl. What could Emily possibly have to say to him that she hadn't said already? When he'd seen her earlier on campus, she had ripped him a new one about how much of an asshole he was for leaving Vivienne. Then she launched into graphic detail about how she was going to remove certain parts of his body if he even looked at her friend again. For someone so bubbly, Emily was quite blood-thirsty.

He pulled the hood of his sweatshirt over his head and unlocked his mobile to re-read the messages from Emily. Then, because he was a masochist, he opened the ones from Vivienne. *We're over. Don't ever call me again.*

Seven words. That was all it took to end his world.

He'd known she was angry and upset that he had to stay in London. Hell, *he'd* been angry and upset. And he knew now that keeping the trial a secret had been a grave error. He'd tried ringing and texting, begging her to speak with him. To let him explain.

And she hadn't responded once.

July had been a terrible month, but by August, Deacon had decided to stop acting like a psychopath and give Vivienne the space she obviously needed. To ride out his sentence and fix things when he got home.

He was an idiot.

There was a faint crunch on the burnt-up grass in his front lawn. He looked up to find Emily coming toward him. "Thanks for waiting," she said. "I got here as fast as I could."

"No problem."

She pulled down the hood of her Kensington sweatshirt; glossy black curls spilled out. "Sorry about being so rude when you stopped by earlier."

"It's all right." Emily had no reason to be nice to her best friend's ex. "I know where your loyalties lie." With Vivienne. As they should.

"That's actually why I wanted to talk to you." She stepped closer; he could see she was biting her lip. "Do you have a good reason for being gone this summer or what?"

Why did she care? Still, there was no reason for him *not* to tell her. "I was on tr—"

Emily held up her hand. "I don't want to hear it. Just answer the question with yes or no."

"Yes. I have a good reason for being gone."

"Then don't give up—on Vivienne, I mean."

"I'm not the one who gave up." Vivienne was the one who had broken up with him. She was the one going out with someone else.

"That's not the way Vivienne sees it. She really needed you, and you weren't there."

Why did Vivienne need him so much? Had something happened this summer that he didn't know about?

Emily shifted in the grass. "I shouldn't be telling you this . . . "

"Tell me anyway." Deacon didn't care that he sounded desperate. He *was* desperate.

"When she got home tonight, she cried herself to sleep. Call me crazy, but I don't think she'd do that if she wasn't holding on to something."

His stomach tensed, and he could feel his skin start to burn with the idea of Vivienne still—

Slow down, he told himself. *It could be nothing.*

"I appreciate you letting me know," he said, trying to sound nonchalant.

Emily nodded, glanced toward the empty street, then took off toward campus.

Deacon stared at his mobile's black screen, utterly exhausted. Why had he thought going out was a good idea?

On the short flight to the bar, he tried to focus on what he'd heard at his second rebellious meeting. It was easy to overlook Lee's disdain for Leadership now that Deacon had his own misgivings. And the man was spot-on about HOOK. It was time they felt the sting they'd inflicted on the PAN for over a century.

Whatever happened in his love life, Deacon wanted to make sure HOOK was too busy picking up the pieces to concern themselves with Vivienne—or any other PAN—for a very, *very* long time.

Then he planned on going back to London and forgetting all about Vivienne.

Or at least that had been his plan up until Emily had come by. It killed him that Vivienne had been crying. But crying meant she had to care—at least a little.

When he reached the bar, the parking lot was full. Some new beer stickers had been added to the ones peeling on the door. The smell of stale alcohol wafted from the sticky floor as he pushed his way past some gritty-looking men in leather jackets and stained denim. A group of young women who looked out of place in short, lacy dresses stood around one of the high top tables across from the bar.

"About time you got here. I thought you were going to puss out." Ethan punched him in the shoulder and laughed when Deacon winced. "What're we gettin' you?"

"The usual, I suppose."

The bartender twisted and pulled down a dark bottle and short glass from the shelves. A moment later, there was a glass of scotch in Deacon's hand.

Ethan held his glass of whiskey and soda toward him. "To suspended sentences."

"I'll drink to that." Nicola lifted her bulbous glass of pink gin; the strawberries floating inside sloshed.

"No idea what that means, but what the heck." Max added his beer bottle to the mix.

Deacon clinked his scotch against their drinks. "I'd rather drink to Tennessee."

"*You're* coming to Tennessee?" Ethan choked, his face turning red.

"Peter gave me one final mission." Deacon took a slow, burning sip, hoping it would help him get a bit of sleep later.

"Hell. Yes!" Ethan punched his fist in the air, drawing the attention of the middle-aged couples at the table beside them, which was never a good thing. Everyone but Max was of legal drinking age, but they certainly didn't look it.

"Back together for one final blowout! I wasn't lookin' forward to it at *all*, but now . . . " Ethan knocked Deacon's shoulder again. "We should get some fireworks like in Georgia—Or, wait! I know. Let's do the toilet paper thing like in PA. Dude, this is going to be *ah-may-zing*. I can't believe your mom's letting you off the leash. How'd you swing it?"

"Turns out I'm not too proud to beg." Deacon rubbed his sore shoulder. Ethan must've been working out.

"It'll be just like North Carolina," Nicola said, bumping his hip with hers. Her smile was brighter than he remembered. The rim of her glass was stained red from her lipstick. Had she done something different with her hair?

"I didn't realize you'd be there too." Deacon couldn't wait to hang out with the happy couple. Brilliant. Just brilliant.

"You don't have to sound so thrilled," Nicola grumbled, rolling her eyes. "Guess who else will be there?" Nicola draped her arm around Max's shoulder, yanked him closer, and roughly patted his head. "This kid right here."

"It's my first time out in the field," Max said, fixing his gelled brown hair.

"And we're so proud of you, little Maxy," Nicola gushed, pinching Max's cheek until it was red. "Owen and Barry will be there too."

"Four of you?" Extraction typically assigned one, maybe two, floaters in case a mission went south. Four seemed a bit excessive. "Why the break from protocol?"

"Peter's not taking any chances after Maryland." Nicola took another drink. "Does Vivienne know you're coming?"

Max and Ethan suddenly found their shoes very interesting.

"I told her tonight." Deacon lifted his glass to his lips— Empty? How was it gone already?

"I bet she was thrilled."

"Thrilled," he muttered. That was hilarious. Deacon set his glass on the bar. It was time to get out of here. He needed sleep.

"Okay. Now I'm completely lost. Why do *you* look like you're going to punch someone?" Nicola hissed at him. "And why can't you two meet my eyes?" She pointed at Ethan, then at Max.

"Dash caught the tail end of Vivienne's date with Beardy McGee," Ethan explained, hiding his smile in his glass.

"*Date?*" Nicola set her stemmed fish bowl on the bar and crooked a pink-tipped finger toward the bartender. "Joe? Will you get this guy another drink?" She nudged her head in Deacon's direction.

"One for me too, Joe." Ethan set his glass beside Deacon's and said far too loudly, "Alex is probably just looking for some of that faux-tox Robert's peddling. You know they don't give it to people unless they marry one of us."

Shit. Deacon hadn't even thought of what would happen if Vivienne and Alex got *married.*

That's what normal people did though—the ones who didn't live forever. People like Alex. They went on dates, fell in love, got married . . . and they did it fast. And kids. *Shit.* What if Alex and Vivienne had kids and—

"Look at the bright side," Ethan went on, sniffing his fresh drink like a sommelier, "Alex will be dead in, what? Sixty, seventy years?"

Deacon didn't think it was possible, but his stomach sank lower. "*That's* the bright side?"

"What the hell happened?" Nicola snapped, forcing a full glass of scotch into Deacon's hand. "I really thought you were smitten this time."

Deacon had been smitten. He still was. And so was Vivienne—but with someone else.

"Yeah, well. Things change." Deacon lifted his glass toward a pair of women in tiny jean shorts smiling at him. What'd he have to lose?

Nicola redirected his chin so that he couldn't see anyone but her. "What. Happened?"

"She broke up with me back in June."

"What did you do?"

"I didn't *do* anything. She was upset because I had to stay in London."

A small wrinkle formed between Nicola's perfectly sculpted eyebrows. "You didn't have a choice though. You were sentenced to—What was that?"

"What?"

"Why'd you make that face?"

Deacon felt his frown deepen. "I didn't make a face."

"You did." Nicola turned to Ethan.

"You made a face, man." He nodded.

She pointed to Max.

"Um . . . I wasn't really paying attention?" Max turned around and ordered another beer.

Was it hot in here? Deacon tugged on the collar of his sweatshirt. The conversations buzzing around them became muffled. Why was it so bloody hot?

"Dash?" Nicola's voice held a warning.

"I didn't exactly tell her *why* I was in London."

Ethan grabbed a handful of peanuts from the bowl on the bar. "That's messed up, dude," Ethan laughed, rocking gleefully on his heels as he popped peanuts into his mouth. "You're a total idiot."

Nicola jabbed Ethan in the ribs with her elbow. He doubled over, wincing and clutching his stomach. When Nicola looked back at Deacon, her eyes were narrowed. "What is it with you and your damn secrets? You have to tell her. She deserves to know."

"What's the point?" Deacon said between drinks. Emily had probably only stopped by earlier because she felt sorry for him. Hell, he felt sorry for himself. "She's made her choice."

"Ethan's right." Nicola smacked Deacon's shoulder. What was with everyone hitting him tonight? "You are an idiot."

"I'm gonna go talk to those girls over there." Max retreated to the table of women in lace. Deacon wished he could join him.

"Going on a date with someone doesn't mean she's made a choice," Nicola insisted. "Vivienne's not even nineteen years into eternity. She's allowed to explore her opt—" Her mouth snapped shut. Who was she looking at?

"Shouldn't you be in London?"

Shit.

Deacon eyed a glowing red sign for the fire exit at the back. How cowardly would it be to make a run for it? He took two gulps of his scotch, set it on the bar, and turned around.

What would the penalty be for punching a sitting member of Leadership?

"Hey, Alex." Nicola's cool, slender fingers wrapped around Deacon's wrist, pinning him to her side. "How are you?"

Ethan's eyes flashed to Deacon's clenched fist. He pushed up his sleeves but didn't step any closer.

"Couldn't be better. Had a hot date tonight." Alex leaned back against the bar, a broad grin on his irritatingly bearded face. "Next round on me?"

Ethan knocked back what was left in his glass and set it down. "We were just leaving."

Joe threw down the white rag he'd been using to wipe up a spill and asked Alex what he was drinking.

Alex ordered a gin and tonic before pulling out his wallet. "What about you, Dash?" His mouth twisted into a mocking smile. "I feel like I owe you a drink."

Alex owed him a hell of a lot more than a bloody drink.

He owed him the last five months of his life back.

Deacon lunged, but Nicola and Ethan blocked him from hitting Alex squarely in his smug face.

"Always fighting. I wonder how long you'll be ordered to stay in London the next time you get into trouble?" Alex clucked his tongue and said under his breath, "No one gets what he wants all the time—not even you."

FIVE

Vivienne narrowed her eyes at Deacon. Why did he have to be so freaking cute? She liked the curl the humidity added to his dark hair. She liked the way his green eyes seemed to light up when he'd greeted her at the door a moment earlier. He still smelled the same, like cologne and fresh air.

Vivienne *really* liked that.

Sweat trickled down her spine. Her deep, calming breath did little to settle her nerves.

After crying way too much the last two days, it was obvious that she still liked *him*. A lot.

Which was insane.

Deacon had ditched her after she escaped from HOOK.

Then he had refused to come home when she needed him most.

What kind of person did that?

Not the kind of person you wanted to be in a relationship with.

By Friday evening, she had decided the mission could end in one of two ways. Either they would leave as friends or as strangers who would never speak again. Then she had received her updated alias dossier Saturday morning.

Not only was Deacon coming along, he would be pretending to be her *brother*.

Emily couldn't stop giggling when she found out they'd be living under the same roof. She'd even suggested a third possible ending to the mission.

But there was no way Vivienne wanted to go down *that* heart-breaking route again.

Then he answered the door, looking all . . . Deacony.

"If I didn't know better, I'd say you look happy to see me, Deacon."

"It's Cal, remember? And I *am* happy to see you, *Amanda*." Deacon appeared to be back to his good-humored self—although he had acquired an American accent.

Vivienne missed his British one.

"If you say so," she mumbled, looking past him into the darkness. "This house is gorgeous."

On her first mission, she had been given an apartment. It had been cute, but it was nothing compared to this sprawling brick rancher on the banks of Old Hickory Lake. The place was like something out of a middle-American dream.

"Richard has always had an eye for real estate. He's been buying and selling property since the 1920s."

She felt like she should know that name. "Who is Richard?"

"Twin number two. Come in, come in." Deacon opened the door wider and executed a sweeping bow worthy of a courtier at Buckingham Palace.

Vivienne dragged her suitcase into the air conditioned foyer. The small, tiled entrance opened into a wide, double-height living room with a suite of beige furniture. Knick-knacks lined the shelves on either side of a dated red brick fireplace. The gorgeous wide windows had been decorated with pink and turquoise floral curtains. Even the half-circle-shaped window cut into the far wall had a matching valance.

An entire forest of oak trees had been sacrificed for the floors, ceilings, doors, and trims. Deacon led her through an arched doorway into the heart of the home. The kitchen cabinets, stools, table, and chairs were all stained the same honeyed hue as the oak floor.

"Amanda," Deacon said, stepping aside to reveal a middle-aged couple waiting by the oak island, "this is our mom and dad."

The petite woman playing Karen Moloney took a halting step toward her new "daughter." "It's nice to meet you," she said. The wrinkles at the corners of her soft brown eyes grew more pronounced when she smiled.

"You too, *Mom*." Vivienne nodded to the man cast as Calvin Moloney, Sr. "Hey, *Dad*."

He nodded back. "Welcome to the family, honey."

"If there's anything you need, anything at all, don't hesitate to ask." Her mom tucked her highlighted brown hair behind her ears with a shaking hand. "We weren't told much about this role beyond the fact that you would be taking care of yourselves. But I'll be cooking while we're here. Don't feel like you have to eat it, although you're more than welcome to join us for meals."

Calvin put his arm around his wife's waist for a reassuring squeeze. "Mel—I mean *Karen*—is an excellent cook."

"Brilliant." Deacon grinned. "I'm an excellent eater."

"Sounds good to me," Vivienne said, fluffing air into the back of her sweaty shirt. They made small talk for another five minutes before their "parents" linked hands and escaped to their private wing of the house.

59

Once they were gone, the tension in the air between Vivienne and Deacon made her want to quit and go back home.

"How was your flight?" Deacon asked quietly, rearranging some rooster-shaped salt and pepper shakers tucked behind the apron sink.

"Fine." Vivienne wiped her clammy hands on her skirt. "Yours?"

"Fine." Silence. "Do you need anything from the store? I was planning on running to WalMart in a bit."

"No. I'm good. Thanks."

"It's really hot outside."

"Yeah, I know."

Deacon looked around the kitchen as if searching for something else to talk about. "There's water in the fridge. Do you want one?"

"I still have a bottle from the airport."

It shouldn't be like this between them.

If they were still together, this would have been the best trip of her life.

But then she would have told him about the impending forgetfulness, and he'd break her heart all over again.

Deacon tilted his head and squinted at her, like he was trying to read her thoughts.

Afraid of what he might see, Vivienne turned and snapped up the handle on her rolling suitcase. "I'm going to find my room."

Deacon jumped in front of her and took the bag. "Let me help you with that." He dragged it out of the kitchen, down the corridor past the living room, and stopped outside two open doors set opposite one another.

On the right side was a sky-blue bedroom with red-white-and-blue striped bedding and chunky mahogany furniture.

"That's my room," Deacon said from behind, making her jump. When she turned around, he was close enough that

60

she could smell his spicy cologne. "I'll give you a tour, if you want."

The last thing she needed was a tour of his bedroom. "No. I'm good."

A muscle in his jaw feathered as he nudged his chin toward the other door. "Yours is over there."

The second bedroom, identical in size, had a purple feature wall, spindly ivory furniture, and a whimsical canopy bed.

Deacon lingered near the entrance, flicking a springy doorstop attached to the baseboard with his toe. "What do you think?"

It was a beautiful room. Not her style, but comfortable, plush, and it smelled brand new.

"Looks good to me." She picked up the remote for the television from the top of the dresser. "I won't have to leave unless I need food," she said toward her private en suite, only half joking.

"Look, I want to say I'm sorry, all right?"

Vivienne jumped onto her bed and switched on the TV. "For what?"

The only sound was the vibrating doorstop. Vivienne was convinced he wasn't going to answer, until he said, "For what happened this summer."

They needed to have this conversation at some point, but not while she was sweaty and tired and irritable. And definitely not while he was looking at her with regretful green eyes and messy hair and wearing a tight blue T-shirt that made his arms look like they belonged in a magazine.

"I don't want to do this right now," she said through her teeth, clicking on a random war movie with lots of guts and gore and violence.

The phone in her pocket let out a cheerful ding. *Miss you already. Did you make it to TN?*

Alex's text made her face flush. It didn't feel right texting him with Deacon standing in front of her, but she did it anyway. *Miss you too. Here safe and sound. And tired. Gonna get some sleep.*

Deacon cleared his throat.

Vivienne kept her eyes on her phone, knowing it was easier this way. "Maybe after we've both had some sleep. Okay?"

The door clicked closed.

She dropped her phone onto the mattress and listened to the gruff-voiced narrator set up the storyline. Her sweat had dried; she could feel the grittiness on her skin between goosebumps.

Maybe if she showered she would feel more like sleeping.

It didn't work.

So she unpacked her bag and slipped her clothes into the chest of drawers and the closet. When she finished, she spritzed her mother's perfume over her pillow, like she did every week at Kensington.

The bottle had been salvaged from the house fire meant to conceal her parents' neutralization. The tube inside clinked against the glass when she tilted it, reminding her to use it sparingly.

But not even the scent of lilacs could calm her stretched nerves.

It could have been her nGh rearing its ugly head. Alex had said insomnia was usually the first symptom to set in. But it was too soon for that, wasn't it? Her Nevergene hadn't even been active for a year. She could ask Alex, but didn't really want to know the answer.

The door across the hall opened and closed.

No. Her sleeplessness was *his* fault.

The longer she laid there, the more she thought about *him*.

To distract herself, she opened her laptop; the browser was already on Instagram.

After Max's comment about making an album for his dad, she had looked back through her sparse camera roll. The first photo was of an ugly pair of shoes Emily had tried to make her buy during their first shopping trip to Albany. And there were photos of cinnamon rolls for some reason, but she wasn't sure when she'd taken those. Emily must have taken it.

A handful of other memories she had captured over the last year sat on her phone, small reminders of the people, places, and events that mattered.

At the airport that morning, she had started a brand-new Instagram account just for herself, with no followers: *Forever-eighteen2020*.

The handle still made her laugh.

She wasn't sure when she would start forgetting, but she hoped the photos would help jog her memory when she really needed it.

In order to log in, she needed the Wi-Fi password. She snuck out of her room in search of the keys to the internet and some junk food.

The cupboards were empty, everyone was gone, and the router was nowhere in sight. Vivienne went back to her room to grab her purse. She left via the back door and flew to a gas station, one situated next to a small grove of trees that concealed her landing.

Country music murmured through the speakers of the small convenience store. Vivienne picked up a pint of ice cream, a family-sized bag of BBQ potato chips, and two chocolate candy bars.

A bell over the door *dinged*, and a rowdy group of guys came in, shouting and laughing in matching black T-shirts with "Ryan's Getting Shackled" printed on the front. All but one of them stumbled around the store, grabbing snacks and roaring obscenities at the guy who ended up waiting in line behind Vivienne.

"Please excuse my friends," he said with an embarrassed chuckle, scratching his buzzed head. "They're all assholes."

"We all know a few of those," Vivienne said with a shrug.

"Yeah, but for some reason, I know *a lot* of them," he muttered before being dragged by the collar toward the beer display.

"You're either having a really good night or a really bad one," the clerk said, scanning Vivienne's items.

"Is it that obvious?"

A dusty prepaid phone card stuck out from behind a stack of CDs. The last time she'd contacted her foster brother Lyle, HOOK had been tapping his phone. Lawrence Hooke himself had called her back in hopes of convincing her to follow in her parents' footsteps and cooperate with them.

"Hello?"

Vivienne shook her head, clearing the memories of that bone-chilling conversation. "Sorry. How much did you say it was?"

"Ten sixty-seven."

Rummaging around her purse, Vivienne mumbled an apology as she pulled handfuls of random items from the cavernous bag. She lost things inside it all the time. Like the tube of mango-flavored lip balm she now found beneath the ripped lining. She'd bought it in June and hadn't seen it since.

The woman lifted her penciled-in eyebrows. "Looks like you need a smaller purse."

"You're probably right." Vivienne freed her wallet from her tangled earbud cord, then paid with her credit card. On her way out, she swiped a plastic spoon and carried the bag to one of the picnic tables in a grassy area next to the parking lot. Her phone dinged.

Assuming it was another text from Alex, Vivienne

ignored it. She undid the lid on her ice cream and dipped the spoon into the pint of cookies 'n cream.

Snap.

Of course. Why wouldn't the spoon break in half? Why would something go right when it could go wrong?

She shoved the container aside to thaw and ripped open the bag of chips. Her phone dinged again. When she checked it, the voicemail icon blinked from the center of the screen.

She popped a chip into her mouth and listened.

"Hey, it's Paul. I wanted to let you know that Leadership has approved your nomination of Lyle Foley . . . "

Vivienne held her breath to keep from squealing with excitement. This was the first bit of good news she'd had all summer.

"There are still a few details to be worked out. But, as of right now, I don't see why you wouldn't be allowed to bring him to Neverland. I'll get on it as soon as I get back from London next week and give you a date."

Lyle was coming to Neverland.

Holy crap.

He was going to freak out when she told him.

All she had to do was survive the next few weeks.

Using what was left of the spoon, Vivienne scraped around the ice cream's softened edges and swallowed a victorious bite.

Lyle was coming to *Neverland.*

That meant he had no connection with HOOK.

Which meant she could finally talk to him.

She fitted the lid onto her ice cream, grabbed her purse, and ran back inside to buy a prepaid cell phone.

After paying for her stuff, she snagged another spoon from the coffee caddy. When she got back to the picnic table, she added minutes to the flip phone, took a hulking bite of half-melted ice cream, and dialed Lyle.

It rang once . . . Twice . . .

Movement in the corner of her eye drew her attention, and she turned to catch Deacon jogging across the parking lot toward her. "Hey, Amanda!"

Vivienne snapped the phone closed and shoved it into her purse. "I thought you gave up stalking me," she said, forgetting momentarily that they weren't on teasing terms anymore.

Deacon ran his hand through his hair, making it stick up at the back. "I'm only here because the truck was empty." He stepped to the side, giving her an unobstructed view of the lone vehicle parked beside the gas pumps.

"I was joking." He hadn't come for her this summer, why would he bother to now? She slid her snacks back into the brown paper bag and hooked her purse over her shoulder. "I'll see you at home."

"Want a lift?"

"I'd rather walk."

"Why do you have to be so bloody stubborn?" he groaned. "You know what? It doesn't matter. If you feel like getting a lift with me to school tomorrow, we're leaving at eight." On his way back to the pump, he kicked a bunch of stones across the parking lot.

By the time Vivienne landed back at the house, her appetite was gone. She stored the melted ice cream in the freezer and brought the rest of her goodies into her room. Then she fell onto her lilac-scented pillowcase and drifted off to sleep.

SIX

Deacon felt like his eyes had just fallen shut when his mobile startled him awake like a fire alarm. Why did high school start so early?

The hot shower did little to revive him. Perhaps he'd feel more human after breakfast.

When he reached the kitchen, the savory smell of frying bacon lifted his mood. "Morning, Mom."

Karen looked up from the cooktop and smiled. "Good morning."

He leaned his hip against the counter and stole a slice of bacon from the paper-towel-covered plate. Cooked to perfection: crispy enough to melt in his mouth. "Bacon is my favorite. How'd you know?"

"You're a teenage boy. I took a chance you weren't a vegetarian. Eggs are right there." She nodded toward a bowl on the counter. "Help yourself."

"You don't have to tell me twice." He filled a plate and slid onto one of the stools at the island.

"Want some juice?" Karen asked, carrying over the salt and pepper shakers.

He could only nod until he swallowed the massive bite he'd stuffed into his mouth. "Please."

It had been a long time since he'd had this sort of interaction first thing in the morning. His father had always been the one to cook breakfast; his mother had stopped eating the meal altogether when he passed away.

Karen filled a cup and sat it beside his plate. "I packed your lunch. It's in the fridge."

He took another bite. "You didn't have to do that. But thank you." His mood lifted a bit more.

"I was happy to. There's a lot of downtime with this job." She set two brown paper bags in front of him. "You might let Amanda know it's here."

His mood fell.

"Did she not come out for breakfast?"

Karen's lips pressed together. "Not yet."

Deacon checked his watch. It was nearly time to go. He finished eating, drank the juice in one go, and brought his dishes to the dishwasher. Karen took the last slice of bacon out of the pan and turned off the burner.

Sneaking another piece, he kissed his faux mother on the cheek. "Thanks again. That was the best breakfast I've had in ages." On his way out, he picked up the two lunch bags. Five minutes later, he was ready to walk out the door, but there was still no sign of Vivienne.

"It's eight o'clock." Deacon pounded on her door. "We need to go." They were meeting Ethan—Bentley—in the school office at quarter past. If they didn't leave now, they'd be late.

"*It's eight o'clock . . .* " He heard Vivienne mimic. Her mobile dinged. When the door finally opened, he could smell lilacs.

Seeing the clothes strewn across her unmade bed made

him smile. She was such a beautiful slob. The green outfit she had chosen showcased her tan, which made him think about her tan lines—

"What're you looking at?" Vivienne hissed, tugging at the hem on her shorts.

"Nothing." His head snapped up. "Here." He shoved her lunch into her arms. "Mom packed lunch."

"She did?" Vivienne looked toward the kitchen.

"You'll have to thank her later," he said, heading toward the garage, "we're late enough as it is."

"Are we taking the truck you had last night?"

"That's the one." Then he added, "I hear you have a thing for guys with trucks," because he couldn't help himself.

He didn't turn around to see her face, but he imagined she was fuming.

She climbed into the cab and slammed the door.

Good. Deacon didn't want to be the only one feeling miserable today.

Once they were on the road, he stole a glance at Vivienne in the passenger seat. The ends of her hair were lighter than the top; ombré strands lifted slightly from the air conditioning blasting through the vent. He liked a bit of heat as much as the next man, but the humidity this far south was ridiculous.

Her mobile dinged again.

Deacon imagined the steering wheel was Alex's neck and squeezed until his fingers ached. Didn't Alex have anything better to do? "Will you do me a favor?"

She didn't look up. "Depends."

Her thumbs flew across the screen like she was writing a damned novel.

"Turn that thing on silent so it doesn't keep me awake tonight."

Vivienne narrowed her eyes and made a show of

pressing the volume button until it vibrated in her hand. "Happy *now*?"

How could she think he'd ever be happy about her texting some other man?

"What do you think?" He flicked the indicator and stopped behind a line of cars waiting to pull into the student parking lot.

Vivienne vaulted from the truck before he'd put it in park. He grabbed his rucksack from the back seat and followed everyone else toward the glass entryway, trying to look anywhere but at Vivienne's tanned legs . . . and short shorts . . . and swaying hips.

Ethan pushed himself away from the flagpole when he saw them. His backwards baseball cap matched his blue runners. "Morning, Moloney children. How are we this fine, humid morning?"

Vivienne offered him a warm greeting and a brilliant smile. Deacon bit back his irritation and followed them through the main door.

Every high school in the States smelled the same. Like canvas rucksacks, sweaty teenagers, and metal lockers. A massive black and gold "H" had been painted in the center of the floor.

When they reached the office, the receptionist escorted them to a row of chairs across from her desk. Before sitting down, Deacon told her they were supposed to meet someone named David Calhoun.

The elderly woman nodded and picked up the intercom. "David Calhoun to the office, please," she said in a raspy voice.

Although they had yet to meet, Deacon felt like he already knew David William Calhoun. David's birth mother had passed away during childbirth; his father, Brian, had married Jane Cheney three years later, only to be killed in a car crash when David was ten. As far as anyone knew, Brian

Calhoun had taken his first wife's secret life as a PAN with him to his grave.

A tall guy with a military-style haircut sauntered into the office wearing a Vols T-shirt, cargo shorts, and flip flops. "Mornin', Mrs. Garrett. Did you need somethin'?"

The receptionist pointed at Deacon, Vivienne, and Ethan with a nicotine-stained finger. "Apparently, you're supposed to show the new kids around."

"No problem." David approached them with a welcoming smile. "Hey, I'm David."

"Bentley."

"Cal." He poked Vivienne in the ribs. "This is my sister, Amanda."

Vivienne jumped and slapped Deacon's hand. "Hey, David."

David nodded to Deacon and Ethan, but his gaze lingered on Vivienne. "Nice to meet y'all. Where's everyone headed for first period?" He may have asked all of them, but it was obvious he only cared about one answer.

Deacon checked the schedule that had been included in his alias dossier against the one in Vivienne's hand. "Looks like we both have Spiker."

"Bender," Ethan said, shoving his schedule into the front pocket of his rucksack.

"I have Spiker first too," David said with a grin, "but both classrooms are upstairs. Follow me."

A handful of nosey teenagers still loitering next to their lockers watched them walk toward the stairs.

"Are you two really brother and sister?" David asked, glancing over his shoulder at them.

Vivienne mumbled, "Unfortunately."

"And you're both seniors? No offense, but you don't look like twins."

Deacon searched the area for exits. There was one at each end of the hallway, and a third, he assumed, down the corridor to his right. "We were born the same year, only ten months apart."

"Oh, right." David stopped at the top of the stairwell and pointed to his left. "Bender is down the hall, past the fire extinguisher."

Ethan thanked him and headed toward the extinguisher without a backward glance.

"Spiker is this way." David turned right and slowed his pace until Vivienne caught up with him. He immediately began asking her questions about where she'd moved from and whether or not she missed it.

"I'm not sure yet," she said, flicking her hair over her shoulders. "We've only been here a few weeks."

"School sucks, but I figure that's kinda a universal thing. But there's a lot happening at the lake, and being close to Nashville is cool." David stopped when he reached a classroom at the end of the hall, then asked if she wanted to sit with him.

Without a sideways glance at Deacon, Vivienne agreed, following David to one of the two open seats at the side of the room, beside a bookshelf. Deacon went to the only other free chair, at the back, next to the windows.

He tapped at the double-paned glass, then checked the handle in the center of the lower frame. It wasn't locked. The opening would be large enough to fit through in the off chance he and Vivienne needed a quick exit.

It wasn't ideal having her so close to the front of the room, but he could make it work in a pinch.

"Lookin' for an escape?"

He focused on the girl to his left. Straight black hair, wide hazel eyes, a diamond stud in her nose, and a beauty mark above her cherry-red lips. "Do you think I'll need one?" he asked with a smile.

"Nah. Ms. Spiker is one of the best teachers in this hell hole." She propped her cheek on her hand as she drew concentric circles on her pink binder. "You won't want to jump out the window during this class. Now, if you have Mr. Harrison for calculus . . . *that's* a different story."

He pulled out his own notebook and searched for a pencil. There was one at the bottom of his bag beneath his black sweatshirt. "What's wrong with Harrison?"

The girl swung her bare knees from under her desk and leaned toward him. "He eats a ton of dairy at lunch—I'm talkin' cheese on *everything*—even though he's obviously lactose intolerant. Get to his class early." She wrinkled her nose. "Sit by the window."

"In case I want to jump?"

"Or breathe fresh air."

Deacon always sat at the back when given the option, so that wouldn't be an issue. "Thanks for the heads-up. I'm Cal."

"Diane. And you're welcome."

When the bell rang, Deacon feigned interest in his classmates' summertime stories and reviewed the syllabus as though he was actually going to complete the assignments.

A minimum of one PAN was in the classroom with David at all times during the day. At lunch, Diane waved at Deacon from a table near the exterior doors. Two other girls he recognized from second period sat across from her.

"Only the first day and you've already got yourself a fan club," Ethan sniggered, following him down the stairs to the lower level of the cafeteria.

After another round of tedious introductions, a girl wearing an HHS volleyball T-shirt named Kate scooted her chair closer to Ethan.

"Where are you guys from?" she asked, twisting her platinum hair around her index finger.

"South Dakota," Ethan said, pulling a turkey sandwich from his lunch bag before launching into a ridiculous story involving a mountain lion. He and Deacon usually tried to top the other with their backstory embellishments, but Deacon didn't feel like it today.

All Deacon told them was that he'd moved from Oregon.

"Are you living close by?" Kate's friend Melody asked. The combination of her thick fringe nearly covering her eyes and the way she chomped her pretzel stick reminded him of highland cattle.

"Not too far." Ethan dumped the rest of his lunch onto the table. "A few houses down from the big Methodist church."

"What about you, Cal?" Diane crossed her legs; her knees brushed against his.

"My parents bought a place on the lake."

"Do you have a boat?" Melody asked, blowing her fringe out of her eyes.

"It'd be a shame if we didn't." He made a mental note to file a request with Julie.

Diane smacked her hands on the table, making the other girls jump. "We should totally go out on the lake this weekend."

Ethan grinned at Deacon over his water bottle. "Sounds good to me."

"Can we do it on Saturday?" Kate pushed her salad from one side of the container to the other. "I'll be gone all day Sunday."

"Saturday works best for me too." Melody crunched another pretzel stick, then turned to Diane and asked if her mom had any wine coolers they could "borrow."

Diane set aside her bag of crisps in favor of a giant choco- late chip biscuit. "Of course she does. The fridge is full of them."

The first bite of Deacon's BLT was amazing. He'd have to thank Karen again when he got home. "I can get us some beer if you want."

Diane put her hand on his knee and squeezed. She

74

smelled like lemons, which was nice. Not as nice as lilacs though. "Do you have a fake ID?"

If only she knew. "A bunch of them."

Something whizzed past Deacon's ear.

Ethan didn't even bother pretending it wasn't him. "You gonna invite your sister?" He plucked another grape from a bunch and rolled it between his fingers.

Deacon snagged one for himself and popped it into his mouth. "We both know she won't want to come." Vivienne had made it pretty clear she wanted nothing to do with him.

"Which one's your sister?" Brushing back her fringe, Melody searched the tables around them.

Kate pointed across the crowded cafeteria. "Cute brunette in the green romper."

The three girls swiveled toward Vivienne's table.

Melody asked why she wasn't sitting with them.

"Because David is obsessed with her and asked her to sit with him first." Diane slid one neon pink nail from Deacon's wrist to his elbow and back again. "You have a girlfriend back in Oregon?"

Deacon watched Vivienne, deep in conversation with their mark. Why was she being so attentive? All she was supposed to do was keep an eye on him and wait for his Nevergene to activate, not become his best friend.

"Nope. No girlfriend." This was the reason he didn't date. Hooking up with girls didn't involve all of this bloody heartache.

"What about you, Bentley?" Melody tapped the face of Ethan's watch.

"Yeah. I have a girlfriend." His answer made Melody and Kate frown.

"Cal?" Melody leaned toward him. "What class do you have next?"

"I'm not sure." He unraveled the tattered schedule from his back pocket. "PE."

75

"Me too," Kate giggled.

Melody gave her a high five. "Same."

Diane glared daggers at the other girls. "Ugh. I have Harrison."

No place was safe. Everywhere Vivienne went the rest of the week, David found her. Which was a good thing, she supposed. After all, there was no need to keep an eye on their mark when the mark never took his eyes off of her.

She speed-walked to the truck, then ducked behind the bed so her heartrate could return to normal.

Ethan was sitting on the tailgate, swinging his legs and scrolling on his phone. "Playin' hide-and-seek with your buddy David?"

"Shut up." Sweat rolled down her back. Something bit her neck; she swatted at it. "David hasn't let me out of his sight all week."

"We noticed." Ethan nodded to a couple strolling hand-in-hand to their car. They gave Vivienne an odd look but didn't stop.

Her right leg started tingling, and she shifted from a crouch to a squat. "Tell me if you see him."

"Will do." Ethan adjusted his Vanderbilt hat and grinned at his phone.

"There you are, Amanda!" A pair of black sneakers rounded the truck and stopped next to her.

"David's here." Ethan's grin grew wider; he still didn't look up.

Vivienne punched Ethan in the thigh as she straightened and tried to make it look like she hadn't been hiding from their mark. "Oh *heeey*, David."

Wiping the sweat from his forehead, David winced at the

cloudless sky. "I wanted to ask if you'd be interested in comin' to a show with me this weekend?"

Her eyes darted to Ethan. This time, he seemed to be paying attention.

"Cal's having that party on your family's boat Saturday." Ethan stood and shoved his phone into his pocket. "*Remember?*"

Had she missed a boat parked at the dock behind their house? "I don't think we own a—"

Ethan's eyebrows rose.

"I mean, yeah. Totally forgot about the party. On a boat. We most definitely own."

Ethan covered his smile and shook his head. "You should come too, David." His light blue eyes widened when she shot him a glare.

"I'll have to clear it with my mom first, but sounds fun." Turning back toward Vivienne, David started scratching his arm. "The show's actually on Friday if you'd still wanna go."

"I would," Vivienne said, linking her arm with Ethan's, "but we're kinda a thing, and I don't want Bentley getting jealous."

"Oh geez. Sorry, dude. I swear I didn't know."

"It's still pretty new," she lied.

"Gotcha." When David turned around, he stumbled.

Ethan's hand shot out to keep him from going headfirst into the line of exiting cars. "You okay, man?"

"Thanks," David muttered, his face turning red. "That's the third time I've tripped today. Not sure what's wrong with me."

Vivienne felt her adrenaline spike. Unsteadiness was the first sign of an activating Nevergene. And if it activated, the PAN only had a short window of time to inject him with a serum to keep his gene active. "I'll go to the show with you," she blurted.

David's eyes widened. "But you just said—"

"I've changed my mind." Vivienne dropped Ethan's arm and shoved him toward his own truck. "He's not even that good of a kisser."

Ethan snorted and gave her a cocky smile. "That's not what you said last night."

It took every ounce of restraint within her, but she ignored him. "What time's the show?"

David looked over her head toward Ethan. "You sure you're cool with it?"

Ethan had the gall to laugh. "My broken heart will mend eventually."

"Sweet. Show's at six. I gotta get to soccer practice right now. Maybe we can talk about it before first period tomorrow?"

"Yeah. Sure. Sounds good."

David waved and jogged across the lot toward the soccer field.

"What have I gotten myself into?" Vivienne groaned, covering her face. Now David was going to get the wrong impression.

"Don't even pretend like you're the victim here. You literally started dating me and dumped me in the same sentence. *And* you said I wasn't a good kisser. I'll have you know—"

"Shut up."

Ethan's lips clamped shut, then he sighed. "But seriously. You shouldn't go out with him. The rules are pretty strict when it comes to that kind of stuff."

"Did you see the way he stumbled? How else were we going to cover Friday night?"

Ethan shrugged. "Cal and I would have taken care of it."

Typical. The two of them wanted to keep her on the sidelines. Had they ever escaped from HOOK? No. But she had. And she was perfectly capable of taking care of herself.

"Now there's no need. I'll take Friday night, and the two

of you can handle him at your little boat party on Saturday."
A bead of sweat tumbled its way from her hairline down her
forehead. Why the heck was it so humid in this place?

Deacon jogged around the back of the truck, looking as
irritatingly perfect as ever. Did he ever sweat? "What'd I
miss?"

"Apparently I'm a shitty kisser," Ethan said, throwing his
backpack into the back of his own truck.

"So I've been told," Deacon said with a smirk.

"By who?"

Deacon pretended to lock his lips and throw the key over
his shoulder.

Ethan kicked the back tire. Then he smiled. "David just
asked Amanda on a date."

Deacon's shoulders stiffened. "Aren't you popular?"

"What can I say? Boys like new toys," Vivienne shot
back.

"Was that a dig at me?" Deacon snarled, chasing her to
the passenger side. When she grabbed the handle, he held
the door shut. "That's not fair."

"Yeah, well, it's true." He'd ditched her the moment the
novelty had faded. Sure, she had been the one to break up
with him. But that was only because he was hiding in
England, refusing to come home.

"Hey, Cal!" A tall, athletic-looking girl in a pair of tight
spandex shorts and an HHS volleyball T-shirt waved from a
few cars away. "Come here for a sec."

"Oh, would you look at that. You have a shiny new toy."

He dropped his hand with a curse and veered toward the
girl. Vivienne ripped open the door, and hot, stifling air
gusted over her. Instead of climbing into the inferno, she
threw her backpack onto the seat and tried to ignore the way
the girl kept touching Deacon's arm. He was laughing and
obviously enjoying being the center of all the female
attention.

"I see the two of you are still fighting," Ethan drawled from the cab of his truck.

"Stay out of it."

"Maybe I would have if you hadn't started a rumor that I was the worst guy you'd ever kissed."

"I never said—"

"Too late now. These things grow legs in high school." Ethan's smile faded as he watched Deacon. "You really need to listen to what he has to say."

"I've listened to every order he's barked since we got here." And she was sick of being told what to do. Her next mission would be a solo one.

"I'm not talking about the mission. The two of you need to discuss what happened this summer."

Crap. "What do you know?"

Had someone told him about her test results?

And if Ethan knew, it was only a matter of time before Deacon found out too.

"Just talk to him, okay?"

She rolled her eyes as more sweat collected at the base of her spine. "Fine. I'll talk to him . . . *if* you give me a ride home."

SEVEN

That evening, Deacon enjoyed a buttery chicken pot pie dinner with Calvin and Karen. There was no sign of Vivienne. How she could barricade herself in her room every day without going completely mad made no sense to him. All he wanted to do was escape.

Since it wouldn't be dark for a few more hours and he couldn't fly, Deacon dragged his running gear from his suitcase and changed. On his way through the living room, he nodded to his parents, who were cuddled on the couch, watching a movie.

The air outside was thick enough to drink, and sweat was burning his eyes before he reached the end of the driveway. He started for the school, then turned down a few side streets with wide, sunburnt lawns and sprawling houses.

About two miles in, his wireless headphones died.

And all he had to keep him company were his useless thoughts of how much he'd screwed up this summer.

You had a choice. You made the wrong one.

What would Leadership have done if he had refused to stay at Harrow?

It was too late to ask that question.

He had stayed. He had done what he thought was right. He had never been so wrong.

When he reached the park, he turned around.

What was he going to do now?

Vivienne wanted nothing to do with him—that much was obvious.

Did he bow out and hope that she'd forgive him in a decade or so? She couldn't be mad at him forever. Could she?

He could always move back to London. Peter would be thrilled. So would his mother.

Or he could go to Limerick. Start over completely at the Neverland there.

By the time he reached the end of the driveway, it was dark. The night was still warm, but a faint breeze blew in from the lake. He would've gone directly to the dock if he hadn't been so thirsty. The air conditioned darkness inside the house made him shiver. There was no sign of his parents in the living room, but the light was on in the kitch—

Deacon hesitated in the arched doorway.

Vivienne leaned on the island wearing a fluffy purple robe.

Should he leave her in peace or force her to acknowledge him?

In the end the choice was simple: he would rather bask in the heat of her irritation than remain invisible for another lonely night.

Vivienne raised her eyes from a magazine on the counter and bit the slice of pizza in her hand. "You're really sweaty."

He used the bottom of his T-shirt to wipe the sweat from his face. "I went running." Still buzzing from the exercise, he rolled his shoulders and crossed to the cupboards. It would take a few minutes before he felt like sitting down.

"Thanks for the invite."

After filling the glass at the tap, he turned around. He had thought about inviting her, but, "I didn't think you'd come."

Her eyes darted toward him, then back to the pizza. "Did you eat yet?"

"Mom made chicken pot pie." How long had it been since dinner? Vivienne's pepperoni pizza smelled amazing.

"Want some?" she asked, scooting the cardboard box toward him.

"Sure." Deacon grabbed a slice and relished the first bite. It wasn't hot anymore but it was good.

When Vivienne finished what was in her hand, he expected her to run away. But she didn't run away. Why wasn't she running away?

She wiped her hands on a crumpled paper towel next to her and took a sip from a can of soda. "I'm ready to talk now if you are."

He wasn't.

He needed a shower and a good night's sleep.

And water.

He took a drink. Then another. "All right. Let's talk."

Vivienne slipped onto one of the bar stools. When she crossed her legs, her bare knees emerged from the gap in her robe. What was she wearing beneath?

"Why didn't you come back this summer?"

Focus, Deacon. Focus.

This summer.

The shittiest summer he'd ever had.

"I told you already. I wasn't allowed."

The stool scraped on the floor when she shoved away from the island. "If you're going to give me the same crap, then I'm going to bed."

"Sit back down. *Please.*"

She sat, but her back and shoulders remained rigid.

Why had he thought it was a good idea to keep this from her? He was some fool.

"I didn't go to London for a normal Leadership meeting." He heaved a breath. "I was on trial."

Vivienne's head snapped up. "*What?*" Her brows drew together. "Why?"

"There may have been a few fights, an arrest, a certain haunting incident, some well-placed Christmas lights on church steeples—"

"That was *you?*"

He nodded. "I nearly got you killed when I asked Joel to give you your exam early. I didn't follow *any* of the rules when I recruited you. And I may have bribed a Neverland official into swapping our mission assignments."

"Holy crap, Deacon!"

He grabbed a second slice of pizza. "It's Cal."

"I can't believe you did all that."

It was hard to tell if her wide-eyed expression was one of horror or appreciation.

Choosing to think it was the latter, he chuckled and leaned his hip against the counter. "And those are only the violations they know about."

"Did you really get arrested?"

"That one genuinely wasn't my fault." Some prick at the bar had shoved him multiple times; Deacon had been defending himself.

A smile briefly came over her lips before her frown returned. "You should've told me."

Deacon wanted to kiss away the despondent lines marring her beautiful face. Instead, he ate what was left of the pizza. "With everything that happened this spring, the last thing you needed was to worry about me and the mistakes I've made. Then you broke up with me and said you never wanted to speak to me again."

Fiddling with the tie on her robe, she kept her gaze on the counter. "I broke up with you because you were back with Gwen."

Gwen? She thought he'd been with *Gwen*? "What are you on about?" He hadn't seen Gwen in ages.

"I called you, and she answered your phone."

"She *what*?" The only time his mobile had been out of his sight was the time he'd forgotten it after dinner. But he'd remembered it before he left Harrow.

"You didn't know?" Vivienne shoved her loose sleeves up to her elbows and scratched her arms.

"Of course not." That explained a lot. "Why didn't you say something to me about it? Give me a chance to explain?"

"It was easier to break up with you than have you break up with me when you found out."

His chest tightened. The pizza in his stomach made him feel queasy. When her mobile buzzed on the counter, he had the overwhelming urge to hurl it against the wall.

"Found out what?" he asked, even though he was certain he didn't want to know.

Vivienne pulled a worn slip of paper from her robe pocket and slid it across the counter facedown. Deacon's hand shook when he picked it up. Printed on the other side were three lines: one green, one orange, and one red.

A hormone chart.

He pointed to the orange line. "Yours?" The numbers were almost double his own.

Vivienne shook her head. "My mother's."

"That means . . . yours is . . . "

No. No. No.

The paper drifted onto the counter, and her tear-filled eyes met his. "Mine's red."

EIGHT

V ivienne watched Deacon pace between the island and
the picture window overlooking the lake. He hadn't
said a word in the five minutes since she had told him about
her hormone levels. But neither had she. He'd kept things
from her to keep her from worrying. She'd kept her secrets
because she was a coward.

"What's your treatment plan?" Deacon asked, stopping
long enough to rake his hand through his hair and curse.

"I . . . um . . . I don't really have one." Her hands and
arms were red and raw from where she'd scratched them.

When he finally looked at her, his eyes were dull. Hollow.
"They have medicine that could help."

"It won't." She tore her eyes from his and folded her
chart with sharp, jerking movements. "I'm in a lose-lose situation. Take meds, lose the ability to fly and, eventually, my
memory. Or I do nothing and get the same result. Or I could
ask HOOK to neutralize me and be done with all of this."

His mouth opened. And closed.

"I don't even know why I'm telling you. It has nothing to do with you. This is my problem and I'll deal with it on my own." The same way she'd dealt with every other problem she'd ever faced. She was strong and independent. She had friends who supported her. And soon, she'd have her brother. And she had Alex.

She didn't need Deacon. "You've made it clear how you feel about a relationship that won't last. I'm pretty sure forgetting who I am qualifies."

"Of course it *qualifies!*" he roared. "I've seen the forgetful PAN—and the people they leave behind. Grieving for eternity for ones who don't even know they exist. It's a fate *worse* than death."

"*Whooo* wants to play Scrabble?" Karen stepped into the kitchen, shaking a cardboard box. When she looked between Deacon and Vivienne, her smile disappeared. "Everything okay?"

"I can't do this." Deacon stormed out the back door and disappeared into the night.

"Amanda? What's wrong?"

"Nothing." The last thing Vivienne wanted was to go back into her silent bedroom and think about what had happened. Deacon had reacted exactly as she had expected. So why did it feel like there was a gaping hole in her chest? "I'd love to play Scrabble."

Karen's gaze dropped, and her eyes widened. "What happened to your hands?"

Vivienne hid them inside her fuzzy sleeves. "They're just really itchy."

"I think I have cream that'll help. I can grab it if you want."

"I'll be fine."

Karen set up the board on the kitchen table and tried to make small talk; Vivienne responded with nods and one-word answers. Eventually, Karen fell silent. At some point,

Calvin came through and checked their progress. After rearranging the tiles on Vivienne's rack to spell the word *sucker*, he winked at her and continued to the living room.

The hour-long game ended with Karen's score nearly double Vivienne's. Which normally would have bothered her. She didn't like losing. But she had already lost so much today that the game didn't even register.

"Rematch tomorrow?" Karen suggested, dropping a handful of tiles into a black drawstring bag. "Maybe we can convince the guys to play."

Vivienne couldn't see Deacon agreeing to that. "Can't tomorrow. I have a date."

"Really? With whom?"

"His name's David."

"David what?"

"Calhoun."

Karen grabbed the notebook they had used to keep score and wrote down David's full name.

Vivienne laughed despite herself. Their date was the least of her worries. "Don't worry, *Mom*. I'll be fine." Maybe if she said it often enough, it would eventually be true.

"Call me if you need anything. And if he's not a perfect gentleman, tell him your dad owns a gun."

"Does he own a gun?"

"No." Karen winked. "But David doesn't know that, now does he?"

"Good point."

Vivienne had seven messages and one missed call from Alex. He knew about her fate and still liked her. She tried to take some comfort in that. "Thanks for packing lunches and cooking all week. I really appreciate it."

"It was my pleasure."

"Night, Mom."

Karen smiled. "Goodnight, honey."

Vivienne nodded to her dad watching TV on the couch

on the way to her bedroom. The first thing she did when she got inside was take off the robe. What had she been thinking, packing something so warm?

When she called Alex, he answered on the second ring. "Hey, everything okay? I got worried when I didn't hear from you."

"It's fine." *Fine. Fine. Fine.* "Sorry I missed your calls. I was playing Scrabble with my mom."

"Who won?"

Vivienne wandered around her room, collecting dirty clothes for the hamper. Humid weather made for a lot of laundry. "Karen crushed me."

"Bummer. How was the rest of your day?"

Terrible. Awful. Horrible. Heartbreaking.

"Fine."

"That wasn't very convincing." Alex sighed. "Not having a good time?"

That had to be the understatement of the year. "It's been a crappy week."

"Here's an idea. How about I fly down Saturday and we do something fun? I can check who's playing at The Opry. Maybe grab some dinner beforehand?"

That did sound fun—and distracting. Unfortunately, "This weekend's no good. My brother's throwing a party on a boat we don't own." And she had a date. But she didn't figure Alex needed to know that. It wasn't a *real* date. And when they'd discussed their "relationship" before she'd left, she had told him that she wasn't ready for labels.

"I didn't realize Ethan was your brother."

"He's not." Life would have been a lot easier if he was. She dropped to the corner of her unmade bed and stretched out on her back. "Deacon's here too."

"Three recruiters for one mark seems excessive," Alex clipped. A car door slammed on the other end of the line. "Did Dash request the assignment?"

"I doubt it." And even if he had, he wouldn't be doing it again.

"Be careful, Vivienne."

"They haven't let me out of their sight long enough to be care*less*," she said, slipping the strap of her tank top back into place. Emily had forced her to buy something cuter to sleep in than her dad's old OHIO sweatshirt. She had to admit, the silky black tank and matching shorts were pretty comfortable.

"I'm not talking about the mission. He's always had a thing for you."

"Not anymore."

"Even so, you should know that he has a reputation around Neverland. I'd hate to see you heartbroken because of someone like him."

If only Alex knew it was too late for that.

The metal dock bobbed up and down on the lapping water while crickets played their music in the long grass. The night was bright enough that Deacon could see silhouettes of the trees along the opposite bank.

High levels of nGh led to catastrophic memory loss. There were no exceptions.

Tootles, his grandad's best mate, never remembered more than a few hours previous. The other patients confined to a drafty country house in the Scottish highlands were the very same. And at night, they lashed out like they were possessed.

It was only a matter of time before Vivienne joined them.

She would be gone.

Just like his father.

Deacon kicked off his shoes and let his feet dangle in the lake. The water felt warm, but he knew coldness hid beneath the surface. He wanted to let it numb him and take away the hopeless thoughts invading his brain. The worry. The regrets.

He had wasted the last five months pining when he should have been moving on. Getting over her. Putting what they could've had behind him. Then the shock of hearing they had no future together wouldn't feel so devastating.

Deacon took off his sweaty shirt and pulled his mobile from his pocket. The screen lit up with a message he hadn't realized was there. *Plan?*

He returned Ethan's text. *Swimming. You in?*

Ethan's response was instantaneous. *B there in 5.*

Inky blackness dulled Deacon's senses when he dove in, and the edges of the moon appeared as fluid as the frigid water surrounding him. At thirty seconds, his lungs burned for oxygen; at a minute, he began feeling lightheaded.

He resurfaced and drank in the humid air.

After three short breaths and one long one, he tried again.

When Deacon came back up, Ethan was on the dock, kicking off his shoes. "Thanks for waiting."

Deacon floated on his back until Ethan got in. It continually amazed him how much effort it took to stay afloat in the water versus the air. The water made him feel sluggish; the sky made him feel invincible.

"I'm surprised you didn't bring Nicola." But Deacon was grateful she hadn't come. The last thing he needed was her female intuition telling her something was wrong, followed by her relentless digging.

"She's avoiding the weirdness between you and Vivienne. I'm heading to her place after I leave." Stretching his arms above his head, Ethan dove in. When he popped up next to Deacon, he nodded toward deeper water. "How far are we going?"

Deacon searched the dark horizon for some point of

reference. The opposite bank was a bit far for a warm-up. "Buoy?"

"Fifty bucks says I beat you."

"You're—"

Ethan lunged and shoved his head beneath the water. Deacon tried to grab for him, but Ethan was already swimming for the buoy.

Despite the head start, Deacon only lost by an arm's length. He flew into the air to catch his breath and give the stitch in his side a chance to ease. "You're a cheating bastard."

"And you're a sore loser," Ethan laughed, pounding the side of his head, trying to dislodge the water in his ears. "Double or nothin' on the way back?"

"Why not?" They dropped into the water in tandem, then raced toward the shore.

This time, Deacon won easily.

"The Mermaids must've taught you a few tricks. You're a lot faster than I remember."

Deacon chuckled as he pulled himself onto the dock and fell onto his back. "Maybe you're just a lot slower." His stomach was in knots. He'd overdone it with the pizza.

Ethan flopped beside him, leaking water all over Deacon's shirt and shoes. "Have anything good to drink inside?"

Karen had stocked the fridge with all kinds of drinks, but there was no way Deacon was going back into the house before he was sure everyone was asleep. "Just get something at Nicola's."

Ethan was lucky. When he left, he was going to hang out with his immortal girlfriend, not a care in the world. Deacon was going to be up all night cursing the fates. "Would you still be with Nicola if she wasn't one of us?"

"You mean if she was an outsider?"

"Yeah." *Or if she was going to lose her memory.*

"I'd be an idiot to pass on Nicola for *any* reason. She's too good for me. Her only flaw is that she doesn't realize it."

Deacon silently agreed. "Do you think your relationship would be any different if she wasn't immortal?"

"We'd probably take this more seriously," Ethan said, sitting up and resting his arms on his knees, keeping his gaze on the water. "It's what outsiders seem to do anyway." A shrug. "All of them are pretty conscious of their biological clocks—especially the women. We don't have that problem."

The fact that Ethan hadn't given a smart-ass answer surprised him.

"Why're you asking about outsiders?" Ethan nudged him with his elbow. "Thinking of that hot Diane girl from class?"

"I'm not interested in Diane." Deacon hadn't given her a moment's thought outside of the few conversations they'd shared at school. She'd asked him to hang out a few times already that week, but he'd put her off until the boat party Saturday.

"You're too hung up on immortality, man. I could hit my head on this dock and drown just as easily as I could live for another five hundred years. There are no guarantees. Gotta do what you want while you can."

What if *what* you wanted wasn't going to last?

What if *who* you wanted was going to forget about you?

"We goin' again?" Ethan asked, pointing back to the buoy.

"Why not?" Deacon stood and stretched. It wasn't like he was going to sleep tonight anyway.

When Ethan left, Deacon stayed outside for another thirty minutes, staring at the dark windows of the house. Collecting his shirt, shoes, and mobile, he crossed the stretch of dry grass to the back patio. The hinges on the door creaked when it opened. He tiptoed to the fridge to grab a bottle of water, conscious of his dripping shorts and the AC freezing his skin. The living room was empty, but Vivienne's light was on.

Deacon thought he heard her voice and hesitated.

Then he heard the unmistakable sounds of sniffling.

He escaped into his bedroom, feeling like an asshole for making her cry. Again.

After throwing his sopping clothes into the hamper, he turned on the shower and hopped in.

Hot water streamed over his face like tears.

Making him think of Vivienne.

How did he know she was crying over him?

Perhaps she was crying over the unfairness of the whole bloody situation. She was going to forget everyone she'd ever cared about—and eventually, they would forget her too.

When the first patients were brought to Scotland, they had visitors for every holiday and birthday. Memories they recalled without prompts were like lifelines to their friends and family, giving false hope that perhaps someday the forgetful would snap out of it and remember.

But that never happened.

For the ones left behind, it became easier to keep away than to sit face-to-face with a person who should know you but didn't.

That was what had happened to Tootles: his family and friends had abandoned him in Scotland.

All of them except Peter.

Turning off the shower, Deacon rested his head against the cool wall tiles.

He remembered asking his grandad why he tortured himself by visiting every week when Tootles wouldn't know the difference one way or another.

Peter had shrugged and said, "He's my best mate."

He'd made it sound so matter-of-fact.

But it couldn't be that simple . . .

Could it?

NINE

Vivienne studied Deacon's sparkling green eyes. His damp hair. The black T-shirt clinging to his chest and arms as heat emanated from his freshly showered skin. When she had heard a knock on her door, she had assumed it was Karen. If she'd known who it really was, she wouldn't have answered.

"I don't care," he repeated, slower this time.

"Yeah, I heard you." Was it really necessary to say it over and over again? To twist the knife after he'd cut out her heart? "You don't care about me. Thanks for the reminder."

"You're not getting it," he muttered, stepping around her and into the bedroom. "I care about you. A great deal, actually. But your levels don't matter to me *at all*."

His words made no sense. Her levels didn't matter? She closed the door, afraid Karen and Calvin would overhear their conversation and start asking questions.

"But you said—"

"I was wrong." The corner of his mouth lifted. "It's happened a lot this year."

Maybe he didn't realize the severity of the side effects. That had to be it. "I'm going to forget *everything*."

Deacon's throat bobbed when he swallowed. "Then I'll have to remind you."

"I can't ask you to do that." She wouldn't let him throw away his life. His future.

"You're not asking me to do anything. I'm volunteering," he insisted, his knuckles grazing her cheek. "I want to be the one reminding you about the time I dragged you to a hospital roof to save you."

Her mouth went dry when his gaze dropped to her lips. "Reminding you about our first kiss on New Year's Day—after you kissed Alex." He frowned and rubbed the back of his neck. "On second thought, I'll edit that part out."

"Deacon—"

"You won't know the difference anyway." Amusement danced in his eyes; his lips curled into a mischievous smile.

She dashed at her tears with one hand and hid her smile with the other. "Not funny."

He was so close, she could smell his soap, feel his warmth. He reached for her hand, lacing their fingers together. Hope sparked at the silent promise in that connection. Leaning forward to whisper in her ear, he said, "And I definitely want to remind you about the time you brought me into a dressing room to try on that sexy black negligee."

She shivered as he slid his finger along her collarbone, toying with the strap on her tank top. The fireflies in her stomach started buzzing. "That's *not* what happened."

"You're the one with the faulty memory, not me." His other hand found her hip and settled on the skin beneath the hem of her top. "Most important of all, I'll remind you how much you love me."

"I-I never told you I love you." She did. Even after everything. It had always been him. Would always *be* him.

"But you do."

Somewhere in the background, her phone started ringing, but she ignored it as he brushed his lips along her throat. Slid his hand higher to stroke her bare waist.

"Do you want to tell Alex?" he asked, nipping her earlobe. "Or shall I?"

Alex couldn't have been further from her mind when Deacon slipped the strap from her shoulder and dragged his mouth along her collarbone, and every bone in her body felt weak and her skin was on fire and her heart was racing—

"You sound awfully cocky," she managed to croak.

"Not cocky." Featherlight kisses tickled her jaw. "Hopeful that you could love me the way I love you."

"What way is that?"

He whispered, "To the point of madness," then captured her mouth with his.

At first his lips were soft and gentle, becoming reacquainted with hers after so long apart. But when she gripped the damp hair curling at his neck and dragged him closer, they turned insistent and hungry. Their tongues met with a sense of urgency. She couldn't get enough. His chest slammed against hers, and a burning sensation electrified in her bloodstream. The carpet disappeared from beneath her as Deacon picked her up and carried her to the bed.

Then everything started spinning when he crushed her into the mattress. Her legs locked around his hips, and she had no intention of ever letting him go except to . . . *Tug. Off. His. Shirt.* And his heat was everywhere as her top rode higher. Skin searing skin.

She traced the tense muscles in his back, clinging to him as he trailed kisses down her throat. Her shoulder. Her chest.

Adrenaline pumped through her veins like she was

about to leap off a skyscraper. "It feels like my whole body's on fire."

"Just wait. It gets better," he murmured. His hand danced beneath her top and over her ribs, leaving a trail of flames in its wake. When he found her breast, she sucked in a breath. Groaning, his hips ground against hers, fanning the inferno. She tried to catch her breath, but all she managed was a moan, and with him moving like that, she never wanted him to stop, except—

He *obviously* knew what he was doing, but she didn't have a clue, and she couldn't couldn't couldn't—

Breathe.

"I . . . feel like . . . you . . . " How could this feel *sooo* good? "Need to . . . *knoooow* . . . "

He shifted his hips slightly, leaving her crying out. If he didn't stop, she was going to come out of her skin, and she didn't know if that was what was supposed to happen or if—

Oh god.

"Ihaven'tdonethisbefore."

His hips stilled and his lips lifted from her skin. "Haven't done what, exactly?"

She fought the urge to push his head back down. To tell him to keep going. Her face flushed with a different kind of heat. "Um . . . anything, really."

He dragged his hand from beneath her shirt, rolled off her, and pressed his fists to his eyes.

No no no!

Was he mad at her?

Why had she opened her stupid mouth? "I made out with a guy at the movies once. He tried to force my hand down his pants, but I told him I had to go to the bathroom." *Stop talking. Stop talking.* "I ended up leaving him there. He called me a tease and broke up with me the following Monday."

Deacon dropped his fists to the mattress and turned to her with wide eyes.

"And when I told my prom date that I wouldn't go to a hotel with him, he ditched me before the last dance. Lyle had to drive me home. And when I was a freshman—"

"Take a deep breath. I'm not going to ditch you or call you a tease."

"It's not that I don't want to . . . um . . . you know. I'm just really nervous." She inhaled. Finally, she could breathe. Some of the tingling subsided. "Sorry."

"I should be the one apologizing. I told you that you drive me mad."

"I liked it. Like . . . *really* liked it." Knowing she could make him lose control made her feel powerful.

"Me too." A tight laugh. "Obviously." Deacon's gaze drifted to the exposed skin at her midriff, then back to the canopy above them.

"Are you okay?"

"Mmmhmm. Just trying to get the blood back to my brain."

She glanced at his shorts, then back to his face. "*OH* . . . Right . . . um . . . okay. Does that mean you don't want to make out anymore?"

He turned his head toward her. "Do *you*?"

She nodded. "But I don't think I'm ready for anything else, if that's okay?"

He laced his fingers with hers and kissed the back of her hand. "Your first time isn't something we need to rush."

She scooted closer and kissed him again. This time, his hands remained clamped on her hips. When yawns kept her mouth busier than he did, he kissed her cheek and rolled off the bed.

"You're leaving?" Every part of her started panicking when he grabbed his shirt from the floor. She didn't want him to go. She never wanted him to leave her again.

His brows drew together. "You'd rather I stay?"

She nodded.

His eyes darted to the door, then back to where she sat on the bed. "Scoot over. I always sleep on the left side."

When he was settled again, she curled into him and closed her eyes, relishing the way he smelled, the heat from his skin, his deep, even breathing, the flash and click from his phone.

Her eyes snapped open in time to see him smiling at his screen. "What the heck? Did you just take a picture?"

"I did."

"That's against the rules."

"This may come as a shock to you," he drawled, rising on his elbow and smiling down at her, "but I don't always follow the rules."

She'd have to get a copy of it from him. This night was definitely one she needed to remember. "I love you."

Pressing a kiss to her temple, he said, "And I love you."

This was what bliss felt like. Deacon was sure of it.

He had finally found a cure for his insomnia—and she smelled like lilacs from heaven's garden.

The strap on Vivienne's black tank top had fallen from her shoulder. Tendrils sprung free from the hair piled on top of her head. She had stolen all the covers. And he couldn't be happier, shivering and staring at the back of the woman he loved.

He reached for his mobile on the bedside locker, careful not to shift too much on the mattress.

Vivienne hummed and stretched in one slow, fluid motion as she turned toward him. Her dark lashes fluttered open, and she smiled sleepily.

Luckily, he was already recording.

"Turn it off!" She covered her face and kicked him in the shin. For such a small woman, she had a helluva kick.

"Don't you want to remember the morning after the first night we slept together?"

Her cheeks turned pink from behind her hands. "Are you going to film everything from now on?"

"Only the good parts." He zoomed in to capture the way her lips curled up at the corners. "What's your name?"

Vivienne dropped her hands to reveal narrowed brown eyes, but her smile remained. "Amanda Moloney."

"Your *real* name."

"Vivienne Renee Dunn."

"And what's my name?"

She rolled her eyes. "Deacon Ashford."

He lowered the phone long enough to say, "My middle name is Elias," then re-centered her in the frame.

"Deacon *Elias* Ashford."

"Do you love me?"

"Yes."

He stopped recording and dropped his mobile onto the mattress. "Nothing wrong with your memory yet."

"Alex said it's a gradual process."

"Let's not talk about him." Deacon pulled her closer to nuzzle her neck. "Kills the mood."

"Don't get into the mood. We need to get up."

"Too late." His grip tightened and her back arched and that damned strap fell off her shoulder on the other side and the black silky material was so thin he could see the outline of her—

"I'd love to stay in bed with you, but—"

"Ah-ah." He nipped her earlobe. "Let's just leave it at, 'I'd love to.'"

When she wiggled free from his grasp, he groaned. "Please come *baaack*."

"Do you know what time it is?"

She said it as though he should care. He told her he didn't.

"It's almost eight. We need to leave in ten minutes."

"Or we could play hooky." He covered his head with her pillow and breathed in the fragrant scent of her shampoo. Why was it so sunny in this godforsaken place?

She lifted the pillow and smacked him in the stomach with it. "Do you really want to get put back on trial for another bird-watching incident?"

Back when he had first started recruiting for Neverland, he'd been partnered with a girl he fancied. Unfortunately, their extra-curricular activities had led to the Extraction team being called in. They'd pretended they had been bird watching, but no one bought it.

"It'd be worth it," he told her. "Can you Google Tennessee's state bird?"

Someone knocked on the door. "Amanda? It's almost eight."

Karen.

"I'm up!" Vivienne shouted, rushing over to turn the lock.

"Have you seen Cal? He's not in his room."

Deacon hid beneath the duvet. It smelled like Vivienne's perfume, and he decided this was where he was going to stay for the day.

"Haven't seen him." There was a smile in Vivienne's voice.

"Okay. Your lunches are on the counter."

"Thanks, Mom!" Vivienne yanked the duvet away. "Hooky's out. Get your butt out of bed." She went back to the door and peered into the hallway. "You're stuck for the minute. Mom's in the living room."

"You think so?" He lumbered out of bed, found his shirt on the floor, and flicked the lock on the window. Before he climbed out, he twisted back toward Vivienne and said, "At least it's not on the third floor."

It wasn't until he dropped into the dew-drenched grass that he remembered he was barefoot. Was there a good excuse for being outside at that hour without shoes? He'd come up with something on the fly if Karen asked.

Moments later, Deacon strolled through the front door, waved at his mother, and jogged into his room. He picked up a pair of nearly clean shorts from the floor and grabbed the least wrinkled shirt from his suitcase.

Within five minutes, his teeth were brushed and he was leaning against Vivienne's door frame. "Are you ready yet? We don't want to be late."

When she opened the door, she glared at him.

"What's wrong?" Deacon checked his shirt for stains. There weren't any he could see.

"You look perfect." She flattened her hair with one hand and tugged on her black top with the other. "And I look like I didn't have time to shower."

"You've never been more lovely." Her brown eyes shimmered with secrets he had helped restore.

"Shut up."

"What? I'm serious."

She pushed past him to collect her rucksack from beside the garage door. "Just shut up."

He laughed in the face of her foul mood. Finally, *finally* this week—this bloody year—was turning around. They went into the garage, and he bypassed the truck to wait by the exterior door.

"Aren't you driving?"

"Bentley is." He caught a bit of her hair and slid the glossy strands through his fingertips. "Unless you'd rather go bird watching."

Her tongue darted out, wetting her lips. "We need to go to school."

"Do we?" He leaned forward and tasted her pout. Mangos and toothpaste.

"Yes?"

Didn't she know that was the wrong answer? His fingers lost their way in her hair, and she responded by wrapping her arms around his neck and stealing his breath with her kiss.

"I see you two finally made up," Ethan said from the doorway.

Vivienne stiffened and tried to pull away, but Deacon kept her close. He'd let her go once. Never again.

"We're a little busy," he muttered. She giggled.

"Geez. Get a room. On second thought, don't. I don't want to be late."

"We really should leave." Vivienne's whispered words trembled along his neck, but her hands curled into the waistband of his shorts.

Leave? They absolutely did not need to leave. They needed to stay and sneak back to her room—or his, it didn't matter—and then—

The groaning sound of the automatic door lifting brought him back to his senses. Ethan smiled from where he was playing with the button.

"Sometimes you can be a real wanker," Deacon shot over his shoulder before releasing Vivienne. His arms had never felt as empty as they did when she left him to follow Ethan to his truck.

TEN

It was still warm when Vivienne and David left the concert that night. She found herself liking Tennessee a lot more after the sun went down. When she checked her phone, there were three messages from Deacon. *Hope you're having a shite time. Save your kisses for me.*

The third one was a picture of a mockingbird—Tennessee's state bird.

A shiver of anticipation snaked its way through her body, and her internal flame sparked to life.

"You can't be cold," David grumbled, wiping sweat from his forehead and adjusting his Vols hat.

"I'm not." But she *was* looking forward to getting home. Sliding her phone back into her purse, she tried to hide her giddiness. But her smile was so big it hurt her face. "Thanks for inviting me tonight. The show was really good."

And David had been a perfect gentleman. He'd held open doors and paid for the tickets and snacks they had shared. He would make a great boyfriend—for some other girl.

"I'm glad you came." A smile. "Are you interested in grabbing some ice cream?"

"Always." If there was one thing Vivienne couldn't resist, it was dessert.

From the corner of her eye, she saw him wipe his hand on his cargo shorts and reach for hers.

"Tonight was a lot of fun," she said, stepping away and tucking her hand into her pocket, "but it also made me realize I'm not really over my ex."

"Really?" A V formed between his brows. "You seemed pretty over him yesterday."

"Not *Bentley*." Thinking of the two of them together made her chuckle. "The guy I dated before him."

David nodded, his mouth a tight line. "I get it." He squinted up at the night sky as they continued up the street. "I'm kinda the same, except my ex is more interested in your brother than she is in me."

She wondered which of Deacon's admirers was David's ex—and hoped it wasn't one of the girls coming on the boat tomorrow.

David knocked his hip against hers. "Doesn't mean we can't get ice cream."

"Lead the way." The words were barely out of her mouth when her phone started buzzing. She apologized as she dragged it from her purse. Adrenaline stirred to life beneath her skin. But it wasn't Deacon. It was Emily.

How r things with ur sexy brother?

Vivienne grinned at the screen as she typed her response. *He had to sneak out my window this morning.*

A bunch of messages came through at once.

Your window???

In your bedroom???

OMG!!!!

Hello?

Don't leave me hanging!

Three dots appeared, then disappeared. A second later, the phone rang. Vivienne pressed the green button and answered with a laugh. "Hey, Emily."

"Don't 'Hey, Emily' me! Last night you were texting me about how sad you were, and this morning Deacon's sneaking out your bedroom window? I *need* to know what happened in between!"

Vivienne gave David an apologetic glance. He shrugged and kept kicking a stone down the sidewalk. "I'm kinda busy at the moment. I'll have to call you back later."

"No way. No freaking way. If you hang up on me I swear—"

She ended the call and apologized again. "That was my best friend from back home," she said, hoping the explanation made her seem less rude.

"You can talk to her now if you want. I don't mind."

"I'll call her back later. She wants to hear all about my first week at school, and that's not going to be a short conversation." Vivienne was about to return her phone to her purse when David's started ringing. "Looks like we're both in demand tonight."

"It's not mine." He showed her the blank screen in his hand. "Sounds like it's coming from your purse."

It did?

She listened.

It did.

Vivienne combed through her purse until her fingers clasped around a buzzing phone hidden beneath the ripped lining.

BLOCKED NUMBER.

Who would be calling her on the prepaid she'd bought at the beginning of the week? It had to be a wrong number. That was the only explanation.

Unless—

"Two phones, huh?" David laughed. "You doin' some shady shit, Miss Moloney?"

Crap. This was bad. So, so bad.

Vivienne had to get rid of it. Then she had to run. She dropped the phone onto the ground, stomped it until the ringing stopped, and threw it into a neighboring yard. When she looked back, David was staring at the lawn beyond the white picket fence.

"We need to get out of here." She grabbed his arm and pulled him off the sidewalk toward a side street.

"What was that about?" He stumbled along beside her with wide eyes.

"I'll tell you later." She found Deacon's number; it only rang once.

"How's the date?" he asked cheerfully. "Do I need to punch David the next time I see him?"

Her heart pummeled in her chest. "We need to go." According to policy, she should have already abandoned her mark. But she couldn't leave David behind.

"What's wrong?"

"They're coming." She didn't know how she knew, but she did. HOOK wasn't done with her.

"Get out of there. Do you hear me? Fly somewhere safe and call Extraction."

"I'm not leaving David."

"Vivienne—"

"I'll meet you at the truck." She hung up, cutting him off mid-curse, and shoved her phone into her purse. "Come on, David. We need to hurry."

"What's going on, Amanda? Who was that? Who's coming?"

"Hello again, Vivienne."

Fear choked the air from her lungs as she slowly turned.

"Boy, am I glad to see you," Jasper Hooke said with a

congenial smile. He looked different without his lab coat, less evil. His strawberry blond curls were gone, his hair cut tight to his head, but he still had on his red shoes.

"Do you know this guy, Amanda?"

Jasper extended his hand toward David and introduced himself. "And you are?"

"Don't answer that," she snapped, pushing David behind her. Deacon called her name from down the road. The lights of the city twinkled in the backdrop as he and Ethan came into view. Both of them were running.

"It's Amanda now?" Jasper chuckled, rubbing a hand over where his curls should have been. "You change your name as often as you change your hair."

Why was he talking to her like they were friends? Like he hadn't stalked her from Virginia to this dark street? "Go to hell. We're leaving."

When she turned, Jasper caught her by the purse. "I just want to talk. Please—"

"Let her go," David snarled, shoving against Jasper's shoulder.

Jasper stumbled back from the force, pulling her with him until she slipped her arm free of the strap. Her purse clattered to the ground.

"I have nothing to say to you." She steadied herself against the car parked beside them to keep from falling over.

"Hear me out. I'm begging you." Jasper took a halting step forward, palms facing her. "I think we can come to an arrangement that'll help everyone."

Deacon and Ethan came to a stop when they reached them. Deacon paused for a beat, then stepped in front of her, cutting off Jasper's line of sight.

Ethan bent to pick up her purse. "You okay?" he asked quietly.

"I don't believe it," Jasper whispered, his voice high with excitement. "You're the Shadow."

Deacon's hands flexed into fists at his sides. "I suggest you turn around and go back to Virginia while you're still able." His accent had returned.

David turned and gaped at Deacon. "Dude, what's up with your voice?"

"All good, Jasper?" A brawny man with a shaved head and a neck tattoo stepped from behind a minivan parked two cars away.

Jasper cursed under his breath. "Just a little misunderstanding," he said, waving the guy away.

Instead of retreating, the guy stepped closer. A second man with slicked-back hair followed behind him.

"That's the girl Lawrence told us to find, isn't it?" Tattoo asked, moving closer.

"Yeah, that's what I thought too, Rhett. But I was mistaken."

Mistaken? Why was Jasper lying? Vivienne peered around Deacon to watch Jasper catch the men by the elbows, halting their advance.

"No. That's definitely her." Tattoo shrugged free and gave Vivienne a crooked smile that made her insides twist.

The men pushed back their matching knee-length coats, revealing identical sidearms beneath.

"I'm really not sure what I got myself into here," David muttered, stumbling away from them, "but I'm . . . I'm gonna go." He slinked behind Jasper and backed toward the quiet houses.

"As much as we'd like to stand around and chat all night, we have places to be." Deacon turned his back to Jasper and the guns. His eyes were wide when they met Vivienne's. "*Run.*"

Run.

She needed to run.

Her muscles tensed as she searched the dark street for a good place to—*there*. Next to a white house. A gap. Heavy shadows. She took off sprinting, ignoring Ethan as he beelined in the opposite direction. Footsteps were heavy behind her. She glanced back, needing to know Deacon was—

"I'm here," he rushed breathlessly.

Here. Deacon was only a step behind.

Fire exploded in her chest, and she veered toward the dark gap and the trees beyond.

Behind them there was shouting and cursing and—

Crap.

Holy crap.

Those were gunshots.

"Stop shooting!"

Who was that? Jasper? Why was Jasper trying to keep them from shooting?

"Don't stop!" Deacon shouted at her back. "They only use—"

Blanks. HOOK always took their victims alive. Should blanks sound so real?

Vivienne pivoted in time to catch Jasper lunging at Tattoo. It looked like . . . *wait.* Was he *defending* them?

That made *no* sense.

Deacon wheezed a laugh.

"We made it!" She twirled victoriously. Deacon was looking down to where his hands covered his chest. Why wasn't he smiling? That had been terrible, but it was also exciting and exhilarating and—

"I don't think"—he moved his hand from his chest—"those were blanks."

Then Deacon fell from the sky.

ELEVEN

Vivienne screamed, lunging toward Deacon with outstretched arms. He was falling too fast. Then someone tackled her midair, knocking the breath from her body. *Ethan*. It was Ethan. And he shoved her onto the sharp shingles of a neighboring roof.

"Let me go!" She punched his chest, but his grip only tightened.

"He'd never forgive me if something happened to you."

Oh god oh god oh god.

"They *shot* him!" Her words trembled as she choked back the bile rising in her throat. Deacon was shot and hurt and falling and HOOK was going to get him if he wasn't dead already.

"No. You're wrong. HOOK only uses blanks. They *always* use blanks." Ethan let her go to crawl to the edge of the roof and peer down at the scene below. Whatever he saw made him curse.

If they'd been using blanks, Jasper wouldn't have been

shouting for his men to stop shooting. Deacon wouldn't have been shot. Bleeding. Dying.

She yanked on the ends of her hair, trying to figure out something useful to do besides hide on the stupid roof while Deacon was down there. "I'm telling you, there was blood on his shirt *before* he went down."

Ethan's face paled. "You're sure?"

She shook so violently that her nod was almost involuntary.

"Shit." Ethan looked between Vivienne and the spot where Deacon had disappeared. "*Shit.*"

"We can't just leave him there. We have to save him. We have to—"

"*You're* not doing anything." He wiped sweat from his forehead, then pinched the bridge of his nose. "And if I leave you, Dash will kill me."

"He won't do anything if he's dead."

Ethan growled at the stars and swore at the ground. "Do you swear you'll stay here until I get back?"

She agreed only because she knew she wouldn't be able to fly even if she wanted to.

"Make the call." He floundered for a moment before vaulting from the roof.

Vivienne pressed the button on her earpiece; the green screen appeared.

"Hello, *Vivienne.*"

"TINK, I need an extraction."

"Sending your coordinates to . . . *Kensington Extraction.*"

A light breeze drifted over her sweat-slicked skin as she waited for the call to connect. Eventually there was an answer on the other side.

"Vivienne, it's Owen. I'm locked onto your location. What's happening?"

Where did she begin? "They knew we were here and Jasper showed up and they shot him and he fell—" Her lungs refused to work and she couldn't breathe and it felt like there was a boulder crushing her chest and *oh god* this was all her fault.

"I need you to try and calm down. Who shot Jasper?"

Jasper? Had she even mentioned him? She couldn't remember. "No one shot Jasper."

Silence.

Owen asked if there was anyone else he could talk to.

"Ethan went to find Deacon."

"Dammit. Okay. Let's try this again. I want you to tell me exactly what happened."

She pieced together the events as best she could—leaving out the call she had received on the prepaid cell phone.

When she finished, the line was silent until Owen said, "You're *sure* Deacon was hit?"

If only she wasn't sure. If only there was a chance he hadn't been shot and that he was fine. "I-I'm sure."

"I need you to listen to me carefully. You have to stay out of sight. When the boys get back, have them call me. Got it?"

Vivienne couldn't bring herself to ask what to do if neither of them returned.

Distant sirens grew louder until red, blue, and white flashes bounced like strobe lights off the buildings below. She could hear the mumbled buzz of police walkie-talkies and people shouting. Boots stomping on concrete. In gravel.

Ethan reappeared, dirt and grime on his hands and forearms and shoes. He fell beside her and made his own call to Extraction. She didn't ask what had happened. Deacon wasn't with him. That's all she needed to know.

Vivienne tucked her knees beneath her chin and wrapped her arms around them, trying to keep herself from shattering into pieces. If Deacon was hurt, he couldn't have gone far. He had to be *somewhere*.

When Ethan's gaze finally met hers, his blue eyes were haunted. "I looked everywhere."

"Did you find *anything*?"

His mouth tightened. "Just a shit ton of blood."

Oh god. No. Please. No. "This is all my fault." She clutched her head in her hands; tears streamed down her face.

"It's not your fault."

"No, it is. It's my fault. I didn't think HOOK was still looking for me and I . . . I called Lyle, even though I knew HOOK had his phone tapped and—"

"*What?*" Ethan scrambled backwards, nearly falling off the roof.

Her body shook so violently that her teeth chattered. Deacon couldn't be dead. He couldn't. She closed her eyes and wished and hoped and prayed that he'd survived.

"Dammit, Vivienne! What were you *thinking*?" Ethan punched the shingles.

That was the thing . . . She hadn't been thinking. At least not of anyone else. She was so selfish. So *stupid*.

"Did you buy a burner phone?"

She nodded.

"Give it to me."

"It's gone. I threw it over a fence."

Rubbing his hands down his face, Ethan exhaled a loud, hissing breath. "You can't tell anyone else about the call."

"But it's all my fault."

"Listen to me." He knelt by her side and took her by the shoulders. His dirty hands left streaks on her skin. "If Leadership finds out this is your fault, there's no telling what they'll do to you. You can't tell them what happened. *Ever.*"

A shadowy figure thumped onto the backside of the roof. Owen crossed the shingles until he was standing right in front of them, intimidating in full body armor. "Where's Dash?" he snapped, his black eyes scanning the night.

Ethan and Vivienne stared wordlessly at him, neither of them willing to make the damning statement.

"*Shit.*" Owen pressed his earpiece. "Max and Barry, I

need you in plain clothes on the ground. Shots have been fired and they were live rounds—I repeat, *live rounds*. Expect police helicopters any minute, so an air search is out of the question until the area is clear. Deacon's still missing." He withdrew a silver object the size of a tube of lipstick from his vest. There was a chime, and the tube disappeared except for a dull blinking light. It reminded her of a lightning bug. The light drifted out of Owen's hands toward the carnage on the street.

"What was that?" she asked.

"A FAIR-E." Ethan kept his eyes glued to the speck of light until it, too, was gone.

Owen explained in short, clipped sentences that FAIR-Es conducted recon when it was unsafe for the PAN to do it themselves. He let off three more, then knelt in front of Vivienne. "I need to get you somewhere safe." Turning to Ethan, Owen asked if he was able to fly on his own.

"Yeah." Ethan nodded toward Vivienne. "But I'm worried about her."

"I've got her." Owen threaded one arm beneath her knees and steadied his other arm behind her back.

"Not without Deacon," she cried, bucking and flailing against his hold as hot, angry tears burned her eyes. Deacon wouldn't have left her alone and hurt. He would have moved the world to get her back.

Owen's arms tightened until she could barely breathe. "If we don't go right now," he snarled in her ear, "the police helicopters will find us, and I don't have time to explain how we climbed four stories to hide on a roof with no access point." His hold loosened, and she gave up fighting as he carried her away from the mayhem.

The flight was a blur of sound and motion, then warm, soothing darkness.

They ended up at the edge of an empty field, the lights of Nashville nothing but a faint halo on the horizon.

A black helicopter landed in the center of the clearing.

"Where's Dash?" Nicola shouted from the open door.

Owen carried Vivienne beneath the swirling blades and set her inside. Vivienne didn't hear his answer, but from the way Nicola's face dropped, she knew it wasn't good. There was a sharp, stinging pain on Vivienne's upper arm and then her entire world went dark.

"28, 29, 30 . . . " With his arms weak and shaking from chest compressions, Jasper took a deep breath and started counting again. "1, 2, 3 . . . "

A pair of dark dress shoes appeared to his right. "Lawrence wants to talk to you," Terry said, shoving the phone in Jasper's face.

"I'm . . . busy . . . 9 . . . 10 . . . "

Flashing lights lit up the bloody sidewalk. *Damn.* There was *a lot* of blood. Jasper was used to blood—worked with it every day. But there was a big difference between handling vials of the stuff and seeing it splattered all around.

"The police are here," Rhett said from somewhere behind him.

"15, 16, 17, 18 . . . "

A paramedic knelt beside the body and snapped her gloves into place. "I'll take over now."

Jasper looked down at his bloodstained clothes and nodded. She took his place and fell into a steady rhythm as a second man raced toward her with a defibrillator. Jasper found Terry standing next to Rhett. Both of their faces were blank masks. As if seeing the PAN fly—shooting them from the sky—was an everyday occurrence. "I told you to call the police, *not Lawrence.*" His brother was the last person he needed to deal with right now.

"I don't work for you. I work for Lawrence. And *he* told

me to call if anything went wrong," Terry bit out, forcing the phone into Jasper's hand. "I'd say this qualifies."

Closing his eyes and praying for patience, Jasper brought the phone to his ear.

"What do you mean you killed someone? Terry? *Terry!*"

"It's me, Lawrence."

"*Jasper?* What the hell is going on there?"

Dread replaced the numbness as Jasper watched the boy's body being loaded onto the stretcher and closed into the back of the ambulance with three paramedics. "Rhett and Terry shot at a bunch of kids . . . and may have killed one of them."

"Terry said you saw Vivienne. Is that true?"

Jasper collapsed onto the edge of the curb. All the sirens made it hard for him to concentrate. "I just told you someone was murdered, and you're worried about *Vivienne?*"

"You're right. We need to figure out how to keep this from becoming a PR nightmare."

"That's not what I—"

"We can say that they used unauthorized weapons, put the blame back on the company I hired them from. People will think we're the victims."

Jasper cursed at the fireflies floating above his head. "They *did* use unauthorized weapons, Lawrence."

"Of course, of course."

A tall policeman approached from where yellow crime scene tape was being stretched. His weathered face looked like it was permanently etched into a grimace. "Sir, I need you to come with me."

Jasper nodded to the officer. "The police are here. I have to go."

"Don't say anything! I'll get a lawyer to—"

Jasper slid Terry's phone in his back pocket and followed the officer to his vehicle.

TWELVE

The first signs of morning lightened the sky outside a single window. In a chair at the corner of the room, Nicola leaned forward, her elbows on her knees. She was still wearing her black-on-black Extraction uniform, and her blond hair had been pulled into a tight bun at the top of her head. Black mascara lines trailed down her cheeks.

The walls were painted a sage green. Generic paintings of landscapes had been framed and hung in a cluster beside a closet. It was a bedroom of some sort, but a lot bigger than Vivienne's. Despite the size of the room, the metal rails on the bed felt like they were closing in on her. A hospital bed, but not in a hospital. Somewhere else.

Vivienne's lips cracked when she opened her mouth to speak. "Where am I?" And why was she so thirsty?

"You're back at Kensington. In Leadership House." Nicola rose and walked past the bed toward the door.

Vivienne touched the IV tubes sticking out of her hand.

Her nails had dried blood beneath them. "Where's Deacon?" They must be keeping him in another room.

Nicola's shoulders stiffened. Instead of answering the question, she stuck her head into the hallway and told whoever was waiting outside that Vivienne was awake.

Deacon. It had to be him.

Who were these people filing into her room? There were six of them, and no one looked familiar until Paul walked in. And if she'd learned anything from being in Kensington, it was that having the Head of External Affairs seek you out was never a good thing.

Behind his glasses, Paul's eyes had dark circles. His mouth pulled into a line when he asked Vivienne to tell them what had happened.

What happened? That was a great question. Vivienne had hoped he would be the one answering that question for her.

She closed her eyes, and the first thing that popped into her head was, "I went to a concert in East Nashville with David."

The concert was good. And they were supposed to get ice cream afterward. But that was all she could—

"Ethan said Jasper Hooke was there."

Her eyes snapped open. Jasper *had* been there. And he had—

Oh god.

She lunged for a pan beside the bed and puked until there was nothing left.

Oh god oh god oh god.

Paul handed her a pink cup of room-temperature water. When it was gone, he refilled it from the jug on the table next to her bed. "Vivienne? We need to know."

"Jasper found us." Her arms were itchy; she had to scratch them, but it hurt so freaking bad—where had all the scrapes come from? "We tried to escape, but Jasper's men had guns."

"Breathe." Paul held the cup toward her.

She shook her head. She didn't want more water. She wanted answers.

Between gasping for air and trying to shut off her mind from the horrific scenes flashing there, it took Vivienne a long time to tell Paul and the others what had happened in Tennessee. When she finally finished, numbness settled into her body.

"How high was Deacon when he fell?" asked a woman with a soft, soothing voice.

"Three stories . . . maybe four. I'm ... I'm not exactly sure."

"He should have survived a fall of that height," the woman mumbled to a man standing next to her.

"What did Jasper Hooke say to you?" Paul asked.

"He wanted to come to an agreement."

"What kind of agreement?"

"I didn't ask because they were *shooting at us*." None of this mattered. None of it. She would talk to them about Jasper for as long as they wanted as soon as someone told her where Deacon—

The door burst open and everyone turned toward a silhouette illuminated by the blinding hall light.

Mary Ashford stood there, her eyes red-rimmed and wild. "*You* did this," she screeched. "*You killed my son.*"

Countless muted hours slipped past while Vivienne, Ethan, and Nicola waited for news from Tennessee. Every time a shadow passed the door, the trio looked up. But no one ever came in.

Vivienne curled onto her side and brought her knees to her chest, praying for the numbness to return because everything hurt. Her heart, her head, her hands, her stomach, her soul. *Everything.*

Nicola perched on the bottom corner of the bed, hugging her long legs against her chest. Ethan alternated between pacing and passing out in the chair.

Every once in a while, Nicola offered Vivienne a melancholy glance.

Ethan refused to look at either of them.

Paul returned sometime in the afternoon, wearing faded jeans and a wrinkled polo with an uneven collar. "I'm afraid I have some terrible news," he said, removing his baseball cap and bending the bill between his hands.

"Stop." Vivienne couldn't even lift her head to shake it. "If you don't have good news, then go away."

Instead of stopping, he kept going. And what he said didn't make any sense. It had to be a lie.

"A John Doe was admitted to Vanderbilt Medical Center at 11:13 p.m. last night with a gunshot wound to the chest. He matches Deacon's description. The surgeons fought to save him, but . . . "

A whimper escaped from Nicola. She covered her mouth as tears rolled down her cheeks. Paul crossed to his daughter and hugged her head to his chest. "I'm so sorry, honey. So, so sorry."

Ethan dropped his head into his hands and sobbed.

"He's *not* . . . he can't be." Paul had to be wrong. There was no other explanation.

"Vivienne . . . " Nicola reached toward her foot.

Vivienne kicked her hand away. "Did anyone see the body?"

Paul kissed the top of Nicola's head before stepping away. "By the time we paid someone off at the hospital morgue, the body had disappeared. We can't be certain, but—"

Ethan shot to his feet; his chair rattled against the tiles.

He was still wearing his dirty plaid shirt and shorts from Tennessee. "It was HOOK, wasn't it?"

"We believe so."

Ethan cursed and kicked the chair. "Looks like they've decided we're still useful dead."

Paul ignored him. "Julie is making the necessary arrangements for the funeral."

This wasn't happening. It just wasn't. "We don't even know if it was him. There's no proof!"

"When HOOK is involved," Paul said, scratching his goatee, "there's hardly ever proof."

"This is bullshit." Ethan stalked toward him, fists clenched and jaw ticking. "What are *they* going to do about it?"

"The rest of the Extraction team is still in Tennessee. I'll be joining them tonight to conduct my own investigation."

"That's not what I meant, and you know it."

"There's nothing more anyone can do."

"Total bullshit." Ethan kicked the corner of Vivienne's bed and stomped out of the room.

"Ethan! Wait!" Nicola ran after him.

"Vivienne?"

Hiding her face in her hands, Vivienne curled into herself because if she didn't hear what Paul had to say, it wouldn't be real. *THIS COULD NOT BE REAL.*

A warm hand touched her shoulder. "Vivienne?"

She opened her eyes, meeting Paul's concerned gaze. "I understand this is going to be hard for you. But when it's all over, you and I need to have a meeting."

She nodded as her tears soaked into the sheets.

How was she going to tell him that Deacon's death was entirely her fault?

THIRTEEN

Peter Pan looked like he had emerged from a movie screen. He had on the same green tunic and tights Deacon had worn last Halloween. Pointed buckskin shoes covered his feet, and a small green hat with a scarlet feather topped his unkempt red hair. A dainty dagger dangled from a leather belt at his waist.

Despite the familiar garb, Vivienne had her doubts regarding Peter's authenticity—until he asked for help reconnecting his missing shadow.

Once the impish silhouette had been sewn to his heel, Peter's green attire morphed into an expensive three-piece suit with golden cufflinks shaped like roosters. An ornate, tarnished gold pocket watch ticked prophetically from the left side of his waistcoat.

"Welcome to Neverland, Vivienne." Peter clicked open the pocket watch, frowned at its elegant face, then returned it to his waistcoat.

His accent and the timbre of his voice was so similar to

Deacon's that Vivienne's response caught in her throat. "Thanks, Peter."

"I wish you could stay. But I'm afraid having you here puts everyone at risk."

Tears streamed along her cheeks, falling in an onyx puddle at her bare feet. "I'm so sorry."

"Apologies won't bring him back."

If she had known they were going to kill him, she would have gladly sacrificed herself. "I'll leave Neverland right now." No one else was going to die because of her selfishness. Her stupidity.

"Not before you pay the price." Peter's kind expression turned malevolent as he circled her. His shadow grew to twice his size, casting darkness over them both. A spidery shiver crawled down Vivienne's spine as he continued advancing in her direction. "HOOK won't stop taking my family until they get what they've been searching for."

Nose-to-nose with the leader of the PAN, Vivienne's question emerged no louder than a whisper. "What's that?"

Peter unsheathed the dagger hidden inside his coat and pressed the blade against her throat. The heat from his breath mingled with the warm drops of blood falling on her stark white shirt. "HOOK wants *you*."

For the fifth time that week, Vivienne woke drenched in sweat after the recurring nightmare involving Peter Pan. What made that morning different from every other one was that today, she wouldn't be able to wallow in sorrow until bedtime.

It was Friday.

It was time to say goodbye to Deacon.

The only black dress Vivienne owned was the one she

had worn to Deacon's house on New Year's Eve—an occasion filled with hope and promises for the future.

Instead of holding the ceremony at the chapel on campus, the PAN met in the much larger Aviary to accommodate the considerable number of mourners expected to attend.

Vivienne hoped to slip in unnoticed, but a trail of whispers followed her through the crowd pushing into the building.

Emily met her by the door with a hug. "Nicola said she's saving a seat for you in front."

"I can't sit down there." Vivienne backed toward the exit. It was bad enough that she was here. She couldn't sit where everyone would stare at her with accusing eyes.

"Don't go." Emily wrapped her slender fingers around Vivienne's wrist. "Sit with me and Max. We're in the nosebleeds."

Vivienne nodded.

Emily kept her grip firm until they reached the top balcony.

Max lifted his hand toward the girls and indicated two empty chairs next to him.

"Thanks for saving us seats," Emily said. "It's *sooo* crowded."

There were very few empty chairs scattered around the lower levels and still lines of people coming in.

"No problem. I thought I'd save a couple just in case. " He rubbed the back of his neck and winced. "I'm sorry, Vivienne. I wish I could've done more. I tried my best to find him."

"This isn't your fault, Max."

It was her fault. All of it.

He nodded and turned away.

Below her, Nicola waited next to two empty chairs in a fitted, dark gray jumpsuit. Ethan came in and made his way to her side. Handsome in a black suit, he said something that appeared to upset her before slumping into an empty chair and dropping his head into his hands.

The crowd parted for a stunning girl Vivienne didn't recognize. Her platinum hair was braided down her back. She sat next to Ethan, but he barely acknowledged her.

Alex was there too, scanning the congregation. Was he looking for her? Vivienne scooted back in her chair. She hadn't seen him since she got back. He'd tried calling her every day, but she hadn't answered.

On a makeshift stage at the far side of the Aviary, a single microphone had been connected to the podium from the chapel. In lieu of an empty casket, a gilt-framed photo of Deacon had been lovingly displayed on a table next to a flickering candle.

Vivienne concentrated on his handsome face, committing to memory his mischievous green eyes and wry smile.

The doors opened, and a hush fell over the congregation. The pastor led a procession down the center aisle to a row of reserved chairs in front of the stage. Mary Ashford—dressed head-to-toe in black—followed him, accompanied by a much older woman with a shock of silver hair. A thin, white-haired gentleman in a navy blue suit brought up the rear.

Last to arrive was a teen wearing a white dress shirt with sleeves rolled to his elbows and a skinny black tie. He nodded to a number of people as he passed and continued to the corner of the stage, where he settled cross-legged next to Deacon's photo.

The pastor trudged to the podium and recited a prayer for Deacon's soul, as well as for the family and friends left behind.

Vivienne tried to pay attention to the service, but her gaze kept straying to the teen on the stage. He fidgeted with his fingers, and his feet never stopped moving. He didn't turn his head as much as he twitched from one side to another, as though he was tuned in to a ghostly argument only he could hear.

The pastor concluded with a passage from Psalms, closed his Bible, and left the stage. Then the white-haired gentleman rose from his chair and climbed the three rickety steps.

"Who is that?" Emily mouthed.

Vivienne shrugged.

The man didn't speak; instead, he lowered the microphone and retreated to the rear of the stage. The entire congregation waited in silence.

The odd teen hopped up and took his place behind the podium.

Staring at Deacon's smiling face, he bent the microphone to his lips. "This is my four hundredth funeral. And I can assure you, it does not get any easier." His formal British accent and the surprising strength in his voice commanded authority. "In being blessed with a long life, we are also cursed to lose far too many loved ones. Yet, there is something precious inside that breaks each time we bury one of our own—one who should have seen at least five hundred more summers.

"I can still remember the first time I held my grandson . . . "

Holy crap. *That* was Peter Pan.

" . . . and the pride I experienced in that moment has only grown as Deacon became the kind of man I was honored to know. I could ramble about his unfailing loyalty and wicked sense of humor. I could share his struggles with this secretive life, his frequent bouts of insomnia that got him into far too much trouble, or the stubborn streak he likely inherited from me. But I won't do any of those things because . . . because I'm still in denial that I will never again make him laugh or see him smile—or reprimand him for breaking the rules.

"Today we've gathered to celebrate a young man we were lucky to know and love. But tomorrow—when life resumes and we slip back into routine—is when we will experience his loss. We will look upon a chair that should hold a promising young leader but remains empty; we will tell a joke or share a story, but there will be one less contagious chuckle to respond; we will pick up our mobiles to make a call, only to realize there is no longer someone to answer.

"We're not expected to handle this bravely, to smile our way through the pain, or to recover quickly. Now, more than ever, we need to lean on one another to survive the dark days ahead until we are able to find the light.

"Hold those you love a bit closer tonight, because tomorrow is not promised to any of us, no matter how immortal a fairy tale tells us we are."

Peter Pan stepped off the stage and took the empty seat next to Mary. He tucked his arm around her shoulders, and she fell against him, sobbing.

After the service, the majority of mourners lingered inside. It took some time for Vivienne, Emily, and Max to reach the exit and emerge into the dreary September day.

When Vivienne saw Nicola waving in their direction, all she could think about was escaping. "I can't do this," she whispered to Emily. "I'm sorry . . . I just . . . I can't talk to people right now."

"Go. I'll see you back home."

No one stopped Vivienne as she raced back to her apartment, but she could feel their eyes on her. Watching. Judging.

Back in the safety of her bedroom, she hid beneath her covers, praying they would smother the guilt churning in her stomach. Everything felt so wrong. So unfair.

She had led HOOK straight to their location.

Her friends should have been attending *her* funeral, not Deacon's.

When she had lost her parents, her entire life had been turned upside down. Her home had become a pile of charred rubble; all her toys and books had been destroyed. She had moved into her first foster home and switched schools. She had been completely alone.

Now her life was mostly intact.

She was still at Kensington with her friends, and life would go on like Deacon had never existed. But she felt more helpless than she had when she was six years old.

From the moment Alex had shared her diagnosis, Vivienne had lived in fear of her impending forgetfulness.

Now she couldn't wait to forget everything.

The sound of bullets being sprayed into the sky.

The last image of Deacon, his eyes wide as a bloodstain bloomed at his chest.

The feeling of watching him fall and not being able to do a damn thing about it.

The—

There was a knock at her window . . . on the third floor.

Vivienne peeked from beneath her covers toward the pulled blinds. She held her breath while she waited, but whoever had been there didn't knock again.

In the aching silence, she crept forward and slid her fingers between the blinds. Someone had taped a piece of paper to the other side of the glass. She opened the window and checked the gray sky only to find clouds and a lone bird. The ground below, the fountain, the crushed stone walkway, and the roofs of the neighboring buildings were all empty.

She pulled the paper free of the glass.

Come to my office.
-Peter

Why did Peter Pan want to see her?

Did he know the truth? That she was responsible for his grandson's death?

Memories of her nightmares over the past week came flooding back. She darted a look at the bag still packed from Tennessee that Extraction had dropped off two days earlier. Should she grab it and leave forever? Go back to Ohio? Go straight to HOOK and let them neutralize her?

In the end, she left the bag and headed for the Hall with empty hands and an emptier heart.

Vivienne deserved whatever punishment was coming.

Vivienne's footsteps echoed in the hollow reception hall. The only light inside was what seeped through the windows. Unsure which office was Peter's, she followed the sound of sniffling to find Julie with her head on her desk, crying. It wasn't until Vivienne cleared her throat that Julie looked up.

"Vivienne?" Julie dabbed at her puffy eyes with a tissue. "Did you need something?"

"I guess Peter wants to see me," Vivienne said, handing Julie the note.

Julie glanced over it and stood, sending a pile of used tissues on her lap tumbling to the ground. "Come with me."

Vivienne followed her through reception, past the grandfather clock, and down the dark hallway to a door at the very end. Nothing set this particular door apart from any of the others they had passed: dark shiny wood, gleaming brass knob. It felt like there should have been some outward indication of the office's fairy tale occupant.

Vivienne raised her hand to knock when Julie stopped her. "If he asked for you, he knows you're coming. Go straight in."

Her feet wouldn't budge.

131

She should have run away when she had the chance. "I don't think I can."

Julie squeezed Vivienne's fingers. "He doesn't like being kept waiting." With that, she left.

Vivienne pushed the door aside and stepped into a room with dark green paneling. A floor-to-ceiling bookcase sat across from a window overlooking campus. Beyond a small table with a chess board inlaid on top, a second door had been left ajar.

"I've told you time and time again, Lee. We are *not* an army and we cannot behave like one. Now is *not* the time for retaliation." Peter's voice sounded so much like Deacon's that, if Vivienne closed her eyes, she could almost imagine he was there.

"I can't believe you won't even retaliate for the death of your own grandson!" Lee bellowed. "How many more of us need to be executed before the loss warrants a reaction from the *great* Peter Pan?"

Vivienne steadied herself against the leather couch, unsure whether or not to wait outside until their argument was over. In the end, her curiosity trumped everything else.

"Inciting a mob of naive individuals who are not privy to *all* the facts, and are fed only a steady stream of propaganda solidifying *one side* of the argument, is unacceptable. It cannot continue."

"It's not up to you."

Footsteps stomped toward the door, and Lee burst out of the inner office. He stopped mid-stride when he saw Vivienne. He'd shaved off his beard. It made him look younger, even though the hair at his temples was going gray. "How are you holding up?" A wince. "Sorry. I don't know why people ask that when the answer's obvious."

She offered him a tight smile. "I'm surviving." *Barely.*

"If you need anything, you know where we are." Lee squeezed her forearm, then dropped his hand.

Vivienne watched him leave.

"I'm sorry you had to hear that."

Her entire body stiffened, and she turned slowly to see Peter Pan frowning in the doorway.

He rubbed his neck and sighed. "Of all days for Lee to even suggest something like this."

"It's fine," she said in a strangled whisper. "I didn't hear much." What was one more lie?

"That's a relief." His green eyes softened, and he eased his shoulder against the doorframe. "You go to his meetings, don't you?"

"I've been to a few."

"Come with me." He waved her into his office and gestured toward one of the chairs across from his desk.

The only items on top of his leather-topped desk were a gold Charlie Bell clock and a picture frame. Vivienne could only see the frame's generic back and gold edges. Was it a photo of Peter's family? Of Deacon?

Peter followed her gaze to the photograph before handing it to her.

Peter, Deacon, and Deacon's mother had their arms draped across each other's shoulders. They were all laughing.

Vivienne couldn't take her eyes away from Deacon's face. He'd been so handsome. So charismatic. So *alive*.

And now? Now he was nothing.

Tears stung the backs of her eyes. She'd spent the entire day trying not to cry, allowing them to build like water in a reservoir. And the dam was about to break.

Peter reached into his desk drawer and handed her a handkerchief with a gold P embroidered on the corner. "I'd like to hear your opinion," he said after she'd regained control of herself.

"My opinion on what?"

"Lee's meetings."

"I've only been here a year," she said, squeezing the handkerchief in her fist. "I'm not really in a position to say anything." With reluctance, she set the photograph back on Peter's desk.

"I disagree." His head twitched to the right. "Unlike most of us, your judgement hasn't been clouded by a century of prejudice and fear. Rebellions are suited to the young." He removed his black tie and undid the top two buttons on his shirt. "If I wasn't who I am, and didn't know what I know, I'd probably join him. I always did love a good rebellion." Beneath Peter's open collar was a wide white scar that appeared to go around his neck. "But that's neither here nor there." He sighed. "I asked you here so I could thank you."

There must be something wrong with her hearing. Peter Pan wanted to *thank* her?

"For what?"

"Deacon has always been a bit unruly. If he'd been ordered to stay in London a few years ago, he would've given Leadership the finger and done the opposite."

Imagining Deacon doing just that almost made her smile. But, "I don't see what that has to do with me."

"He told me the only reason he stayed was because he didn't want his actions to blow back on you." Pushing back from his desk, Peter laced his hands behind his head. "He's grown up a lot in the last year—and I attribute a good deal of it to his relationship with you."

"I miss him so much," she confessed, her vision turning watery as she stared at the photograph. "What if I forget him?"

"Your mother said the same thing about your father when she started forgetting."

Her mother had been forgetful too?

How had she never connected the dots? Anne Dunn's nGh levels had been the highest on record until Vivienne came along. It made sense that her mother's memory could have been affected.

"That's why William struck a deal with Edward Hooke," Peter went on. "In exchange for donating blood, Edward promised them a vial of poison."

Last year, when Lawrence Hooke had claimed her parents were helping them . . . that had been true? "But they were past the ten-year mark." And for a PAN with a Nevergene active for more than ten years, the poison would've been lethal. Her parents had died from neutralization, but she never believed the rumors that they had taken their own lives.

"They weren't going to take it," Peter explained with a shake of his head. "William believed that we could develop a milder version that wouldn't completely deactivate the Nevergene. He thought it could help us find a cure."

"For forgetfulness?" If she wasn't so bent on forgetting the last week, she would have said she felt hopeful.

Peter twisted a cheap looking plastic watch he wore around his left wrist. "And the Nevergene itself."

"A cure for immortality?" That made no sense.

"Losing loved ones and fighting constant battles gets tiresome when there's no end in sight. Some of us, myself included, wouldn't mind growing up," he said quietly, turning the frame face down on his desk. "Unfortunately, Edward Hooke didn't hold up his end of the bargain. Now the poison is nearly inaccessible."

"You really think the poison can do all that?" she asked, tucking her cold hands beneath her thighs. Maybe there was something she could do for the PAN after all. Vivienne already knew Jasper Hooke. Could she convince him to give her some of their poison in exchange for her cooperation? It was definitely something to consider.

"Your father believed so. And that's why Lee wanting to attack HOOK isn't feasible. If we go after them now, we may never get our hands on it. We need to focus on helping the living, not seeking retribution for the dead."

"Why are you telling me all of this?"

His smile made the skin around his green eyes crinkle. "If Lee hears it from me, he'll think I'm lying or that I have some sort of ulterior motive."

"And you want me to tell him?"

Peter chuckled. "Despite what Lee preaches, I'm not some dictator shouting orders. I prefer to give facts and let you decide what—if anything—to do with them."

She nodded as though she knew what he meant. Her decision making had been crap lately, so she kind of wished he'd tell her what to do. "Thanks for telling me."

"Before you go, I have something to give you," Peter said, handing her a black thumb drive from his desk drawer.

"Um . . . thanks?"

His smile was sad. "You're welcome."

FOURTEEN

A lex was the last person Vivienne expected to find waiting for her in reception. When he saw her, he stood and stepped away from the mustard-colored couches. He was still in a black suit, but his tie was balled up in his hands. "Hey."

"Hey." She crossed her arms, trying to keep herself from falling apart.

"I'm not going to ask how you are," he said, his eyes on his black dress shoes, "but I thought you ought to know that there are a lot of people waiting for you at your apartment."

Sitting around with her friends would only make the fact that Deacon wasn't there to join them harder. "I don't feel like seeing them right now."

His brows drew together, and he scratched his stubbled cheek. "You're welcome to come with me."

She thought about it for a second before nodding.

Julie wasn't around to see them leave the Hall together,

and the stone driveway was empty except for Alex's truck. Vivienne slid into the passenger seat and tucked the thumb drive Peter had given her into her bra. Alex tapped the steering wheel with his thumbs but didn't try to make conversation. At the main road, he turned left.

In the year she had been at Kensington, she had never gone in that direction.

They drove with nothing but static on the radio, which suited her. Sad songs would have made her feel worse; happy songs would have reminded her that she'd never be happy again. After ten minutes, Alex stopped at the first brick house with black shutters in a row of houses that looked exactly the same.

"Is this your house?" The grass needed cut and the shrubs could have done with a trim.

"It belongs to Tootles. But it made more sense to live here than to look for a place of my own when I already have a house in California." He climbed out and crossed the driveway to the black door.

Vivienne drifted along behind him, waiting while he unlocked the door and hung his keys on the hook next to the other ones. When he slipped out of his shoes and placed them beside the door, Vivienne did the same.

A black blanket had been folded into a perfect square and centered on the back of the couch. The coffee table was empty except for a single remote.

"Would you like anything to drink?" he asked.

"Water would be great."

Alex went past a hallway and into the kitchen. Not even a toaster or bowl of fruit sat on the bare butcher block counters. There were no dirty dishes in the apron sink. A small table with one chair had been turned into a desk, with papers and files stacked neatly beside a mason jar of pens.

Alex retrieved a glass from one of the navy blue

cupboards. Instead of filling it from the faucet, he pulled a filtered jug from the fridge. "Here you go."

She accepted the glass with muttered thanks. Her throat was sore from trying not to cry, but the cool liquid did little to sooth the ache.

Alex leaned against the counter, bracing his hands on either side of himself. His mouth tightened as he watched her drink. When she finished, she handed him the glass.

"I'm worried about you," he said, loading it into the dishwasher.

"I'm worried about me too."

She would survive. She would move forward. But she would never forgive herself.

Vivienne made her way back toward the living room and sank onto the couch. The skirt of her dress rose over her knees. She pulled it back down. Alex took off his coat and draped it over the back of the couch. When he sat down, he left a cushion between them.

What was she doing? She shouldn't be here. Alone with another guy when Deacon—

"You and Dash were . . . The two of you were close." Alex looked down at his flexing hands. "Probably closer than I want to know."

"Yeah. We were."

"There's nothing I can say that'll make this any better. You need to take time to feel how you need to feel. But, Vivienne"—he reached for her hand—"I want you to know I'm here for you. Even if it's just to give you an empty space to grieve. A place to hide away. A shoulder to cry on. Whatever you need."

What if she needed to forget?

"Who knew I'd end up looking forward to becoming forgetful?"

Alex stiffened. "You don't mean that."

Her eyes welled with tears. Remembering the good times she had with Deacon hurt nearly as much as reliving the bad. "Right now I do."

With her eyes locked on the blank TV screen, she scooted close enough to lean against Alex. His weren't the arms she wanted around her, but they were strong, and steady—and there.

Alternating between heavy, gut-wrenching sobs and soft, quivering tears, Vivienne allowed herself to cry until her eyes were so sore, even blinking hurt. Alex handed her tissue after tissue from a box he'd retrieved from the bathroom.

"Sorry I'm such a mess." She wiped her nose and closed her eyes. It felt good to cry. It felt good to be held.

"You don't have to apologize." He rubbed the face of her watch with his thumb. "But it's getting late. It's time I dropped you home."

The thought of going back to Kensington made her sick to her stomach. Emily would want to talk about what happened. Vivienne never wanted to talk about it again.

"It wouldn't be fair to you if I stayed," she whispered.

"It's pretty clear we both want different things." His ribcage expanded and contracted as he sighed. "Until we're on the same page, I really don't think you should."

She studied his tortured expression through puffy eyes. "That's not a 'no.'"

His brow furrowed. "I know."

"Staying won't mean anything." It couldn't. Not yet. She needed him to understand that.

Alex brushed her hair back from her face and said, "I know."

"But I don't want to go back there tonight."

"I know."

"It's just—"

His rough thumb pressed against her lips. "You don't

need to explain anything to me. I get it." He replaced his thumb with his lips for a soft, reassuring kiss. "You can have my bed. I'll stay here on the couch."

"Would it be okay if I stayed with you for a little longer?"

His answer was to pull the blanket over them and settle her head against his chest.

He didn't try to kiss her again.

Eventually, Alex's sweet murmurs of comfort were replaced by deep, even breathing. Vivienne stared at the shadowed ceiling, waiting for sleep to overtake her. But memories of what she had done haunted her every time her eyes drifted shut.

If she was ever going to sleep again, she needed to get something off her chest. "Tennessee was all my fault."

Alex's limp arms went rigid. "Did you say something?" he asked groggily.

Her arms started to tingle and itch as she explained what had happened in Nashville.

Alex withdrew his arm and lifted himself against the back of the couch. "Have you told Paul?"

Her hair rustled against his chest when she shook her head.

"*Will* you tell him?"

That question had plagued her since she had returned to Kensington. "I don't think I could live with myself if I didn't."

Alex shifted in his sleep, startling Vivienne awake. The living room was still dark. What time was it? She twisted her wrist to check her watch.

Five o'clock.

She managed to lift his arm off her and slip off the couch without waking him. After pulling on her shoes, she sneaked out the front door and crossed through the frosty grass to the backyard. The sun was barely visible on the horizon, but she took a chance and flew back to Kensington.

When she arrived at her apartment, she typed her PIN into the keypad.

It didn't work.

She typed it in again.

Nothing.

2-9-5-2

Or was it 9-5-2-5?

Neither worked.

Instead of knocking and waking Emily, she flew to the front of the building and took the stairs. When she finally got inside, she pulled off her wet shoes and abandoned them beside the others next to the door.

Empty wine and beer bottles littered the coffee table and counters. Three pizza boxes sat on the kitchen table. Vivienne found a slice left inside and took a bite.

"Where in the world have you been?" Emily hissed from the hallway. "I stayed up all night waiting for you. You didn't answer any of my calls or texts or—"

"All right, *mom*," Vivienne groaned, taking another bite and squeezing past her friend.

"Where *were* you?"

If Vivienne hadn't been so tired, she would have tried coming up with something better than, "I went to Alex's."

Emily grabbed her arm. "You spent the night with *Alex*?"

"Nothing happened." Vivienne glared at her and shook free. "I needed a friend, and Alex was there for me."

Emily's expression darkened. "*I'm* your friend. *Max* is your friend. *Ethan* and *Nicola* are your friends. And we were all here waiting for you. Alex is—"

"He's *what*?"

"I'm not sure he has your best interests at heart right

now." Emily's hand balled into a fist. "I feel like I need to beat him up for taking advantage of you."

"If anything, *I* took advantage of *him*," Vivienne muttered, pushing open her door.

"I get that you're spiraling, I do. But I don't want to see you make a mistake you're going to regret for the rest of your life."

"Yeah, well, it's a little late for that now isn't it?" Vivienne slammed her door and fell onto her bed. She was exhausted and wished she could sleep. But every time she moved, she smelled Alex's cologne on her skin—and felt Emily's disappointment in her soul.

She stripped out of her dress and turned on the shower. When she picked it up to stuff it in her hamper, the thumb drive Peter had given her fell onto the floor.

With steam tumbling from the bathroom, she threw on her robe and opened her laptop.

The hard drive contained three files.

The first was the photograph Deacon had taken of the two of them in bed the night before he died.

The second was the video he had filmed the following morning.

The third file was a grainy video of Deacon in what looked like a bar. "Hey, Vivienne. It's me. The guy you love. Right now you're having the worst date of your life—or at least I hope it is. I've been doing research on the mockingbird. I'll tell you all about it when we get home—" A broad smile spread over his lips. "Speak of the devil . . . "

The screen went blank.

Deacon must have been recording when she had called him about Jasper.

Never knowing it would be his last.

Extraction must have found Deacon's phone; it was the only explanation for how Peter had gotten the files. Vivienne wasn't sure how she felt about Deacon's grandfather having access to those private moments. Then she realized it didn't matter.

He had shared them with her. That's what mattered.

She hid the files on her computer and deleted them from the drive. After showering, she wrapped herself in her covers and cried herself to sleep.

FIFTEEN

V ivienne's phone sprang to life, waking her from her first dreamless sleep since returning to Kensington. Her bleary eyes made it hard to read the name on her phone.

Max? Why was he calling her this early in the morning?

"It's happening," he said in a harsh whisper. "We're going to Virginia."

Why would they go to Virginia?

HOOK.

HOOK was in Virginia.

Vivienne sat up and pushed her hair out of her face. "Who's going?"

"Me, Lee, Ethan, and a few others. We're catching a flight in fifteen minutes."

"You're only telling me this *now*?" She shoved the covers aside and searched her closet for something to wear. Even if she flew all the way to the airport, she'd never make it.

"I've been trying to convince Ethan that you had more of

a right to be here than anyone. But he keeps saying it's not what Dash would have wanted."

Deacon hadn't been her boss when he was alive, and he wasn't going to dictate her life now that he was gone.

"What's the plan?" she asked, pulling on a pair of black tights.

"We're landing around noon. And tonight, we're gonna burn HOOK to the ground."

How satisfying would it feel to watch everything their enemy had built go up in flames?

All their research, their legacy, their poison—

Crap. The poison—"You guys can't burn HOOK." Where the heck was her purse? "You have to stop them."

"Are you hearing yourself right now?"

In the background, she could hear a flight attendant make the final call for boarding.

"Trust me on this, Max. HOOK has something Peter needs, and if they burn it down, it'll be destroyed." Along with any hope of curing his father's forgetfulness.

"What does HOOK have—"

"There's no time to explain. Talk some sense into Lee—or at least get him to wait. I'm begging you."

She pulled her black sweatshirt over her head, found her purse in the living room, and left for the airport. The only flights available were standby, and there wasn't a seat free until the afternoon. Once she knew Max's plane had landed, she tried calling again, but his phone went straight to voicemail.

The moment she disembarked in Dulles, she tried again. No luck. Getting out of the airport took a bit of time, between waiting for the underground train and the escalators rolling at a snail's pace. It was still too bright to fly, so she was forced to take a forty-minute cab ride to the HOOK facility. The driver gave her a skeptical look when she asked

146

to be dropped next to a barren corn field just after dusk, but accepted her money with a mumbled, "Thanks."

She waited for the silver Chevy to make a U-turn before trudging into the muddy field. Once she was far enough from the road, she launched herself into the sky.

"Hey, TINK," she said, her hand on the earpiece as the wind whipped through her hair, "I need you to call Ethan."

"Calling . . . *Ethan.*"

Every ring made her heart beat faster until—

"Kinda busy at the minute, Vivienne. Everything okay?"

"No, it's not *okay*. Deacon is dead, and now you're trying to burn down HOOK."

"How did you—*Dammit*. Doesn't matter. These bastards deserve everything that's coming for them." A dial tone punctuated Ethan's wooden reply.

The ridge surrounding the HOOK research facility came into view. The last time she had been there, Deacon had come to save her.

This time, there was no Deacon.

There was only emptiness—and smoke.

Too late. She was too late.

Billowing clouds distorted the left side of the largest structure; flames erupted from the bottom windows. There was no hope if the poison had been kept on the lower levels, but if it was upstairs . . .

Her phone rang in her ear, and Ethan's name flashed across the screen.

"Where the hell are you?" he roared.

The wind changed, blowing acrid air in her path. She coughed and sputtered, "HOOK."

He cursed and ended the call.

A disembodied hand emerged from the darkness, dragging her toward six masked men watching the destruction from the empty parking lot.

"Do you have a death wish?" Ethan snapped from beneath his ski mask.

Vivienne shoved him away and tried to take off again. He caught her by the ankle.

"I have to go in!" She kicked at him with her free leg, but his grip tightened.

"And kill yourself? Not happening, girl." He yanked her down, caught her by the waist, and threw her over his shoulder.

Of all the humiliating—"Let me go!" She pummeled his back with her fists, hating the way the others turned their masked heads toward them.

Ethan didn't seem to notice. She bounced as he carried her toward the trees at the back of the—

From the corner of her eye, she saw a top floor light flick on.

"Someone's inside!" And that person could tell her where they kept the poison.

"The last employee left hours ago." Ethan picked up his pace. "It's probably just a motion light."

She stopped struggling. In her calmest voice, she asked him to put her down.

"You have to promise to leave."

"I promise."

The moment her feet hit the pavement, she shot into the air and flew toward that light. Ethan shouted her name, but the sound faded into the heat pulsing around her. The bottom level windows exploded, sending shards of glass across the lawn, and she tumbled for a split second before righting herself.

She had to get to that light.

She had to get the poison.

And if someone was inside, she had to save—

Jasper Hooke.

He was on the ground inside a room filling with smoke,

crawling toward the window. He stood, coughing, then stilled when he saw her. The lenses on his glasses were dirty, but she could see when his eyes widened. His words were muffled, but Vivienne knew he'd said her name.

Gravity tugged her body downward. She closed her eyes and focused on keeping herself afloat.

Jasper forced the window open and sucked in a ragged breath. "Will you help me?"

What choice did she have? Without Jasper, she'd never get the poison. "Climb out," she shouted.

His glasses fell to the ground as he crawled awkwardly through the opening onto the surrounding ledge and gripped the window frame with white knuckles. "What now?"

She flew close enough to touch the stains on his blackened lab coat. "Put your arm around me."

"I'm too heavy. I'll make you fall too."

"I should be able to get you on the ground if—"

"Get the hell out of the way, Vivienne," Ethan barked, appearing through the smoke. He jerked Jasper's arm around his shoulders and carried him to a field at the back of the building.

Jasper fell onto the ground, gasping toward the starless sky. When he caught his breath, he narrowed his eyes at Ethan. "How does it feel?"

"What the hell is that supposed to mean?" Ethan's hands flexed at his sides; the veins in his neck bulged.

"Flying," Jasper clarified, looking between Vivienne and Ethan as he struggled to a seated position. "What does it feel like? Are there any odd internal sensations, or does the air feel differently than before? Or—"

"I'm not answering any of your damn questions," Ethan snarled, kicking a mound of dirt toward Jasper. "But you'd better answer mine, or else I'm going to pick you up and show you exactly how it feels to fly." A smirk. "Or in your case, to fall."

"What questions could you possibly have for me?" Jasper asked.

"I want to know what you've done with the body."

Jasper's pale blue eyes went blank. "I don't know what you're talking about."

Ethan lunged, grabbing Jasper by the collar. "Don't lie to me! I just saved your worthless life. You *owe* me!"

Vivienne managed to get between them and push Ethan off Jasper. He stumbled away and cursed at the sky.

Jasper drew gasping breaths into his lungs; his eyes were wide and panicked. "*Body?* You think we have a body?" Ethan twisted and stalked toward him, only stopping when Jasper winced and held his arms over his face defensively. "We have no cadavers on site," he rushed, his voice shaking. "I swear. Please don't hurt me. I swear I don't know what you're talking about."

Jasper was a liar and a murderer, but for some reason, Vivienne believed him. Ethan must have too, because he froze and raked his hands through his hair before swearing again.

"Where's the poison?" Dampness seeped through the knees of her tights when she knelt next to Jasper in the grass.

"What poison?"

What had he called it back in April? "The *treatment* you use to kill us."

"*Kill* you?" He shook his head. "I've never killed anyone. I swear, I—"

"Where is it?" She didn't want to hear more lies. She wanted to get the poison, go back to Kensington, and give it to Peter. It wouldn't atone for her sins, but at least she'd be doing something to help the PAN instead of hurt them.

"W-we don't keep it in the main facility—at least, not much of it."

"I need it, Jasper. *Please*."

His eyes searched hers, and eventually he told her that his brother kept all the spare vials in a safe in his office.

She stood and started for the administrative building. Maybe her luck was finally changing. It was the only one that wasn't on fire.

"Are you insane?" Ethan caught her arm. "You can't go back there. The place will be crawling with first responders." Sirens echoed in the distance.

If she hurried, maybe—

Her phone started ringing, blaring in the silence.

"Don't answer that," Ethan warned.

"I just want to see who it is."

Greenview Regional Hospital.

Why would a hospital be calling her? It had to be a wrong number. Right?

"Hello?" Silence. "*Hello?*"

"Vivienne! I just told you not to—"

"When a hospital calls, I'm going to answer it." Whoever had been on the other line must have ended the call.

"Hospital? Which one? Where is it?"

Opening a new web browser, Vivienne typed the name into the search engine.

Greenview Regional Hospital was in Bowling Green, Kentucky.

An hour away from Nashville.

SIXTEEN

Vivienne's heart clattered against her ribs as she stared at the beige hospital. The building was six stories high, with rotating doors at the main entrance and an ambulance parked by the emergency room.

Her body was so tired from flying the whole way to Kentucky that if she tried going back now, she'd fall right out of the sky.

"Do you want to go inside or just stand here gawking at the sign?" Ethan muttered, opening his wallet and handing her a stiff twenty-dollar bill.

The plan was to buy flowers and balloons from the gift shop to keep from looking suspicious. Then they were going to split up and search for Deacon. Vivienne was to start at the top and work down, while Ethan went from the bottom up. The first person to find something promising was going to text the other.

"I made it this far without asking this," she said, swallowing the fear in her throat, "but what if it's not him?"

Instead of looking at her, Ethan spoke to the building, "It *has* to be him."

Ten minutes later, Vivienne exited the sparse gift shop with a wilting bouquet of Gerbera daisies in hand. Ethan carried a foil balloon for a new baby boy down the hall in front of her. After wedging herself into the elevator between two doctors and two other visitors, she watched Ethan navigate through the outdated waiting room toward the first ward.

Starting with the top floor, Vivienne scoured the bustling hallways and read every name tag next to every door. By the time she reached the third level, her hope had been replaced by resignation.

Feeling utterly defeated, she called Ethan. "Tell me you've had better luck than I have."

"Nothing. And I'm almost to the third floor."

"That's where I—"

A trio of policemen stood at the end of a quiet corridor.

The chances that Deacon was in this particular hospital—over an hour outside of Nashville—were slim. But if he had made it all the way to Kentucky with a gunshot wound to the chest, surely the police would have been called.

"Vivienne? You okay?"

Two of the officers left their posts and walked toward her.

She whispered, "Come quick," when the men had passed, deep in conversation with one another as they vanished behind the steel elevator doors.

"Two seconds."

When the doors opened again, Ethan pushed past the other passengers and beelined straight for her. "What'd you find?"

She inclined her head toward the lone uniformed man outside room 312.

Cocking his head to the side, Ethan grinned. "Looks like

that officer is responsible for making sure someone stays *inside* the room."

Vivienne nodded but kept her eyes on a water cooler between a pair of chairs. "There were three of them, but the others went for dinner."

"Hold this."

"Why?"

"Because I'm about to get arrested." He shoved his balloon into her hand and headed toward the guard with a pronounced stagger. "Hey, man," he slurred. "Is my no good, piece-of-shit brother in there?"

The policeman's hand went to the gun holstered on his belt. "Sir, you can't come in here."

"Calvin, can you hear me?" Ethan kicked at the wall. "I'm gonna kill you for worryin' Momma."

"Sir, lower your voice." The officer blocked him with his forearm. "Do you know who is in this room?"

"I have a feeling it's my drunk ass brother. He got himself into trouble again, didn't he?"

A cluster of wide-eyed hospital staff gathered alongside Vivienne to witness the drama unfolding at the end of the hall.

The officer told Ethan to calm down. Although Ethan didn't resist, the officer grabbed his wrists, jerked them behind his back, and led him through the captivated crowd. "Can one of you get back to 312?" the officer said into the walkie-talkie attached to his shoulder. "I have a guy here who claims to know the victim."

"*Victim*?" Ethan stomped his foot. "Don't tell me he's gone and done something stupid like get himself shot."

Ethan winked as he passed Vivienne. She let the balloon drift toward the ceiling and strolled through the murmuring group of onlookers straight into room 312.

The space was as dark as the sky outside. A blue curtain had been pulled around one of two beds; the only noises were a chorus of humming machines and heavy, steady breathing.

As anxious as Vivienne was to throw aside the final barrier, she first took cover on the far side of the empty bed. Her knees connected with the floor just as one of the officers opened the door, throwing a beam like a searchlight across the room.

"All good, Frank?" a man asked.

"Looks okay to me."

The door fell closed, and Vivienne was once again swallowed by darkness. She counted to one hundred before emerging from the corner and making her way to the curtain. Her trembling fingers connected with the thin, papery material and moved it aside.

SEVENTEEN

Deacon hit the ground with a thud, a crunch, and a curse. Somehow, he managed to land a block east of the bullet-soaked scene on Woodland Street. He shifted to his knees in the sludge next to three wheelie bins and pulled his demolished mobile from his pocket.

Well, shit. He dropped the useless thing into the muck.

His hand flew to his right ear. TINK was missing. *Shiiit.*

An invisible, sadistic demon stabbed him in the chest with a red-hot fire poker. His left arm hung limp by his side. Moving it made the pain more unbearable. He dragged his jacket across his chest and somehow managed to zip it enough to conceal the bloody smears ruining his T-shirt. Hopefully no one would notice the bullet hole.

The bin clinked and jingled when he used it as a handle to struggle to his feet. Putting weight on his left leg left him cursing. It probably wasn't broken, but it still hurt like hell.

He staggered down the alley, away from the screaming sirens and red and blue strobes.

Although the sidewalk was packed, there were no taxis waiting along the curb.

Instead of going into a restaurant where no amount of ambient lighting would conceal his bloody trail, Deacon fell into one of the moody, dark bars lining the streets of Five Points.

Inside were clusters of patrons at different stages of drunkenness, bustling bartenders, and frowning employees rounding up empty glasses strewn around the liquor-soaked tables.

After locating a group of college-aged women toasting with fruity cocktails, he beelined for the epicentre of riotous chatter. "I'm sorry to interrupt, ladies," he said, mustering a smile, "but I seem to have lost my mobile *and* my friends. Would one of you mind calling me an Uber?"

As usual, the winning combination of questionable female sobriety, buzzing neon lights, and his accent worked like a charm.

A nice girl named Cindi—with an *i*—agreed to call him a cab.

She also offered to buy him a drink *and* bring him home to her momma. As much as Deacon hated being rude, he was forced to say no. After all, he was standing in a sizeable puddle of blood that somehow no one had seemed to notice yet.

"You don't look so good," Cindi said, twisting a toothpick floating in her green martini.

"Don't feel so good either." Did she have a twin or was he seeing double?

Her mobile lit up, and she squinted at the bright screen. "Your ride's here."

Deacon thanked her and miraculously made it outside the crowded space without anyone bumping into his left side.

Dropping into the car, he fought a losing battle with the seat belt.

"Sorry, man," the driver said, turning down the stereo. "I'm waiting for a girl named Cindi."

"Cindi requested you for me. I smashed my mobile."

"Smashed your phone, huh? Wild night?"

"You could say that."

The driver adjusted the rearview mirror and asked where Deacon wanted to go.

He wanted to go find Vivienne. But he needed to go to . . . "The hospital."

"Dude . . . " The driver twisted to glare at him. "If you need an ambulance, it looks like there's one around the corner. Wonder what happened?"

"I'm just feeling a bit dizzy. That's all." Deacon felt the same way he had when his Nevergene had finally activated.

"Fine. I'll bring you. Just don't puke in my car." The driver pulled away from the curb, indicating toward the ring road that danced around Music City.

"Do you mind bringing me to a hospital outside of Nashville?"

"Think you'll make it?"

Slumping against the door, Deacon muttered, "I hope so."

"How far outta town do you want to go?"

The hospitals in and around the city would be on high alert for gunshot victims after what had happened. And with HOOK out there, he needed to get out of Tennessee. "Kentucky?"

The driver's eyes met his in the mirror. "That's gonna be expensive."

"Whatever the fee is, I'll double it." Deacon slid down until he was lying across the back seat. The fruity smell of the leaf-shaped air fresheners dangling from the mirror left his stomach rolling. The car swayed through traffic and bumped over potholes.

"Do you mind turning up the heat?" he asked. It was bloody freezing.

"Get up, man. We're here."

Deacon squinted against the dazzling lights. Where was he?

"Why are you covered in blood?"

Why was this stranger poking him? He needed to go away and let Deacon sleep.

Somewhere in the background, a woman screamed.

He tried to apologize for all the blood but wasn't sure any real words came out. His cumbersome eyelids closed, and he drifted toward a blinding white light.

EIGHTEEN

He was alive.

Deacon was *alive*.

But what if he wouldn't wake up—what if he *couldn't*? What if he was in a coma or on life support or had brain damage or was going to be a vegetable or—

"Deacon, wake up," Vivienne whispered.

Nothing.

"Deacon? *Please* wake up." White bandages peeked from beneath his patterned hospital gown. Vivienne placed her warm hand in his cold one and squeezed.

His lashes fluttered open, but his green eyes remained unfocused. "What took you so long?"

Tears stung the back of her eyes, and she choked on her relief. "I'm so happy to see you."

The corners of his lips lifted. "Prove it."

The forgotten bouquet in her hand spilled petals onto the bedcovers as she dropped it and cupped his jaw. Vivienne's lips crushed against his, and she kissed him with every ounce of fear and elation she'd felt over the last week. "I thought you were dead," she whispered, leaning her forehead against his.

"Dead, huh? Were you devastated?"

"Nope. I didn't cry at all," she said, tears clouding her vision. "As a matter of fact—"

Voices. Outside. In the hallway. They got louder and louder, then stopped.

He put his finger to his lips. "*Hide.*"

The doorknob jingled, and Vivienne raced to the far side of the other bed. Her heart clattered against her ribcage as she pulled her knees to her chest. The blue curtains around Deacon's bed ruffled when the door opened.

"Hey, Dr. Blue Eyes," he greeted. "How was the wine?"

Who the heck was Dr. Blue Eyes? Vivienne peered beneath the curtain but could only see a pair of nondescript white sneakers and blue scrubs.

"Everything I imagined it would be," Dr. Blue Eyes said. She sounded young. "I see one of your fans brought you flowers."

"My biggest fan."

Crap. The flowers. Vivienne had forgotten all about those.

"You're going to leave behind a lot of broken hearts, Casanova."

Vivienne frowned at her clenched fists and forced herself to stretch open her hands. Just because the doctor sounded young didn't mean she was. She could be shriveled and old and nearing retirement. After five minutes of flirtatious small talk, the doctor told Deacon everything looked good. When Vivienne heard the door close, she jumped up and went back through the curtain. "How are we going to get you out of here, *Casanova*?"

Deacon gave her a sheepish smile. "Unless you'd like to

deal with the police guarding my door, I'd suggest calling Extraction."

Vivienne rolled her eyes even as she pressed the button on TINK and asked her to call Extraction.

Owen answered on the first ring. "Dammit, Vivienne, if you tell me something's wrong, I'm going to have Peter chain you to Kensington Hall."

"Nothing is wrong, but I need an extraction," she said, grabbing Deacon's cold hand.

Owen cursed. "I've locked on to your location. Why are you at a hospital? Are you hurt?"

"No, but Deacon is."

"Holy sh—*Dash* is with you?"

Deacon kissed her hand and tugged her closer.

Owen's questions were short and to the point. After Vivienne explained everything, including the fact that Ethan was probably in jail, Owen promised to be at the hospital in two hours.

Vivienne spent most of the time curled into a ball below the window, biting her tongue when nurse after nurse stopped in to "check on" Deacon and giggle and comment on his "cute" accent and ask if he needed any more pillows. Seriously, how many freaking pillows did one guy need?

Vivienne nearly cheered when she saw Owen's message on her phone. *Open the window.*

She opened one of the wide windows, then resumed her position in the corner. A moment later, Owen crawled through with a black bundle tucked beneath his arm. He was wearing a pair of black cargo pants, a long-sleeved black thermal top, and a black beanie over his dark hair.

He didn't say anything to her, just pointed to the dividing curtain.

She nodded and gave him a thumbs up. The last nurse had left ten minutes ago, so they should have a bit of time before anyone else came in to give Deacon another stupid pillow.

Owen pulled the curtain aside and . . . laughed? Was that what the gruff sound was?

"I see Extraction's response time is still shit," Deacon said with a grin.

"I see you're still a dick." Owen sniggered and threw a pair of black sweatpants and a black button-up shirt onto the bed. "Get your ass covered, but leave the shirt under your pillow. We don't want to draw any *more* attention to ourselves, now do we?"

"Just like old times, isn't it?" Deacon pulled aside the covers. His left ankle was wrapped in bandages.

Owen cleared his throat and narrowed his black eyes at Vivienne. "Can you give me a sec to get his clothes on?"

"She can help if she wants." Deacon wiggled his eyebrows.

"God, I hate you," Owen grumbled, yanking the curtain closed.

After a bit of cursing, Deacon was clothed from the waist down but still wearing the hospital gown on top. Owen dragged the covers back over Deacon's legs before checking the screen on the IV.

Feeling completely useless, Vivienne asked if there was anything she could do to help.

"See if you can find gauze and tape. There may be some over there." Owen indicated a wall of cabinets as he glanced at Deacon's chart.

Sure enough, the cabinets were full of extra medical supplies, and she set the requested items on the end of the bed.

Owen returned the chart, then went to the sink. "If you want to help, you'll need to wash your hands too."

When their hands were cleaned, they slipped on some

rubber gloves from a box above the sink. Per Owen's instructions, Vivienne ripped off a bit of tape and opened the gauze. Owen folded the gauze over on itself four times, then held it over the needle on the back of Deacon's hand. In one fluid motion, he removed the needle and taped the gauze in place.

Voices sounded outside the door, and Vivienne smacked Owen in the knee. He didn't flinch as he added a second piece of tape.

The curtain fluttered, sending Vivienne's adrenaline through the roof. Why was no one else panicking?

Nicola slipped between the curtains with an ID badge secured to the waistband of her blue scrubs and a stethoscope around her neck.

"Hey, Dr. Mitter." Deacon waved at her with his right hand.

Nicola glared at him, but it looked like she was fighting a smile. "You look like shit, Dash."

He laughed. "Could be worse."

Nicola's lips lifted as she picked up Deacon's chart. It was hard to believe that only few days ago they were at his funeral; now he was sitting beside her, a wicked gleam in his eye and mischievous smile on his lips. If Extraction hadn't been so close—

Wait. *Why* had they been close?

"How'd you guys get here so fast?" There was no way they had made it from Massachusetts to Kentucky in under two hours.

Nicola flipped to the second page and handed the clipboard to Owen. "The body in the morgue ended up being David Calhoun's. So we knew this idiot had to be out there somewhere."

David?

Oh no. Oh god.

Vivienne steadied herself against the bedrails to keep

from collapsing. She thought David had escaped. That he had made it home. Deacon grabbed her hand, and she held onto him as though her life depended on it.

Deacon was alive, but Vivienne had still killed someone.

"What's the status on our lift?" Owen asked, replacing the chart again and clearing the bits from the bed.

"Ten minutes out," Nicola said. "If you want, I can get him to the roof. You and Vivienne can—"

There was a click, and the curtain fluttered.

Vivienne, Owen, and Nicola flew to the other side of the far bed and hunkered down.

"Who took this out?" a woman hissed.

Vivienne recognized the doctor's voice from earlier. Dr. Blue Eyes.

"Took what out?" Deacon asked with a lazy yawn.

Beside Vivienne, Nicola checked her watch.

"Your central line."

"How should I know? This is your hospital."

Owen and Nicola shared a look Vivienne couldn't decipher. They both nodded at the same time, and Owen heaved a breath before disappearing around the curtain.

Vivienne heard the door's lock engage.

Something clattered the floor.

"Ease up," Deacon scolded. "You're scaring the poor woman."

Vivienne shot to her feet and ripped the curtain aside. Owen had his hand around the doctor's mouth. Her blue eyes were wide with terror when her gaze landed on Vivienne and Nicola.

Deacon held out his hand like he was trying to calm a scared animal. "You're not going to shout, are you, Dr. Blue Eyes?"

The woman shook her head; some of her wild red hair slipped out of its clip.

"Dammit, Dash. I can't wait till you're out of the field." Owen released the doctor with another curse. He yanked her name tag from her scrubs with one hand and lifted the other to his ear. "Hey, TINK, call Julie." There was a pause. "Julie, I need information on a Dr. *Hilary Carey* . . . " His voice faded as he stalked into the bathroom.

Nicola wiped her hand across her forehead and groaned. "Looks like we're kidnapping a doctor."

Dr. Carey's eyes narrowed as she glanced toward the locked door. "I'm not going anywhere with you."

"You may want to reconsider," Deacon muttered. "*She's*" —he nodded to Nicola—"actually quite violent."

"Fine." Dr. Carey crossed her arms over her chest and seemed to reassess Nicola. "But you have to tell me what's going on."

Nicola rolled her eyes and pushed past Dr. Carey to the bed. "We're getting him out of here."

"There's no way I'm letting him leave this hospital. He still needs medical attention."

Nicola hummed a noncommittal response as she tucked the bed's remote between the railing and the mattress. There was a loud snap when she kicked the release on the bed's brakes.

"If you come with us," Deacon said with a lazy grin, "you can give me all the attention I need."

"To where? Prison? Because that's where you're headed."

"I'd love to see them try to put me in prison," Nicola muttered on her way to the bathroom door. "Hey, Owen? We have three minutes."

"Three minutes for what?" Dr. Carey asked.

"Three minutes to get him to the roof," Owen said on his way out of the bathroom. He tossed the doctor's name tag back at her. "She's good to go."

"Good to go *where*?" Dr. Carey hooked her nametag on

her pocket and shoved her fallen hair from her face. "Who *are* you people?"

"All you have to do is wheel him outta here with me." Nicola steered the bed toward the door. "And if you alert anyone—" She bent close to whisper something in the woman's ear.

Dr. Carey's eyes bulged, and she nodded. "All right. Um. Okay. Let's see. If you have any hope of getting out of here without the guards accompanying us, he's going to have to pretend to sleep."

Deacon closed his eyes, and his head lolled to the side.

Nodding toward Vivienne and Owen, Dr. Carey asked how they were planning on getting out.

Owen told her the truth—that they were going out the window.

"But we're three stories up."

"Your point?"

Vivienne lifted her hood to cover her hair and followed Owen. He let her fly out first before following her to the rooftop.

Deacon, Nicola, and Dr. Carey emerged onto the roof at the same time a hulking black helicopter landed on the empty helipad. Barry jumped out and helped Owen get Deacon inside. Nicola climbed in after him.

Vivienne watched Dr. Carey silently take in the confusing scene around her. Wind from the propellers twisted her wild red hair around her shoulders. "You'll be happy you helped us. I promise." The words would have been more effective had Vivienne not been forced to shout them.

Dr. Carey nodded, her lips tight.

"There's only room for one more," Owen yelled at the doctor. "We won't force you to come with us if you don't want to."

Dr. Carey squared her shoulders. "I'm coming."

Owen nodded. "Vivienne, get in."

"What about you?" Dr. Carey called as he turned toward the edge of the roof.

Owen grinned, banishing the shadows from his face, and said, "I'll race you there." He took off running and dove over the edge.

NINETEEN

J asper watched as two-thirds of his family's legacy turned to ash in the course of a few hours but couldn't summon an ounce of remorse for what had been lost.

Treatment for those with the Nevergene was part of the protocol. He was responsible for diagnosing them, collecting blood and tissue samples, and administering treatment. Every potential PAN he had met since being employed at HOOK had been a dead end, so the final step had been redundant.

Until Vivienne.

She possessed the active gene they needed to continue their research. Although he already had her blood samples, Jasper's father had insisted they find her.

His obsession was becoming unhealthy.

At one point the previous summer, Jasper had attempted to bring Lawrence to his side on the matter, but his brother had vehemently disagreed.

When Jasper had asked why it mattered which subject

they had, the only response he had received was that the answer was "above his pay grade."

Now he found himself at odds with his family. There had to be some explanation. Perhaps Vivienne had been mistaken when she had called the treatment poison. Or maybe the side effect was something no one else had documented.

"Lawrence?" He knocked three times before entering his brother's office. "I need to speak with you for a minute."

"If it's not important, it'll have to wait," Lawrence grumbled, sorting through a stack of papers on his desk.

"It's very important."

Lawrence cursed but dropped the pages and gave Jasper his undivided attention. "You do realize we're in the middle of a crisis, don't you? I'm trying to get shit sorted with the insurance company so *you* can get back up and running."

"I know." Jasper took a halting step closer. "It'll only take a minute."

Lawrence pressed some buttons on his phone and flashed Jasper the countdown timer on his screen. "*One* minute."

"Very funny."

"Fifty-five seconds."

"My question is about the treatment we give our subjects."

Lawrence's dark eyebrows lifted. "That doesn't sound very important to me."

Of course it didn't. Lawrence didn't care about anyone or anything beyond himself. "I was wondering how well the side effects of the injection have been documented."

"Sounds like that's your area of expertise, Mr. Head of Research."

"True. But I haven't been required to administer treatment since I've been employed here."

Lawrence's eyes dropped to the page in front of him. "I

think the stuff you're looking for is in Storage." He rummaged for a pen and signed the page.

Jasper tapped the red X at the bottom of the countdown. "Would you look at that? Two seconds to spare."

The fire had been contained to the largest research complex. Firemen had fought for hours so that the smaller office building remained untouched. From inside, the only indication there had been a fire was the occasional smell of acrid smoke drifting through the air vents.

Jasper reached a black door at the end of a stark hallway marked STORAGE. His hand connected with the flimsy handle, and stale, musty air wafted toward the opening door. Despite the blackness within, he had no trouble locating the light switch. Fluorescent tubes sputtered to life, bathing the wall of filing cabinets in a blue-tinged glow.

Three ancient computers with black screens, an outdated, boxy television set, and a VHS player sat on a table in the middle of the room.

Jasper took a deep breath and opened the first filing cabinet near the entrance.

After hours of searching through purchase orders, receipts, and tax returns, he had given up hope of locating anything of use. And then he found it.

Buried within the seventh filing cabinet was a thick tan envelope with the name *Sophia Tierney* scrawled on the front.

Inside the folder was a copy of hospital admission records from a facility he had never heard of and a few scraps of prescription paper scribbled with dated notes.

August 10 - Subject presented signs of active NG-1882
August 17 - Subject confirmed PAN
August 23 - Tests administered
September 4 - Exhibiting significant memory loss/confusion
October 1 - Treatment administered via local injection
October 3 - Subject grounded, showing signs of rapid aging

October 4 - Subject deceased

Jasper read—and reread—the final entry; bile burned the back of his throat.

Subject deceased

Jasper, along with his father and brother, had been under the illusion the work their family was doing was for the good of mankind. HOOK was the front-runner in discovering a way to eliminate aging in the human race. And their groundbreaking research aimed to control the next leap in evolution by isolating the genetic ingredients that allowed the PAN to fly.

But Edward Hooke had been keeping a big secret from all of them.

They had been naive to believe such breakthroughs could have been made without first paying an unconscionably high cost: the life of every PAN ever injected with the NG-1882 treatment.

Perhaps justice had been served the night Peter's people had taken a match to their facility. It felt mutinous to think along those lines, but Jasper knew it would be better to end their harmful research before another life was taken.

He checked his watch.

It was late, but his father and Lawrence would still be around the office for at least another hour.

Before he left the room, he attempted to open the last filing cabinet in the line, only to find it locked. He searched the room for keys; there were none. He'd have to ask his father about them after he told him of his discovery.

Jasper burst through his father's door without knocking. "Thank God you're still here."

Dr. Charles Hooke sat at the desk in his small office as arrogantly as any king had ever sat on his throne.

His medical degrees and awards were showcased in matching frames on the wall. There were so many, the color of the paint behind them was a mystery. On the edge of his desk sat a cluster of photos from the various ceremonies held to honor him for his philanthropic work in the local community and beyond.

"What're you still doing here, Lab Rat?" Lawrence asked, coming into the room and clapping him on the back hard enough to send Jasper stumbling forward.

"I've been doing research, *Lawrence*," Jasper said, shrugging off his brother's heavy hand. "Isn't that what you pay me to do?"

"This week's been tough enough without the two of you bickering like children." Their father removed his glasses and rubbed the bags beneath his eyes. "What do you need?"

"I need to speak with you about our treatment serum."

His father tossed his glasses aside and adjusted his heaving bulk in the too-small chair. "What about it?"

"I don't know how to tell you this," Jasper said, drawing in a steadying breath, "but I'm fairly certain it kills them."

His father and brother shared an unreadable look and then did something so surprising that Jasper would never forget it.

They *laughed*.

"Can you believe him?" Lawrence asked, still bent over in hysterics.

His father's wheezing subsided long enough for him to exhale an, "I know," before losing his composure again.

"It's *not* funny." Jasper smacked the damming envelope against his thigh. "I'm being completely serious."

His father stopped laughing and clapped his hands together on the desk. "How'd you stumble upon this conclusion?"

"I found this," Jasper bit out, thrusting the evidence toward him.

His father opened the parcel and flicked through the pages before his face grew solemn. Lawrence sauntered behind the desk to look over his father's shoulder. "Where'd you get this?" his father clipped.

"It was in Storage."

"Why the hell were you in the storage room?"

"Lawrence suggested I look for what I needed in there. I know how upsetting this must be for you. I was shocked myself. "

"It's not a big deal, Dad," Lawrence said, shifting closer to the door.

"Not a *big deal*?" their father growled, rising from his chair and bracing his hands on the desk. "The storage room is off limits. Do you hear me? *Off. Limits.*"

"*What?*" Surely Jasper hadn't heard him correctly. His father was barring *him* from accessing vital research?

"There's nothing in there you need to see."

Jasper studied his father and brother. Neither of them appeared ruffled or even surprised. "Did you *know* the side effects?"

Dr. Charles Hooke stood to his full height and glared at Jasper. "Of course I knew."

"How could you be so naive, Rat?" Lawrence drawled. "What did you think we were doing? Giving them some vitamins and sending them on their merry way into the clouds?"

Although Jasper had known both men his entire life, he now felt as though he was seeing them for the very first time.

His father shoved the notes back into the envelope and locked it inside his desk drawer. "This isn't going to be a problem, is it, Jasper?"

"No, it isn't." For the first time in his life, Jasper lied to his father's face.

"Good. Now head home and let your brother and I finish our work so we can do the same."

That night, every time Jasper's eyes drifted closed, he found himself gazing into the sightless eyes of a faceless woman with gray, wrinkled skin named Sophia Tierney.

The next morning, he bypassed his office and went directly to the storage room, only to be greeted by a gleaming padlock on a new, industrial fire door.

Defeated, Jasper returned to his temporary workspace in the prefab lab to figure out what he was supposed to do now that he knew he was a villain.

TWENTY

It was physically impossible to get comfortable in a hospital bed. Pillows, blankets, extra pillows, no blankets, no pillows—none of it mattered. Nothing worked. Deacon had spent the last two days tossing and turning and trying not to ask Dr. Carey for more painkillers before breaking down and begging her for something to ease the pain in his shoulder.

Where was the remote? He searched the tangle of sheets until he found it between the plastic mattress and the metal bed rail.

"Shouldn't you be in a morgue?"

Deacon jerked around so quickly he swore his spine snapped. Then he groaned.

Bloody shoulder.

But the pain in his shoulder was nothing compared to the pain in his head when he saw the jaw-dropping woman smiling at him from the doorway.

Of all the days for her to show up.

"What are you doing here, Gwen?"

Gwen carried a bouquet of red roses to the bedside locker and replaced the daisies Vivienne had given him with her own. Wiping her hands on her tight leather leggings, she sank onto the chair. "Someone very close to me died last week."

Deacon dragged the infuriating hospital gown Dr. Carey had forced him to wear back over his shoulder, knowing Gwen would see his current state of undress as either a weakness or an opportunity. "How tragic."

Plucking at the corner of his gown, she settled the material into place. "Not really. It turns out he's far too stubborn to *actually* die."

"How inconsiderate of him, especially seeing as you traveled all this way."

"He is quite inconsiderate. And selfish. And immature." She swept a platinum wave from her cheek. "But he has a few good qualities too." She traced a nail along the sheets covering his legs. "Shall I list them . . . one . . . by . . . one?"

~~YES.~~

No.

No. Absolutely not. Bad idea. Terrible, terrible idea.

Deacon stopped her hand before she reached her final destination, removing it from his inner thigh and placing it on the bed rail. "Gwen, we had fun. But as I told you this spring—"

"There's no need to remind me," she snapped. "I remember all the awful things you said."

Awful? He'd said that he wasn't interested in seeing her anymore. That wasn't awful. It was honest.

"I was so angry and thought I could never forgive you," she went on, reaching for his hand, "but then I heard what happened in Tennessee. I was crushed, and I cried the whole way here. I kept thinking: what would I do if I had one more chance? Things could be different between us. Better."

I was angry.

I could never forgive you.

I don't care about you, only about myself and what I want and how I feel—I I I I I.

"Only you could make *me* getting shot all about *you*." Some things would never change.

"Must you be so callous?" Gwen whined, her full lower lip jutting forward. She adjusted the hem of her black T-shirt, and the V at the neck dipped lower.

Perhaps he was being too hard on her. "I'm sorry." He offered her a smile. "You know how cranky I get when I'm not sleeping well."

"Perhaps there's something I can do to help you"— turquoise eyes dropped back to the sheet—"with that."

Was it hot in here? Damn he was thirsty. Deacon grabbed a cup from the bedside locker and gulped the tepid water until it was gone. "I . . . um . . . What I mean to say is, Dr. Carey is bringing me some pills. That should help. Help me sleep."

Gwen wore a knowing smirk as she relaxed against the back of the chair and crossed her arms, making her chest look—

STOP looking at her chest. Look at the wall. LOOK AT THE WALL.

It was a nice wall. Sage green with patterned wallpaper behind the tele and—

"How long have you and I been doing this?" Her tinkling laugh made him cringe. "One of us gets distracted for a month or two, but we always find our way back to each other. It's only a matter of time before you come to your senses."

Deacon glanced back at her. "You're wrong." Yes, they had been back and forth for the past five years, but this time it felt different.

"Am I?" Without warning, she leaned forward and pressed her mouth to his.

Wrong wrong wrong.

This was wrong. So wrong.

Her tongue slid across his lips, but he kept his mouth clamped shut because this was wrong and she had no right to kiss him. With his good arm, he found her shoulder and felt her smile against his mouth . . . until he pushed her away.

Her eyes narrowed into slits when he wiped at the lipstick he knew was all over him.

"Don't do that again."

"What's the matter? Can't handle the temptation?" she whispered, brushing her fingertips along his collarbone.

"Gwen?" His hand covered hers, halting the familiar caress.

"Yes?"

"Get out of my room."

"Who is *that*?" Max nodded toward a gorgeous teen scanning the tables inside The Glass House.

Vivienne had been too busy enjoying her breakfast burrito to notice the girl come in. But she looked awfully familiar. "Wasn't she at the funeral?"

The stranger's leather leggings left little to the imagination; her shirt—like the one Vivienne wore—had been tucked into her waistband, accentuating her small waist and curvy hips.

Something warm spread down Vivienne's thigh. Groaning, she slammed her burrito onto the plate and tried wiping the oozy cheese with a napkin but only ended up spreading it around and making it worse.

Emily took a bite of her bagel sandwich; butter dripped down her fingers. "That's Gwen."

Now she was going to have to change before seeing Dea–

"Did you say *Gwen*?" Vivienne choked.

"Yeah," Emily garbled, mid-chew. "I think . . . she's from . . . London."

Crap. Crap. Crap.

Vivienne shifted in her seat, rubbing her sweaty palms on her pants. She would be unlucky enough to meet Deacon's ex-whatever wearing the same shirt and covered in cheese stains. She cursed the way her own Kensington shirt gaped over her nearly flat chest. In contrast, Gwen's chest stretched her shirt to capacity.

When Vivienne looked back up, a pair of blue-green eyes stared back at her. "Is your name Vivienne?"

Vivienne nodded. Gwen's regal accent made her feel like a peasant.

"I need to speak with you."

Vivienne turned to her friends for support; Max's eyes glazed over as he gaped toward Gwen's abundant chest, and Emily's eyebrows raised as she took another bite of her sandwich.

"About what?"

Gwen's red lips twisted into a smirk. "Your '*boyfriend*.'" She made quotations with her fingers.

Vivienne's arm started to itch. "Go on then."

"People are afraid to say anything bad about him because he's Peter's grandson. But I don't have the same reservations. Take it from me: you're only wasting your time there. Behind that handsome exterior is an immature, fickle little boy with serious commitment issues."

"He's never been fickle when it comes to me." If anything, Deacon had been surprisingly consistent, and Vivienne had been the fickle one.

Gwen bared her white teeth and bent to whisper, "If you

don't believe me, ask your friend Nicola. The two of them love to go birdwatching."

Surely Gwen wasn't suggesting that Nicola and Deacon—

Gwen straightened, smirked, and swept out of The Glass House.

Max blinked and shook his head as if breaking out of a trance. "That was *hot*."

"Shut up, Max." Emily cleaned the butter from her hands and smacked him in the shoulder. "What a jealous bitch. How dare she come in here and talk to you like that. She doesn't even know you."

"It's fine, Emily." Vivienne picked up her burrito, but her appetite had been replaced by a gnawing, twisting sensation in her gut that tasted like jealousy. The smell of food made her want to puke, so she pushed her plate aside and took a sip of water to settle her stomach.

"You gonna finish that?" Max asked, nodding toward Vivienne's breakfast.

She shoved the plate across the table. "It's all yours."

Nicola and Deacon?

Deacon and Nicola?

Vivienne had a hard time imagining the two of them together. Sure, they seemed close. But had they ever been closer? Had Nicola been the one Deacon had slept with during the whole bird-watching fiasco?

She hoped not.

Vivienne could handle Gwen. Like Emily said, Gwen was jealous.

But *Nicola*?

Was there any truth to it? If so, why had Deacon never mentioned their relationship? Surely Vivienne deserved to know if he had hooked up with one of her friends.

"You coming home with us or going to see Deacon?" Emily asked, waving her napkin in front of Vivienne's face.

181

"Deacon." His name felt like a lifeline. She needed to talk to him, to get rid of this awful gnawing feeling. He could tell her this was all a big misunderstanding.

Outside was unseasonably warm for this late in September. The water in the rooster fountain bubbled quietly as she passed. Vivienne nodded to the people she knew but didn't have it in her to stop and chat. Joel waved at her from Kensington Hall's roof, and she returned the gesture.

One of the apartments in Leadership House had been transformed into a makeshift hospital room. Dr. Carey had set strict visiting hours; no one was allowed in before nine. And when they did show up, no more than two visitors were allowed in at once. The kitchen-living room was used as a waiting area. There were pastries set out on the coffee table, and the basket of coffees next to the coffeemaker had been restocked since yesterday.

Vivienne checked her watch before knocking on Deacon's door. When he shouted for her to come in, the tension in her body eased a fraction. Deacon sat on his bed, one leg drawn up, tenting the covers. His dark hair was still rumpled from sleep, and his hospital gown fell over his wounded shoulder, revealing tanned skin and white bandages.

When he looked up from the phone in his hand, his mouth broke into a grin. "It's about time you showed up. I missed you."

All Vivienne could see was a bright red smudge staining the corner of his lips.

"Did you?" She swallowed her misery; it settled into her stomach next to the jealousy.

"Of course I did." His head tilted to the side and his brows came together. "What's wrong?"

"I met Gwen."

"Brilliant," he muttered, closing his eyes and rubbing his temples.

Vivienne's heart sank deeper in her chest.

"I told you I was with her before."

"But not anymore?"

His eyes opened; something crossed his face. Regret? Pain? Irritation? When he finally answered, his voice was tight. "Of course not."

Did he think she was an idiot? He had her lipstick all over him. "What about Nicola? Were you with her before too?"

Deacon stiffened. "Vivienne, listen to me—"

"Yeah . . . no." Wiping the corner of his lips with her thumb, Vivienne showed him the red smudge on her finger. "I've heard enough lies today."

Deacon dragged the back of his hand across his mouth, removing the rest of Gwen's lipstick. "It's not what you think."

Vivienne backed slowly toward the door. "Whatever you say, Casanova."

How could she have been so stupid? It shouldn't have surprised her that Deacon and Gwen were still hooking up. Vivienne couldn't compete with girls who had legs that went on for eternity, jawlines that could cut glass, and boobs big enough to use as tray tables.

Vivienne grabbed another tissue from and pulled her covers tighter to her neck. It felt like she had lost Deacon all over again.

"Hey, Vivienne!" The door muffled Emily's call. "You have a visitor."

Was it Deacon?

No, it couldn't be. He was still bedridden for at least another day or two.

Was it Alex?

Vivienne hadn't run into him since the night of Deacon's

funeral. She wasn't looking forward to *that* confrontation.

Maybe it was Gwen again.

God, she hoped not.

"Who is it?" she asked, not moving from her bed. "Never mind. It doesn't matter. Tell them to go home." After crying all morning, she didn't feel like seeing anyone.

Nicola came in and closed the door behind her. "Yeah, that's not happening."

Vivienne scrambled to sit upright while avoiding her reflection in the mirror. She already knew she looked like crap.

Nicola glanced toward Vivienne's pile of tissues but didn't comment. "I hear you met our lovely Gwen." The mattress dipped when she sat at the bottom of the bed. She was dressed in tight blue athletic pants and a neon printed tank top, revealing her toned arms.

"Deacon told you?"

"Yeah. And he begged me to come talk to you since you're refusing to answer his calls. Again." Nicola wiped at a thin sheen of perspiration glistening on her forehead with her shirt. "Can I give you a bit of advice?"

"Thanks, but I think I've had enough advice for the day."

"From who? Gwen?" When Vivienne nodded, Nicola snorted. "She's a psychopath. I wouldn't listen to a thing she said. In fact, I'd probably do the exact opposite. She's always treated Dash like her plaything, and she's just pissed that he's not falling for it anymore."

"I don't want to hear about them."

"Yeah, well, if you want to date Dash, you're going to have to learn to deal with it." Nicola folded her hands together on her lap. "And if you don't get a handle on your jealousy, you'll drive him away."

"Is that what you did?"

Nicola's blue eyes flashed. "You don't get to speak to me

like I'm the bad guy here. If you want to know about my relationship with your *boyfriend*, all you have to do is ask."

"Fine." Vivienne scratched at her forearm, avoiding the scabs left from Tennessee. "What happened between you two?"

"It's none of your business."

"You just said—"

"*But* I'll tell you because I have nothing to hide." Leaning back against the wall, Nicola adjusted her watch. "I had a thing for Dash when he first came to the States. I mean, come on. Those eyes and that accent. Plus, it doesn't hurt that he looks like a handsome devil you'd gladly follow to hell," she said, toying with the ends of her ponytail, twisting the strands around her finger. "Whatever it was, it was short-lived. I was young, and he was new and British." She shrugged, as if those two reasons excused all of it.

"I thought you came here to make me feel better." Instead, Vivienne felt worse. Much, much worse. And she needed another box of tissues.

"I came here to tell you the truth. If that makes you feel better, great. If it doesn't?" Another shrug. "I assumed when you two started hanging out that you knew about his reputation."

The itchiness got worse. "I mean, I know he's gone out with a lot of girls."

"*Gone out with?*" Nicola sniggered. "What is this? Middle school? He's probably slept with more women in Neverland than he hasn't."

Vivienne knew it was bad, but didn't think it was *that* bad. No wonder most of the girls she met gave her strange looks or whispered behind her back. She had assumed it was because of her parents or HOOK, but this made a lot more sense.

"Look," Nicola went on, "we all have things in our past

that we aren't particularly proud of. But we can't let our mistakes define us—or keep us from moving forward."

Vivienne understood exactly what she meant about mistakes. She had already made too many to count—and she was only eighteen.

"Dash *doesn't* date." A laugh. "Or at least he never used to. But if it's any consolation, he seems different with you. Like he's actually trying. Which is a pretty big deal for him. So," Nicola said, pushing herself upright, "next time you have an issue with him, at least let him explain himself. He's not going to lie."

Vivienne could only nod.

"And don't wait too long to clear things up. I'm sick of seeing him mope around the place because of you." When Nicola opened the door to leave, Emily nearly fell on top of her.

Nicola gave an exaggerated sigh and helped Emily right herself before saying goodbye.

Once the front door closed, Emily jumped onto the bed. "What'd she say?"

"Don't even pretend you weren't eavesdropping the whole time," Vivienne grumbled.

Emily smiled. "I couldn't hear *everything*."

"I've had enough coddling! I'm going home." Deacon's frustrated curse echoed through the apartment.

"You're not leaving until you can get around without doing more damage."

Vivienne recognized Dr. Carey's voice from inside Deacon's room.

The last thing she wanted was an audience for their conversation, so she backed toward the door.

"I can . . . *ow* . . . get around . . . *ow* . . . just fine."

"Try keeping your arm still when you—"

"I know how to put on a bloody shirt!"

Vivienne took another step back. Just a few more and she would be out of the apartment and—

Her leg collided with the couch. Something clattered onto the wooden floor. Batteries rolled by her foot.

Stupid remote.

Deacon's door swung open.

"Who is it?" he asked from inside.

Dr. Carey stuck her head out. When she saw Vivienne, she smiled. "Hey, Vivienne."

"This seems like a bad time." Vivienne collected the batteries and remote and threw them onto the couch. "I'll come back later."

"No. Come in. Now. *Please.*" Dr. Carey dragged her by the wrist into the room. "You may be able to talk some sense into him."

Deacon stood unevenly at the foot of the bed, keeping most of his weight off his left leg. The unbuttoned blue shirt he wore gaped open, revealing taut muscles and a dark blue sling.

Vivienne dragged her eyes away from his abs and looked toward the far wall.

Ethan waved at her from where he was perched on the windowsill, grinning. "Take a seat and enjoy the show."

"Show?"

"Yeah. Those two are having a little tiff."

Deacon pointed an accusatory finger at Dr. Carey. "*She* keeps telling me that I have to sit on my ass for the foreseeable future."

"I never said you had to *sit on your ass!*" Dr. Carey stomped her foot and dragged on the ends of her hair. "Even immortal bodies need time to heal."

"*Heal?*" Deacon tried to hook the buttons on his shirt. "I'm beginning to atrophy in this cell."

Ethan laughed. Deacon glared at him. Ethan laughed harder.

"You're only a few weeks into recovering from being *shot*," the doctor pointed out.

"As if I need a reminder." He still hadn't gotten the first button. "Who brought me this damn shirt?"

"I did," Ethan said with a smirk. "You're welcome, by the way. Were you always this ungrateful?"

"I told you to leave on the gown," Dr. Carey muttered.

Did Deacon just *growl* at her?

Vivienne stepped closer to Deacon and reached for his shirt. He dropped his hand and stood completely still.

Goosebumps raised on his chest as she closed the first button.

"Everyone needs to get out," he barked.

Dr. Carey stepped closer. "But your physical therapy—"

"Can wait five bloody minutes."

With a huff, Dr. Carey nodded and left the room.

Deacon peered around Vivienne toward Ethan. "Don't you have somewhere else to be?"

"Nope."

"*Get. Out!*"

"Good luck, Vivienne. He's awfully cranky." Ethan slipped out the window and flew away.

Deacon closed his eyes and sighed. "I'm *never* alone anymore."

Alone. He wanted to be alone. Of course he did. He'd had visitors all day and was probably exhausted. Vivienne dropped her hands and turned toward the door.

"That does not apply to you." He caught her by the elbow and sank onto the side of the bed. Before she could protest, he settled her between his knees and hugged her against him with his unbound arm.

She inhaled the smell of his shampoo and threaded her fingers in his hair, almost black from dampness. "I'm sorry about this morning. I was acting jealous and petty. Gwen is gorgeous, and I'm—"

"You are perfect," he whispered, brushing her hair away from her shoulders. The soft kisses he dotted along her collarbone sent chills through her.

Perfect? Hardly.

His hand slipped beneath the hem of her shirt to draw lazy lines along the skin at her waist. She clung to him as his kisses grew more insistent . . . and trailed lower . . .

What had they been talking about?

It didn't matter.

All that mattered was that he didn't stop—

"Deacon?" There was a staccato knock on the door. "Physical therapy. Remember?"

Groaning, he pinched the bridge of his nose. "That infernal woman is going to be the death of me, you know."

"Stop whining." Vivienne giggled, stepping away and adjusting her shirt. "Stand up and I'll help you get your shirt on."

"I have a better idea." The corner of his mouth lifted into a crooked smile. "How about we lock the door, and I'll help you take yours off?"

She laughed again, but Deacon was sitting there smiling like he meant every word he said. "You're not serious." The fireflies in her stomach jumped around, screaming. "You're broken," she said, gesturing to his bandages.

"I'm still in perfect working order. Lock the door and I'll prove it."

"But Dr. Carey—"

"Vivienne? Do you want to lock the door and make out with me or not?"

"Yes, but—"

"Then lock the damn door."

Vivienne tiptoed across the room, not sure why she was trying to be stealthy. Dr. Carey already knew she was there.

With the door locked, she turned around to find Deacon texting someone.

"There," he said, tossing his phone onto the bedside table. "She won't be back for at least an hour."

An entire hour alone in a bedroom with Deacon? *Heck yes.*

He managed to get himself to the top of the bed with only a few muttered curses and scooted to the left side, making room for her.

"How is this supposed to work, exactly?" she asked, eyeing all his wounds.

Patting the free spot with his unbound arm, he said, "Get up here and we'll figure it out."

Vivienne climbed in next to him but couldn't get comfortable. Deacon started kissing her, and she tried focusing on his mouth, but all she could think about were the metal railings digging into her back and worrying that if she moved, she would hurt him.

"What's wrong?" he asked, pulling away with a frown.

"I'm not very comfortable."

"We don't have to do anything."

"No, no. I want to. I definitely do. But this bed is a bit small. That's all. Maybe we could sit up?"

Deacon fumbled for the bed's remote. When he pressed a button, the back lifted with a mechanical whine. "Hospital beds have their advantages," he teased, settling himself against the pillows.

Vivienne rose to her knees so she could straddle his hips. "That's better."

"Much better," he said hoarsely, reaching for the back of her neck to bring her mouth to his.

She loved kissing him. The way his tongue swept into her mouth and stole her breath. The way his lips felt against hers: hot and insistent.

When Vivienne worked the buttons free on his shirt, Deacon murmured, "If mine comes off, yours does as well."

Oh. My. Gosh.

"Deal." She dragged his arm free and tossed his shirt onto the floor. He clutched the hem of her top and started tugging, then cursing and complaining about his shoulder, and Vivienne decided to help him out.

Deacon's heated gaze raked down her body, igniting her internal fire, and she was so incredibly grateful that Emily had insisted she buy some new bras. Vivienne crushed her mouth against his, and his arm came around her waist, holding her against him. She could feel him through his jeans and adjusted her position so—

OH. *Ohhhh.*

Deacon groaned as she shifted again. When he cursed, she froze. "Did I hurt you?"

"No." His hand tightened on her waist and he lifted his hips, urging her to move again. "Don't stop."

She kept moving and kissing him until they were both breathless and gasping, and her heart was beating so fast she thought it would burst. Deacon buried his face in her chest and cursed again, his grip on her so tight it was almost painful.

Then he fell back onto the pillows, his eyes hooded and a sheen of perspiration on his brow.

"Did you just—"

"Shit." He rubbed his hand across his eyes, his bare chest heaving.

"That's all it takes?"

His laugh was gruff and a little embarrassed. "Having the beautiful woman I'm in love with straddle and grind against me? As mortifying as it is to admit, yes, that's all it takes."

"It felt really good."

"Too good, obviously." Grinning, he told her to turn around.

"What? Why?"

"Because I only have one working hand at the minute."

That made no sense, but Vivienne turned around, and when he told her to lie down on his chest, she did that too. Her head fell in the space between his neck and his shoulder, their hips in line with one another. His hand traced from her throat to her navel and lower. And *looooower*.

"Does this feel as good?" The heat from his whisper tickled against her ear.

Good? What he was doing felt so amazing that she never wanted him to stop. Vivienne's "Yes," was a breathless sigh.

"Shit, Vivienne. I really want to touch you."

"You are." He was touching her, and she wasn't embarrassed or nervous or freaking out.

She felt his head shake. "Under these," he said, dipping a finger beneath her waistband.

His heart pounded against her back, and he was breathing as heavily as she was, and if it felt this good *over*, it would probably feel even better *under*, so she nodded.

"Tell me you want me to."

"I do."

Deacon's fingers breached the elastic at her waist. She screwed her eyes shut and held her breath until they reached their destination.

A low growl rumbled in Deacon's throat as he kissed her neck. His fingers were moving and exploring and igniting and stealing every thought in Vivienne's head. Heat pooled in her stomach and she was dying and coming to life and if he didn't stop she was going to spontaneously combust and—

HOLY. CRAP.

TWENTY-ONE

T*ick.*
    Tick.
Tick.

The pendulum on the grandfather clock made the slightest ticking sound as it swung back and forth. And back. And forth. Vivienne darted a look at Julie, who was still on her phone at her desk, speaking in low tones as she swiveled on her chair.

The day of reckoning had finally come: Paul Mitter wanted to talk to Vivienne about what had happened in Tennessee.

Ethan and Alex were the only other people who knew the truth about Nashville. Vivienne had planned on confessing everything to Deacon, but hadn't gotten around to it.

Liar.

Okay. Maybe she'd totally chickened out.

Now it was too late.

Tick.

Tick.

Tick.

On the other side of the hall, the door to the underground lab opened. Vivienne seriously considered dropping to the floor and rolling under the couch. But Alex caught sight of her, and she knew there'd be no escape. He froze mid-stride, and his lips pressed together in a slight grimace.

Don't come over here. Not today. Please. Not today.

But this day was destined to be crap, so of course Alex straightened his shoulders and started for where she was sitting.

Vivienne jumped to her feet. She was short enough, and sitting for this confrontation only put her at more of a disadvantage. Alex halted when he reached the clock. Instead of speaking, he stared at the black and white tiles beneath his boots.

Tick.

Tick.

Tick.

He had obviously come over to say *something*. Why couldn't he get it over with? The silence was killing her. If he didn't say something soon, she was going to end up saying something stupid. Like, "So I've been meaning to come by the lab—"

"Do I look like an idiot to you?" he ground out. "If you wanted to see me, you could have walked the two minutes it takes to get from your apartment to where I spend every waking moment of every day trying to find a cure for what's going to happen to you."

The gut-wrenching anger in his tone sent her a step backward. "Alex, listen to me." Vivienne reached for his arm, but he jerked away. The flat look in his eyes sent ice through her veins. "Look, I'm sor—"

"Don't apologize. I get it."

"Get what?"

"How you really feel about me." Alex sneered. "You think I'm good enough to fill in the gaps, but that's it. He breaks you, and I get to pick up the pieces."

Deacon hadn't broken her. He had *died*. Or so she'd thought. "Come on. That's not fair."

"You're right. It's not fair. *At all*." Alex pulled the zipper on his black leather jacket up to his chin and shoved his hands into his pockets. "I'm not settling for second place anymore. The next time he leaves you—and he will—don't come flying to me. Not unless you're planning on sticking around and giving me a real chance."

All Vivienne could do was stare as Alex stalked away. The heavy door slammed behind him, echoing off the paneled walls. Julie stared at her from the desk, her brows disappearing into her frizzy hair.

Everything Alex had said was true. Vivienne would never be able to give him what he wanted as long as Deacon was in her heart. Yet she had willingly used him as a substitute when Deacon wasn't around.

Vivienne felt like a terrible person.

She *was* a terrible person.

And it was time to confess just how terrible she had been.

Paul barely acknowledged Vivienne when she came into his office. He gestured to the deep-buttoned leather sofa across from him and continued staring at the papers inside an olive-green folder. His finger tapped against the wood of his desk, alternating with the solid tick of a Charlie Bell on the bookshelf.

Tap.

Tick.

Tap.

Tick.

There was a new framed photo on the desk that hadn't been there the last time she'd been in his office, after HOOK. It was a picture of Paul and Nicola and a gorgeous blond woman who Vivienne assumed was Nicola's mom. They were at the beach, smiling as they lounged on colorful sun chairs. It was strange to think of the Head of External Affairs ever relaxing.

"I'd like to tell you a story," Paul said, finally closing the folder. He rubbed his graying goatee before removing his glasses and discarding them on top of the folder. "There once was a girl who had a fantastic opportunity to live in a magical kingdom. This kingdom was ruled by a gracious king whose subjects never wanted for anything. But in order to live in the kingdom, all of his subjects had to follow a few simple rules. With me so far?"

Vivienne's stomach sank as she nodded.

"Now, instead of *following* the rules, this particular girl chose not to listen. And her actions put a lot of people in danger—including the heir to the kingdom." Paul reached into his briefcase and slid a plastic baggie across the desk. There was a crushed flip phone inside. "What do you think happened to that girl?"

Why had she thought throwing the stupid phone over a stupid fence had been a good way to get rid of it? Why had she bought the stupid thing in the first place?

"Vivienne? Did you hear my question?"

Vivienne shifted in her chair, tucking her hands beneath her thighs to hide their trembling. "I don't know."

Paul tented his fingers beneath his chin, and his mouth turned down into a disapproving frown. "Do you think she was allowed to *stay* in the kingdom?"

The door burst open.

Deacon limped in, wild-eyed and disheveled. A navy blue sling secured his shoulder, and he rested his weight against a crutch in his right hand. "Tell me it isn't true." His gaze landed on the cell phone in the baggie. He jerked back, colliding with the door frame. "Dammit, Vivienne! *You gave HOOK our location?*"

How could he think she would do something like that? She had screwed up, but she wasn't a traitor. "No, I didn't. I swear. I just . . . I called Lyle . . . and HOOK was tapping his phone . . . and—"

Deacon twisted and disappeared into the hall.

"Deacon! Wait!"

Paul didn't try to stop her as she clambered for the exit. Even injured, Deacon was fast.

She finally caught up to him at the end of the hallway. "Please, listen to—"

He froze, his back and shoulders rigid. "Did you sleep with Alex after my funeral?"

His strained whisper cut through her like a knife to the heart. How had he heard about Alex? Emily was the only one who knew, unless . . . *Alex.* He must have left her and gone straight to Deacon's room. Told him everything.

Vivienne's face burned with shame, and she wished the ground would swallow her whole as she said, "I slept *beside* Alex."

Slowly, Deacon twisted and tried adjusting his weight on his crutch, but then he was cursing and throwing the thing against the wall. It clattered to the ground, the noise ringing in the hallway. Deacon's face was dark, his green eyes dull and lifeless. "With him. Beside him. *On top of him.* It makes no bloody difference!" he spat, raking his hand over his face. "You jumped into bed with him like—"

"Couch."

Deacon's brows shot up beneath the dark hair falling across his forehead. "What?"

"I slept *beside* Alex on his *couch. Not* in his bed," she clarified. Those details mattered.

Deacon's eyes narrowed and he leaned forward, close enough for her to feel his heat. And in a voice laced with quiet rage he said, "I wasn't even dead a week and *you*. *Slept*. *With*. *Alex*."

This was bad. But it wasn't the worst thing in the world. Nothing had happened that night with Alex. Besides that one tiny kiss. But now wasn't the time for *that* confession. Once Deacon calmed down, they could discuss it like rational adults.

There was something more pressing that needed to be dealt with first. Something Vivienne wasn't sure was as forgivable. "So you're just mad about Alex and not Tennessee?"

"This is about *all* your lies, Vivienne. Not only did you call Lyle, you didn't even care about me enough to tell me. You told *Alex*, but not me. You trusted him. Not me."

"I'm sorry, okay?" Vivienne seemed to be saying that a lot lately.

His expression tightened, then went blank. When she reached for him, he limped away. "You could have had Neverland, but you refused to let go of Ohio. We could have had each other, but you couldn't stand by your decision to love me long enough to let go of him."

"Deacon—"

"Maybe this is just who you are—an indecisive girl too afraid of being abandoned to commit to anything. Or anyone."

"You are such a freaking hypocrite! Mister 'I don't date.'" She was the one in the wrong here, and Deacon was trying, he really was. But the double standard was infuriating. "Yeah, I spent the night with Alex. But I thought you were *dead*."

"Right." The muscles in his jaw flexed as he ground his teeth together. "Well, it's good to know I'm replaceable. That you won't have any trouble moving on."

This time when he left, she let him go.

It was all true. Vivienne had been given a life out of a fairy tale, and in return she had broken rules meant solely to keep the PAN safe. She'd had Deacon's love, but every time he was gone, she had turned to Alex for comfort and companionship. She'd been so afraid Deacon wouldn't commit to her that she had never really committed to him.

Now it was too late.

Vivienne went back to Paul's office, prepared to face her fate. It was easier to accept that her time in Neverland may be over knowing that Deacon would never forgive her.

Paul was still in his chair, but he wasn't alone. Nicola and Owen waited next to the open window, both in full tactical gear, with a black suitcase by their feet. She could hear laughter outside. A breeze drifted over her, as cold and unyielding as Nicola's blue eyes.

"Vivienne Dunn," Paul said, rising and bracing his hands on his desk, "your access to Neverland and its resources has been terminated. Hand over your cell phone and helmet."

Her fingers shook as she withdrew her phone from her pocket and TINK from her ear and set both on the edge of the desk.

"If you tell anyone about our existence or location," Paul went on, "appropriate action will be taken."

Did he really think she would expose the PAN to outsiders out of spite?

One look at his pinched expression, his mouth turned down in disapproval, answered her question.

"I'll just get my things."

Owen kicked the suitcase. It rolled across the tiles and banged against her knee.

Had her entire life really fit into one bag? The handle opened with a snap, and she held onto it for support. "Can I say goodbye to my friends?"

Owen sneered at her. "Did David's stepmother get to say goodbye? Did Deacon's mother get to—"

"That's enough," Paul snapped. "No, Vivienne. You will leave here immediately and not speak to anyone."

Something behind her rustled. She turned to see Nicola approaching, her beautiful face devoid of emotion. Without a word, she wrenched Vivienne's sleeve above her elbow and jabbed her with a needle.

Vivienne didn't fight the darkness dancing at the edge of her vision as the sedative took hold of her, dragging her under. It felt like she was neck-deep in wet concrete, unable to move or fight. Not that she would have fought even if she could.

She deserved this.

PART TWO

TWENTY-TWO

One month later

If Vivienne was quiet enough, she could hear the neighbor's phone conversation through the shared wall. It sounded like the woman was making a vet appointment for her cat Tootsie or Bootsie. Something with an "ootsie" at the end. If she breathed deeply enough, she could smell the woman's cigarettes too.

The brownish-yellow stain on the ceiling above her bed looked bigger. She'd have to ask the landlord to check if the bathroom upstairs was leaking again.

"Come on, Viv," Lyle called from the living room. "We're gonna be late."

Her foster brother had managed to get her a job at the diner where he had been working since graduation. Waitressing wasn't so bad. It passed the time and forced her to be semi-sociable. And every once in a while, she'd have a table that left a decent tip.

Life post-Neverland was duller than before, like the color

had been leached from the world. The trees seemed to have forgotten autumn altogether; they had gone from green to brown to empty in the course of a month. Gray clouds stretched above her. They had been there so long, it felt like the gray had replaced the blue. She could have flown past them to remind herself of the colorful sky. But she didn't.

Vivienne never wanted to fly again.

Flying was another reminder of everything she had lost.

And she didn't need any more reminders.

Vivienne rolled off the bed. She had been lying there for so long, she felt dizzy when she stood. Her apron was on the nightstand, but where was her purse? It wasn't on the dresser or in the bathroom or near the pile of dirty laundry next to her closet. It must have been in the living room somewhere.

"Looking for this?" Lyle stood at the door, the brown pleather bag Vivienne had bought at Goodwill swinging from his finger.

The freckles across his nose looked more pronounced now that his tan was fading. His mousy brown hair was shorter than it had been when she'd first left Ohio; it made him look older.

What was she thinking? Lyle *was* older.

He had turned nineteen a few days ago. Technically Vivienne was nineteen too, but she didn't look any older than when she had left a year ago.

And she never would.

Unless she went to HOOK.

Her mumbled thanks was lost in the sound of a car horn blaring outside. She slipped the strap over her shoulder and followed Lyle through the apartment and down three flights of stairs to the street below. The wind tore away the few stubborn leaves still clinging to the barren trees along the street.

She tugged her coat zipper to her chin out of habit. It

didn't actually keep away the cold. The cold had settled into her bones and refused to leave—like those persistent gray clouds. Her internal fire was nothing more than ash in her chest.

The passenger door on Lyle's black Corolla looked like it had a new dent. He hadn't been concerned with the last one, so Vivienne didn't bother mentioning it as she swiped some candy wrappers from the seat onto the floor with the others.

"Are you ever going to clean this thing?" she grumbled, searching her purse for her phone. Zero messages. No missed calls.

Apparently, disappearing for a year and not telling anyone where you were turned friends into unforgiving strangers.

"I'll clean it when you buy a new phone." The car sputtered to life when he turned the key. He patted the dusty dashboard and thanked the heap of crap for starting.

"You know I can't afford it." The cash the PAN had put in an envelope and stuffed into her bag was going to run out eventually. Sharing an apartment with Lyle helped, but without a decent income, it wouldn't last long.

"How do you even text on that thing?"

"You're the only person I text—and I can usually just shout at you from my bedroom."

The drive to the diner took ten minutes in late-afternoon traffic. Vivienne was already looking forward to ten o'clock, when she could go back home and pretend this wasn't her life now.

She spent the first few hours wrapping silverware with Lyle and waiting on the handful of tables trickling in. There was a rush at six that lasted for two hours—longer than most days since it was Friday.

Adjusting the apron around her waist, Vivienne filled one of her pockets with straws. She never remembered the straws.

A woman with orange hair waved to her from the first booth. "Can we get some ketchup?" she asked, pointing to her plate of chicken tenders.

The guy across from her dripped hot sauce onto his burger before reassembling it and taking an enormous bite. Cheese oozed out the far side, plopping into a heaping basket of fries.

"No problem." Vivienne went into the kitchen, put in the order for a table of elderly women, and collected two orders of cheese sticks. After she dropped the appetizers at a table of rowdy young soccer players, she passed by the end booth.

"*Ketchup?*" called the orange-haired woman.

"Sorry. One sec." Vivienne went back to the kitchen.

"You look confused." Lyle popped a cherry tomato from the salad station into his mouth. He dropped some lettuce into a bowl, added two tomatoes, and sprinkled on way too much cheese.

"I came back here to get something." But she couldn't remember what it was.

He added croutons to the salad. "An order?"

The stainless steel counter beneath the heat lamps was empty, and there wasn't a cook in sight. "No orders."

"Salad?" He offered her the one he had made.

"No. That's not it either." She went back out to check on her tables.

The orange-haired woman glared at her.

Crap. Ketchup. She had forgotten the stupid ketchup. "Ketchup, ketchup, ketchup," she chanted quietly. There was a red plastic bottle on a table previously occupied by the teens standing at the register.

The woman ripped it out of Vivienne's hand with a muttered, "It's about time."

Vivienne smiled tightly, gritting her teeth. "Can I get you anything else?"

"More like can you *for*-get anything else."

Thankfully, the floor manager told Vivienne that she didn't need to take any more tables after that. Vivienne didn't go back to the orange-haired woman's table until it was time to hand over the bill. The woman stuffed her credit card inside the black checkbook without even glancing at how much it was. Vivienne ran the card, returned the checkbook, and hid in the kitchen until they were gone.

"Let me help you with that," Lyle offered, setting a bus tub beside her as she stacked plastic baskets on top of the plates.

"Thanks, Lyle." He picked up the cups while Vivienne stuffed the discarded napkins and bits of straw paper into the tub. It wasn't until everything was gone that she worked up the nerve to flick open the black checkbook. The woman had signed the receipt, but the amount on the bill was the same amount written on the line marked TOTAL.

Tears pricked the back of her eyes when a shiny nickel fell out of the flap.

Lyle's eyes widened, but he kept silent as he carried the bus tub to the dishwasher in the back. When she finished her side work, Vivienne waited for her foster brother in the cold car. He came out twenty minutes later carrying a small Styrofoam box.

"This is for you." He sat the box on her lap and started the car. After hitting the radio with the heel of his hand, '80s hair-band music burst from the driver's side speaker—the only side that still worked.

Inside the box was a slice of peanut butter pie. "Thanks. Peanut butter is my favorite." She'd have it after she ate the leftovers from the day before—assuming she felt like eating.

Rolling his eyes, Lyle muttered, "Yeah, I know."

Along with the duller colors in a post-Neverland world, all the food she had eaten in the last month had tasted like chalk.

"Cheer up, girl. You had a bad night. So what?" Lyle said with his typical devil-may-care attitude.

A bad night? Try a bad freaking *year*.

Lyle had a pocketful of cash; he had a year's worth of job security; he had a life.

What did Vivienne have? A crushed heart, shattered dreams, and $22.05.

And a piece of peanut butter pie.

And Lyle.

Lyle used the steering wheel as a drum kit; Vivienne's head was the cymbal.

She sighed. What would she do without him?

"Why are you in such a good mood?" she asked, giving his hand a half-hearted swat.

"Why wouldn't I be in a good mood? The sister I *actually like* came back from the dead a few weeks ago."

What had it been like for him when she'd run away? Had he felt as abandoned as she did? She glanced at him beneath her lashes. It didn't look like he was holding a grudge over it. The hardest part for him seemed to be the fact that Vivienne still refused to tell him where she had been.

When they reached their apartment, there were cars blocking hydrants, covering double yellow lines, and abandoned in the front yard. The brick building pulsed with blaring music, and—

"Lyle?" She turned to find him wincing. "Why are there people on our balcony?"

"I was going to tell you, I swear. But then you had such a shitty night, and I chickened out." He pulled in behind a jacked-up old Bronco and shifted to park. "Maren gave me fifty bucks to let her have a few people over. You know she can't bring them to Mom's."

Vivienne's foster sister, Maren, had opted to save money and live with Lynn while attending the local community college. The two had never gotten along—mostly because Maren was evil incarnate.

"I'll give you a hundred bucks to make everyone go away," she said, sinking deeper into the seat. Would it be too cold to sleep in the car?

"Lighten up, Viv." Lyle nudged her shoulder. "You may even have fun."

Could a person have fun in hell?

TWENTY-THREE

The living room was crammed with teenagers Vivienne recognized from high school. She coughed as she forced her way to the kitchen. Someone was definitely smoking weed. They had better be on the balcony, otherwise the place was going to stink for a week.

The leftovers she had planned to have for dinner had been spread across the counter like a makeshift Styrofoam buffet. A guy who used to play on the football team leaned against the counter, dipping into some cheese sticks. He smiled at her, but the look didn't reach his glassy, bloodshot eyes.

Vivienne twisted away to find the sink filled with ice, bottles of generic liquor, a carton of milk, and a tub of butter.

"Excuse me." A guy with patchy stubble leaned around her to grab a brown bottle from the fridge door. He opened it with a bottle opener from his breast pocket, and the lid bounced off Vivienne's shoe. "Aren't you the girl who got abducted by aliens?"

Aliens? Close enough. "That's me."

He took a swig. "Cool."

"Outta the way, Jack." Lyle nudged him aside to snag an entire six pack from the fridge. "Come on, Viv." He pulled two forks from the drawer, picked up a container of spaghetti, and headed toward the bedrooms.

Someone turned up the volume on the music until Vivienne could feel the bass vibrating against her shirt.

Three girls who had played on the basketball team were grinding against each other in the hall, crushing discarded red plastic cups under their heels. A circle of guys—all wearing plaid shirts and backwards baseball caps—stared with slack-jawed interest, red cups and beer cans in their hands.

Vivienne and Lyle reached the safety of her bedroom, but the thumping music and buzz of conversations forced its way through the walls.

Beside Vivienne, Lyle's can cracked open with a hiss. She hadn't planned on drinking tonight, but a cold beer sounded fantastic—after she washed the stench of other people's food out of her hair.

"I'm going to shower," she said, putting her Styrofoam box on the floor next to the bed. "You can have a bit of pie if you save me some spaghetti." Lyle dropped to the floor and gave her a thumbs up.

There was a loud crash from the living room and a wave of cheering.

Vivienne didn't even want to know what it was. "I hope Maren knows—"

"Knows what?" Maren shouted from Vivienne's bathroom.

"That you're cleaning up tomorrow," Vivienne said, stifling a groan.

"This place is such a dump, it'll probably look better *after* the party." Lyle's twin sister teetered out on three-inch heels.

Her black fishnets were ripped above the knee, but the short black dress she wore looked—

"Where'd you get that dress?" Vivienne hissed.

Maren tossed her shoulder-length brown hair away from her freckled face. "Ugh. Don't give me that look. I'm only borrowing it."

"That's *my* dress." Vivienne had kissed Deacon in that dress—and had worn it to his funeral. It belonged in a glass display case, not on Satan.

"Stop being dramatic. Where'd you get all this cute stuff?" Maren flicked through Vivienne's closet like she was shopping in a store. "Looks expensive." She stopped on one of the chiffon dresses Vivienne had been given for her mission in Tennessee. "Oh, I *love* this one."

"Take it off. *Now.*"

Maren rolled her eyes. "Don't be such a bitch."

"If it's her dress," Lyle managed between bites, "you've gotta take it off, Mar."

Maren shoved the dress back into Vivienne's closet and stomped over to her brother. "Why do you always take her side? *I'm* your sister. You should be on *my* side."

His eyes widened. "Mar—"

She kicked over his beer. "Oops."

"What the hell? What's your problem?" Lyle rolled away from the spill seeping into the stained carpet. He righted the can and ran to the bathroom, returning with a towel.

Instead of helping him, Maren turned to Vivienne, her eyes narrowed and full of hate. "Don't worry about your stupid dress. I'll give it back eventually."

She was gone before Vivienne could respond.

"Sorry about the witch. On the plus side," Lyle said, scooting the spaghetti toward Vivienne like a peace offering, "I'm leaving you all of this."

"I'm not hungry anymore." Vivienne brought a pair of

JENNY HICKMAN

tights and a T-shirt into the bathroom, stripped out of her uniform, and hopped into the shower.

It was just a dress. That was all. Just a dress that reminded her of the best and worst days of her life. Her tears faded into the spout of water spitting from the broken shower head.

When she came out of the bathroom, Lyle was still sitting on the floor, two open cans of beer at his side and a third in his hand, scrolling on his phone.

She was about to reach for her pie when an urgent knock thudded against her door.

"Use the bathroom down the hall!" Vivienne shouted, scrunching her wet hair with the towel. The last thing she wanted was some drunk person peeing all over her bathroom.

"I don't need to use the bloody toilet," grumbled a voice on the other side.

Lyle looked up from his phone, his eyebrows raised in silent question.

Vivienne's mind must have been playing tricks on her because she could have sworn the guy had a British accent.

The person pounded again.

For the first time since she had left Neverland, her skin tingled to life and adrenaline zinged in her veins and hope bloomed in her chest and she ripped the door open and— "Peter?"

Peter Pan slipped through the opening wearing a black Kensington hoodie and a pair of black skinny jeans. He forced the door closed and pressed his back against the wood, heaving a sigh of relief.

"Hello?" It sounded like a dog was scratching at the door. "Are you in there? Hellooo?"

Peter's green eyes widened, and he offered Vivienne a pained smile. "Help me," he mouthed.

212

Vivienne pointed to the bathroom. Peter nodded and disappeared inside.

When she opened the door, a girl with an unnaturally red pixie cut and earrings climbing both her lobes fell into the room.

"Where is he?" she asked, adjusting her short jean skirt. Was her name Megan or Mary or Mae? It definitely started with an M.

"Who? Lyle?"

Lyle saluted her with his beer.

"Not *Lyle*," M spat. "Hot guy. Black sweatshirt. This tall." She held her hand a few inches above her head. "*Seeexy* British accent."

"There's no one in here but us."

With a dejected sigh, M turned back to the crowded living room. This time, when Vivienne closed the door, she locked it.

"I appreciate the assistance," Peter said, strolling out of the bathroom and shoving his sleeves up to his elbows. "We didn't know you were having friends over, otherwise we could have waited until tomorrow."

We? Who was *we*? Was someone with him?

Peter crossed to the window and opened it. Vivienne half expected him to jump out and return to Neverland. Instead, he came back to where Lyle was sitting and pointed to the half-eaten spaghetti. "Are you finishing that?"

"If Viv doesn't want it, it's all yours," Lyle said, shoving it toward him. "Fork on top's clean."

"Vivienne?" Peter dropped cross-legged on the floor.

"Go for it."

He twisted the pasta onto the fork and took a bite. When Lyle handed him a beer, Peter opened it and took a drink.

Why the heck was Peter Pan eating leftover spaghetti on her bedroom floor?

"Do I know you, man?" Lyle asked, watching Peter shovel in another bite.

"We haven't met." Peter put down the fork and extended his hand; his knees bounced as he waited for Lyle to take it. "I'm Peter Parker."

Lyle laughed. "Dude, is your name *really* Peter Parker?"

Peter's head tilted, but his face remained impassive. "You find that humorous?"

"Ah, yeah. It's pretty *humorous.*" Lyle took another drink, using his sleeve to wipe his mouth. "You know who Peter Parker is, right?"

Peter's eyebrows drew into a confused line.

"Never mind." Lyle drank some more.

Peter finished the spaghetti, took another sip of beer, then asked Vivienne why she wasn't getting ready to go home.

Home? Surely he wasn't suggesting she should go back to Neverland. Before she could ask, the handle on her door jiggled.

Every muscle in her body tensed, and her stomach started doing somersaults.

With her heart in her throat, she unlocked the door. A familiar frame lunged through the gap before locking it again. "Why is Maren wearing your dress?"

Deacon was here. He was really here.

His outfit was the same as Peter's. He'd gotten his hair cut since she'd last seen him. It was tighter on the sides but still unruly at the top. It looked good. Not that she could tell him that.

"I know you're in there," Maren called from the hallway, pounding on the door. "Come out here, and I promise I'll make it worth your while."

"That woman is relentless," Deacon muttered, shaking his head.

"If you're thinking of unlocking that door, you're gonna need this." Lyle held a beer toward Deacon.

Deacon shook his head. "My girlfriend would kill me."

Girlfriend? Vivienne had only been gone a month and he already had another girlfriend? If he was going out with Gwen again, she was going to curl up and die.

As if hearing her mental freak-out, Deacon turned to her with narrowed eyes and asked why she wasn't packing.

"Peter Parker just asked the same thing." Lyle jerked his thumb toward Peter.

"The Peter Parker joke *again*?" Deacon rolled his eyes. "It's getting old."

Peter grinned over his beer. "Still gets a good reaction though. You thought it was funny, didn't you Lyle?"

Lyle's eyes ping-ponged between Deacon and Peter. When they didn't say any more, he took a long, slow sip of beer. "Who wants to tell me what's goin' on?"

Why were Deacon and Peter looking at her? Vivienne had no freaking clue what was happening. The last time she'd seen Peter, Deacon had been dead. And the last time she'd seen Deacon—

"Didn't Vivienne tell you?" Deacon sank onto the corner of her bed and smoothed his hand over the patchwork quilt her foster mother had given her.

Now three guys stared at her with raised brows and expectant looks.

"Paul told me not to say anything to anyone, so I didn't."

"What weren't you supposed to tell me?"

Peter's knees bounced higher. Seeing him grin made it easy to forget he was over a hundred years old. "About Neverland."

Lyle's eyes bulged as he raised the can to his lips, muttered, "Neverland," and finished his beer.

Leaning his elbows onto his knees, Deacon fixed his eyes on her. Peter opened the Styrofoam pie container, sniffed, made a face, and closed it again.

"Sounds like you should'a told me your name was Peter *Pan* instead of Peter Parker." Lyle cracked open another beer.

Peter's head tilted. "Then it wouldn't have been a joke."

"Yeah. Okay." Lyle sniggered. "*Peter Pan.* I suppose you're going to tell me you flew here."

Peter deadpanned. "I did."

"Right. Okay. Right. You're Peter Pan, *I'm* Tinkerbell,"— Lyle pointed to Deacon—"and this guy, he's probably Mr. Smee or some shit."

"Don't be ridiculous." Peter checked the plastic watch on his wrist. "That's my grandson."

"Vivienne's boyfriend," Deacon added with a half-smile that made Vivienne's pulse race.

Flicking the tab on the top of his can with his finger, Lyle asked, "Are you going out with Peter Pan's grandson, Viv?"

"I mean . . . I *was.*" She had been pretty sure getting kicked out of Neverland meant their relationship was over. "I guess *technically* he never broke up with me, but I assumed it was over."

Deacon's mouth tightened. What did he expect her to say? Their last conversation hadn't been about their relationship status.

"Now that you've served your sentence, you can come back," Peter said, stretching his legs and crossing them at the ankles.

"I didn't realize that getting drugged and thrown out of Neverland was only a temporary thing."

"I told Peter he should've contacted you sooner," Deacon grumbled, shoving Peter's shoulder, "but *he* insisted it wouldn't have the same effect as letting you believe you were banned permanently. He also thought you'd fare better with a swift, severe punishment from him than waiting for Leadership to decide."

"I didn't *think.* I *knew.* Deacon put Christmas lights on a few steeples and was sentenced to six months of service.

What would they do to the woman who they thought got a recruit killed? Deacon had his connection with me to protect him. Vivienne had no such luxury."

"Holy shit," Lyle choked. "Did you really get someone killed?"

Vivienne ignored him. "Wait a minute. What do you mean *thought* I got someone killed? Are you saying David's death wasn't my fault?"

Peter and Deacon shook their heads in tandem.

Relieved wasn't a strong enough word to describe how Vivienne felt. But if HOOK hadn't traced the call, then, "How—"

"It's complicated," Peter said, drumming his fingers on his knees, "but suffice it to say your call to Lyle was not the reason HOOK found you."

"Hook? As in the curly-haired pirate with one hand and a mustache?" Lyle asked, curling his index finger into a makeshift hook.

The question made her wince. "Should we really be doing this in front of him?"

Lyle gave her the finger.

"Why wouldn't we be doing this in front of him?" Peter clapped her foster brother on the shoulder. "You're coming with us, aren't you?"

"I don't know what drugs you're on," Lyle said, leaning away from Peter, "but I want some."

The moment Vivienne had been kicked out, she had been convinced her adventure was over. She still couldn't believe it, but there was no denying the fact that Peter Pan was sitting on her bedroom floor, asking her to come back to Neverland—and bring Lyle.

"I suggest you both gather your things quickly." Peter dragged the suitcase from beneath her bed and rolled it toward her. "We're leaving in ten minutes."

Lyle didn't budge.

"Lyle, I know this sounds crazy," Vivienne said, stepping toward him, "but it's true."

Lyle opened the last beer.

Why wasn't he saying anything?

He was sitting there, sipping away like this kind of stuff happened to him every day. He tilted his head back, and his Adam's apple bobbed as he chugged. Then he slammed the can on the ground next to the other empties and said, "I guess I could grab a few things."

"Brilliant." Peter hopped up and offered Lyle a hand. "I'll meet you outside shortly." He crossed to the window, slipped beneath the raised pane, and jumped out.

"Did he just—"

"Jump out a fourth-story window?" Vivienne laughed. "He's Peter Pan. Remember?"

"I must be drunker than I thought." Lyle shook his head and left the room.

The moment the door clicked closed, Vivienne became painfully aware that she and Deacon were alone in her bedroom. And he was still on her bed, watching her with shuttered eyes.

Silence made the space between them feel like a bottomless pit. There was so much she needed to say, but she didn't even know where to begin.

"I didn't think I'd ever see you again," she whispered.

Deacon was off the bed in a flash. Then he was in front of her, so close she could smell the spicy cologne and fresh air clinging to his sweatshirt. "When I told you I loved you, I meant it."

His thumbs skimmed her bottom lip, and all she could do was stare at his mouth.

After everything she'd done . . . "You still feel that way?"

His hands dropped, and he stepped away from her. She desperately wanted to bring back that connection.

"I'm allowed to be angry. I'm allowed to be disappointed

and hurt. This isn't some fairy tale where we get to end our story with happily-ever-after. We're going to disagree. We're going to fight. But eternity is a long time to go without forgiveness."

Forgiveness.

She hadn't expected it.

She really didn't deserve it.

But the man she loved was offering it to her anyway.

Forgiveness became a bridge between them. She crossed it in two strides, threw her arms around his neck, and tugged him down until his lips crashed against hers. His hands slid around her waist and his mouth tasted like spearmint gum and she couldn't get enough of his taste or his tongue or the feeling of his hands roving possessively over her body.

"I missed you." Deacon's fierce words turned into a fiercer kiss. He caught her by the hips and dragged her with him to the bed.

"Tick-tock," Peter called from the darkness.

Vivienne tried to step away.

"He can shove off." Deacon yanked her back by the hem of her shirt. "I've been waiting too damn long for this." And then his mouth was on hers again, but she was the one pushing him onto the mattress, straddling his hips, wanting to show him exactly how much *she* had missed *him*.

She lost her fingers in his hair and her mind in the way his tongue swept into her mouth and—

Something hit her foot.

She ignored it.

Thwack.

Thud.

Deacon tore his mouth from hers with a curse. There was a stone on the mattress behind him. "*Dammit, Grandad,*" he groaned, pinching the bridge of his nose. Vivienne rolled off him and tried to get her breathing back to normal by staring at the light fixture above her bed and ignoring the fire under her skin.

Deacon stalked to the window and slammed it closed right as another stone pinged off the glass. "We may as well pack your things, because he's not going to stop." Another stone hit the window, punctuating Deacon's sentence.

"Can't you just tell him to go away? That we'll meet him in, like . . . an hour?"

The mattress shifted as Deacon braced his hands on either side of her and pressed a kiss to her temple. "What I want to do with you would take all night," he whispered, leaving the hairs on the back of her neck standing on end. "And probably a bit of the morning as well." He grinned wickedly when he pulled back and offered her a hand up. "And I doubt my grandad or the Extraction team waiting outside would be very pleased with me afterwards."

The last thing Vivienne needed was to piss people off and have them refuse to let her come back. So, she rolled over and grabbed her suitcase. Starting with the dirty clothes next to the closet, she semi-folded and stuffed them into the bag. Deacon offered to help, and she told him to empty the dresser while she worked on the closet.

"I think that's everything," she said, dumping a wet bottle of shampoo, her makeup bag, and her mother's perfume onto the bed.

"Not everything." Deacon nodded to the dresser. The top drawer had been left open—the one where she kept her bras and underwear.

Heat crept up her cheeks as she tucked her underthings into the front part of her suitcase. She couldn't zip it fast enough.

Deacon cleared his throat and handed her a pair of lacy black underwear that had fallen onto the bed beside him. "Perhaps I *will* tell Grandad to come back tomorrow."

Vivienne ripped them out of his grasp and stuffed them into the suitcase.

The bedroom door slammed against the wall, sending her adrenaline skyrocketing. Music poured in from the hallway.

Lyle stumbled in with a small duffel bag over his shoulder. "Got my stuff. I assume Neverland has electricity, right?" He held up his cell phone.

"You can't bring that," Deacon said, pulling the suitcase from the bed and lacing his fingers with Vivienne's.

"Hate to tell ya this, Smee, but I don't go anywhere without my phone." Lyle's slurred words sounded like he was brewing for a fight.

The couple making out in the hallway stopped to stare into Vivienne's bedroom with glassy-eyed interest.

"How about we talk about this outside?" Vivienne suggested, squeezing Deacon's hand and heading for the exit.

In the living room, there was one girl still swaying to the music by herself. Everyone else was either making out on the couch or drinking on the balcony. On his way through the kitchen, Lyle snagged another beer from the fridge.

"Where do you think *you're* running off to?" Maren screeched, hobbling toward them. A guy with a sleeve of tattoos glared at them from the corner of the couch, his mouth covered in Maren's lipstick.

Vivienne watched in horror as Maren snaked her arms around Deacon's waist.

"I'm bringing my girlfriend home." He tried to politely nudge her off of him.

Maren's eyes fell on Vivienne, and her smile faded. "Very funny. Vivienne doesn't have a boyfriend."

Deacon let go of Vivienne's hand long enough to unhook Maren's arms. Then his warm fingers found hers. "Shall we leave, my love?"

Having Deacon make such a solid claim in public felt so weird. But in a really, *really* good way. Vivienne linked her finger through the belt loop on Deacon's jeans and said, "Get your own boyfriend, Maren. This one's mine."

Vivienne's apartment in Kensington felt like a palace compared to the place she'd been living the last four weeks. She filled her lungs with the scent of the sandalwood candle Emily had lit and snuggled deeper under her covers. It was a relief to breathe in and not feel like she needed to spray disinfectant everywhere.

The look on Lyle's face when he'd seen the black helicopter parked in the clearing behind their apartment was nothing compared to when he'd watched Peter Pan shoot into the sky like a bottle rocket.

Even Vivienne couldn't believe how fast he was.

According to Deacon, Peter's adrenaline ran high. Which also explained why he always seemed to be moving and fidgeting.

Speaking of moving and fidgeting—

"Don't you want to go to your own bed?" Vivienne mumbled.

Emily squeezed tighter. "Nope. This is your punishment for disappearing on me."

Vivienne had had enough punishments to last a long time. Still, having Emily refuse to leave her side wasn't so bad. Deacon probably wouldn't agree—Emily had kicked him out an hour ago, saying it was her turn to catch up. Vivienne didn't have the heart to tell Emily that she and Deacon hadn't had any time to catch up either, not with Lyle asking her questions the entire flight to Kensington.

"I told you—"

"They kicked you out, blah blah. I'm not letting you out of my sight."

"You sound like Deacon."

Emily's arms finally loosened, and she propped herself up with her elbow. "He's been a wreck since you left."

It was kind of twisted, but Vivienne secretly hoped Deacon had been as miserable as she was. "Tell me more."

Emily's eyes gleamed as her mouth quirked into an evil smile. "I may have ripped him a new one after I saw all your stuff was gone. He swore he didn't know what they were going to do. He marched right into Peter's office and said something along the lines of, 'If she's gone, I'm gone too.'"

Deacon had been willing to leave Neverland for her? Vivienne tucked that thought away for later analysis. She imagined Deacon storming in like an avenging angel, his face drenched in shadows, his eyes dark and dangerous. "What'd Peter do?"

"He laughed."

That sounded about right.

Vivienne couldn't help but smile.

"Then Peter explained everything," Emily went on. "Deacon said a lot of cuss words, but Peter eventually calmed him down. It was so frickin' entertaining to watch. Like something out of a soap opera."

Tennessee, Ohio, Maryland—even the fire in Virginia—all had one thing in common: Vivienne Dunn.

Vivienne shuddered when she thought about what would have happened if Leadership had decided her fate. She knew for a fact that she wouldn't be in Neverland, lying beside her best friend. After everything she'd done, Vivienne deserved a lot more than a month-long stint in Ohio.

Peter Pan's decision had saved her . . . but at what cost?

TWENTY-FOUR

D eacon told himself to focus on what was important: Vivienne was back.

He should be happy. He *was* happy. But it was difficult to maintain that happiness while staring at three pairs of Lyle's muddy shoes discarded by the sofa.

And his crumbs covering the coffee table.

And his sweatpants draped over the stool.

And his tower of unwashed dishes getting crusty in the sink.

Paul had objected to Lyle living on campus—Kensington flats were traditionally reserved for PAN only. And Neverland liked its traditions.

Then Deacon had been foolish enough to suggest that Lyle move into his home.

It was only temporary, until they could acquire more suitable accommodations—a month at most, Paul had assured him.

But these last few weeks had taught Deacon that a month could feel like a decade.

While Vivienne had been exiled, Deacon had focused on his own recovery. Dr. Carey had worked extensively with him on regaining the full range of motion in his left arm. It still ached, but at least he didn't have to wear the sling anymore. He had tried to find something—*anything*—to occupy the time until he was allowed to collect Vivienne from Ohio.

Going to the gym with only one good arm had been a waste of time.

Everything he'd tried to cook ended up tasting like shite.

Ethan's constant nagging to join him at the bar had gotten old after the first four hangovers.

Spring cleaning his entire house had only taken two bloody days.

And there was only so much tele a man could watch without going mad.

"Lyle?" Deacon called, throwing his keys into the bowl beside the door. An empty soda can sat next to it.

"Hey, Smee." Lyle clambered down the stairs and looked past him. "Where's Viv?"

Deacon gritted his teeth but forced them apart before he gave himself a headache again. He grabbed the can and crushed it in his fist, imagining it was Lyle's smirking face.

"Vivienne is at Kensington." The last time Deacon had brought Vivienne over, Lyle spent the entire evening on the sofa beside her, reminiscing about Ohio. Since then, Deacon had opted to meet her on campus—where he had to share her with Emily and Max.

But at least it wasn't Lyle.

"And I would appreciate it if you used my real name." Deacon kept his tone light and carefree. If Lyle knew how much the nickname bothered him, he would only use it more.

"Eh, I'm gonna keep callin' you Smee." Lyle stepped over his shoes on his way to the kitchen. "Can you ask those personal shoppers of yours to get avocados?"

After two weeks, Deacon had hoped the novelty of using Kensington's personal shoppers to run frivolous errands would have worn off. Every time he reminded Lyle that there was a grocery store a brisk ten-minute walk from the house, Lyle's response was, "Why would I buy groceries when someone else can do it for me?"

Deacon had stopped putting in orders last week and started going to the store himself to give the shoppers a break—and to get away from Lyle. "Write whatever you want on the list."

"It's easier if I just tell you." Lyle hummed as he opened the fridge, then his head snapped up. "Did you eat all the yogurt?"

Deacon shrugged out of his coat and settled it on the hook. One of Lyle's coats was balled up in the corner; Deacon hung it beside his own. Beneath the coat was a T-shirt. Deacon sighed as he collected it along with Lyle's sweatpants. "I didn't *buy* any yogurt."

"Dude, seriously? I asked you to get some."

"But did you put it on the list?"

Lyle groaned and yanked a pen from the drawer. He grumbled as he wrote with exaggerated movements. Then he threw the pen against the backsplash. "Happy *now*?"

"Immensely." It was a small victory, but a victory none-theless. "Perhaps you'll learn to do your dishes next."

"The last time I put something in the dishwasher, you told me I was doing it wrong."

Lyle hadn't bothered to rinse the bowl beforehand and had somehow managed to make it take up more room on the rack than a pan. "I simply said the bowls go on the top."

"Whatever." Lyle swiped an apple from the fruit bowl, sidestepped his discarded shoes, and went back upstairs.

Out of curiosity, Deacon checked the notepad.

Get some yogurt and avocados you prick.

"Are you alone?" Peter kept his face deep in the shadow of his hooded raincoat. Raindrops bounced off his shoulders and fell onto Deacon's welcome mat.

"Lyle is in the kitchen." Deacon was surprised his grandad couldn't hear the wanker complaining about the avocados not being ripe.

"Hurry then. I don't want any witnesses." He caught Deacon's arm and pulled him into the rain.

"Let me lock up first." Deacon couldn't trust Lyle after he had left the door wide open all day on Tuesday. A feral cat had done a number on Deacon's sofa, and it had taken him an hour to find and remove the damned beast.

Using his coat as an umbrella, Deacon twisted the key in the lock, then ran to a car idling with one wheel on the curb. After driving for over a century, his grandad still didn't know how to park.

Once Deacon's seat belt clicked, his grandad spun out of the puddles and headed toward Worcester. "What's wrong?" Deacon asked, steadying himself against the dashboard.

"Why would you think something is wrong?" Peter flicked the wipers to a higher speed. Even at the fastest setting, they struggled to clear the window.

"You showing up at night, dragging me out of my house in the pouring rain, and driving like a lunatic makes me a *little* suspicious."

His grandad wove in and out of traffic, seemingly oblivious to the horns honking around them. "You're coming to DC with me. We need to make a delivery." Peter touched the

227

button above his head, and the overhead lights illuminated two bulging duffel bags on the backseat of the rented coupe.

The last delivery Deacon had made with his grandad had involved a bunch of sheep and Tootles's garden.

Deacon poked one of the bags to see if it *baa*-ed. Whatever was inside felt hard.

"Don't touch them!" The overhead light clicked off. "I want it to be a surprise."

The deluge had stopped by the time they reached the tarmac at Worcester Regional Airport. Peter handed Deacon one bag—it wasn't as heavy as it looked—then slung the second over his own shoulder before collecting a small backpack from the boot. Together they boarded a private jet and strapped in for the two-hour flight to the nation's capital.

The PAN owned so many shell corporations that Deacon had stopped keeping track years ago. But Pane Aviation, Inc., a company that commissioned private jets to anyone who could afford the luxury, was by far the most lucrative.

"Sir? Would you like something to drink before we take off?" a peppy stewardess in a starched green uniform asked. She was young, early twenties, with straight red hair, and cute—and she was eyeing his grandad with blatant interest. Peter didn't seem to notice.

"Two glasses of scotch, please." Peter's tight voice held not an ounce of charm.

Perhaps he *had* noticed.

The stewardess sauntered to the bar to collect their beverages. Peter's eyes never left the gold ring he spun around his little finger.

Deacon's grandmother, Angela, had been gone for decades. Surely his grandad deserved to find someone again —if not for love, then at least as a distraction.

Peter Pan could be the most charming man in the room . . . when he wanted to be. He had taught Deacon everything he knew about dealing with the opposite sex. But

Deacon had never seen him so much as flirt with anyone under the age of fifty.

When the stewardess returned, Deacon accepted the drink, swirling the fragrant liquid in his crystal glass. "I think she likes you," he said in a low voice once she left.

His grandad snorted and saluted Deacon with his glass. "She's much closer to your age than mine."

Deacon took a sip, relishing the way the scotch set fire to his throat. "I don't know many one-hundred-and-fifty-year-old women who look like *that*."

"I'm not in the market for another wife."

"And I'm fairly certain she's not looking for a husband."

Peter choked on his drink. "I take relationships more seriously than your generation does."

The disapproval in his words made Deacon wince. "Forever is a long time to be alone."

"And you believe having a woman in my bed, whom I do not care for, would make me *less* lonely?"

Deacon knew the answer to that was a resounding, "No."

"Just because I'm alone doesn't mean I'm lonely." He nudged Deacon's foot with his own. "What about you? Are you one of the lucky ones who's found someone to share forever with?"

Forever.

What an unfathomable question. Deacon was only twenty-six years into eternity.

He loved Vivienne. He had never felt this way about anyone else.

Couldn't that be enough for now?

"I don't know how to answer that." Deacon reached for an air vent above his head, twisting it until a blast of cold air wafted over him.

"Do you plan on abandoning her when she forgets who you are?"

Deacon's last sip of scotch went down the wrong way.

Did his grandad really think he could be so callous? One look at Peter's serious expression answered his silent question.

The stewardess hurried over with a bottle to refill both glasses.

Deacon turned to the darkness outside the window; lights from houses and buildings below them were few as they flew over a stretch of rural landscape.

Tootles usually had about thirty minutes of conversation in him before his mind would reset. On the rare occasions Deacon accompanied his grandad to Scotland, it wasn't Tootles's forgetfulness that plagued him, but the heaviness that followed Peter back to Harrow: his slumped shoulders, the weariness in his eyes, the sheer helplessness.

The forgetful were blissfully unaware.

The people they left behind were the ones who really suffered.

Deacon knew all of this. He worried about it constantly. But he would never abandon Vivienne to save himself the pain. "Of course I'm not going to abandon her."

"Then I'll ask you again: are you one of the lucky ones?"

One of the lucky ones.

Seeing his grandad's hollow eyes, the ring he still wore for his dead wife who was never coming back . . .

Perhaps committing to forever wasn't the burden Deacon thought it was.

Perhaps Deacon *was* one of the lucky ones.

A car pulled into a neighboring driveway, and Deacon crouched lower behind the chimney. Although the wind around them was light, it still carried the promise of winter. "Are you sure this is where he lives?" The townhouse below them was much smaller than he had expected.

"Of course I'm sure."

Deacon pulled a Charlie Bell from one of the dark duffel bags. The rest of the clocks inside glinted like treasure in a chest. Charlie Bells had been one of Tootles's favorite gifts before he discovered eBay. His grandad had an entire room in his home filled with them. "What's the time?"

"Midnight."

Deacon wound the timepiece until the small red hand pointed north. "Where will we leave them?"

"I've enough for every window on the second floor."

"And a few for the chimney and gables?"

"Why not? Let's go mad."

"Will we do the same for Lawrence?" Deacon asked, counting five windows at the front of Jasper Hooke's townhome before collecting five clocks from the bag.

Peter handed Deacon two more. "I have something special in mind for dear Lawrence." He slung the bag over his shoulder and jumped off the roof.

Instead of waiting for midnight at Jasper's house, they flew across town to Lawrence's two-story brick home in the center of a quiet gated community. After assessing the steep pitch of the roof, Deacon suggested leaving a few there, as well as on the windowsills.

"Set yours for midnight," Peter said, collecting clocks to plant around the garden, "and I'll set mine for one o'clock."

The clock in Deacon's hand ticked like a bomb waiting to explode. He had always loved a good prank. His favorite had to be the time he and his grandad had stolen a bunch of traffic cones and created a diversion through Tootles's front garden.

At the stroke of midnight, the chiming bells made the house sound like a church on Christmas morning. A light in one of the upstairs windows came on, and Lawrence swept aside the curtains. Even though there was no way Lawrence could see them from their perch in the evergreen at the end of his driveway, Deacon's heart rate spiked.

Lawrence lifted the sash, cursing as he snagged a clock from the sill. He did the same for every other clock clattering in the windows. Then he stormed out the front door in his dressing gown to check the line of alarms on the roof. "Those little *bastards!*"

Peter's laughter was so contagious, Deacon had trouble catching his breath. "Keep it down," Deacon scolded, the muscles in his stomach aching. "I don't fancy getting shot again."

"I know you're there, you obnoxious little mosquitoes," Lawrence shouted to the sky. "And when I catch you, you'll be sorry you were born." The door slammed shut.

"I haven't laughed that hard in years." Peter sighed, rubbing tears from his eyes. "He'll be even less impressed in another hour. I can't wait to tell Tootles about this."

What would be the point? It wasn't as if Tootles would remember the story the next day.

"Shall we grab something to eat during the intermission?" Deacon wiped sap from his hands onto his jeans, leaving sticky smears everywhere.

"You read my mind." Peter used the branch as a springboard and launched himself into the air.

They flew to a Wendy's across town. His grandad claimed it was because they had the best fast-food burgers, but Deacon thought he simply enjoyed eating in a restaurant called Wendy's.

"I return to London this weekend," his grandad said after taking a long sip from his straw. It was his third cup of soda. He loved anything and everything that should have rotted his teeth; somehow, he had never had so much as a cavity.

Deacon finished chewing the chip he'd popped into his

mouth. "I thought you weren't going back until the next Leadership meeting."

"There are certain preparations that must be made before then," Peter said in a tight voice.

Preparations for yet another trial.

While Vivienne had been exiled, Lee Somerfield and his followers involved in the attack had received summons to appear before Leadership. Deacon longed for the days when Leadership had occupied themselves with deciding on crest colors and outsider nominations.

Pushing his burger aside, Deacon wiped his hands on a napkin. "Can we discuss what happened?"

"The moment they took matters into their own hands, they took the outcome out of mine. The case will go to Leadership, and those responsible will be delivered consequences appropriate for their actions."

"What consequences would you deem *appropriate*?"

A shrug. "I suppose we'll find out in two weeks."

Two weeks.

"I don't see why there should be any consequences at all," Deacon said, dumping the rest of his chips onto his burger wrapper. "We've been going back and forth with HOOK forever. Look at us tonight. Do you really think that what we're doing is that different from what Lee did when he set HOOK on fire? I'll admit, Lee's response was extreme, but HOOK *shot* me."

Peter sipped his soda until his straw made an annoying slurping sound, his eyebrows raised and green eyes wide. "I can see where you're coming from," he said, setting the cup aside and stealing one of Deacon's chips. "But Leadership is determined to handle the situation before Neverland spirals out of control."

"Surely you, of all people, can do something."

His grandad leaned back in the booth and rubbed his

hand across his eyes. "I'm afraid I used my one and only trump card for Vivienne."

Peter had made an executive decision that had likely saved Vivienne from something far worse. If he tried to do the same at the meeting, then Lee's claims that Neverland was a dictatorship would ring true.

"I don't believe I ever thanked you for what you did." Deacon had been angry and said some awful things to his grandad. Then he had been accepting. But he had never said how grateful he was in the end.

"I couldn't save her parents, but I could save her . . . from something, at least."

He must have been referring to Vivienne's forgetfulness.

The lab in Harrow was searching tirelessly for a cure, but Peter had made it clear that Deacon shouldn't hold out false hope. And if Vivienne's family history was anything to go by, she could start exhibiting symptoms within the next ten years.

The only time Deacon had tried to speak to Vivienne about it since her return, she had cut him off. She promised to discuss it, but not in front of Lyle, who was blissfully unaware of her diagnosis. And since Lyle was *always* around—

Peter clapped his hands, then checked the plastic Casio watch on his left wrist. "Come. We wouldn't want to miss the next performance."

Instead of returning to the trees at the end of Lawrence's driveway, they took refuge behind the brick chimney. While they waited, Peter reset the roof clocks for half past one.

On the hour, the clocks hidden like Easter eggs in the landscaping rattled to life.

A light in the upstairs window turned on, and Lawrence burst through the front door. "I'm going to *kill* you!" he bellowed, finding the first of five clocks and stomping it on the tarmac.

By the time he located the fourth clock, a man from a neighboring house had come outside. "What the hell is that racket, Lawrence?"

Lawrence threw what was left of a mangled clock into his neighbor's front lawn. "Mind your own damn business!"

"If you wake up my kids, I swear—"

"It's not my fault you chose to procreate."

Mumbling, the man retreated back into his house.

"What's that noise?" A slender black-haired woman in a fuzzy dressing gown called from the doorway.

"Go back inside," Lawrence said, his voice tight but softer than it had been a moment earlier.

"It sounds like a bunch of alarm clocks."

Peter snorted but stifled the noise with his hand.

"I said go back inside, Louise!"

The woman disappeared, leaving Lawrence to locate the final clock in the oak tree.

"I didn't know the devil was married." Deacon watched Lawrence try to knock the clock from the barren branches with a handful of decorative stones.

"Good shot, that one." Peter took another bite of the Frosty he'd insisted on buying. "Louise is his girlfriend," he explained, setting the cup on the edge of the fireplace before unzipping his backpack.

What was that godawful smell? The food, barely settled in Deacon's stomach, churned, and his eyes started watering.

Peter swayed two plastic bags of rancid white meat toward him. "On tonight's menu, we have a filet of cod, aged to perfection."

Noticing a window Lawrence had left ajar, Deacon grinned and said, "I know just where to put it."

TWENTY-FIVE

As far as Vivienne knew, there had been no news from Lee Somerfield's faction since the attack on HOOK. It was almost as though they had disbanded for good. And after meeting Peter, she didn't feel like he expected people to blindly follow him like Lee had suggested. If anything, Peter seemed to want what was best for everyone.

But when a message came through about a meeting that night, Vivienne felt like she needed to attend, even if it was just to explain why she wouldn't be coming anymore. After what Peter had done for her, she couldn't go against him.

The only car in Lee's driveway was his own black truck. When she went around the back of the house, the basement entrance was dark.

"Hey!" someone shouted.

Vivienne turned to find Ethan rounding the corner wearing all black. "It's only a small meeting tonight," he said, waving her toward the main entrance, "so we're not in the basement."

She followed him around to the front, up crumbling concrete steps, and through a squeaky screen door. In the living room, a path had been worn into the carpet between a leather recliner and what she assumed was the kitchen. A single canvas stretched across the stark white walls, bold green strokes mixing with softer blue ones.

Vivienne waved to Max, who sat on one of two stiff-cushioned beige loveseats. There wasn't a decorative pillow or snuggly throw in sight.

Lee came out of the kitchen carrying two boxes of pizza. When he saw her, he frowned. "Isn't Deacon with you?"

"Should he be?" Why would Lee want Peter's grandson to be there? Deacon had always been vocal about his disapproval of the rebellious meetings.

"I've tried him a couple times," Ethan said, dropping onto the couch and flipping open the top box, "but he didn't pick up."

Max grabbed a slice.

Vivienne sank onto the couch beside Ethan and picked up a piece. She had skipped dinner and should have been hungry. After one bite, she realized she wasn't. She slipped the slice back into the box, then cleaned the grease off her fingers with a napkin.

Lee looked pointedly at Vivienne, then at Ethan. "Has Deacon said anything to either of you about the trial?"

"What trial?" Vivienne gasped, crushing the napkin in her fist.

Max said, "We're going on trial . . . at the next . . . Leadership meeting," between bites. "For the fire."

"He didn't say anything to me about it," she muttered, picking at a bit of pepperoni.

What else had happened while she had been in Ohio? And why hadn't Deacon told her? Was he hiding anything else?

"Dash told me he's going to put in a good word with

Peter." Ethan settled himself deeper into the stiff couch and ran a nervous hand through his unkempt blond hair.

"Won't help," Lee grumbled. "Peter hasn't voted in decades. He prefers to remain *neutral.*"

"He wasn't neutral when it came to Vivienne." Max winced, then apologized. "My mouth's a few steps ahead of my brain."

Vivienne's stomach tightened. "It's fine."

The entire meeting—if she could even call it that—consisted of the guys brainstorming plausible punishments for their actions. And with each one, Vivienne's worry grew. She knew Lee had disobeyed a direct order from Peter but had never considered the consequences of their actions.

From the worried looks on their faces, neither had Max or Ethan.

But Lee seemed almost resigned.

"Do you think they'll neutralize us?" Ethan asked, wincing and rubbing the back of his neck.

Max's eyes bulged. "No way. I mean, they thought Vivienne got someone killed and all they did was kick her out for a month. Sorry."

"You don't have to keep apologizing, Max," she told him. "It's the truth."

"That's enough speculation for tonight." Lee closed the empty pizza boxes and carried them to the kitchen.

Vivienne left Max and Ethan whispering to follow him. Lee's back was to her, his shoulders deflated and forehead resting against the upper cabinets.

"Is that really a possibility?" Would her friends be neutralized?

His back stiffened. When he turned around, his eyes were heavy. "I honestly don't know. I doubt it, but . . . I don't know."

She sank onto one of the two chairs at the tiny kitchen table.

How had it come to this? Neverland was meant to be a place of magic, a community. Their goal was to *activate* dormant Nevergenes, not *deactivate* them as punishment.

That would make them no better than HOOK.

Vivienne found herself staring blankly at a collage of photos on the wall. In one picture, a fresh-faced teen had his arm around another boy who could have been his twin. "Is this *you*?"

Lee glanced toward the collage, then turned back to the window. "Yeah. It's me and my brother. Feels like a lifetime ago."

The handsome pair had mischief in their eyes and goofy grins on their faces. She studied Lee as he studied the darkness. The mischief had been replaced by something she knew all too well: grief. Her heart ached for what had happened to them.

In another picture, Lee and his brother lounged in a red-and-white booth, the table littered with remnants of a meal. Her parents sat across from them. "That's my mom and dad."

Lee's smile was sad. "The four of us were inseparable."

"They didn't have rules about taking pictures back then?"

"There's always been a rule about photos." Lee laughed bitterly. "But I've never liked being told what to do."

At the bottom of the collage was a picture of a dark-haired girl sitting next to Lee on the edge of a dock, their feet dangling in the water. Lee had his arm around her shoulders, and she leaned into the embrace. She smiled at the camera, but Lee was smiling at her.

She looked like . . . *Holy crap.* No. It couldn't be.

Except it was.

Why was Lee Somerfield in a picture with Deacon's mom?

"I'm freaking out." Max shifted from one foot to the other, like he wanted to run away but wasn't sure which way to go. Ethan had stayed behind to talk to Lee, but Max couldn't get out of there fast enough.

"It'll be fine," Vivienne assured him, having no idea if it was true. There were cars driving past Lee's, so they went around the back and waited for a gap in traffic to take off.

"That wasn't very convincing." Max's frown turned into a grimace. "I feel like I should go see my dad next week. Just in case they kick me out too. Where the hell am I going to go?"

Vivienne couldn't think of anything to say that would make him feel better. Max didn't need more guesses. He needed answers.

"Instead of freaking out, why don't we swing by Deacon's place and ask him if he knows anything?"

For the first time that night, Max looked almost hopeful. "Yes. Absolutely. I was gonna suggest that but didn't want to bother him. Do you mind?"

"Not at all. And neither will he."

Her internal fire sparked to life, and she flew toward the treetops. When they reached Deacon's house, his car was in the driveway, and she could see someone moving around inside through the partially open blinds.

Since returning from Ohio, she and Deacon hadn't been able to spend any time alone together. She had felt obligated to make sure Lyle was comfortable in Neverland—he was her nominee, after all. But once Lyle got his own place, she and Deacon were going to seriously make up for lost time. Even the thought of being with him made her lightheaded.

Vivienne knocked and tucked her cold fingers into her coat sleeves. Lyle answered the door in a pair of gray tracksuit pants and his old high school soccer sweatshirt. "Hey, Viv. What's up, Max?"

She didn't want to make it seem like they were only there for Deacon, so she didn't ask about her boyfriend right away. "Just thought we'd swing by to say hi."

"You're just in time. Game's just started." Lyle opened the door wider and stepped aside. The Patriots game was on in the background, but there was no sign of Deacon in the living room or kitchen. Lyle picked up a beer can from the coffee table and flung himself onto the couch.

"Got any more of that?" Max asked, nodding toward Lyle's beer. "It's been a pretty crappy night, and I could really use a drink."

"There's a whole case in the fridge, man. Help yourself."

Max went to the fridge and pulled a can from the cardboard box inside. "You want one, Vivienne?"

"No, thanks." She listened for signs of life upstairs, but the only noise was the TV and the hiss of Max opening his can. "Is Deacon asleep?"

"He left a few hours ago. Haven't seen him since." Lyle sipped his beer, his eyes fixed on the TV screen.

That was weird. He hadn't mentioned any plans when they'd spoken earlier. Deacon had said he was tired and was going to stay home.

She sent him a text to make sure everything was okay. The meeting at Lee's still had her on edge. "Guys, I'm going back to campus." It didn't feel right being in Deacon's house without him there. "Emily said she wants to do something tonight."

"Will you have a few drinks if we come with you?" asked Lyle.

If she sat around all night wondering where Deacon was, she'd go crazy. "Why not?" A few drinks with her friends could be fun.

"Sweet." Lyle grabbed a thirty-pack and handed it to

Max. Then he pulled a few bags of chips from the pantry and collected his coat from the hook.

Her brother had always been a bit of a slob—and that was saying a lot, considering she wasn't much better. Vivienne was happy to see he was actually picking up after himself now that he was living in someone else's home.

They were almost out the door when Lyle stopped and groaned. "You guys didn't drive here, did you?"

"No." Max narrowed his eyes at him. "If Vivienne gets the beer, I could probably carry you."

"Yeah, that's not gonna happen." Lyle grabbed Deacon's keys from the bowl and tossed them at her. "Viv can drive us."

"I'm not stealing Deacon's car."

"If Smee minds you borrowing his car, then you probably shouldn't be dating him."

"Yes!" Emily yanked Vivienne in for a hug the moment she, Lyle, and Max arrived at the apartment. When she saw the box of beer, she dropped Vivienne and hugged the box. "*Hell* yes! Are we having a party?" she squealed, her eyes wide with excitement.

"I wouldn't exactly call this a party," Vivienne mumbled. Emily's grin was infectious. "But we have beer and snacks."

"*Sooo* it's a party." Emily peered into the hall before shutting the door. "Where's mister sexy pants?"

Emily had taken to calling Deacon that ever since the day after Vivienne had returned from Ohio. Deacon had worn a pair of old jeans that were so ripped up that the bottom of his boxer briefs peeked through. Emily thought they were the sexiest pants she'd ever seen. Vivienne had to agree.

Instead of saying she didn't know where her boyfriend was—which would lead to a whole bunch of questions—

Vivienne said Deacon was busy. Emily accepted it with a shrug and a muttered, "His loss."

Max made a quick trip to his apartment for a sleeve of red plastic cups and two ping pong balls. Vivienne partnered with Lyle for a few rounds of beer pong, but they lost every single one.

"Looks like I'm a bit rusty." Normally they crushed the competition.

"Maybe if you put your phone down and actually paid attention, you'd play better." Lyle threw the beer-soaked ball into the sink and combined the last cup with the one in his hand.

"Yeah. Sorry about that." But if she didn't check her phone, she could miss a text from Deacon.

"If he wanted to talk to you, he would have called or texted already." Lyle snagged her phone out of her hand and tossed it on top of the cupboard.

"What the heck?"

Before she could fly up to get it, he caught her by the sleeve. "You can't have fun with us if you're staring at a screen all night."

Emily and Max buried their hands into the chip bag and pretended not to be listening.

Vivienne yanked free and flew to grab her phone from the disgusting layer of dust at the top of the cabinets. When she was back on the floor, she took her phone and her beer to her bedroom.

Stupid Lyle. He didn't know anything. Deacon definitely had a good excuse for not being at home tonight. Of course he did. Still . . . she tried calling him. Just in case something was wrong.

No answer.

Not a big deal. He'd get ahold of her when he could.

The boisterous laughter from the kitchen made her feel bad for snapping. Lyle was right. Being on her phone all night was rude. She plugged it in next to her bed and went back out to her friends.

"What's everyone laughing at?"

"Nothing." Emily smirked from where she sat on the counter and nodded toward Lyle. "Your brother thinks we should play a different drinking game."

"What game?" Vivienne asked, pulling a beer from the fridge. The can was so cold it made her shiver.

"Never have I ever." Lyle's smile grew wider. "To play, you—"

"I know the rules," she clipped. And Lyle knew how much she hated this game. Still, it was three against one, so Vivienne resigned herself to an empty chair between Emily and Max, with Lyle was directly across from her.

"Me first!" Emily squealed, crossing her long legs beneath her. "Never have I ever kissed Peter Pan's grandson."

Vivienne rolled her eyes and took a drink.

Lyle said, "Never have I ever flown."

The three PAN drank.

Vivienne, Emily, and Lyle looked expectantly at Max. "Oh. Sorry. My turn. Um . . . " He closed his eyes. "Never have I ever had a roommate."

Vivienne, Emily, and Lyle drank.

"Never have I ever stolen something." Vivienne couldn't believe it when everyone else drank. "Geez, remind me to lock up my valuables."

"I was only, like, four or five." Max laughed. "I stole an extra eraser from the teacher's prize box."

"Me too," Emily said, drumming her multicolored nails against her can. "I took a plastic pony from my pre-school."

"Not me. I stole a pair of sunglasses from a gas station this summer." Lyle scooped a chip into a jar of salsa and shoved it into his mouth.

"My turn again." Emily took a drink even though she hadn't asked a question. "Never have I ever . . . had sex."

Max and Lyle drank.

Vivienne felt like she should drink to get Emily to stop staring.

Seriously. Everyone needed to quit looking at her. This was exactly why she hated this game. Alcohol and secrets did not mix. "Moving on . . . " Vivienne kicked Lyle from beneath the table.

"Never have I ever kissed two different people on the same day."

Vivienne was the only one who drank. Had Emily told Lyle about New Year's Eve?

The knowing look Emily and Lyle exchanged was all the confirmation Vivienne needed. For some reason, her best friend and foster brother were ganging up on her. Still, she kept playing until there were two empty cans in front of her and another one with only a few drops left in her hand, and the one over there. Was that hers or Emily's?

Her face felt like . . . nothing. There was a word for that, but she couldn't remem—*numb*. That's what it was. Completely numb. Even when she pressed on her lips, she couldn't feel it. And Lyle looked fuzzy. She wished he'd stop moving around so much. Why hadn't she eaten that pizza earlier? She really should have eaten that—

"Never have I ever . . . kissed my brother."

Emily was supposed to be her best friend, but she was a stupid traitor. Vivienne forced her eyes to narrow and glared across the table at Lyle; he smiled right back at her.

Stupid Lyle. He must have told Emily about playing spin the bottle at his and Maren's joint sixteenth birthday party. Stupid drinking games.

Emily nudged her. "Did you hear me?"

"I don't *have* a brother," Vivienne bit out.

"Fine." Emily rolled her eyes. "Never have I ever kissed my fost—"

"You already had your turn," Vivienne said, covering Emily's mouth with her hand. Then Emily *licked* her.

Why the heck were her friends being so obnoxious tonight? Except Max. Max was nice. Maybe he would be her new best friend. Vivienne wiped her spitty hand on her pants and turned to ask him.

With a wolfish smile, Lyle said, "Never have I ever kissed my *foster* brother."

"Traitor." Vivienne finished her beer and set the empty can beside the others. "That's it. I'm not playing anymore."

"Why not?" Lyle asked.

"You two jerks are ganging up on me, that's why. You guys didn't drink at all!"

"Told you she'd figure it out," Emily said to Lyle in what was probably supposed to be a whisper.

"I hate all of you." Vivienne stood up as gracefully as she could with the floor tilting back and forth like a cheap funhouse. On the way to her room, she had to steady herself against the walls. Whoever thought of the word wall? Wall. Wall. W-all. Words were so weird. One foot in front of . . . the other. Slowly. Carefully.

Ding.

Her phone. That was her phone. She burst through the door and tripped over her desk chair on the way to her nightstand. Deacon. It had to be Deacon. No one else would be texting her this—

Don't hate me. Not Deacon. Lyle.

Stupid Lyle was the least of her concerns.

Where in the world was Deacon?

She clicked into Deacon's messages and sent her missing boyfriend another text.

"You're not allowed to hate me," Emily said from the

doorway. "Lyle said you're funny when you're drunk, and I wanted to see."

"I'm gonna kill him," Vivienne groaned, dropping her phone onto the mattress. Yes, it was time for Lyle to die.

"You'll have to wait till morning. He's passed out on the couch."

"He's an idiot. So obnoxious. I don't even know why I wanted him here. He's a garbage human. Garbage."

Garbage. Another funny word.

Gar-bagé

Garb-age

Garbage.

"So, I need to know something." The mattress dipped when Emily sat next to her. She offered Vivienne a drink of her beer, but Vivienne shook her head. Even the smell made her stomach revolt. "And since I'm your best friend, you can't lie to me," she said, nudging Vivienne's knee with hers. "Have you and mister sexy pants really not done it?"

"Oh my *goooosh.* Emily!" Vivienne hid her burning face beneath her hands. She did *not* feel like talking about this right now.

"What? I don't have a guy in my life, so I have to live through you. I just assumed the two of you slept together in Tennessee."

"We did sleep together." Vivienne rolled her eyes when Emily started bouncing up and down. "Emphasis on *sleep.*"

"Ugh! At least tell me you've put that mouth of his to good use."

"I mean, we've made out a bunch. So I know he's a good kisser. Like, mind-blowingly good." Thinking of kissing Deacon made her feel all tingly and gooey inside. Where the heck was he? She'd like to kiss him right now.

"Aren't you curious if he's good at other stuff too?" Emily asked with another nudge.

Deacon *was* good at other stuff. But Vivienne wasn't

drunk enough to tell her about that time in the hospital bed. "Okay . . . I'm going to tell you something, but if you tell *anyone*, I swear I won't ever speak to you again."

Emily giggled even as she pinky-promised to never tell a soul. Vivienne launched into the story of that night in Tennessee while Emily alternated between saying "*Ohmygosh*" and pretending to faint.

"*Gaaah*! I can't believe you were *this close* to doing it with him and stopped. If he told me to take off my clothes, I'd be naked before he finished the sentence."

Vivienne's eyes widened.

Emily rolled hers. "*Hypothetically.* You must have some serious willpower."

"Not sure I'd call it willpower. I freaked myself out. I mean, I had no clue what I was doing and then I started babbling about other guys I'd dated and totally killed the mood and Deacon is . . . well, *Deacon* and—" She stopped herself. Thinking of Deacon with anyone but her made her want to vomit. "What about you? I remember you talking about your exes. Have *you* done it before?"

Emily toyed with the ends of her curly hair, tugging on it, then letting go. It bounced back into place like a spring. "I went out with this guy at the beginning of junior year and we messed around a bit. But I haven't really dated anyone since. The guys I go out with start annoying me after two or three dates, so we never really get to the point of doing anything but make out."

"I want to make out with Deacon," Vivienne whined, grabbing her phone and texting him to tell him just that. Why wasn't he here? He should be with her. She told him that too.

"Why do you have that goofy look on your face?"

"Shut up." Vivienne tried to stop smiling but couldn't. If Deacon didn't show up after that string of text messages, there was something wrong with him.

"What are you saying to him?" Emily asked, poking Vivienne in the side with her glittery nail. "Are you telling him you want to have his British babies? Because you definitely should."

Emily was right. Vivienne should tell him that.

"OMG do you know what you should do?"

"No. What?"

"You should call him."

"I should call him," Vivienne agreed, tapping the phone icon and waiting for the call to connect.

TWENTY-SIX

Water. Deacon desperately needed water. He reached for his bedside locker. Instead of a glass, he found a coin. Hadn't he left a glass of water there the night before? With a groan, he heaved off the duvet and forced himself upright. It felt like the entire room shifted as well. When his feet hit the floor, he found the glass of water—and accidentally kicked it over.

He nudged a dirty shirt on top of the puddle, picked up the overturned glass, and carried it to the bathroom sink. His stomach lurched when he smelled the lemon-scented hand soap. What had he been thinking, trying to match his grandad drink for drink? Deacon was some fool.

When he went back into his room, the coin on his bedside locker caught his eye.

Not a coin.

A ring.

The conversation he'd had with his grandad the night before came back in snippets.

But he was fairly certain Peter had given him Angela's ring so he could give it to Vivienne.

What had he been thinking?

Deacon wasn't ready to get *married*.

The doors to the guest room and Lyle's room were closed. Lyle must've slept like the dead, because they had been anything but quiet when they returned from Washington.

Steadying himself after each stair, Deacon swallowed back the bile rising in his throat on his way to kitchen. After making a cup of coffee, he brought a box of yesterday's croissants to the island.

Pounding on the door matched the pounding in his head. He wanted to shout and tell the person to stop, but that would've made his headache worse. Stepping over his discarded sweatshirt and shoes, Deacon trudged to the door, ready to tell off the person on the other side. He was going to eat and then go back to bed for the day.

"*Vivienne?*" Deacon winced at the golden sunlight glistening off her hair.

"I brought your car back," she said, dropping a set of keys into his palm.

When had she taken it? He caught a whiff of alcohol when she swept past; was it coming from him or her?

"Looks like I wasn't the only one having a party last night," she muttered, picking up one of the glasses next to an empty bottle of bourbon on the coffee table.

"You had a party?" He frowned when he noticed her bloodshot eyes. "And didn't invite me?"

Her brows lifted. "Maybe you should've answered your phone."

Where was his mobile? He'd left in such a rush he'd forgotten it. Eventually, he located it beside the microwave. "Did you really call me seven times?" He had five missed calls from Ethan and two from Lee as well. *"Ohhh, this is interesting."*

"What?" She worried her bottom lip with her teeth, drawing his eyes to her mouth. Vivienne had a lovely mouth. And he loved the way she—

Not now. Later.

Dragging his gaze from her lovely mouth, he focused on his screen. "You were looking for me at three o'clock this morning. You are aware that nothing virtuous happens between the hours of one and four a.m."

"Whatever." Her eyes rolled heavenward. "Where were you?"

"Running an errand with my grandad." He skimmed through his messages from Ethan and Lee. When he got to Vivienne's, he nearly dropped his mobile. *I miss you. I tried calling. Hope you're ok. I'm getting worried. Whre are yuo? I need your hot British mouth. I wnt yuo. We shuld have babies. Lots of babies.*

"What's wrong?" she asked.

He shook his head and tried to keep from laughing.

"Seriously," she pressed, smacking his good shoulder. "What is it?"

The last thing he wanted was to embarrass her, but the moment she checked her own messages, she would figure it out. "Apparently, I have a hot British mouth and you want to have my children."

Vivienne's cheeks turned the same shade of red as her shirt. "I . . . um . . . obviously I didn't mean to . . . " She covered her face with her hands and whispered the cutest curse. "I think I'm going to die."

"Oh look! You left a voicemail. I wonder what it says?"

"Do NOT listen to that," she begged, swiping for his phone.

"Too late." The message consisted of giggles and someone—Emily he assumed—prompting Vivienne to say what she wanted to do with him. All relatively mild compared to what he wanted to do with her. Chuckling, he ended the call and said in a serious voice, "I'm up for all of it. Did you really buy handcuffs?"

Vivienne's face paled and she started shaking her head. "Handcuffs? I didn't—I can't believe I said—"

He couldn't hold it in any longer. A laugh burst from his chest and he doubled over, gasping for breath.

"I hate you so much right now," she growled, shoving him into the island.

"That's not what you said last night."

She opened her mouth to respond, then jerked toward the staircase. "Is someone here?"

"It's probably Lyle." Peter didn't usually rise before noon.

Her frown deepened. "Lyle stayed at my apartment last night."

Lyle had stayed the night with *her*? In her two-bedroom apartment? Where had he slept?

"Do you have a girl upstairs?" Vivienne's whisper-shout jolted him back to the present.

"You must be joking." How could she think he'd do that to her? He'd hardly given her a reason to distrust him. Where was this coming from?

Peter came in wearing the cotton shorts and faded Kensington T-shirt Deacon had loaned him. "Good morning, you two," he said, saluting them on his way past. "Lovely day out there, isn't it?"

How the hell was he so chipper? It was maddening. "Morning, Grandad." Deacon waved toward the kitchen. "Help yourself to what's there. Make some coffee if you need it."

"I absolutely need it." Peter rifled through the cabinets until he found a coffee mug.

When Deacon turned back to Vivienne, he couldn't help but grin at her.

"Sorry," she whispered. "I thought . . . "

Deacon knew exactly what she thought. He leaned close so that only she could hear him say, "Why would I need anyone else when my girlfriend has such wicked plans for me and my mouth?"

"You're seriously saying that with your grandfather in the room?"

"I booked the tickets you asked about last night," Peter announced, adding milk to his coffee.

Tickets? What tickets?

"You're going somewhere?" she asked.

Deacon vaguely recalled mentioning that he'd like to visit the island, but nothing had been set in stone. "Apparently so."

"Don't worry, Vivienne. There's one for you as well," Peter said with a smile before bringing his coffee mug and croissant back upstairs.

"We're going away?" Vivienne's eyes widened, and her mouth, her lovely, lovely mouth, lifted at the corners. "Just the two of us?"

"And Ethan and Nicola." That much he remembered. Peter had been adamant about the need for chaperones. As if Ethan and Nicola would qualify.

"Can I invite some of my friends too?" She grabbed a croissant and pulled it apart, offering him half.

"Why don't you ask Emily and Max?" he suggested, taking a bite. His stomach didn't revolt as he'd expected it to.

"Max can't come. He's going to London. What about Lyle?"

Lyle? She wanted bloody *Lyle* to join them? Perhaps she'd like to invite Alex as well. Her foster brother was the reason

Deacon wanted to leave Kensington in the first place. Lyle was a thorn in his side and—

Vivienne's eyes sparkled with excitement, and he heard himself say, "The more the merrier."

Lyle hadn't moved from Vivienne's side since they'd left Massachusetts that morning. Deacon had ended up sitting by Emily during both flights. There was nothing wrong with Emily, but he wanted to sit beside his girlfriend.

That was the entire point of this holiday.

He thought of the ring tucked inside his suitcase. All right. Not the *entire* point.

Before they'd left, his grandad had explained that commitment on this level was a shift in mindset, from "Could she be the one?" to "She *is* the one."

Peter made it sound so simple.

But if it was that simple, more PAN would be married, and there wouldn't be so many rules regarding relationships.

Deacon still wasn't sure what to do, but the more time he spent with Vivienne, the clearer the decision became. He loved her and couldn't imagine being with anyone else. Time was a luxury they didn't have. There were a lot of memories and experiences he wanted to share with her while she could still remember them—and he wanted something to cling to when she couldn't.

Emily, Ethan, and Nicola splashed in the azure water bordering vibrant Belize City. Deacon and Vivienne had decided to wait until they reached their accommodations before getting sandy.

And Lyle.

Lyle had opted to wait too.

"When are we checking in?" Vivienne asked, peeling the

corner of her cotton shirt from her sweat-dampened skin. "I could really use a shower."

"You and me both," Lyle grumbled from her right, wiping his face with the bottom of his T-shirt.

"It'll be another few hours. We aren't staying in a hotel here." Deacon nodded toward the water. "We're staying out there." Vivienne was going to love flying over the sea. It was one of Deacon's favorite things about coming here. His only regret was that it would have to be after dark.

"Out where, exactly?" Shielding her eyes from the sun, she squinted toward the horizon.

Deacon explained about Peter's island. Instead of looking impressed, Vivienne propped her fists onto her hips and asked how he thought Lyle was going to get there.

Lyle. Lyle. *Lyle*.

This wouldn't have been an issue if he had stayed at Kensington. "Lyle can ride on the boat with the bags." And, if Deacon was lucky, the boat would sink.

"By *himself*?" Her warm brown eyes narrowed. "That's not fair."

Today was off to a brilliant start.

"It's fine," Lyle said, poking her in the side. "I don't mind."

Vivienne ignored Lyle and continued glaring.

What did she expect Deacon to say? When this holiday was first booked, there were only supposed to be PAN present. Admittedly, it had been planned by two inebriated individuals, but he and his grandad had thought of everything.

Everything except bloody Lyle.

Deacon could offer to carry him—an offer Lyle was sure to refuse. And he couldn't guarantee he wouldn't drop Lyle in the middle of the sea and leave him to the sharks.

But then Vivienne would be cross.

And if he *did* ask her to marry him, she'd probably say no.

Emily jogged out of the water and across the beach to the boardwalk where Deacon and Vivienne—and Lyle—waited next to the bags. "What's the plan, folks?" she asked, withdrawing a pink towel from a pile.

"Apparently we're staying somewhere offshore," Vivienne clipped.

Emily's eyebrows shot up as she wrapped the towel around her waist. "And that annoys you because . . . ?"

"Because Deacon wants to fly, but *some of us* are grounded."

"I already told you that I didn't mind going on the boat," Lyle said, resting a hand on Vivienne's bare shoulder. Deacon wanted to chop it off.

"I'll go with Lyle," Emily said, wringing the water from her curly ponytail.

Deacon felt like hugging her.

Something flickered across Vivienne's face. She said, "You don't have to do that," but sounded hopeful.

Emily shrugged. "I want to. I'm too tired to fly anyway."

"Excellent. Problem solved." Deacon would have to find a way to thank Emily for her sacrifice.

Fifteen minutes later, he got a call that a boat was waiting for them. He reached for Vivienne's hand, but she shifted away.

Brilliant. Now she was mad at him.

At the docks, Deacon helped a man load the bags while Vivienne said goodbye to Emily and Lyle—as if they wouldn't see each other in a couple of hours.

He watched her out of the corner of his eye; the sunset added a soft pink glow to her face. Her shoulders were stiff, and she kept her gaze trained on the boat disappearing over the horizon. "I'm starting to think inviting Lyle was a mistake."

Finally, something they agreed upon. "You read my mind."

"I should've stayed home with him."

"I can't believe you right now." He raked his hands through his hair, damp with sweat and sea spray. "The entire reason I wanted to come here was to spend time alone with you, and you wish you'd stayed back at Kensington?"

Her eyes widened in surprise. Lilac perfume washed over him when she shifted closer. "If you wanted to be alone with me, then why the heck did you invite Ethan and Nicola?"

"Because my grandad is under the impression that I won't try to seduce you if we have chaperones."

Her lips curled into a slow smile—the first genuine one she'd given him since that morning. "Seduce me, huh?"

"That *was* the plan," he groaned, "before you invited *Lyle*."

TWENTY-SEVEN

Black shadows rose from the water as Vivienne flew over blips of land dotting the ocean below. After forty minutes, they reached an island covered in palm tree silhouettes. A sprawling villa with walls of glass faced the beach, nestled amidst thick, luscious foliage. The pool outside glowed a bright blue, and tiki torches lit the beach like an airport runway.

When Deacon had told her about Neverland, this was what she had imagined. Exotic and warm and dreamy. Not that Kensington wasn't wonderful, but this place was magical. Her feet sank into the cold, soft sand at the water's edge, and she never wanted to leave.

Deacon's arms slipped around her waist from behind. "Do you like it?" he whispered against her neck. The warmth from his words sent shivers down her spine.

"It's gorgeous. I didn't think places like this really existed." And she certainly didn't think she'd ever be in one.

"It's about time you guys got here," Lyle called from the house. He had changed into a pair of striped trunks and a CCAD T-shirt. "Hurry up so we can go swimming!"

Deacon groaned and muttered something about drowning her brother.

Vivienne jabbed him in the ribs with her elbow. Lyle was just enthusiastic. And it had to be intimidating entering the world of the PAN without having the same abilities.

Ethan jogged toward the house, then turned around abruptly and asked if any mermaids were coming. The silly grin he wore made Vivienne smile. As much as she would have loved to be on her own with Deacon, vacationing with her friends was a close second.

She glanced back at the dark water, imagining a girl with a shimmering tail washing up on the shore. "I'd love to meet a Mermaid."

"No you wouldn't," Nicola mumbled as she swept past. It was the first time she had spoken to Vivienne all day. They hadn't been on great terms before Nicola had escorted her from Neverland, so she didn't have very high hopes for their relationship now.

That was why Vivienne had wanted Emily there. At least she would have an ally. And she didn't want Emily feeling like a fifth wheel, so she had suggested Lyle.

Vivienne hadn't even considered the fact that, without her friends, it would have been two couples on a private island—everyone minding their own business.

Deacon held her hand along a crushed-shell path, past the in-ground pool, and into the main part of the house.

A large kitchen opened to a dining room and living area with an ivory sectional. Three bags sat next to the coffee table—none of them were hers. "Where's my stuff?"

"In here!" Emily's call echoed off the hall walls.

She followed the sound of her voice to the first door.

Vivienne's bag sat next to one of the two single beds draped in white mosquito net canopies.

Emily was lying like a starfish on the other. "This place is a palace."

Vivienne laughed in agreement.

"Check this out." Emily bounced off the bed to a glass wall overlooking lush vegetation and flicked a switch. The scenery disappeared. "Privacy glass. Pretty cool, huh?"

"Very cool." This place kept getting better and better. "I think we're going swimming. You coming?"

"No. Sounds like a terrible idea. Who wants to go swimming on Peter Pan's private island?" Emily giggled, grabbing her bathing suit and disappearing into the bathroom.

Vivienne laid her suitcase flat on the floor and unzipped it. Shorts, tank tops, running shoes, cover up, a pretty dress, something cute to sleep in—just in case she wasn't on her own . . . The thought made the fireflies in her stomach flutter. Deacon hadn't said anything about sharing a room, but the night was young.

Where were her bathing suits?

"Geez, Vivienne. I was only gone for two minutes and the place is a disaster!"

Vivienne mumbled an apology as she shoved everything into a sloppy pile. Where the heck were they? She remembered putting them on her bed. How had she forgotten to put them in her bag?

"What's wrong?" Emily asked, dropping onto the edge of the bed and slipping her gold sandals onto her feet.

Vivienne frowned at her stuff. "I forgot my swimsuits."

"You're joking." Emily laughed. "That's basically the only thing you're going to be wearing all week."

"Yeah. I know."

"Lucky for you, I have a bunch of new ones you can choose from." Emily rummaged around in her own suitcase before throwing three bikinis with tags on her bed. Vivienne picked up a black one and brought it to the bathroom.

"Does it work?" Emily asked with a knock.

"Yeah. It fits."

In the kitchen, Deacon was bringing down glasses from one of the cabinets. When he saw Vivienne, his brows came together. "Did you really forget to bring swimwear?"

She knew what he was thinking, but it had been a simple mistake. "I'll probably find it in my bag tomorrow."

His mouth drew into a disapproving line, but he didn't make a big deal of it. Ethan, wearing pineapple-print shorts, used a corkscrew to open two bottles of wine.

"I'm never going back to Kensington." Emily swiped two drinks and handed one to Vivienne.

"You said it." Ethan gave one to Nicola, then filled his own glass to the brim. Deacon collected his, but there was still one drink left.

Vivienne looked around the room, but there was no sign of her foster brother. "Where's Lyle?"

She was pretty sure Deacon said, "Who cares?" under his breath, but ignored him.

"In his room." Nicola closed her eyes as she lifted the wine to her nose and inhaled.

"This joyous occasion calls for a toast." Ethan raised his glass toward the ceiling. "To our friend and gracious host, the revered Prince of Neverland. May you be quick enough to dodge bullets and smart enough not to get shot in the first place."

One. Two. Three. Four. Five. There were *five* empty bottles of wine. Vivienne could barely keep her eyes open. Emily had gone to bed an hour earlier. Ethan lay upside down on one of the sun loungers next to the pool. His sunglasses made it impossible to tell whether or not he was asleep.

Beside him, Nicola was drinking directly from a sixth bottle of wine.

It was unclear who had suggested taking shots, but Deacon and Lyle were the only two still sitting at the patio table with a bottle of liquor between them.

"I'm going to bed . . . if anyone cares." Deacon didn't even acknowledge her. They hadn't so much as kissed since they'd arrived. And seeing him sitting there in nothing but his blue shorts made her want to do more than kiss him.

If only she knew how to be seductive. Bathing suits. They were seductive. She shimmied out of her cover up and kicked it under the table. But ponytails weren't. She pulled out her hair tie and finger-combed the damp strands. Her hair was such a tangled mess. She should have left it up.

This time, when she said she was going to bed, both Deacon and Lyle turned toward her.

Deacon's eyes widened as they roved down her body. "Bed. Yes." He shoved the liquor bottle aside and shot to his feet.

"I'm tired too." Lyle stood, then steadied himself against the table edge.

"Hey, Lyle?" Nicola caught him by the elbow before he fell. "Vivienne tells me you have a twin sister." She sounded way too sober for a woman who had drunk an entire bottle of wine by herself.

Smiling at Nicola, Lyle sat back down. "Maren? Yeah. She's the evil twin."

"Run," Deacon mouthed, grabbing Vivienne's hand and hauling her through the bright kitchen and around the corner into the darkened hallway. They reached her door, and she found herself trapped between the wall and Deacon's bare chest.

His lips bruised against hers, hot and urgent and

flavored with whiskey. She clung to his neck, keeping herself upright. The way he devoured her made her feel strong and weak, and her head was spinning, but that could have been the wine. Her spine ground into the wall, and the friction between their bare skin ignited her internal fire.

Bed. She wanted him to bring her to a bed, but Emily was asleep. "Which one's your room?"

He squinted into the darkness. "One, two, three. Three doors down."

She kissed him again, stopping long enough to murmur against his mouth, "How big is the bed?"

He let out a low groan, nipping at her lower lip. "Come with me and I'll show you."

"Are you guys drunk? Cuz I am sooo drunk."

STUPID LYLE. Why had she invited him again?

Deacon cursed and drew away from her. Vivienne glared at her foster brother as he stumbled toward them.

"Those shots were *not* a good idea. I haven't done shots in *ages*." He forced his way between Vivienne and Deacon so he could give her a hug. "Thanks for inviting me to Neverland. You're the best. I mean it. The best."

"You're welcome." From over Lyle's shoulder, her eyes met Deacon's. He looked like he wanted to murder someone.

The door handle jiggled behind her as Lyle fumbled with it. The door clicked when it opened, and she found herself nudged deeper into the dark room. Before Lyle closed the door, he grinned. "Sweet dreams, Viv."

Knowing better than to sneak out right away, she pressed her ear against the wood and listened. It sounded like Deacon was angry, and Lyle was . . . *Wait*. Was he laughing? He was so strange when he got drunk. And chatty. They'd probably be out there for a while.

And Vivienne really had to pee.

She ran into the bathroom, then changed into the cute pj's Emily had picked out. Three doors down. That's where

Deacon was. Was Lyle ever going to shut up? She sat on the edge of her bed to wait.

The mattress was so soft and inviting. She should probably lie down. Just for a minute. And close her eyes. Just for a minute.

TWENTY-EIGHT

W *ine.*
　　　　Whoever had invented it deserved a punch in the face.

It didn't even taste good, never mind the hangover it gave you. Grapes were supposed to be healthy, but Vivienne did *not* feel healthy.

The last thing she'd wanted this morning was to go running. But Nicola the sadist had told everyone it was the best cure for a hangover. She was a big fat liar.

Vivienne felt the same way about Nicola as she did the wine.

The humid morning boasted clear blue skies that stretched beyond the horizon. Eerily still, the waves lapped more than crashed. Bits of seaweed spread like fingers across sand whiter than snow and nearly as fluffy.

"Hurry up!" Nicola shouted from out of view.

"Someone didn't drink enough last night," Ethan grumbled, slowing the higher they climbed the rocky terrain. The back of his gray shirt was drenched in sweat.

Vivienne silently agreed.

"Your idea of hangover recovery sucks," Lyle called from the back, gasping for air. He'd never been very athletic. "I should'a stayed at the house with Emily."

"Why didn't you?" Deacon muttered. He had started out jogging but had been flying the last ten minutes because of his sore shoulder.

"Whatever, dude." Lyle cursed and shoved a branch out of his way. "Not everyone's been taking breaks like you."

"Deacon needs to rest his shoulder," Vivienne reminded him.

"Well I need to rest my legs, but you don't see me stopping."

From above, she heard, "Perhaps you could rest your mouth instead."

"Deacon! That's not—"

"I can see why someone shot you."

"Lyle!"

"Both of you need to shut up," Nicola shouted from a clearing up ahead. "You're spoiling the view." Her legs looked even longer in her tiny black running shorts.

The lush jungle ended abruptly at the sheer face of a dangerous cliff. Sea birds swooped toward the water and back to their nests in the dark rock.

How did places like this even exist? It was so beautiful, Vivienne could have stared out at the endless ocean, glimmering and undulating, forever. She continued jogging until she reached the very edge, her adrenaline spiking with each step. All she wanted to do was jump off and feel the sunshine and salty air slipping past her skin as she plummeted toward the aquamarine water.

Deacon landed on a pile of small boulders beside her, his

face flushed. He winced as he raised and lowered his left arm.

"I was skeptical at first, but this was a good call, babe." Ethan caught Nicola by the waist and pressed a smacking kiss to her cheek.

"Gross! You're all sweaty!" She squirmed free and wiped her forehead with the back of her hand even as she giggled. Besides a few beads of glittery sweat, she looked as fresh and perfect as ever, fluffing her hair like she was in a shampoo commercial.

Ethan kicked off his shoes, peeled off his socks, and climbed the boulders to stand beside Deacon. "What's the plan, Dash? We swimmin'?"

Was he nuts? Of course they were swimming. Vivienne's arms started to itch, and she bent down to take off her own shoes.

"That's a stupid question." Deacon pulled his shirt over his head and let it fall next to Ethan's shoes. Ethan had made fun of him for being out of shape, but there was absolutely nothing wrong with Deacon's shape. Nothing at all. Seriously. *W-o-w.*

Lyle walked past Vivienne and kicked a loose pebble into the void.

Crap. Lyle.

Vivienne didn't need to count the seconds it took for the stone to reach the waves gnashing at the base of the island to know it was way too high for him to jump without getting hurt—or killed.

Lyle frowned; he must have thought the same thing.

"I'd rather go back to the beach or the pool," Vivienne announced, tying her laces again.

"You're kidding, right?" Ethan leapt from the boulders and flew to her side. "We can literally jump off a cliff in broad daylight, and you want to swim in a *pool*? Are you insane?"

"Not all of us can fly." From the corner of her eye, she noticed Deacon removing his shoes as well. "You're not going with him, are you?"

"Why wouldn't I?" Deacon's shoes landed next to her. Then his rolled-up socks.

"Come on, Lyle. We can go back." As much as she wanted to jump off the cliff with her friends, it wouldn't be fair to her brother.

"It's not a big deal, Viv," Lyle said quietly. "Stop making it one."

Deacon sauntered backward to the ledge, his eyes focused on Vivienne. "You don't have to come if you don't want to." When his heels hit the air, he winked at her . . . then disappeared.

He fell with his face toward the sky and his left arm tucked protectively at his side. Halfway down, he twisted, and right before he reached the water, he leveled out, skimming the tops of the waves with his fingers. He cut through an approaching swell before spiraling back toward the crisp, bleached clouds.

"You comin', sweetheart?" Ethan asked Nicola, pulling her against him for a hard kiss.

Nicola pushed him away with a flirtatious swat. "No kisses till you wash yourself."

"Done." Ethan launched his body into the air in a front-flip and continued spinning as he fell. Nicola stepped without fanfare into the breeze and dropped out of sight.

When Deacon returned, he sat on the ledge, dangling his legs over the drop like he was relaxing on the edge of the villa's pool. "You're missing out, Vivienne," he said, his face upturned to the sun. Seeing the nasty purple scar on his shoulder made her stomach sink.

Vivienne didn't want to miss out on anything.

"You'll regret it if you don't, Viv."

Later. She could come back later—maybe on her own, or with Deacon. *Then* she'd jump.

Lyle rolled his eyes, and kicked a stone at Deacon. "Think you can help me do it?"

"No!" Had he lost his mind? "You can't fly."

"I'll be fine. Your boyfriend won't let me die. Will ya, Smee?"

"Would you like to call me by my real name before you ask me that?"

Deacon's threat hit its mark. Lyle rephrased his question, called Deacon by his real name, and even said please.

When Ethan landed, he pounded his head a few times to get water out of his ear. Nicola drifted to the ground as gracefully as she'd left.

"Come on, Vivienne. Are you seriously not gonna jump?" Ethan asked her, his shorts dripping on the stones beneath his bare feet.

"She'll go after Lyle." Deacon stood and motioned her brother closer. "You'll need to brace your weight across my—"

"Don't be stupid, Dash. If you take his weight, you'll end up hurting your shoulder," Nicola snapped, tying her hair into a ponytail. "Ethan and I'll do it. Put your arm around me, Lyle."

"I won't say no to that." Lyle scooted closer and slid his arm around her shoulder.

"Eyes up or I'll drop you," Ethan warned, draping Lyle's other arm over his shoulder.

On the count of three, the trio fell out of sight.

Vivienne watched as they hurtled toward the ocean. They were going too fast. Shouldn't they be slowing down? If something happened to Lyle—

A pair of damp arms wrapped around her waist. "It's your turn," Deacon whispered in her ear.

Her adrenaline surged, leaving her body on fire. "Just let me make sure Lyle—"

Deacon's grip tightened and he dragged her over the edge.

Deacon retreated back to the hallway before Lyle could see him from where he was sitting in the kitchen. If he was going to do this, he needed to be stealthy. He knocked quietly on Vivienne's door.

Emily answered in a pink bikini. "Vivienne's in the shower."

"I actually wanted to see you."

Her eyes widened. "Do you want to tell Vivienne or should I?"

"Funny. I need your help."

"With?"

"Lyle."

Understanding lit Emily's eyes. She pulled her hair into a ponytail and nodded. "Hey, Lyle?"

"Yeah?" Lyle called from the kitchen.

Emily waved Deacon into the bedroom and shut the door. From the hallway, he heard her say, "Get off your butt. We're going swimming."

A stool scooted across the tiles. The glass door slid open . . . and closed.

Deacon sank onto the edge of Vivienne's bed and tried not to think of her showering. Naked. The water slipping down her—

Nope. He had to think of something else. Anything else. Like the clothes spilling from her suitcase on the ground. She was such a slob. For some reason, that fact made his heart swell. Seeing her mess made him want to kiss her as much as seeing Lyle's made him want to put his fist through his irritating face.

Lyle hadn't let Vivienne out of his sight all bloody day. First there had been the almost-disaster at the cliff. Then that afternoon, he'd made her lunch and asked her if she wanted to sit by the pool and then go down to the beach. Lyle needed to find his own damn girlfriend and quit stealing Deacon's.

A bottle of perfume sat on the bedside locker. It clinked delicately as he turned it over in his hand. It smelled like Vivienne. This whole bed smelled like her.

The humming shower stopped.

Deacon turned his back to the bathroom when he heard the door open. "I'm in here," he announced, replacing the bottle on the locker. "Don't come out naked—or do. It's up to you."

Vivienne giggled. "What're you doing?"

"Hiding from everyone else."

There was a smile in her voice when she said, "For a big house, it does seem pretty crowded."

"Would you like to escape with me?"

"I thought you'd never ask. Give me a sec to change." He heard her rummaging in the bag next to his feet. The devil in him wanted to peek; he squeezed his eyes shut and prayed for self-control.

"Okay. Ready."

She stood before him in a paper-thin white dress with an impossibly deep V neck over a dark bikini. He couldn't wait to get her out of at least one of them.

Vivienne crossed to the glass doors, but he caught her hand before she reached them. "Not that way. They'll see us."

He peered into the hall.

Clear.

They managed to sneak to the back door without being

caught. And when they emerged beneath two palms bent across the path, they were free and clear. It was dark, but Deacon knew the way by heart. When he was little, he had buried countless treasures back here. He had planned on becoming a pirate when he grew up.

His mother hadn't been impressed.

His father had bought him an eye patch, and Peter had bought him a sword.

He ran all the way to the beach with Vivienne's hand clasped in his. After the exercise that morning, the jostling made his shoulder ache, but he didn't complain.

They were finally, *finally* alone.

"This place is amazing." Vivienne's sigh resonated with contentment. She leaned against him and tucked her head beneath his chin, smelling like shampoo and soap.

"It's my most favorite place on earth," he confessed, pressing a kiss to her damp hair. If only they could stay there forever, just the two of them.

Drawing closer, she toyed with the buttons on his shirt. "Thank you for bringing me here with you." Her fingers were cold when they slipped between the gaps.

"It should be obvious by now that I'm incapable of leaving you behind."

Even before they had properly met, when HOOK showed up to the hospital in Ohio and he had been ordered to abandon Vivienne to her fate, he couldn't leave her. Even now, understanding that in a few years she wouldn't know his name, he couldn't leave her.

She was it for him.

In that moment, he realized there had never been a decision at all. His fate had been sealed the moment he saved her from the hospital.

Deacon captured her mouth with his. She opened her lips, and their tongues met, forcing a moan from deep in his throat. *Damn,* she smelled good, but she tasted even better.

Like mint and vanilla and he couldn't get enough. He tangled his hands in the damp strands of her hair and dragged her closer so every curve of her body conformed to his. He wanted to touch her, but the only bits of skin not covered by her dress were her arms, and he'd never hated a garment as much.

He slid his hands from her hair to her shoulders, taking the straps of her dress with him on the way, lower and lower. Vivienne broke their kiss long enough to tug her dress down over her swimsuit, and it fell to the sand at their feet.

Everything about her was beautiful. Her round face and delicately pointed chin. Her wide brown eyes, hooded with promises of things to come. Her slim body barely covered in that tiny bikini. A bikini he hoped would shortly meet the same fate as the dress.

"And here I thought I was the one seducing you," Deacon said, forcing himself to take a breath. Every part of him was on fire, and if he didn't slow down or get ahold of himself—or get ahold of her—he was going to burst into flames.

"You were taking too long," she said from over her shoulder as she waded into the sea.

"Maybe you shouldn't have invited Lyle," he muttered, fumbling with the buttons on his shirt. Buttons. The most irritating things in the entire world at the moment. He got four open, gave up, and yanked his shirt over his head. It landed perilously close to the lapping waves. The sea could have it for all he cared.

The water was warm on his feet at first, but the deeper he went, the cooler it got—which was probably a good thing. He needed to cool off.

Vivienne waited for him in shoulder-deep water. When he reached her, she threw herself into his arms. "I love you."

He would never get tired of hearing those words fall from her lips.

"And I love you." He tried focusing on something besides the feeling of her legs wrapped around his waist, but then she shifted, and it was *all* he could think about.

He tugged the string tied around her neck. It slipped through his fingers, then caught. He pulled again, harder this time. "A double-knot?"

Vivienne smiled against his mouth. "I can't make things too easy on—" She jerked out of his arms.

"What's wrong?"

"Something touched my leg," she said, searching the water around her.

"Um . . . yeah . . . sorry about that." Deacon adjusted his shorts. "I got a little caught up in—"

"Not *that*." She twisted toward deeper water, still looking down. "It touched the *back* of my leg. Maybe some seaweed?"

The water rippled behind her

Deacon's stomach twisted. "We need to get out. *Now*." He lunged for her, but it was too late.

Something dragged Vivienne beneath the water.

TWENTY-NINE

D own . . .
      Down . . .
Down.

The more Vivienne thrashed, the tighter the thing gripped her ankle.

Deeper and deeper. Her eyes stung as she searched the blackness for a way out.

Then it just . . . let go.

She kicked and grabbed for something, anything solid, but there was only darkness and water.

Up.

Up.

Which way was up?

Her internal fire tried igniting, but the sea doused the spark. Her lungs screamed for air, but there was none, and even knowing that, she had the overwhelming urge to take a breath.

Don't breathe in.

DO NOT breathe in.

Her mouth opened and saltwater forced its way into her throat.

THIRTY

G *one.* Vivienne was gone and Deacon knew what had happened to her.

A Mermaid. And not just any Mermaid. A white-blond head popped up from the water and Aoibheann laughed. Like this was some sort of bloody joke.

"Find her!" Deacon roared, dragging air into his lungs and plunging into the dark water. His eyes burned and blurred, and everything was so black, and if anything happened to Vivienne, he would never forgive himself. No matter how deep he swam or how much area he covered, he couldn't find her. His lungs begged for oxygen and he couldn't stay under any longer and if he couldn't stay under, then there was no hope for Vivienne. She hadn't known what was coming for her. Hadn't taken a fortifying breath before being pulled under.

Deacon kicked to the surface in time to see Aoibheann swimming toward the shore with a body in her arms. Vivienne's dark hair floated on top of the water, and she wasn't moving.

Cursing wouldn't help the situation, but Deacon cursed anyway as he followed the Mermaid to shore.

"Dammit, Aoibheann!" His voice cracked as his knees slammed into the sand. Vivienne was pale, so damn pale, and her lips had no color.

"It was an accident, Dash," Aoibheann cried, falling down beside him. "I swear, I didn't mean to—"

"For once in your life, do something useful and get help!"

Aoibheann shot to her feet and hurtled down the beach toward the house. Deacon turned Vivienne's head to the side; water drained from her nose and mouth into the sand. *Shit.* How much had she inhaled? Tilting her head back, he pinched her nose and forced four strong breaths into her mouth. Pressing his fingers to her neck, he checked for a pulse. Where the hell was her—*there*. It was faint, but her heart was still beating.

Again, he pinched her nose and pressed his lips to hers and begged and prayed that Vivienne would wake up or that this was all a nightmare and he would be the one to wake up.

When he pulled away, there was a faint gurgling sound, and he rolled her onto her side in time for her to vomit in the sand. Vivienne's groan was music to his ears.

"What did you do?" Nicola shouted, flying toward him with Ethan and Emily right behind her. Lyle was running, Aoibheann and Caoilfhionn, another bloody Mermaid, were a good bit behind.

Emily landed first. "No, no, no . . . " Her dark hair swayed as she shook her head.

"She's breathing now," Deacon assured her—and himself.

"Yeah, but do we need to bring her to a hospital?" Emily

asked, one hand over her mouth, the other pressed to her chest.

How the hell was he supposed to know?

"Out of my way," Nicola hissed, shoving Emily aside.

"Shit, Dash." Ethan raked his hand through his hair. "I thought she could swim."

"She *can* swim, you idiot," Lyle snarled, skidding to a halt beside them, kicking up a wave of sand.

Aoibheann and Caoilfhionn stayed in the shadows near the palm trees.

"What happened?" Nicola checked Vivienne's pulse and watched with wide, worried eyes as Vivienne dragged in halting, ragged breaths.

"Aoibheann tried to drown her."

"I told you it was an accident!" Aoibheann cried from the shadows. Caoilfhionn had an arm around her like Aoibheann was the victim.

"Say no more," Nicola said, holding up her hand. "We need to get her inside. I'll call the mainland for a doctor."

Deacon slid his hands beneath Vivienne's limp body, taking half the beach with him.

"I'll help," Lyle offered, reaching for Vivienne's legs.

"Don't touch her," Deacon snarled, clutching her to his chest. No one was going to touch her but the doctor and Nicola.

Nicola barked orders and his friends ran this way and that, complying without question. But all Deacon could focus on was how fragile and lifeless Vivienne felt in his arms as he carried her into his bedroom.

"Her room is down there," Lyle said, gesturing toward the room Vivienne had shared with Emily.

"Shove off, Lyle." Deacon would've said more, but Vivienne stirred and moaned. He rushed into the room and settled her on his bed.

"The doctor will be here in an hour," Nicola told him from the door.

"What do I need to do?" he asked, gathering Vivienne's wet, sandy hair and spreading it across the pillowcase so it could dry. The duvet was already tucked beneath her chin, but she was still shivering.

"There's not much you can do."

"If I don't do something, I'll go mad."

Nicola sighed. "Just keep her warm and make sure she's breathing. If it sounds like she's struggling, let me know. She'll be all right, Dash."

Not trusting his voice to remain steady, Deacon nodded and prayed Nicola was right.

Vivienne should be fine. The doctor had said so. She was going to wake up and be fine. Except . . . what if the man was wrong?

Deacon shifted on the chair he had commandeered from the living room, trying to find a comfortable position. Vivienne still looked as pale as she had when Aoibheann had dragged her from the sea. Had the doctor noticed that? Had the man heard her ragged breathing? It sounded like her lungs were still full of seawater. Should Deacon call him back? He should probably call him back. Just to make sure. The boat couldn't be far from the island.

"Deacon?"

She was awake. Thank God, she was awake. "I'm here."

"Oh, good," she sighed, her lips lifting in the barest hint of a smile.

Deacon hadn't left her side all night, and he had pains in his neck and shoulder to prove it.

When Vivienne started coughing and gagging, he grabbed the bin and held it toward her. That doctor didn't know a bloody thing. Deacon was going to haul his ass back here and hold him hostage until he was sure Vivienne would be all right.

"What happened?" she asked when the fit subsided, clutching her stomach and curling on her side toward him.

Deacon grabbed a glass of water from the bedside locker and offered it to her. Her throat must burn like hell. "You met a Mermaid," he said, rage building in his chest.

"A Mermaid?" she gasped, her dark eyebrows coming together over panicked brown eyes. "Mermaids are *real*?"

"I've told you about them before."

"I thought you were joking!"

"If only," he muttered, running a hand across his tired eyes. "The real Mermaids aren't like in the stories, with tails or scales or anything like that. They have a different genetic mutation that lets them stay underwater for a long, long time. It has something to do with the way their bodies process oxygen. So instead of flying, they're really good swimmers. Better than good, actually. They practically live in the water."

Deacon took the glass back from her and set it on the nightstand next to his watch.

Vivienne twisted away and stared toward the sheer white canopy, fluttering softly in the early morning breeze. "Is this your room?"

"It is."

When she groaned again, he grabbed for the bin. "I'm sorry," she cried. "I'm destroying your bed."

"I don't give a toss about sandy sheets." He reached for her hand and drew idle circles on her knuckles with his thumb. "I thought . . . " Panic squeezed his chest, and his adrenaline surged. "I thought you were—"

"Deacon? I'm fine."

Some of the color and returned to her face and, despite the dark circles beneath her eyes, she did look fine. Better than fine. She looked deliciously rumpled, and for the first time since last night, he remembered that she was wearing nothing but her black bikini, all her silky skin on display, begging to be explored and—

"Will you sleep in here tonight?" When her eyes widened, he added, "There's no pressure. I just can't stand the thought of you being away from me."

Vivienne's lips curled into a smile. "Okay."

The tension in his chest eased until he remembered their unexpected guests.

It was time to deal with the Mermaids.

Deacon told Vivienne he would be right back, collected the empty glass, and carried it into the hallway. Sounds of low conversations and running water emerged from the kitchen. Deacon paused, attempting to get his anger under control. What had Aoibheann been thinking? Had she been thinking at all?

He intended to find out.

Emily rushed over when he walked into the kitchen, asking if Vivienne was awake. Deacon nodded, and she took off down the hall at a sprint.

"I don't see what all the fuss is about. The doctor said she'd be fine." Aoibheann tossed her white hair over her shoulders and curled onto the stool next to Lyle. "She wasn't under more than thirty seconds."

Deacon drew in a slow, steady breath. "Who told you we were here?" He'd asked his grandad to keep their holiday a secret for this very reason. The Mermaids brought with them a whole host of problems beyond his girlfriend's almost-drowning.

"Does it matter?" Caoilfhionn muttered, dragging her fingers through her mahogany hair. She didn't seem to notice the puddle of seawater at her feet. "We wouldn't have come if we'd known you'd brought your feathered friends."

There was a half-eaten blueberry muffin on a plate in front

of her.

Aoibheann scooted her stool closer to Lyle. "Speak for yourself."

Lyle smiled down at Aoibheann's skin-tight iridescent wetsuit like he was looking for the zip. It wasn't in the front. It was at the back beneath her—

"Lyle isn't one of us," Deacon said before he could stop himself.

"*Really?*" Aoibheann walked her fingers across Lyle's knee. "We don't spend much time with outsiders. Especially not ones as cute as you."

"Why the hell are the two of you here?" Deacon snapped, slamming the empty glass on the counter. "And why the hell did you try to drown Vivienne?"

"I wasn't trying to hurt her, Dash," Aoibheann insisted, rolling her blue eyes heavenward and reaching for an apple from the fruit bowl. "It was meant to be a joke. How was I to know she couldn't swim?"

"You dragged her under the water when she wasn't expecting it. She could have died."

"Calm down. I've already apologized a hundred times."

Vivienne appeared in the hallway with Emily at her side. Her hair was wrapped in a white towel, and she'd changed into a pair of short black shorts and a Kensington T-shirt.

"That's Caoilfhionn and that's Aoibheann," Emily said, pointing to each Mermaid.

Caoilfhionn bobbed her head.

Aoibheann smile and waved. "Hey, Vivienne. I'm sorry about last night. I was trying to be funny, but it obviously didn't work." A sigh. "Are you feeling better?"

"Yeah. I'm okay." Despite her words, Vivienne still looked understandably wary. "I really didn't expect to meet a Mermaid on this trip. I didn't realize you really existed."

Caoilfhionn's hands clenched into fists. "That's because

Neverland doesn't think we're as relevant as the rest of you feathered fowl."

"Spoken like a true fish," Deacon bit out. Caoilfhionn had no right to be rude. *They* were the ones who had arrived uninvited.

"Ah, but no one shoots a fish," Caoilfhionn teased, tapping the scar on Deacon's shoulder before sauntering toward the sun-drenched patio.

"Our existence is an anomaly," Aoibheann explained, rolling a red apple between her long, pale fingers. "As far as we know, our genetic mutation only occurs in a small percentage of descendants with Irish mothers and PAN fathers."

"Why don't you have tails?" Lyle asked, knocking Aoibheann's foot with his.

She returned the gesture and giggled. "Because we don't need them."

Leaning his elbow on the counter, Lyle toyed with the ends of Aoibheann's hair, tinged green from her underwater exploits. "Are you staying tonight?"

Emily frowned at the back of Lyle's head.

"That depends on Dash," Aoibheann said, peering at him from beneath her thick lashes.

What was Deacon supposed to say? Peter would expect him to be a gracious host, but he knew better than to expect the Mermaids to keep from causing trouble. "You're welcome to stay if you'd like."

Lyle jumped off his stool and grabbed Aoibheann's hand. "There's a spare bed in my room."

If Aoibheann touched Deacon's arm one more time, Vivienne swore she was going to rip her ridiculously big eyes out of her beautiful head. All day, the slimy Mermaid kept him engaged in conversation, laughing at inside jokes and offering him secretive looks.

Deacon hadn't done anything inappropriate, per se, but he hadn't done anything to discourage her either. He had obviously forgotten that Aoibheann had tried drowning his girlfriend last night.

Vivienne watched Deacon refill Aoibheann's outstretched wine glass before frowning at her own empty glass next to her half-eaten plate of carbonara. When she looked up, she met Nicola's wide eyes from across the table. Nicola's mouth pinched as she picked up the bottle and filled Vivienne's glass, then her own.

Ethan was talking quietly to Caoilfhionn, but Nicola didn't seem to mind. If only Vivienne had her confidence.

"Is anyone interested in a late-night swim?" Aoibheann threw Deacon a pointed look, then turned to smile at Lyle. "How about you?"

"Hell yeah!" Lyle practically fell off his chair. "I'll grab my trunks."

"Before you go, would you mind helping me out of this?" Aoibheann lifted her blanket of white hair, showing him a zipper at the back of her ridiculously tight wetsuit.

Once Lyle unzipped it, Aoibheann peeled herself free, revealing a stringy black top that didn't cover much of anything and a matching black thong.

"I'm going to bed." Emily jolted to her feet. "Vivienne?"

"I'll probably just go to bed too." And, if she was lucky, Deacon would join her.

Ethan tossed his napkin on the table. "We'll go swimming."

Nicola whispered something in his ear, and his eyes widened. "Never mind. We're going to bed," he choked, hauling a laughing Nicola into the house.

"What about you, Dash?" Aoibheann asked. "I know you don't fall asleep this early."

Vivienne's stomach twisted, and she held her breath as Deacon finished what was left of his wine.

"Yeah, all right. Sounds fun."

Emily reached for Vivienne and squeezed her elbow. "Come on."

"Wait for me," Deacon called. When they got to the hallway, he smiled down at her as though nothing was wrong. "I'll change my sheets, so you don't end up covered in sand."

"Yeah, I'm *not* sleeping in your room."

His brow furrowed. "But I thought—"

"You thought what?" Vivienne clipped, hating the stupid confused look on his stupid handsome face. Was he really that clueless? "That I was going to sit around and wait for you to come back from your little 'swim' with Aoibheann?"

"So come with me."

"Not happening, jerk." She hadn't gone near the water all day for fear Aoibheann would play another "joke" on her. Vivienne reached for the door handle, but Deacon blocked her with his arm.

"You think I'm the one being a jerk here? Aoibheann and I have been friends for ages," he said, his chest rising and falling in irritation beneath his black T-shirt, "and I'm not going to be rude and ignore her because my girlfriend is being jealous for no bloody reason."

"No reason? She's been toying with you all day, and you're just lapping it up." And to make things worse, Aoibheann had been using Lyle for her little mind games. "For someone who 'can't stand the thought of being away from me,' you sure are quick to jump into the water with the monster who nearly drowned me."

Vivienne didn't like Aoibheann. She had tried to keep an open mind. Tried to be friendly with the Mermaid. But after an entire day in Aoibheann's company, Vivienne knew they would never be friends.

And she was totally okay with it.

"Look," Deacon huffed, squeezing his eyes shut and pinching the bridge of his nose, "if you don't trust me, then how the hell are we supposed to make this work?"

"I trust you, Deacon. But I sure as hell don't trust Aoibheann." Vivienne shoved him aside and slammed the door in his face. She held her breath as she waited, hoping he'd knock and apologize for being an idiot.

He didn't.

"Stupid Mermaids. Seriously. Who even invited them?" Emily grumbled, ripping her nightgown out of the drawer.

"Tell me about it." And Vivienne had thought Gwen was bad.

"Did you see Lyle drooling like an idiot? Ugh. Disgusting." The dresser rocked when Emily shoved the drawer closed. "'Let's go swimming. Help me with my zipper. Do you like my scales?'"

Vivienne dropped onto her bed and groaned. "I hope they're gone tomorrow."

"Tomorrow? I hope they leave tonight."

"What took you so long?" Aoibheann called from the water. There was no sign of Lyle or Caoilfhionn.

Deacon had briefly considered not coming. Perhaps if Vivienne had discussed her concerns with him like a rational adult instead of jumping down his throat, he would've been more inclined to listen. It wasn't like he was going to *do* anything with Aoibheann.

Deacon was going for a swim. He'd been swimming with her today, and Vivienne hadn't freaked out. And everyone else had been invited. It wasn't his fault the others were too tired to join them.

If he went back now, Vivienne would think he couldn't

control himself around other women. And he could control himself.

He'd turned Gwen down, hadn't he? Aoibheann was no different.

"Not all of us live in our swimming costumes," Deacon said before diving beneath the waves.

When he resurfaced, Aoibheann was waiting for him. Water droplets rolled down her face, clinging to her lips. "Are you any faster than you were the last time?" Her white teeth were a flash in the darkness when she grinned.

"Let's find out." He launched himself into deeper water. By the time he reached the sandbar, he was out of breath and in excruciating pain.

"Are you sure you didn't fly the last five meters?" she whined, shoving her hair back from her face.

"You won," Deacon chuckled. "Why does it matter?"

"I usually trounce you."

It was true. She was the fastest swimmer he knew, which meant he resorted to cheating when they raced.

"Where's everyone else?" The only sound he could hear was the waves lapping against their skin. Palm silhouettes swayed in the breeze on the distant shore.

"I don't know where Caoilfhionn is, but your cute friend needed a break," Aoibheann said with a laugh. "You know how tiring it is trying to keep up with us."

"Lyle isn't my friend." Deacon didn't know why the distinction mattered. But it did. "He's Vivienne's foster brother."

"Really?" Her mouth crooked up at the corners.

"We should—"

Her tongue darted from between saltwater drenched lips.

What had he been about to say?

Deacon cleared the thickness from his throat. "We should get back."

"What's the rush?" Aoibheann lifted her arms and

289

propelled herself backwards. "Everyone else is probably asleep."

She had a point. And it would be a while before Deacon felt like doing the same.

"Five more minutes then." He allowed the cool water to ease the aching in his shoulder and did a few of the stretches Dr. Carey had given him.

"Why didn't you tell me you were coming?" As Aoibheann floated on her back, the moonlight made her pale skin glimmer. "I could've been here waiting for you when you arrived."

What a disaster that would have been. It was bad enough she had shown up last night. "That's why I didn't tell you."

She circled him, her movements as fluid as the sea. "Are you still in the same room you usually sleep in?"

"Don't start."

"Start what?" she drawled, spinning through the water like a fishing lure.

Deacon ducked beneath the waves and welcomed the way it dulled his senses. When he came back up for air, she was waiting for him.

"Let's see who can stay under longer." She pushed him back down and held him there until his breath had nearly run out and he came up sputtering.

"I'll help you beat your old record," she whispered into his ear. "It'll be just like old times—only your mother isn't around to ruin the fun." Aoibheann dipped below the waves and tugged on the bottom of his shorts.

Deacon caught the waistband before she could pull them off. "Stop, Aoibheann. I'm not doing this with you."

Aoibheann untied the top of her swimsuit, unconcerned when the current took the material.

Tearing his eyes away, Deacon cursed the pale moon for reminding him of her skin.

The water rippled as she closed the gap between them. "Don't you like what you see?"

"I told you that I was with Vivienne."

"Then why are you swimming with me?"

"Because we're friends and—"

"Friends? You honestly think we can be friends after everything?" Her shrill laughter sent shivers down his spine. "Look at me, Deacon. Look at me and tell me you feel nothing."

Deacon turned, keeping his eyes on her face, and said, "I feel absolutely nothing for you, Aoibheann." Then he caught her top and threw it toward her before alighting toward the cliffs.

Vivienne had been right. Tonight was a mistake. What the hell had he been thinking?

Deacon felt like a total cad. He *was* a cad. No friendship was worth jeopardizing his relationship with Vivienne. If only he had figured that out *before* going swimming with Aoibheann.

By the time he returned to the beach, the tiki torches along the path were no longer lit. The soft blue light from the pool reflected off the walls of glass in the dark villa.

When he saw a woman lounging on one of the chairs, he cursed. "Aoibheann, I—"

"I'm pretty offended you think I look like that shark."

Not Aoibheann . . . *Nicola*.

"Shouldn't you be in bed?" Deacon asked, dropping onto a chair next to her.

"I could ask you the same question." She saluted him with her glass of wine. "Did you and Aoibheann have *fun*?"

He grimaced and picked up the bottle. "Not particularly," he said before taking an uncomfortably large gulp.

Nicola took a slow sip, her eyes sharp despite the darkness. "Look, it's none of my business. But if I were Vivienne, I wouldn't put up with your shit."

"Excuse me?" he choked.

"You heard me. She already feels insecure enough without you swimming with that succubus. Stop thinking about your dick and focus on your girlfriend."

He leaned back in his chair and stared into the starry sky.

Nicola wasn't wrong.

"That's why it didn't work with us, and you know it. I really like Vivienne, and she may be willing to put up with a lot. But if you keep doing this, you may as well kiss your *relationship* goodbye."

"Nothing happened."

"If Vivienne doesn't believe you, then nothing you say is going to convince her otherwise."

Deacon sighed and lifted the bottle to his lips.

"Stop feeling sorry for yourself," she hissed, ripping the bottle out of his hands, "and go to bed."

Deacon glanced toward the dark glass at the end of the house and winced. "I'm afraid Aoibheann is in my room."

Nicola groaned. "You're the worst."

"No, I mean I'm *actually* afraid she's in there. I left her in the water and flew to the cliffs." It was the type of thing she would do to stir up trouble.

Nicola frowned, then reached for his hand. "Let's go."

"I'm better off sleeping on the couch."

"Don't worry," she grumbled, hauling him toward the bedroom. "I'll check under your bed for monsters."

THIRTY-ONE

"I should've let you drown."

Vivienne clutched the towel rail next to the bathroom sink until her heart returned to a normal rhythm. The last person she had expected to see standing beside her bed was a wraithlike blond Mermaid. "Get out of my room, Aoibheann."

The greenish tint to Aoibheann's platinum hair made her look like a ghost returning from a watery grave. "He's not yours—and he never will be."

"My relationship with Deacon is none of your business." Vivienne stepped over the clothes littered across the floor. Emily was going to kill her when she saw them in the morning.

"Relationship!" Aoibheann's laugh was as grating as it was musical. "Deacon Ashford, with his wandering green eyes, doesn't *do* relationships."

Emily turned over in her bed and murmured something unintelligible in her sleep.

"He does now."

"You have no idea what you're getting yourself into," Aoibheann said, retreating a step toward the open glass door. "He's one of the many Neverboys who will never grow up. He's going to use you the same way he used every other girl before you. And then he's going to move on to the next girl in line."

Closing her eyes, Vivienne pressed her fingers to her aching temples. "Get. *Out.*"

She didn't open them again until she heard the door slide closed. Stupid Mermaid with her stupid perfect body. What did she know? Deacon had grown up so much in the last year—Peter had said so himself. And he wasn't using Vivienne. They were in love.

As exhausted as she was, it took forever for her to fall asleep. She awoke with a start some time later, her legs tangled in the sheets.

It sounded like two people were talking outside her room. A guy and a girl. The more she tried to ignore them, the more she wanted to eavesdrop. Eventually, her curiosity got the better of her, and she ended up peering into the hallway. Empty. As were the kitchen and patio and living room. There was only darkness under the first three bedroom doors, but in the fourth room—Deacon's—the light was on.

The voices were coming from his room.

It was probably nothing. Vivienne needed to go back to bed and pretend that he wasn't in his room with another girl.

Why was her hand knocking on the door?

The voices inside grew louder.

"Deacon?" she called, knocking harder. "I need to talk to you."

The door opened, and the light inside burned her eyes.

Deacon's cologne permeated the air, strong but not over-powering. She tiptoed to the bed and pulled the netting aside in time to catch her boyfriend shoving a blond head beneath the covers.

"Dammit, Vivienne! You should've knocked."

She clutched her throat, gasping for air. This was worse than drowning. Her cry lodged in her chest and she couldn't . . . *breathe*.

Muffled giggles emerged from under the sheets. He nudged one of the lumps, and the laughter got louder.

"Did you come to join us?" he asked, the corners of his mouth curling into a wicked smile.

"*Us*?" She shook her head, sure she had misheard him.

Then he flipped over the duvet.

Aoibheann was wrapped around Deacon's torso; Nicola and Emily clung to his legs. There was a noise from behind her; Caoilfhionn and Gwen came out of the bathroom wearing matching black negligees.

"Get to the end of the queue, Vivienne," Deacon commanded, lacing his fingers behind his dark head and leaning back on a gold pillow.

She couldn't stop her feet from bringing her to stand in line behind Gwen. "I thought you loved me," she whimpered. Her stomach sank as Aoibheann climbed up Deacon's body until she was straddling his hips and kissing his neck . . . his jaw . . . his mouth . . . and he was kissing her back, and the floor felt like it was quicksand and it was going to swallow her and she couldn't stop it. Didn't want to stop it. She wanted to disappear.

Deacon stopped kissing Aoibheann long enough to laugh and say, "I loved them first."

Vivienne jerked upright in her bed, searching the darkness with tear-filled eyes. Emily's soft breathing whispered from the bed next to her.

There was no way she was going to get back to sleep after *that* dream.

Vivienne tiptoed down the hall and raised her hand to knock on Deacon's door. Just like in her dream, she thought she heard voices from inside. But she was probably paranoid from that nightmare. Before her hand connected with the wood, the door jerked open.

"Nicola?" she choked, stumbling into the far wall.

Nicola was wearing a black tank top and short gray shorts. She rolled her eyes, muttering, "You're on your own, Dash," before heading for the room she shared with Ethan.

Deacon hauled Vivienne into his bedroom, blocking the exit with his body when she tried to escape. "I know what this looks like," he rushed, holding his hands in front of him, "but I can explain."

He could explain why his ex was in his bedroom at four in the morning? This ought to be good.

"Go on then."

"All right." He dashed his hand through his hair and winced. "Nicola came in to make sure Aoibheann wasn't hiding in my room."

That was supposed to make her feel better? "Why the heck would Aoibheann be in your room?"

His pained look shifted into a grimace. "Because she took off her top and—"

"She *what*?" Vivienne needed to get away from him. Aoibheann had been right; he just wanted to use her.

"No. Stop. Vivienne, listen to me." Deacon reached for her, but she jerked out of his grasp, knowing if he touched her, she wouldn't be able to think straight. "I thought Aoibheann understood that I wasn't interested in her because I'm with you," he explained, the words flooding out, "but she assumed that I wanted to, well, you know, but I didn't. She took off her top, but I threw it back at her and flew to the cliffs. I swear nothing happened."

Nothing besides Aoibheann getting freaking naked for him. "Did you kiss her?"

He shook his head. "No. Absolutely not."

Deacon had never lied to her before, but he had omitted plenty. "Did you *touch* her?" Even thinking of his hands on that stupid fish made Vivienne's blood boil.

"No. I would never—"

"Never what? Leave me to go off with some other girl? Because you just did."

Deacon rubbed the back of his neck and sighed before moving past her to drop onto the end of the sandy bed. "Until recently, many of my decisions have been dictated by my"—he cleared his throat—"well, *not* by my brain or my heart. I've changed a lot since I met you, but apparently Aoibheann didn't get the memo."

"You made me feel like I wasn't enough for you." Saying it aloud felt pathetic, but Deacon needed to know that the whole situation had crushed her confidence.

"Vivienne, you are everything to me. If I lost you, I honestly don't know . . . I don't know what I would do. All I can say is, I'm sorry. So very, very sorry."

She didn't want to lose him. Didn't want one bad decision to come between them. Still . . . "I'm *so* mad at you."

"I know." A sigh. "I'm mad at me too."

"I need to go to bed." Maybe after some sleep she would be able to think clearer.

When Deacon reached for her hand again, she didn't pull away. "I can imagine you're wrecked. Perhaps even too tired to go all the way back to your own room?" He bounced a little on the mattress, a small smile playing on his lips. "And I have this big empty bed right here."

"Is this an invitation from your head, heart, or the *dictator*?"

A laugh. "Can it be all three?"

As angry as Vivienne was, she didn't want to sleep alone.

She wanted to feel Deacon's arms around her, holding her, keeping the nightmares at bay. And, most importantly, she wanted to pretend like tonight had never happened.

Vivienne awoke the next morning to an empty bed and silence. The first thought that popped into her head was that maybe Deacon had gone off with Aoibheann again. Which was stupid. He'd told her before they'd fallen asleep that the Mermaids had already left. Good riddance. If she never saw another Mermaid again, it would still be too soon.

While she was in the kitchen grabbing a blueberry muffin, she caught sight of Deacon and Ethan bobbing up and down in the waves. Emily and Nicola were already lounging in the sun chairs.

She went back to the bedroom she shared with Emily to find her bathing suit still damp and sandy from two nights earlier. The thought of putting it on—or getting into the ocean—made her shudder. Instead, she slipped into a pair of running shorts and a printed bandeau top. From her nightstand, she grabbed her sunglasses and a paperback romance she had bought at the airport.

The air outside was warm and muggy, but the sky was cloudless and blue. Vivienne followed the tiki-torch-lined path to where her friends were enjoying their last day on the island.

"It's about time you woke up," Emily said, patting the empty sun lounger next to her. Lyle was face-down on the far chair with a T-shirt over his head.

Vivienne kicked off her flip flops. The sand was hot on her feet before she climbed onto the free chair. "What's wrong with him?" she asked, nodding toward her foster brother.

A muffled, "I'm never drinking again," emerged from beneath Lyle's T-shirt.

"Turns out drinking with Mermaids is nearly as bad as swimming with them," Emily muttered.

Vivienne wasn't sure she agreed. If Deacon had been drinking with Aoibheann, they would have stayed at the house where there were witnesses instead of going off on their own, under the romantic moon, and—

No. She couldn't go down that rabbit hole. Deacon had sworn nothing had happened. And she trusted him.

Slipping on her sunglasses, Vivienne watched her boyfriend swim toward the shore. Deacon shoved his wet hair back from where it had fallen over his forehead and jogged up the beach toward her.

Broad shoulders and toned torso and tanned skin and lean waist. *Seriously.* Guys shouldn't look like that. It wasn't fair. She was going to have to get him to start eating more carbs or something. He looked too good.

Geez, it was hot. Definitely the hottest day so far that week. And if Vivienne didn't stop staring at Deacon, she was going to turn into a puddle of goo. It took a lot of effort, but she forced herself to look down at the forgotten book lying open in her lap.

"Good morning." Deacon dripped water on the edge of her chair when he leaned in for a quick kiss. His trunks were the same color as the foliage. "How did you sleep?"

"Okay, except *someone* stole all the covers."

He chuckled. "You stole them first."

"Ugh! It's hot," Lyle groaned, sitting up and throwing his shirt into the sand. "I'm getting in."

Emily shouted for him to wait up and followed Lyle to the water. Vivienne was really glad they were getting along again.

"No swimming today?" Deacon asked, tugging on the

hem of her shorts as he lifted her legs and sat down, settling her feet onto his lap.

"I'm sticking to dry land for now." Maybe forever.

Beside them, Nicola was quietly smoothing coconut-scented tanning oil over her arms and legs. When she finished, she offered Vivienne the bottle. Before Vivienne could grab it, Deacon plucked it from Nicola's hand and said he'd do it for her.

"I can do it myself," she told him.

"Then what excuse would I have to touch you?"

"You don't need one."

He squeezed some into his hand, then set the bottle upright in the sand. Starting with the tops of her sandy feet, Deacon rubbed the slick liquid onto her skin. The way his hands glided over her shins and around her calves and up to her knees made the fireflies in her stomach quiver. When he ran out, he raised his eyes to hers and arched his brows. "It'd be a shame to have a tan line right here," he said, tracing the shiny line above her knee.

"Such a shame," she whispered, nudging the bottle closer to him.

His smile was smug as he drizzled oil onto her thighs. With slow, strong strokes, he massaged it into her skin, higher and higher, and when his fingertips danced beneath the hem of her shorts, she—

"Do I need to leave?" Nicola clipped.

Vivienne had completely forgotten that Nicola had been sitting two chairs down. And from the redness creeping up Deacon's neck, so had he.

"I'm going to . . . um . . . get back in," he stuttered, handing Vivienne the bottle before walking stiffly down the beach.

Ethan loped out of the water, said something to Deacon, and continued to where Vivienne and Nicola sat. "Will you judge the contest?" he asked Nicola.

Nicola didn't even look up from her book when she told him, "No."

Ethan turned to Vivienne, hope brightening his blue eyes. "What about you?"

"Sure." Whatever "the contest" was should take her mind off the overwhelming sensations coursing through her body. She watched Deacon and Ethan fly twice as high as the palm trees, hold their positions, then drop with their legs tucked against their chests.

They landed in sync with two identical splashes.

"You're judging the splash," Nicola explained, flipping to the next page in her book.

The two guys resurfaced and turned toward the shore. Vivienne voted for Ethan so she didn't seem biased. Deacon dunked Ethan before round two. Emily joined in at round six; Deacon and Ethan picked up Lyle for rounds seven and nine.

"If you're tired, just keep picking Dash," Nicola said, reaching for a bottle of water by her chair. "Ethan will get pissed and not want to play anymore."

Sure enough, after three rounds of Deacon winning, Ethan gave up and grabbed a football from the beach to play catch with the others.

It was the first time Vivienne had been alone with Nicola since the incident in Paul's office. And after what had happened the night before, she wasn't feeling very comfortable with the silence. "It's so beautiful here."

"Yep." The pages in Nicola's book rustled as she turned them.

"Are you looking forward to going back to Kensington?"

"I'm going to London with Ethan for the trial."

Oh, right. The trial.

"Um . . ."

The book snapped closed. In one fluid motion, Nicola twisted toward Vivienne and shoved her glasses to her forehead. "Is there something you want to say to me, Vivienne?"

Was there something she wanted to say? "I guess, I want you to know that I'm not mad at you for what happened in Paul's office."

"You mean when you got kicked out?" Nicola's eyebrows came together when Vivienne nodded. "Why in the world would you be mad at me? You did something wrong and got punished for it. I was only following orders."

Everything Nicola said was true, but it still made Vivienne feel like crap. She opened her book and stared blankly at the text. Would it be cowardly to pretend her stomach hurt and hide in the bedroom until Deacon was finished swimming?

"Sorry," Nicola groaned. "That sounded bitchy. I hated doing it, but I knew Dash wouldn't let it be forever. How are you feeling after everything?"

"My throat is still sore, but my stomach feels a lot better."

"I wasn't talking about the near-drowning."

Right. She was talking about Deacon going off with a Mermaid. "I'm okay." She was, wasn't she? "Still a bit irritated, but okay."

"A *bit?*" Nicola snorted. "I'd kill Ethan if he left me to go off with his ex for any reason."

Wait. Aoibheann was Deacon's *ex?* Why hadn't he mentioned it?

It didn't matter. Vivienne had forgiven him. It was in the past.

"We talked about it last night. He knows what he did was wrong, and he's sorry."

"He's only sorry until it happens again." Nicola pulled her glasses back into place and picked up her book. "Dash has never done the whole *boyfriend* thing. He's great, but you need to remember that he's not the only guy in the world.

Don't let him take advantage of the way you feel and use it to walk all over you."

Images from Vivienne's nightmare invaded her mind. The way she had fallen in line behind the other girls because Deacon had told her to. It had been a dream—but also the reality of dating someone with such a promiscuous past.

Was that what Vivienne was doing? Letting Deacon take advantage of her?

She didn't think so. He had forgiven her for Alex—and she had actually kissed Alex. All Deacon had done was swim with Aoibheann. Forgiving someone wasn't the same as letting them walk all over you. Was it?

THIRTY-TWO

The sun had been swallowed by the horizon, but residual heat lifted from the patio, tangling with the breeze.

Deacon was waiting for Vivienne on one of the low chairs beside the pool, wearing dark trunks . . . and nothing else. Her mouth felt dry, and her stomach was doing that thing it always did when he smiled at her. All she could hear was the shuffling of palm fronds and rhythmic waves kissing the shore. Her heart beat double-time when Deacon stood and came over to her.

"Where's everyone else?" she asked.

"Walking on the beach," he said, teasing his hands up her waist. "Tonight's our last night, and I'm not sharing you."

After the incident with the tanning oil this morning, the thought of being alone with him made her fireflies go into overdrive. She knew she would never again smell coconut-scented anything without thinking of his hands sliding up her thighs.

"Should we get in?" he suggested.

Vivienne hadn't been in the water since the Mermaids had shown up. "As long as you promise not to let me drown," she said, only half teasing.

"Don't worry." He laced his fingers with hers and brought her to the pool's edge. "I'm not going to let you go."

She sat on the side and dipped her legs into the warm, clear water. Deacon lowered himself in before moving to stand between her knees.

He had the most beautiful eyes. So clear and green, with flecks of gold like sparks. She traced his dark brows, high cheekbones, the strong line of his jaw, his mouth . . . She *really* loved his mouth.

He kissed her fingertip and smiled when she shuddered.

The vicious purple scar below his collarbone left her shuddering for a different reason.

His wet hands left drops on her skin as he dragged them from her knees to her waist. "I've been doing a good deal of thinking lately."

"About?"

"Before I answer that, I want you to know that I love you."

Oh no . . . What if this wasn't a *good* conversation? What if he wanted her alone because he was going to break up with her? *Wait.* That was dumb. He just said he loved her.

"I love you too," she said warily.

"You're sure?"

She nodded.

"Then to answer your question, I've been *thinking*," he said, his lips lifting into a seductive smile, "about the best way to show you exactly *how much* I love you."

Oh my gosh. Oh my gosh.

Breathe.

Vivienne focused on expanding and contracting her lungs.

This was it. It was actually happening. She was ready. So, *so* ready.

She couldn't think straight and her body started tingling and—why was he reaching into his pocket? *Wait* . . . He wanted to do it *here*?

The fireflies in her stomach died. She didn't want her first time to be on a hard stone patio, worrying that her friends would come back and catch them in the act. "Not *here*," she choked.

His eyebrows drew together, and he frowned down at his trunks. "Why not?"

Why not? *Seriously*? "I'm afraid someone's going to see us."

"Why should that matter? They're going to find out tomorrow anyway."

"*How*?" Would she look different? Would she walk funny? "I'm not going to tell them." Although Emily would probably get it out of her eventually.

"Then you're not ready," he sighed. A glint of gold flashed in Deacon's hand before he shoved it into his pocket.

"Wait!" She dragged his hand back from the water. *Oh my gosh. Oh my gosh.* "Is that a *ring*?" A petite gold band winked at her from his palm; its dimpled texture reminded her of a thimble.

"What did you think it was?"

She shook her head.

"Vivienne?"

"I thought it was a condom, okay?" Could a girl die of embarrassment?

"A con—" His mouth snapped shut and he shook his head. "As you can see, it is not a condom." His smile faded as he spun the ring between his fingers. "I believe we can both agree that I've been a shit boyfriend. I've never fully committed to anyone, and I think that, even with you, I've been holding back. But I don't want to hold back anymore.

"Vivienne, I cannot imagine ever loving anyone the way I love you. And if you agree to marry me, I swear to commit every part of myself to you . . . if you're willing to do the same for me."

Holy. Crap. Deacon wanted to marry her. Like . . . for real. He had a ring, and he was asking if she wanted to marry him, and she did. She *really* did. But it was insane to even consider his proposal when she was only nineteen, right? And Neverland didn't do divorce, so if she and Deacon decided to do this, he would be her forever.

She touched his scar and thought of her impending forgetfulness.

But it wouldn't be forever—not really. Not for her.

Did Deacon *really* want to tie himself to someone who may not know his name in a few years?

"And when I lose my memory?" she asked, telling herself that she wouldn't be disappointed if he changed his mind.

"We'll make enough memories beforehand to last for a thousand lifetimes. I'll take so many pictures and videos, you'll go mad."

She had no doubt he would.

"And when you forget who you are," he went on, tracing her lips with his damp fingers, "I'll tell you about all our adventures together. That you are my wife, and the woman I adore. And when you forget who I am"—he grinned—"I'll tell you my name is Theo Swanson, a reformed jewel thief from Essex. Or Hunter Atkinson the third, the youngest of four sons to a disgraced earl from some obscure town in the midlands. I haven't decided which."

"You're ridiculous."

"I know." He chuckled. The blue light from the pool danced along the sharp planes of his face, flirting with the shadows. "And then I'll sweep you off of your feet again and again and again. And, if I'm really lucky, you'll let me kiss you with my hot British mouth for all of eternity."

A giddy giggle rose from her chest. "Are you ever going to let me live that down?"

"Are you ever going to give me an answer?"

"I'll marry you on one condition," she said, pressing a kiss to the corner of his lips.

"What's that?"

"You have to swear that you'll always tell me your real name."

"Deacon Elias Ashford it is," he mumbled before bringing his mouth to hers. She poured every ounce of love and joy and fear into their kiss, drawing from his strength, taking solace in knowing that, whatever was going to happen, Deacon would be at her side through it all.

When he pulled away and reached for her fingers, his hands were trembling. "This was my grandmother's, ring. You're meant to wear it on the smallest finger on your right hand."

Plop.

Vivienne stopped breathing.

Deacon swore and dove under the water.

Vivienne jumped in after him. Her hair floated in her face, and her eyes burned as she scoured the bottom of the pool for her engagement ring. Deacon reached for something near the drain and gave her an underwater thumbs up.

When they resurfaced, they were both laughing so hard, they were gasping.

"Take this bloody thing before I lose it again," he muttered, slipping the cool metal onto her finger.

"You're *so* romantic."

"Excuse me? I think I've been quite romantic up until that last part." He lifted her hand to his lips and considered her smallest finger. "Now," he began, his teeth flashing when he smiled at her, "shall we discuss what you *thought* I was suggesting?"

The fireflies in her stomach surged, their wings beating double-time with her heart. "How about we talk about it in your room?"

Deacon was out of the water and hauling her from the pool before she could blink. She giggled when he lifted her into his arms and threw her over his shoulder. "I feel like I should point out how romantic I'm being right now. Carrying you across the threshold and all that."

"So romantic. I've always fantasized about being treated like a sack of potatoes," she teased, watching his feet leave wet footprints on the stones. He didn't put her down until the exterior door to his room was shut and the privacy glass obscured the palm trees from view.

The air stirred by the leaf-shaped ceiling fan made her shiver. Vivienne shifted in the puddle forming on the tiles, more nervous than she'd ever been in her life. "We should probably change into dry clothes?"

His dark eyebrows raised, and the corners of his lips crept upwards. "Or we could take these off."

Off. Right. "I should at least dry my hair." She lifted her hand to unstick her hair from her shoulders. "We don't want to sleep on a damp bed."

"I was hoping we wouldn't be going to sleep for a while."

She swallowed and forced a smile.

Deacon sighed. "What's wrong?"

"I'm sorry. I'm just *really* nervous."

"Then we don't have to do anything." He went into the bathroom and came back wearing dry shorts and carrying two towels.

Vivienne dried her body, scrunched her hair, and wrapped the towel around her like a fluffy shield. Her bag sat on the floor next to the bed, but the thought of changing into more clothes, creating more barriers, didn't appeal to her either.

Deacon threw his damp shorts over the bathroom door and used the second towel to clean up the puddles.

"What if . . . " She stopped when he looked up at her. *Just say it.* "What if I *want* to do something?"

The way he rocketed to his feet made her giggle. "Yes. Whatever you want."

"Okay. Um. I'm not exactly sure what to do. That sounds dumb. I mean, I know what to do, it's just that I haven't done it before, so—"

"Vivienne? Breathe."

She did.

"Why don't we just take things slow?" he suggested, reaching for her towel and loosening the corner tucked beneath her arm. "And if you feel uncomfortable at any stage, tell me."

She nodded.

His thumb brushed across her lips. "Preferably with words."

"Y-yes. I'll tell you."

Deacon traced the lines of her top, trailing his fingers down her neck, over her collarbone, and along the sides of her breasts. His warm touch continued down her ribs until his hands came to rest on her hips. She dragged in halting breaths as her body caught fire. One of his hands slipped around to her bottom, and he pressed her closer to him. His other hand danced back up her ribs until his thumb brushed across her top.

And. She. Stopped. Breathing.

He must have noticed, because he dropped his hand.

She caught his wrist and brought his hand back to her body. He groaned against her mouth and caressed the damp material covering her. If it felt this good *over* her swimsuit—

"I didn't double-knot it," she whispered, not sure she had the nerve to tell him exactly what she wanted him to do.

Deacon found the string tied at her back and tugged. When he did the same to the string at her neck, the material fell away.

She squeezed her eyes shut, too embarrassed to look at his face.

"Vivienne?"

Her eyes flashed open, and for a second, she forgot she was topless. When she remembered, she folded her arms over her chest. "What's wrong?"

"*Wrong?*" he choked. "I'm in my bedroom staring at my half-naked fiancée, trying my best not to lose my bloody mind. There is absolutely nothing wrong. But" —his throat bobbed when he swallowed—"I need to know if you want to stop. And if you do want to stop, it's totally fine. I'll just need to run to the bathroom for a . . . um . . . a few minutes."

Biting her lip, she forced her arms back to her side. "I don't want to stop."

"Oh, thank god," Deacon breathed, closing the gap between them. His chest pressed against hers as his lips grazed from her collarbone to the shell of her ear. One of his arms wrapped around her waist, and he urged her toward the bed. Clinging to his neck, she fell back, dragging him onto the mattress with her.

"I love you," Deacon whispered, his eyes burning into hers as his hands seared the skin over her ribs. With damp hair falling across his forehead, he nudged her legs apart so he could fit his hips between them. Her nerves tried to take over, but then he kissed her, slow and patient, before trailing kisses down her neck to her throat and lower still. Her back arched, and a moan escaped her lips, letting him know *exactly* what she thought of what he was doing with his tongue.

She couldn't think straight. Didn't want to. She just knew

that she never wanted him to stop as she threaded her fingers through his damp hair, keeping his head in place. His chuckle vibrated against her chest and he took his time exploring every inch of newly exposed, uncharted territory.

Then he brought his lips back to hers, and his hips started moving, slowly at first, matching his kiss. She met him with her tongue and her hips, rocking and succumbing to every sensation, allowing the fire building inside of her to steal her senses and drown her fears. Deacon fell to his elbows, cursing and burying his face in her neck.

Her heels dug into his back, pulling him closer as he picked up his pace.

Drawing her hands down his body, she found the waistband of his shorts. Her fingers slipped beneath the elastic. When he stilled his movements, she whimpered. "Why did you stop?"

"We're going slow, remember?" he ground out, his breathing ragged.

"Maybe we should go a little faster."

He pulled back to look into her eyes, his brows furrowed. "Are you sure?"

Vivienne nodded.

"Words."

"Very sure."

Deacon's lips curled into an arrogant smile as he reached for the ties at the side of her bikini bottoms and tugged.

THIRTY-THREE

Vivienne slept in Deacon's arms, but he couldn't find the will to do the same. When it came to women in his past, there had been one barrier none of them could break through: his aversion to commitment.

Now he found himself lying next to his fiancée.

And for the first time he could remember, Deacon felt content.

He kissed a freckle on Vivienne's sun-tanned back, and her lips lifted into a dreamy smile. Every so often, her impossibly dark lashes fluttered as her eyes searched some invisible horizon. He hoped she found what she was looking for.

"It's time to wake up," he said an hour later, hating to disturb her when she looked so peaceful. But the boat would be there in a bit, and he didn't want to waste their last few hours on the island sleeping.

"I don't want to," she whined, arching her back into him

as she stretched. The light sheet wrapped around her body slipped lower.

Deacon lifted his mobile from the bedside locker and switched on the camera. He frowned at himself on the screen and tried to flatten his hair. It desperately needed a cut. Then he pressed the red button. "This stunning creature, wearing not a stitch, has agreed to marry me." He pretended to flash the camera toward her, but actually winked at himself instead.

Vivienne yanked the covers over her head. "Off. *Now.*"

Her irritation made him chuckle. "I cannot imagine why she said yes, but here's proof." He tugged her right hand so that it was in the frame. His grandmother's ring fit like it had been made for Vivienne's dainty fingers.

"The engagement is off if you don't get that phone out of my face." There was a smile in her voice.

"She's terribly cross before breakfast," he told the camera. "But I plan on marrying her anyway. Vivienne?"

She peeked from beneath the sheets. "What?"

"Tell the camera how excited you are to marry me."

"*So* excited."

"Is there anything else you'd like to remind your future self about this morning? Or perhaps *last night*?"

"Off!"

"All right, all right." He dropped his mobile onto the mattress. "Now that you're awake, we need to discuss meeting with Peter. I'd like to do it tomorrow, but you'd have to come with me to London."

When she agreed, he kissed the tip of her nose and suggested she grab some breakfast while he organized her flight. Vivienne wrapped the sheet around her shoulders like a cape and dragged her bag into the bathroom. He brought his mobile outside into the balmy air.

The morning sun glistened off the pool and danced in the undulating waves.

It took ten minutes to book a seat for Vivienne on his flight from Atlanta later that evening.

If the meeting with Peter went well, he could ask for Leadership to approve their marriage after the trial was over. They had done things backwards by getting engaged first, but he figured asking late was better than not asking at all.

And he was going to marry Vivienne no matter what, so they could go and shite if they had a problem with it.

When he went back into his room, the disarray made him frown.

But seeing Vivienne's bikini top on his floor brought back a rush of memories, and he took a picture of it. He couldn't wait to remind her in explicit detail of exactly what had happened.

His stomach rumbled, so he dragged on a shirt and went into the kitchen.

Vivienne was spreading jam on her toast. Ethan sat at the island, eating from a comically oversized bowl. Glass clinked together as Nicola cleared empty beer and wine bottles from the table.

"Geez, Ethan. Do you think you have enough?" Vivienne asked, snagging a grape from his bowl.

"Takes twice as much of this healthy junk to fill me up," Ethan grumbled, stuffing in another bite of fresh fruit. Nicola must have been trying to get him to eat better.

Deacon said good morning to his friends before crossing to Vivienne, kissing the top of her head, and dropping the last two slices of bread into the toaster.

"Why do you look so tired?" Ethan made a face as he removed a chunk of mango from his bowl. "You were already in bed when we got back from the beach."

"Doesn't mean I was sleeping." Deacon winked at Vivienne and snagged the mango.

She swatted his chest, her cheeks flushed.

"You guys missed a good night." Nicola brought a damp

315

cloth from the sink to wipe the table. From the looks of it, someone had spilled a good deal of drink at the far end.

"You may have had a good night," he said, reaching for Vivienne's hand and twisting the gold band around her finger, "but I can guarantee our night was better."

"*Holy shit!*" Ethan shoved away from the counter. "Did you guys get *engaged*?"

The cloth in Nicola's hand fell to the floor.

"*Engaged?*" Emily came running into the room with a towel around her hair. "Who's engaged?"

Deacon kissed Vivienne's hand. "We are."

"*Ohmygosh, ohmygosh!*" Emily's exuberant hug nearly knocked Vivienne to the floor. "Ahhh! I am *so* happy for you!"

"What're we happy about?" Lyle asked from the hallway, a towel draped across his bare shoulders.

Emily grabbed Vivienne's hand and waved it for her. "Vivienne and Deacon got engaged last night! Ahhh!"

Lyle froze, and his eyes bulged. "Seriously, Viv?"

"Seriously, Lyle." Did Vivienne's smile waver, or was Deacon imagining things?

Before Deacon could ask her about it, Ethan caught his sleeve and dragged him outside. He let go when they got to the patio but continued stalking toward the sea.

Deacon assumed he was meant to follow.

The moment Ethan's feet hit the sand, he whirled around. "What the hell, Dash?"

"I believe the appropriate response is 'congratulations.'"

"Maybe if I was *happy* for you. But I'm pretty sure you've lost your damn mind. You're twenty-six years into eternity and you just asked a teenager to get married."

Eternity? Hadn't Ethan been the one rambling on and on about how nothing was promised? How Deacon was too hung up on immortality? "Tell me again how *eternal* my life is," Deacon growled, wrenching the neck of his T-shirt aside, forcing Ethan to look at the unsightly scar beneath.

"Okay. Fine. You got shot. But you survived, didn't you? And if you avoid getting shot again, you're going to live for a long-ass time." Ethan threw his arm toward the house. "Is this because she's not putting out?"

"Say that again, and I'll break your jaw."

"Geez. Relax. I'm sorry, okay? It's just, you've never gone this far for a bit of—"

If Ethan said one more word, he was going to—

"For a girl," Ethan rushed, his hands raised in silent apology. "I can't think of one good reason for you to throw your life away."

"The woman I love isn't going to remember who I am in a few years, so instead of pissing about playing games, I've decided to have a life with Vivienne while I can."

Ethan's hands fell to his side. "Shit. I'm sorry, Dash. I didn't know."

"That's because it's none of your bloody business!" Deacon hoped Vivienne would forgive him for sharing her secret. "Don't tell anyone, all right? She doesn't want it getting out."

"I won't, I won't," Ethan promised, raking his hand through his hair. "But are you sure you know what you're doing? You've seen the forgetful."

"I know what I'm doing," Deacon said, looking back toward the villa and watching Vivienne laughing with Emily. Deacon was one of the lucky ones who had found his forever.

THIRTY-FOUR

The erratic hustle and bustle of London Heathrow felt unnatural after the joyous solitude on the island. Babies screamed at parents, protesting their confinement; tardy travelers raced with rolling bags bumping along behind them. It felt like every single person walked—or ran —with a purpose.

Everyone except Vivienne. She drifted along behind Deacon, watching and listening and taking it all in. If she had been able to sleep on the plane, maybe her head wouldn't feel like a balloon without a string.

She was just nervous about asking Peter Pan for permission to marry his only grandson. It had nothing to do with Lyle's reaction to the news of her engagement. Or at least that's what she told herself.

Lyle had actually had the nerve to tell her she was an idiot for wanting to get married at nineteen. And then he had called her fiancée a prick.

Deacon had supported Lyle's nomination with Leadership.

And let Lyle move into his home.

And tag along to Peter Pan's private island.

Deacon wasn't the one being a prick.

Vivienne linked her arm with Deacon's and let him propel her toward the exit. The cold air outside held the kind of dampness that settled into a person's bones. It wasn't raining but felt like it could start at any minute.

Deacon hailed one of the bulbous black cabs waiting in a line. The driver, sitting behind a steering wheel on the wrong side of the car, asked where they were off to. Deacon muttered a convoluted address; the man bobbed his bald head and pressed a button on the meter.

"What time are we meeting Peter?" Vivienne asked, settling in the back seat and closing her eyes.

"I thought we'd go straight away."

Good. She wanted to get this over with and then get some sleep. Deacon had suggested they stay in his mom's apartment until Mary Ashford arrived for the Leadership meeting. Vivienne was looking forward to seeing where he had grown up, but *not* seeing his mom.

A red double-decker bus pulled up beside them at a stoplight. If someone would have told her last year that after fourteen months in Neverland she would be in London seeking marriage approval, she would have laughed.

The gold band felt heavy on her finger. How long would it take for her to get used to wearing it?

"You look worried." Deacon put his hand over hers. "You're not having second thoughts, are you?"

Second thoughts? If anything, she wanted to marry him more than she had when he first asked her. Knowing Deacon would be at her side for eternity made what she was facing seem more bearable.

"I'm actually more worried Peter's going to tell us we *can't* get married," she confessed.

"Peter isn't going to say no."

The way he emphasized Peter's name made Vivienne wonder if Deacon thought the rest of Leadership would have a different response.

Their driver cut in and out of gaps in traffic that seemed way too small for his cab. At one point, she was sure they were going to lose their bumper to another car, but they squeaked by without a tap.

When the cab slowed for yet another bout of gridlock traffic, Deacon unbuckled his seatbelt. "We're here," he said with a smile. A moment later, the driver whipped into an empty spot, one tire on the sidewalk and the rear of the car blocking the line of cars behind them.

Vivienne hadn't given much thought to what Peter Pan's house should look like. But if she had, she would have imagined it looking exactly like the skinny three-story house painted a muted yellow with white cornices and a floral finial in front of her.

"It looks like a fairy tale." She could imagine the Darling children flying out of the upstairs window to begin their own adventure in Neverland.

"It's just a building," Deacon said, retrieving their bags from the trunk.

"You said the same thing when I got to Kensington." And he had been so very, very wrong.

Iron railings shaped like fancy spears lined a small, manicured front lawn, herding them through a low gate and up a short walkway of black and white geometric tiles.

Deacon banged on the door with a heavy brass knocker, rattling the fragile stained-glass panels. A milky curtain in one of the lower bay windows shifted, then fell back into place.

"Good morning, Deacon," the older man she recognized

from the funeral greeted on the second knock. "Vivienne, welcome to London." His dove-gray button down was tucked neatly inside navy blue trousers with sharp pleats.

"Thanks." Vivienne adjusted the wrinkled sweatshirt she had bought on their layover in Atlanta. She had packed for the beach, not the UK.

"Good morning, Donovan," Deacon said. "Is Grandad in?"

"He'll be down momentarily. Why don't you wait for him in the study?" Donovan reached for their bags and set them on the patchwork tiles in the foyer. Vivienne followed Deacon past a parlor with an eclectic mix of ornate, Victorian-era furniture alongside more modern pieces. At the end of a short hallway, a mahogany staircase climbed upward around a crystal chandelier.

To her left, a hallway led to what looked like a kitchen; to her right was a six-paneled door.

Deacon opened it and went inside.

From the windowsills to the ornate plaster coving, Peter's study was filled with Charlie Bells and memorabilia from the numerous books and movies dedicated to his fairy tale existence.

He had decorative plates on stands, marketing cutouts featuring the lost boys in animal-skin onesies, and framed newspaper advertisements with cocky Peter Pans promoting every product imaginable. Vivienne sniffed a boxed bar of Peter Pan beauty soap that smelled like baby powder.

"I swear he has more junk every time I visit," Deacon muttered, lifting one of the cherub-faced porcelain figurines lined up in front of the more modern plastic toys, "and there's never a speck of dust on any of it."

The hinges on the door creaked, and Vivienne dropped the soap back onto the shelf. A woolly gray dog padded into the room.

Peter Pan had a dog?

It was such a normal thing, owning a pet. She didn't know why the fact surprised her so much.

"What's her name?" she asked, sweeping hair out of the dog's guileless brown eyes.

"That's Nana." At hearing her name, Nana nudged Deacon's fingers with her head, and he obediently scratched behind her ears. "All Peter's dogs are called Nana."

Of course they were.

"Where'd Peter get all of this stuff?" she asked him, studying the framed movie posters hanging beside the window.

"Mostly from Tootles," a voice answered from behind her.

Vivienne whirled around to find Peter standing in the doorway. Nana followed him to his desk and plopped down at his feet. "He found it amusing to come into my home and have them displayed like I'm some sort of narcissist. eBay was his favorite pastime for over a decade."

Vivienne would have loved to meet Peter's best friend. Unfortunately, he was in Scotland with the rest of the forgetful PAN.

"I trust you had a pleasant flight," Peter continued.

"It was long, but uneventful." Deacon reached for her hand and gave her fingers a reassuring squeeze.

"Why don't you sit. It looks like poor Vivienne is ready to fall over," Peter said, settling into his overstuffed wing-back chair. "Tea is on its way."

Vivienne and Deacon sank onto the couch. Even after being on a plane all night, she still found her legs sighing in relief.

"Vivienne, I've arranged a flat for you at Harrow for as long as you need it." Peter picked up one of three Montblanc pens scattered on his desk and tapped it like a metronome against the edge.

Sliding his hand onto Vivienne's knee, Deacon said, "She's staying with me, Grandad."

"Are you sure that's wise?" Peter grabbed a second pen to perform an elaborate drumroll. After hitting his Tiffany lamp hi-hat, he pointed his "drumsticks" at Deacon. "Your mother arrives tomorrow morning."

"An apartment sounds great," Vivienne rushed. As much as she didn't want to stay by herself in a strange apartment, it sounded a lot better than staying in a house with Deacon's mom.

"Brilliant. Now, on to more important matters." Peter kicked his knockoff sneakers onto the corner of the desk. "I see Miss Dunn is wearing some beautiful new jewelry."

"She is." Deacon's broad smile eased some of the tension in her stomach.

"This calls for a celebration." Peter reached into his desk drawer and withdrew a sleeve of brown cookies with chocolate on top. He took two for himself, then handed the pack to Deacon. Deacon took one and offered the sleeve to Vivienne.

Chocolate and—

She broke it apart and sniffed.

Oranges? Peter and Deacon looked at her expectantly, so she took a small bite. It was soft and dry on one side, crunchy and chocolatey on the other, and squishy and orange in the middle. She liked chocolate as much as the next girl, but the combination was strange.

"I'm not sure I can marry you if you don't like Jaffa Cakes," Deacon said, his voice flat. He finished his cookie and withdrew a second one.

Vivienne shoved the rest in her mouth and smiled, determined to swallow it. "It's *sooo* good."

He laughed, then turned to Peter. "We'd like to go for approval as soon as possible."

The cookie lodged in her throat. When Deacon had said they were going to talk to Peter, he hadn't mentioned anything about speaking with Leadership. She had assumed they'd enjoy their engagement for at least a little while before actually getting married.

Dropping his feet, Peter sat forward in his chair, knocking over one of the figurines on his desk. "You need to wait. The last thing you want is for Leadership to think you're rushing into this."

"And if we don't want to wait?" Deacon asked, tapping the cookie against his knee.

"Then I cannot guarantee you will get the answer you're looking for."

"Surely once they understand our situation—"

"What situation?" Vivienne demanded.

Deacon turned to her, his dark brows drawn together. "Your levels."

He knew how she felt about people knowing her diagnosis. The last thing she wanted was anyone's pity. "We're not telling anyone about my nGh."

"Why not?"

Peter stood and started for the door, mumbling, "I'm going to find the tea."

Once he was gone, Vivienne searched Deacon's pinched expression. "I told you that I don't want everyone to know," she said carefully. "They're just going to feel sorry for me or think that my forgetfulness is the only reason we're getting married."

"I'm marrying you because I love you."

"I know that," she sighed, wiping her sweaty palms on her leggings, "but it feels like you're rushing because of my diagnosis. We have time. Let's just wait like Peter said."

"You've changed your mind, haven't you?"

"No, that's not it at all."

"Then why does it matter if we get married tomorrow or ten years from now?"

"Peter just said we wouldn't get approved."

"If you think I care whether or not Leadership approves us, then you don't know me at all."

In the course of a week, Deacon had gone from swimming with Aoibheann to getting engaged to Vivienne to wanting to get married.

Was he *really* that anxious to marry her?

Or was *he* the one having second thoughts?

"Deacon, I want to wait."

He gave her a tight nod. When she reached for him, he pulled away. "Perhaps we should just call the whole thing off."

"Stop acting like a baby. You had time to sit around and think about asking me to marry you, and I had all of thirty seconds to give you my answer." When he opened his mouth, she put her hand across his lips. "Before you say anything, I *don't* regret saying yes, but I would like a bit of time to let it all sink in."

THIRTY-FIVE

The meeting had been a complete disaster.

Why had Deacon expected it to go any other way? He glanced at Vivienne from across the back seat of the cab. The only way she could have been further away was if she opened the door. Her face was angled toward the window, and she hadn't spoken to him since they had left Peter's.

I want to wait.

Deacon had never been very good at waiting.

And waiting gave people time to change their minds.

Vivienne was far too good for him, and it was only a matter of time before she figured it out too.

Plus, the longer they waited, the more time he had to screw things up.

Glancing back at Vivienne, he wondered if he had screwed up too much already.

He placed his hand palm-up on the empty seat between them and left it there, a silent peace offering. Vivienne's head barely moved. A minute later, she laced her fingers with his. She was still looking out the window, but it was a start.

The black hackney cab dropped them off beside a single-story limestone house with arched doors and windows. Beyond the house, an ancient set of iron gates sat between two towering stone walls.

An old man with deep wrinkles and a bristly white mustache hobbled out of the gatehouse. "Apologies for missing your funeral," he grumbled, his words flowing together in a gravelly mix of English and incoherent mumbles. "Can't stand the bloody things."

Deacon had always been fond of the gatekeeper at Harrow; Martin used to give him sweets when he was little. "It's quite all right," Deacon told him. "I decided to skip it myself."

"Still bringing in strays, I see." Martin dropped a pinch of tobacco into a scrap of rolling paper.

"This is Vivienne." Deacon wanted to call her his fiancée but refrained. Before they left, Peter had pulled him aside and asked that he keep the news of their engagement a secret until after the trial. Deacon wasn't sure why it mattered, but he had agreed. "Martin has been our gatekeeper at Harrow for over fifty years, but he's never been inside the gates."

Martin's laugh was more a wheezing cough than a chuckle. "They don't pay me to go inside." He lit the cigarette; a puff of smoke lifted from his lips.

Deacon clucked his tongue and shook his head. "Those things are going to kill you."

"Who wants to live forever anyway?" Martin took a second drag, then reached inside his door. The gates jerked once, then eased open.

It would have been quicker to fly, but Deacon chose to walk down the long, serpentine driveway, dragging their two bags behind him. The sights and sounds of the outside world, teaming with oblivious outsiders, soon faded to nothing.

Between winter-barren branches rose a gothic style sandstone manor. The original facade had been a warm golden hue, but dampness and age had painted the walls black and gray. Fragments of the original color peeked beneath the rims of the eight chimneys that had always reminded Deacon of crooked hats.

Vivienne's lips lifted into a smile; she'd worn the same dreamy look when she had first arrived at Kensington.

Beside Harrow Hall was a quaint gray church with a fantastic rose window below its sword-like spire. In its shadow stood a smaller converted carriage house and a modern block of flats, looking as awkward as a teenager in a room full of distinguished fellows. Behind a second, much larger church sat an unassuming brick shed.

"*Two* churches?" Vivienne asked.

"St. Peter's Cathedral is used for Aviation." Peter had bought the area purely because of the cathedral. "Named before Grandad acquired the property. He claims it was fate."

Deacon reached for Vivienne's hand, but she stepped away.

"Peter uses the old library here at Harrow Hall as his office," he went on, trying to hide how much the slight bothered him. "Michael's Rest is this way."

They made their way through the campus to the flats. Deacon waved at those he knew as they passed, but kept up his pace to deter conversation. He didn't want to talk to anyone but Vivienne. And then he wanted to sleep.

The key in his hand dropped onto the bowing hardwood floor in the reception area outside Vivienne's ground-level flat. He snatched it up and jammed it into the lock.

The flats had been renovated since he had been there that

summer. The gray cabinets were new, as were the shiny kettle and granite countertops.

And the space was freezing.

After turning on the boiler in the hot press, the rads sprang to life. "What do you think?" he asked, watching Vivienne peer into the small fridge

"It's nice," Vivienne said, her dark hair swaying as she twirled to survey the space, "but it seems haunted."

Seems haunted.

Their relationship was up in the air and she wanted to talk about ghosts? He tried to think of a good segue to discuss their engagement, but the best he could come up with was: *Speaking of things that don't exist, let's talk about my patience.*

"Shall I check under the bed for ghosts?"

"Okay." She gave him the barest hint of a smile.

He strolled into a modest bedroom at the end of a short hallway. The duvet and pillowcases were crisp and white against a dark walnut headboard. The furniture was sparse: two bedside lockers and a matching armoire.

He supposed it would do for the time being. He didn't plan on staying long in London, and until he told his mother about the engagement, there was no way he was bringing Vivienne there.

Vivienne stepped into the room, and he squatted down to check beneath the bed for signs of the supernatural. "No ghosts under here," he said, standing and straightening his jeans.

"What about in there?" Vivienne gestured toward the armoire.

There was nothing in the armoire but a rack of empty hangers. "Ghost-free as well."

"Good." She shivered.

He tapped his fingers on the rad beneath the window; it

was still cold. There could be something wrong with the heating; he'd have to call someone to fix it.

Vivienne sat on the edge of the bed, looking small and fragile and unhappy.

Enough was enough. Deacon wanted to figure this out before anyone else learned of their engagement in case she wanted to call the whole thing off. Then he could move to the island and live in solitude for the next few decades. "Vivienne, I—"

"I'm really tired." She yawned and rubbed her eyes. "Can we talk about it later?"

He wanted to beg or shout or curse. Instead, he nodded and turned for the door.

"You're leaving?" She kicked off her shoes and slipped out of her sweatshirt.

"No?" He stood there like a total idiot, watching Vivienne undress to her bra and knickers and slip beneath the covers.

"Hurry up. I'm c-cold."

He'd never taken his clothes off so fast. Once he was beneath the duvet, Vivienne shifted closer. And the way she molded against him, soft and warm and feminine and—

Tipperary . . . Wexford . . . Waterford . . . Dublin . . .

She rubbed her back against his chest, and her hair fell down her shoulder, exposing her neck. How did she always smell so good?

LimerickCarlowCavanClareCorkDerry . . .

Get yourself together. She's just cold.

Vivienne reached back and pulled his arm around her, leaving his hand resting on her stomach. He could feel her ribs expand and contract with each deep breath she drew in.

Close your eyes and go to sleep.

She wiggled closer.

Aaaaand he wasn't tired any more.

Once she fell asleep, he'd slip away and go to his mother's. Otherwise, he'd go completely mad.

When he pressed a kiss to her shoulder, she leaned into it so his lips skimmed the hollow at the base of her throat. Goosebumps rose on her skin as he brushed his fingertips along her bare stomach. "How tired are you?" he asked, stifling a groan when she rolled her hips.

"Not as tired as I thought," she panted, twisting and drawing his mouth to hers.

THIRTY-SIX

Vivienne shifted on the couch and drew the duvet around her shoulders. The heating wasn't going to be fixed until tomorrow, but the cold seeping into her bones was from more than the dampness in her apartment.

The trial started in thirty minutes.

She closed her eyes and tried to remember what Deacon had told her about what was going to happen.

Leadership consisted of four tiers. The first tier of seven core members—eight, counting Peter—were allowed to vote on the most sensitive issues, which included today's trial.

The second tier of surrogates were allowed to step in if a core member could no longer do his or her duty. They were also given a vote on lesser issues. Each surrogate could nominate two representatives; Deacon and his aunt Ida were representatives for his mother Mary.

And finally there were the witnesses. She had agreed to be one after Deacon assured her she'd have no responsibilities other than watching and listening.

On the other side of the wall, the hum of the shower stopped. Neither she nor Deacon had been able to sleep the night before, but they had found plenty to take their minds off of what was happening today. Some of the warmth returned to her body, until a knock sounded at the door.

She considered bringing the duvet with her, then thought better of it. By the time she reached the door, she was shivering again.

"Geez, Vivienne, it's colder in here than it is outside." Ethan pushed past her with a bottle of dark liquor tucked beneath his arm.

Nicola followed behind him; the long blue coat she wore over her black jumpsuit made her look taller than usual.

Neither of them had said congratulations—or anything—about the engagement.

Deacon came out of the bedroom, his hair still damp, and her heart constricted in her chest. They had finally come to an agreement regarding their wedding: wait until Peter thought they would be approved by Leadership.

But she had a feeling the more time they spent together, the harder it would be to wait.

"Is that what I think it is?" Deacon said to Ethan, nodding toward the bottle with a grimace.

Ethan shook it and laughed. "I figured we could all use a little liquid courage today."

Deacon muttered a curse but went to the cupboard to retrieve four cups.

Both guys wore dark waistcoats with button-down shirts and dark jeans. Peter insisted on formal attire for Leadership meetings. Seeing how good Deacon looked in a waistcoat made Vivienne thankful for the dress code. She'd have to ask him to wear it more often.

Ethan pressed a glass into her hand. Whatever was inside smelled like licorice.

She hated licorice.

Deacon put his arm around her waist and kissed the top of her head. "Bottoms up, my love."

From the corner of her eye, she saw Nicola stiffen. Ethan shifted from one foot to the other. They were probably stressed about the trial. That's why they were acting so strange.

After taking the shot—which nearly came back up when she swallowed it—and refusing a second, she followed everyone out of her apartment.

She had assumed Leadership met in the cathedral or a room in Harrow Hall. Deacon bypassed both and crossed the soggy grass to an odd brick structure at the far edge of the walled campus.

The shed didn't even look big enough for the four of them.

A silver padlock had been left hanging on its hook next to thick black doors opened to the misty breeze.

Inside was a surprisingly bright, windowless room with a glass ceiling. An ornate, wrought iron railing surrounded stained-glass tiles decorating the center of the floor. Beyond the masterpiece was a single door, carved to look like the trunk of a tree. Behind the door was a curved staircase lined with antique bronze lamps.

Vivienne had never been in a dungeon, but it felt like that was where they were headed until the creepy staircase opened into a brilliant amphitheater.

If she hadn't just trudged down a bunch of steps, she wouldn't have believed they were under ground. Instead of smelling damp or musty, the comforting scent of cedar permeated the air in the bright chamber. Rainbows from the glass ceiling danced on her hands.

Plaster fairies peeped from the coving, and mischievous mermaids swam along the baseboards that bordered patch-work tiles. The extensive wood paneling in the room resembled the roots and branches of a great tree.

"What's with the trees?" Eight trunks had been painted around the chamber. They varied in size and style, and seven of them had knots the size of a baseball protruding halfway up their length. The eighth tree's knot was much lower.

"Each one opens an escape hatch to a different building on and around campus," Deacon told her. "The one in the back is for those who are grounded. It comes out in the cellar at The Wendy Bird."

The Wendy Bird was a pub across from campus where the Harrow PAN liked to go drinking. She had asked Deacon to bring her there two nights ago, but he hadn't wanted to leave the apartment. Apparently, he didn't want people knowing about their engagement until *after* the trial. She had offered to take off her engagement ring, but he'd insisted it stay on. It felt like there was more to his reluctance, but she hadn't pushed.

Vivienne trailed her fingers along an oak tree's brush strokes, wondering if the escape hatches were really necessary or if they were there to add drama to the room.

Four rows of stools curved amphitheater-style around eight empty chairs placed at the front of the chamber. At the far side, between the congregation and the chairs, sat a larger chair carved to look like a throne. Beneath the throne was an ornate gold Charlie Bell.

Deacon brought her to the row at the back, in front of an autumnal maple. "I'll be right here," he said, hopping over the stools below her to sit next to a guy with mahogany hair.

Nicola sat beside Vivienne but didn't say a word.

Mary Ashford descended the staircase with a gray-haired woman at her side. Deacon's shoulders slumped as he shifted on his stool. Vivienne had tried to get him to talk to his mother before the meeting, but he had claimed he had enough stress in his life.

Mary smiled and waved at him, then her eyes found

Vivienne and narrowed. Deacon's mom was going to like her even less when she saw the engagement ring.

Aoibheann glided down the stairs, her long, green-tinted blond hair plaited in intricate braids around her crown and falling in soft waves down her back. She looked more like an elf from a fantasy movie than a wicked Mermaid.

What the heck was *she* doing here?

Deacon hadn't mentioned she would be at the meeting. Was Aoibheann the reason he hadn't wanted to go to the pub?

Vivienne leaned forward and tapped Deacon on the shoulder. "What's Aoibheann doing in front?"

"The Mermaids have been pushing for a place in Leadership for years. It appears they finally got one."

Crap.

If Aoibheann was a voting member of Leadership, they were screwed.

Alex sat down next to her. His caramel-colored hair had been cut short, his beard trimmed to stubble.

Double crap.

There were at least two people now to vote against her marriage.

Focus.

She didn't need to worry about that now. There was much more at stake today than her wedding.

"If everyone would finish their conversations," Donovan announced, "this session is about to begin."

The boisterous exchanges echoing around the chamber came to an abrupt stop; those present took their seats, while Peter remained perched on the ledge of the steps. His legs dangled into the branches of a birch tree.

Donovan lowered himself onto the throne, but the front stools remained empty.

Mary and the other surrogates filled the second row. Gwen

sat next to her. The handful of witnesses and any remaining stragglers filled in the stools at the back. Vivienne didn't recognize any of them, but from the quizzical looks a few of the girls gave her, she had a feeling they knew who she was.

Another woman sat next to Alex.

"Who is that?" Vivienne asked, feeling like the dark-haired woman looked vaguely familiar.

Nicola reluctantly told her the woman's name was Maimie Ward.

Maimie Ward. Vivienne's great-grandmother.

According to Nicola, the brown-haired guy next to Maimie was Richard One—one of the twins. He had an easy smile and relaxed into his chair with confidence. Beside him, Richard Two—the second twin—was covered in freckles and had a shock of red hair springing from his head. His spine remained straight as he seemed to drink in every detail of the people surrounding him. Nibs—short, blond, and athletic—was next, followed by tall and lanky Slightly. The last member of leadership, Curly, had black hair gelled into a swoop. His dark eyes darted around the congregation like he wasn't comfortable being up front.

"Before we begin," Donovan said, withdrawing a small leather notebook from his waistcoat and setting it on his knee, "Peter has asked that each surrogate and representative nominate one additional witness to take part in future proceedings. We will accept appointments until one week prior to the next session."

A collective murmur emerged from the crowd.

Slightly's thin lips turned down at the corners. "It is unprecedented to allow so many new individuals to take part in such important discussions."

From the step, Peter said, "Everyone shares in the consequences of the decisions we make. A larger sample would be beneficial to our cause."

"Some of the items on the docket are better left to the select few allowed in the negotiation room."

The murmurs turned into mutters of agreement.

"I'm afraid I'm decided on this, Slightly," Peter said, bouncing his heels against the wall.

Slightly didn't look pleased by the dismissal but said no more.

"Right. We all know why we've been called here today." Donovan flipped open his notebook. "It's time to bring in the accused."

Lee Somerfield and the six other dissenters filed down the stairs to take their places on the stools in front of the congregation, facing Leadership. Although every man had entered under his own free will, they reminded Vivienne of a chain gang of criminals being led into a courthouse for sentencing. All of them had their heads bowed except for Lee, who met Leadership with a defiant glare.

Paul Mitter stepped forward from where he waited next to Donovan, an ominous red folder tucked beneath his arm.

Vivienne shifted on her stool, trying to find a comfortable way to sit on the unforgiving wood.

Lee, Ethan, Max, Joel, Ricky, Kyle, and Jason.

Seven defendants and eight stools.

Her arms began to itch.

It was probably a coincidence. Someone had miscounted. There was no reason for her to be—

Paul's eyes met hers. "Vivienne, would you come forward?"

Her breath hitched.

No, no, no—

Aoibheann's mouth quirked upward in a slow, menacing smile. Alex's face went pale.

Deacon rocketed to his feet. "She had nothing to do with this! The fire was set before she arrived."

Ignoring the murmurs around them, Vivienne pulled him back by his sleeve. "It doesn't matter. I was part of it." And she was responsible for the incident that had spurred them to take action. She belonged up front.

"Come on, Peter," Deacon mumbled. "Do *something.*"

Peter shrugged from the staircase and continued looking unconcerned.

Vivienne walked past her fellow witnesses, through the representatives and surrogates, to sit next to Max—directly across from Aoibheann.

Max pinched the bridge of his nose and apologized. "I never should've called you."

"It's not your fault." If HOOK hadn't been looking for her, none of them would be there.

"Tell that to Deacon." Max glanced over his shoulder. "He looks like he wants to kill someone."

Deacon leaned forward on his stool, clenched fists hanging between his knees, eyes narrowed into slits, the muscles in his jaw ticking. Worrying about him would have to wait.

Vivienne needed to worry about herself.

Paul flipped open the cover on his folder and cleared his throat. "On the night of September fifteenth, the PAN before you retaliated for the presumed death of a recruiter by setting fire to the main research facility at HOOK." He paused long enough to adjust his glasses. "This unsanctioned attack nearly cost the lives of Jasper Hooke and one undercover PAN agent."

"Undercover agent?" she asked under her breath.

Max shrugged, and his frown deepened.

It sounded like everyone in the chamber was asking the same question.

Donovan stood and thanked Paul. The whispering stopped.

"Today, we are charged with deciding the appropriate course of action in the aftermath of this attack," Donovan said in a deep, rich voice that carried around the chamber. "Lee Somerfield, you are the leader of this faction."

Lee stood and shoved the sleeves of his shirt to his elbows, exposing the damage from HOOK's poison. "I am."

Vivienne and her fellow accused sat taller in their chairs.

"This is your opportunity to defend your actions."

Lee took his time moving to the space between his followers and their jury. "As all of you know, HOOK murdered my brother"—he traced his black veins—"and sentenced me to death. How did Leadership respond?" Curly and Maimie dropped their eyes to the floor. "They did *nothing*."

Lee pointed to Joel, who said, "HOOK neutralized my uncle."

"And Leadership's response?"

"They did nothing."

He moved in front of Ricky and nodded. "They got my cousin."

"And Leadership's response?"

"Nothing."

Lee stepped to Kyle.

"We have the gist," Slightly drawled. "Why don't you get to the point?"

"It's our turn to speak," Lee snapped, turning back to Kyle and telling him to go on.

"HOOK neutralized my father."

"And"—Lee locked eyes with Slightly—"Leadership's response?"

"They didn't do anything."

Lee asked Jason, Ethan, and Max the same question, and

their responses mirrored the previous ones. Then Lee reached Vivienne.

His warm smile gave Vivienne the confidence to say, "HOOK murdered both my parents and my aunt. They tried to neutralize me, and I thought they killed my boyfriend."

Settling his warm hand on her shoulder, Lee said, "And what did"—he pointed across to Slightly—"*they* do?"

Vivienne inhaled a steadying breath. "They didn't do anything."

"But *we* did something, didn't we?" With his followers nodding behind him, Lee continued. "We didn't riot in the Neverlands or expose HOOK's depravity in case they exposed us to outsiders. We marched to our enemy's head-quarters under the cover of darkness and burned it to the ground."

Lee twisted toward the Leadership panel, his spine rigid and his hands clenched at his sides. "What gives you the right to judge us for seeking retribution for loved ones stolen from us, for futures taken away without consequence, when your *inaction* has been a staple since this committee's inception?"

"Nearly all the cases you've highlighted have involved recruiters," Slightly said with a flick of his wrist. "And recruiters understand the position comes with a number of risks."

"Is that why you only allow the youngest, most inexperienced PAN to recruit? Because they're expendable?"

"Stop right there!" Slightly bellowed, thumping his fist against his chair. "You're making us out to be the villains."

Lifting his right palm, Lee said, "You force *children* to do the most dangerous jobs because you don't value their lives as much as your own." He raised his left palm. "And HOOK uses us for unsanctioned experiments because they don't see us as humans." The "scales" balanced. "What's the difference?"

JENNY HICKMAN

"What would you have us do?" Peter demanded, walking down the stairs until he came toe to toe with Lee. Donovan moved to stand behind him.

"The same thing I've always wanted us to do. I want to fight back."

Peter pressed a button on his watch. It beeped once, then a second time. "By setting buildings on fire and risking the lives of innocent PAN?"

"At least I did *something*."

Peter's head snapped up. "I've told you time and again, we do not declare war on our enemy because we're *not* an army."

"Says the guy giving orders from his wooden throne," Lee snarled, kicking Peter's chair.

"You've leeched off of Neverland for your entire life, yet you've shown time and again that you have no respect for our rules." Slightly raised to his full height. "Instead of bringing your concerns to us, you've taken matters into your own hands—and taken the rest of your followers down with you. Lee Somerfield, you are nothing more than a selfish coward."

"I'm not the one hiding in Harrow with my fingers in my ears!"

"Enough!" Peter shouted. "Slightly, you *will* sit down." When Slightly was back in his chair, Peter twisted toward Lee. "*You* assumed I had no contingency plans in place if we were to lose another PAN to HOOK. It has taken us years, but we have someone on the inside at the research facility, and your little *stunt* nearly killed him."

"I didn't know—"

"Because you've been too busy preaching rebellion to work *with* us! I told you not to retaliate, yet you still chose to disobey me."

Lee sneered. "I don't remember ever pledging my allegiance to the *great* Peter Pan."

Donovan whispered something into Peter's ear. Peter nodded once and took a deep breath. "This conversation has become unproductive. Lee, it's time for you and your people to go upstairs."

Lee stomped toward the staircase, then turned around and scanned the crowd. "What's the point in trying to change minds that were made up a hundred years ago?"

THIRTY-SEVEN

Leaning her forearms against the iron railing, Vivienne stared at the colorful glass below her. The sounds of Ethan's pacing and muttering killed any chance of hearing what was happening downstairs. Max sat beside her, hugging his knees to his chest. "We're screwed," he said, banging his head against his knee.

Ethan stopped to say, "Don't be so dramatic," then resumed his pacing.

"Did you *hear* them?" Max pointed a shaky hand toward the closed door. "They think we're a bigger threat than HOOK."

"We've known their views on our faction from the beginning." Lee leaned against the doorway, watching the rest of the dissenters by the wall outside. He didn't seem concerned by the rain blowing across his shoes. "At least they're consistent."

"And if they're that consistent," Ethan said, "then maybe they'll do nothing."

Shouting lifted from the chamber below.

Max dropped his head. "Doesn't sound like nothing."

"It's called optimism. Try it sometime."

"Fighting amongst ourselves isn't going to help." Lee shifted so his back was against the door. "What's done is done."

"How can you be so calm?" Max asked, adjusting his hold on his legs.

"What're they going to do to me?" Lee laughed, covering the crook of his arm with his hand. "I'll be dead in a few decades."

"That doesn't mean they won't neutralize the rest of us." Max's eyes filled with tears, and he wiped them with his shirtsleeve.

Vivienne wished she could make him feel better, but the truth was, she felt as hopeless as he did. Maybe more so, considering they were here because of her. Still, she said, "They won't neutralize us," with as much confidence as she could muster.

No one looked convinced.

"They won't neutralize *you* because you're dating Peter Pan's grandson." Max squeezed his knees tighter. "But the rest of us are screwed."

Just because she had gotten a reprieve the last time didn't mean she would get one today. It felt like her luck had run out. "They won't neutralize *us* because they don't have any poison."

Ethan came to her side and gripped the railing. "They'll probably sacrifice us in exchange for a few vials."

"They're not going to do a damn thing because they're an elitist, self-elected body that's never been given the authority to enforce their own rules," Lee ground out, kicking his heel off the door. "Peter should be thanking us, capitalizing on what we started. Instead, we're holding a pointless trial, giving HOOK the chance to rebuild."

The chamber door opened.

Vivienne's stomach dropped when she saw Alex, his face pale. His wide eyes met hers. "I need to speak with you in private."

Beside her, Ethan stiffened. She shot him a glare, and he kept his mouth shut.

The last thing Vivienne wanted was to piss off a voting member of Leadership, so she nodded and went outside into the mist. Alex followed her around to the back of the shed, but he seemed more interested in biting his lip and staring at the bricks than talking.

She waited, wanting—and not wanting—to hear what he had to say that was so urgent it couldn't wait until after the trial.

When he finally looked at her, the wrinkles at the corners of his eyes seemed more pronounced. "If I asked you to leave with me, would you?"

Her chest constricted.

Why would she want to leave?

What was happening downstairs?

"Alex, you're scaring me."

"I'm not going to lie. It's not looking good. So I'm asking you to leave . . . *with me*. It doesn't have to be forever," he sighed, reaching for her hands, "not like I have forever anyway. But we can catch a plane back to the States and disappear until all of this blows over."

If he was willing to give up his seat in Leadership *and* his life in Neverland, the situation inside must be downright hopeless.

He touched the ring on Vivienne's little finger and his brows drew together.

She took a deep breath. "Deacon—"

"Do you honestly think he'd leave this behind for you?"

Her knee-jerk response was yes. Deacon loved her and wanted to marry her despite the fact that she was going to become forgetful. Of course he would be willing to leave Neverland for her.

But when she thought about it a bit more, she wasn't so sure. Deacon had grown up in Neverland. His mother was here; his granddad was Peter-freaking-Pan. The only life he had ever known had been inside these walls, under a veil of secrets.

Would Deacon *really* give that up for her?

"You don't have to answer right now," Alex said quietly, brushing her damp hair back from her face. "But if the verdict doesn't go in your favor, I want you to know you have an out."

"For those of you who feel they cannot participate in this debate, feel free to leave the chamber now." Donovan swept his hand toward the staircase.

Stools clattered and scraped as witnesses, representatives, and surrogates fought to be the first to escape.

Deacon's heart sank. "I thought at least a few of them would stay."

"Your mom and Ida are still here," Nicola whispered, nodding toward the row ahead.

Having his mother there wasn't necessarily a good thing. She had never bothered to hide her disapproval of Vivienne. And as the woman in charge of Kensington, she would surely want to make an example out of Lee and his followers.

The only other non-Leadership members in the chamber now were Nicola, Paul Mitter . . . and Gwen.

Of course *she* would stay.

Deacon's collar felt like a noose around his neck. He unbuttoned the top two buttons.

It didn't help.

"Those of you in the back should come forward to help facilitate a more effective discussion," Donovan instructed, indicating an empty stool beside Gwen.

There was no way in hell Deacon was going to sit there.

Nicola, the saint, settled in beside Gwen, and Deacon took the stool at the end—directly across from Aoibheann. His mother leaned forward and told him that she needed to speak with him as soon as this was over. Deacon nodded, even though he planned to slip away before that could happen.

Gwen narrowed her eyes at him, and he turned forward only to catch Aoibheann's lips lifting into a menacing smile.

This day had become his personal circle of hell.

"In keeping with tradition, members of Leadership will be called to vote at the end of a *civil* discussion." Donovan paused to throw Slightly a pointed look. "The rest of you are free to share your opinions until then."

Aoibheann leaned her chin on her hand, as though she was bored already. "I'm new to this, but since they've admitted they're guilty, don't we just need to decide on the consequences for their crimes?"

"*Crimes*?" Was she serious? "They avenged my death."

"Yet here you sit," she said, wiggling her fingers toward his legs.

"Aoibheann is right," Peter said from where he hovered, studying the painted oak leaves with his hands clasped behind his back.

Deacon stared at him in horror. Who was this imposter and what had he done with his grandad?

"They thought Deacon was dead," Peter went on, "and instead of following protocol and bringing their concerns to Leadership, they took matters into their own hands."

"Exactly my point from earlier." Tugging at the bottom of his waistcoat, Slightly puffed out his chest. He was an insufferable ass.

Deacon imagined hitting him in his smug face and felt marginally better.

His grandad landed cross-legged in his chair and pressed the buttons on his watch—something he did when he was nervous. "It's time to break our pattern of inaction."

"I agree with Peter. We've been idle long enough," Richard Two said, swiping a hand through his unruly red hair. "This cannot be allowed to become the norm."

"It's happened once in a hundred and fifty years," grumbled Nibs. "I hardly think there's a threat of it *becoming the norm*."

Slightly elbowed him. "If there are no consequences, then what's to stop someone else from attacking HOOK?"

"Would that be such a bad thing?" Deacon's mother asked. "We've lived our entire lives under constant threat. What's wrong with fighting back?"

Deacon couldn't believe it. His own mother siding *with* the dissenters. As a surrogate, she didn't have a vote, but being Peter Pan's daughter meant her opinion carried a good deal of weight with those who did.

Nibs snorted. "Someone still has a soft spot for Somerfield."

Somerfield? What the hell did that mean?

Deacon glared at Nibs.

Then his mother.

But she refused to meet his eyes. Why wouldn't she look at him? What was she hiding? And what did it have to do with Lee?

"Of course she has a soft spot," Maimie said, her smile warm and indulgent, "they're engaged."

His mother's face went red. "That was a long time ago."

No. This couldn't be happening. Lee Somerfied and his mother . . . *engaged?*

They really *did* need to talk.

Peter's nails tapping against the arm of the chair

reminded Deacon of a woodpecker. "Let's save the merits of going on the offensive for another day."

"I agree with Peter," Richard Two said.

Tap. Tap.

"Of course you do," muttered Nibs.

Tap. Tap. Tap.

"Back to consequences," Slightly said with an exasperated sigh. "Does anyone have suggestions?"

Tap. Tap. Tap. Tap.

Why weren't they saying anything? Did they already know what they were going to do? Was it too awful to say aloud? Was no one going to speak up and say outright how wrong all of this was?

Deacon looked to his grandad for support. Peter raised his eyebrows and kept *tap, tap, tapping*—

Nicola's face was pinched but she didn't speak up. Her boyfriend was on trial. The least she could do was say *something* on his behalf.

Tap.

Tap.

Tap.

Deacon glared across at Alex.

Surely *he* had something to say. He had a vote. He had a voice. And he was too busy staring at his *bloody* shoes to say a *bloody* thing.

Tap.

Tap.

The infernal *tapping* was driving Deacon mad.

Couldn't Peter do something useful?

Deacon's previous indiscretions made his opinion with Leadership worthless, but he'd had enough *bloody tapping*. "How can you even think of punishing them?" he demanded, struggling to keep his voice level. "Every single one of you would have done the same thing if you were in their situation."

The tapping stopped.

"We've all lost friends and loved ones to HOOK." Slightly waved toward his fellow PAN. "But none of us have charged unprepared into battle."

"Justify it any way you'd like, Dash." Aoibheann's wide blue eyes were cold and unyielding. "What they did was wrong."

"It appears the majority of us believe there must be some sort of punishment for this." Richard Two nodded toward Peter. "Even Peter."

"I never said such a thing," Peter drawled, fiddling with the buttons on his dark green waistcoat. "In fact, I agreed with the choice of the word *consequences* in lieu of the word 'punishment.'"

Slightly put his fists over his eyes and groaned. "Brilliant. Now we're arguing over semantics."

"I believe you're missing a fairly obvious point," Nibs said. "HOOK doesn't know for sure it was us, right? Isn't this a bit of a no-harm-no-foul scenario?"

"That's not entirely true." Paul removed his glasses and slid them into his breast pocket.

Deacon locked gazes with Paul and shook his head.

Don't say it. Please, don't say it.

Dropping his gaze, Paul said, "Vivienne helped Jasper Hooke escape from the third floor . . . and she wasn't wearing a mask."

Aoibheann smirked at Deacon. "Her way of thanking him for getting rid of you?"

"Perhaps Vivienne's punishment should be a bit harsher because of her carelessness," Gwen chimed in.

"Thanks for the *unbiased* opinions," Nibs said under his breath.

"No one would have gone to HOOK," Slightly ground out, "if *Somerfield* had been dealt with two decades ago like I had suggested."

"You said he needed to be dealt with"—Nibs laced his fingers behind his head—"but never suggested *how*."

"Can we focus instead of bouncing from one topic to another?" Maimie put her hands on either side of her head. "These tangents are too hard to follow."

"The only punishments at our disposal," Slightly said, closing his eyes, "are banishment or neutralization."

"Excuse me." Alex slid out of his chair and jogged up the stairs.

He was such a bloody coward.

"How can you even suggest neutralization?" Deacon growled. "You didn't give them their Nevergenes and you have no right to take them away."

"We gave them the injection to keep their genes active," Slightly said.

"If you neutralize my fiancée, you may as well stick a needle in me too." Deacon yanked his sleeve to his elbow. They could do it right then and there for all he cared. These people were the ones charged with keeping everyone safe. This whole trial was bullshit.

"*Fiancée?*" Gwen, Aoibheann, and his mother all jerked toward him.

Peter jumped up and threw his hand toward the exit. "Get out."

Deacon crossed his arms and narrowed his eyes, refusing to be ordered around like a child. Peter stalked to the base of the stairs and crooked his finger at him.

At first he considered ignoring it. But what was the point in fighting? Lee had been right; Leadership's mind had been made up years ago.

Slipping off his stool, Deacon ignored the satisfied smirk on Gwen's face.

"You need to leave," Peter said under his breath, the muscles in his jaws ticking.

"If I go, there will be no one left to fight for her."

"What the hell do you think *I'm* doing?"

The heat of Deacon's anger seeped from his body, leaving him cold, deflated . . . helpless.

Peter cursed and rubbed his temples. "And you certainly didn't help matters with your little *announcement.*"

The one thing his grandad had asked him to do was to keep his engagement to Vivienne a secret until *after* the trial. And he couldn't even do that.

"Go upstairs, Deacon."

Deacon wanted to protest.

He wanted to beg for leniency.

Instead, he nodded and trudged up the stairs.

THIRTY-EIGHT

You have an out.

Did Vivienne need one? How could she leave with Alex when she didn't love him? But she could leave on her own. She could run and never look back. Alex squeezed her fingers once more before dropping her hand. When they rounded the corner, the first person she saw was Ethan, his arms crossed and eyes narrowed.

Then she saw Deacon. How long had he been upstairs?

His jaw ticked as he watched Alex walk stiffly to the stairs and shut the door. "Do you mind telling me what *that* was all about?"

"Later." Or never. Never sounded good. "Why are you up here?"

"Peter kicked me out." Deacon's lips pressed into a flat line. "Apparently, I'm only making the situation worse."

Was that even possible? "Isn't *anyone* on our side?"

"Why the hell are you asking me? I'm sure Alex told you everything."

"Stop it," she snapped, stomping her foot. "Stop it and tell me what you know."

Deacon raked his hands through his hair and swore. He said they had Nibs and Maimie. And she knew Alex would vote in their favor. The twins were split down the middle, and Curly wasn't saying much, but he usually sided with Slightly—who was definitely against. "And if it were up to Aoibheann," Deacon went on, groaning, "she'd neutralize everyone in the chamber except Peter."

The door opened again.

This was it.

This was the end.

Donovan avoided looking at any of them as he escorted Maimie out of the building to where a red-haired woman raced across the green to meet them.

"What do you think they're saying?" Vivienne asked, clutching Deacon's arm. Donovan and the woman exchanged words. Whatever it was didn't look positive.

Deacon put his hand over hers and promised to find out. When Deacon reached them, Maimie and the red-haired woman turned to leave. Where were they going? Donovan started speaking to Deacon; Vivienne watched the color drain from Deacon's face.

This was bad. Very bad.

Dampness seeped through Vivienne's dress as she ran to where he stood, shoulders hunched, staring blankly toward the gray clouds leaking rain.

"Tell me what he said."

Deacon lunged for her hand and started pulling her toward the cathedral. "We need to go."

She stumbled along behind him, glancing back toward the darkened doorway where Ethan, Max, and Lee waited. "What? Why?"

"Maimie's forgetful. They're not letting her vote."

"Is anyone taking her place? Surely they're going to let her surrogate—"

He cursed and dropped her hand. "It's Gwen. *Gwen's* her replacement, and she's out for blood. It's over. We need to leave *now*."

"Where the heck are we going to go? We don't have any money. We don't have a place to live. We don't have anything—"

"We have each other."

He didn't know what he was saying. Hadn't thought this through. If she took him away, he'd end up resenting her for it. And that was worse than facing neutralization.

What was she trying to save anyway? She was going to forget everything. Why did it matter if they neutralized her now? She'd lose her immortality, but at least she'd have her memories.

"I'm not running."

"Vivienne, listen to me." He gripped her shoulders and brought his face to hers. "They're talking about neutralization. I can't . . . I can't let them do that to you."

"This is *my* fault, Deacon. *All* of it." She forced back the tears blurring her vision. "I'm going to go in there and take whatever punishment they give me, because I deserve it."

"*Dammit.*" He pressed his fists to his eyes and nodded. "All right. All right. We're in this together. Whatever happens, I'm by your side."

"Deacon—"

"I'd rather have one lifetime grounded with you," he said, cupping her face in his hands and rubbing his thumbs over her cheeks, "than a thousand years flying alone."

Seeing Gwen sitting in the chair Maimie had occupied for the last century felt wrong. The whole trial—*the entire situa-*

tion—was wrong. Neverland, the land of fairy tales, had become a place of nightmares.

Vivienne's blunt nails dug into the back of Deacon's hand as they descended the staircase. The lights on the walls flickered, as if they didn't want to watch either. Rainbows no longer danced around the room, and the raucous laughter and conversations had been replaced by heartbreaking silence.

Donovan told Deacon to continue to his seat when he stopped next to Vivienne.

Lee and the others were already sitting down.

Vivienne's, "I love you," sounded like goodbye. She dropped his hand and took her place at the end next to Max.

Deacon glanced toward the empty stools at the rear of the chamber, then back to his fiancée. If he hadn't been shot, he would have been up front with the rest of them. He didn't belong with the spectators. He belonged with the accused.

So he picked up a stool, carried it to the front, and sat beside the woman he loved. He'd meant what he said. They were in this together.

Nicola stood from where she sat with the other witnesses and brought her stool to sit behind Ethan. His mother—*his own mother*—dragged her stool to sit beside Lee.

Leadership and the rest of the congregation watched in silence.

Peter's heels clipped with each step he took, echoing off the walls as he made his way from the back of the room to the front. When he reached the dissenters, he stopped.

"Before the verdict is read," Peter said, speaking directly to Lee, "there is something I would like to say to you. In your defense, you continually cited Leadership's inaction as the reason behind your decision to march on HOOK. Did you ever consider that what you perceived as inaction was, in itself, a response?

"Lee, what happened to you and Nicholas was a

tragedy," he went on, shaking his head and opening his hands. "But you were caught by HOOK because you didn't follow procedures put in place to ensure recruiter safety. And you expected us to retaliate, risking more lives because of your unfortunate error."

Lee's gaze dropped to the floor.

Peter moved to the center of the line, in front of Ethan. "Every action—or inaction—has consequences. It's time to stop blaming outside forces and look inward for the answers to our problems. Yes, HOOK is inherently evil and bent on destroying us"—he turned slowly to face Leadership—"but if we continue as we are, there will be *nothing* left for them to destroy."

Donovan went to move from Peter's chair, but Peter waved him away and flew to sit on the edge of the steps.

Slightly stood and cleared his throat. His stance was rigid, his face unreadable. "Lee Somerfield, you have been found guilty of disobeying a direct order. You proved once again that you have no respect for Neverland or its policies. The rest of you are guilty of knowingly participating in an event that had no approval from Leadership . . . "

Guilty.

Guilty.

Guilty.

There had never been any doubt that Lee and the rest of them were guilty. The question was: what was Leadership going to do about it?

Guilty.

They were guilty. All of them.

Vivienne reached for Deacon's hand, holding onto him while she still could, knowing she couldn't live with herself if anything happened to him. If he gave up his immortality.

Clothes rustled and stools scraped as the dissenters shifted in their seats. Beside her, Max picked at his nails; Ethan dropped his head into his hands; Lee's hands balled into fists in his lap.

Deacon brought their joined hands to his lips and brushed them across her knuckles. "You and me," he whispered.

Vivienne could only nod as tears stung the back of her eyes.

The silence in a room with so many people was unnatural.

Peter's watch beeped from the stairs. Once. Twice.

Then he stood and dragged a hand through his dark hair. "HOOK has taken so much from us already," he said quietly, his voice piercing the silence. "I refuse to let them tear us apart from the inside. And *this*"—he gestured between Leadership and where Vivienne and the rest of the dissenters sat —"is going to be the end of Neverland . . . "

The end of Neverland.

Over.

This was over.

Vivienne's heart thudded in her chest.

Adrenaline coursed through her veins.

She tried to breathe through the surge, but it wasn't helping, and her skin was crawling and the walls were closing in and she needed to escape. To fly away.

"*If* we don't *fix it.*"

Deacon's grip on her hand tightened.

Fix it? Did Peter just say something about fixing it?

"In light of what's been lost," Peter went on, his voice growing stronger, more resolute, "*I* have determined your sentences have been served."

Peter . . . *not* Leadership.

Once again, Peter Pan was sticking his neck out for her— and for the rebels.

359

And from the menacing look on Slightly's face, there would be consequences. "So that's it?" Slightly snapped. "All's well that ends well? You're only asking for mutiny now, Peter. Surely they deserve more than a slap on the wrist."

"I stand by Peter's decision." Richard Two went to Peter's side.

"And you're not offended that he made the decision without us?" Aoibheann clipped.

"You made it clear during the *civil* discussion that I was the only one who wouldn't allow emotions to cloud my judgement or use this opportunity to settle old scores." Peter waved a hand toward Vivienne and her fellow dissenters. "And I've chosen to offer grace."

"So much for consequences," Aoibheann muttered.

"You want to discuss consequences? Because of this man"—Peter pointed to a slack-jawed, wide-eyed Lee— "HOOK has never been more vulnerable." He stalked back to his chair and grabbed the Charlie Bell. "*Now* is our chance to capitalize on their weakness."

Nibs covered his eyes and shook his head. "Here we go again . . . "

"Peter," Slightly began, his tone chiding, "your imaginary Crocodile *doesn't exist.*"

"It *does* exist," Peter insisted, a grin brightening his youthful face. "And it's time to fight back."

THIRTY-NINE

J asper looked up from the notes he had been trying to focus on for the last hour to find Lawrence staring at him with narrowed eyes. His dark beard really needed a trim. "My office, Lab Rat. Now."

Jasper winced but hid his discontentment from the employees stealing glances at him from behind their goggles. Turning on his heel, Lawrence stalked past the security guard standing at the exit.

He had been on a rampage ever since the fire and showed no signs of stopping. The last thing Jasper wanted to do was make it worse by making him wait, so he closed his notes in a folder and slipped them into his desk drawer.

When he stepped outside into the frigid air, he was sorry he had left his jacket on his chair. He started to turn back, but heard the employees inside arguing.

Being cold was better than playing referee again.

With his breath coming in white puffs, Jasper held his lab

coat closed over his T-shirt and jogged to the admin building.

The moment he stepped into Lawrence's office, he choked.

"I thought you had someone take care of the smell." Jasper pinched his nose, knocking his glasses askew. It had been weeks, and there was still a stink of rotten fish.

"Didn't work." Lawrence finished tying his shoe, then dropped his foot from the edge of his desk. "My whole damn house and all my clothes still reek of fish guts. Stench follows me everywhere"

"You shouldn't have left it vacant for so long." After the PAN had played their little prank, Lawrence had moved into his girlfriend's house for a few weeks.

"I couldn't live there with alarms going off every hour." Lawrence pulled a can of air freshener from his desk and clouded the room with cotton blossom. "I didn't expect the little terrorists to put fish in my dryer vent."

Jasper hid his smile behind his hand. "They must've run out of fish by the time they reached my house."

"You're lucky, Lab Rat. I'm still finding clocks and maggot-ridden lumps around the place."

Jasper's hands clenched into fists. Lab Rat. Lab Rat. *Lab Rat.* Jasper hated the demeaning nickname. He was a hell of a lot more than a lab rat. "Stop calling me that in front of my people."

"It's a term of endearment," his brother mumbled, skimming a memo on his desk.

"It's belittling, and you know it." How could Jasper expect his employees to respect him when Lawrence obviously didn't?

"Fine." Lawrence crumbled the page and tossed it into the trash. "I won't call you Lab Rat in front of your employees."

"Thank you."

"No problem, Lab Rat."

Jasper thumped his fist against the desk. "I just said—"

"Ah-ah." Lawrence clucked his tongue and wagged his finger. "Your employees aren't here."

Understanding no good would come from an argument, Jasper sighed. "Why did you need to speak with me? I'm weeks behind and need to get back to work." It had taken over a month to organize a new workspace; they were only now starting to get back to their research.

"We need to talk about staffing." Lawrence handed him a letter of resignation from Jasper's administrative assistant, Kelly.

Why had she given it to Lawrence?

Kelly was the third employee to give notice in as many weeks.

R&D had relocated to makeshift prefab labs, with desks practically on top of one another and access to only a fraction of the equipment they needed. And with winter coming, they'd be lucky to have the new building finished before summer.

"If you'd let us rent a lab space, as I've suggested multiple times"—Jasper found a stick of gum at the bottom of one of his cluttered pockets—"then we could—"

"Are you *nuts*? Moving off site would stretch our security too thin. Not to mention the astronomical rent we'd be shelling out. It's not in the budget."

"If you're worried about costs, then you may as well close down the lab until construction is complete." Jasper tugged on the retractable key card attached to his lab coat. If Lawrence expected them to be productive in their current environment, he was going to be disappointed.

Lawrence's dark brows came together. "It's that bad?"

It was worse than bad. Jasper was working in hell. "I'm so busy managing tense relationships between the people we have left that I haven't opened my own notes in over a week. One of these days, the pressure cooker is going to explode."

Just that morning, two of his employees had nearly gone to blows over coffee mugs. *Coffee mugs!*

Rubbing his hand across his beard, Lawrence promised to see what he could do. Jasper left the office feeling more upbeat than he had since their conversation about the serum.

From the end of the hall, he saw his father muttering to himself over a stack of papers. The fluorescent lights reflected off his bald patch as he shook his head.

"I didn't realize you were coming home today," Jasper said to him. Normally his father's pro bono trips took at least a week.

"I didn't feel comfortable working elsewhere for free when it's obvious you need my help here." His father looked like he had aged a decade in the three days he'd been gone. "Why aren't you in the lab?"

Jasper followed him into his office and explained the meeting he'd had with Lawrence.

His father draped his coat over the back of his chair and dropped his briefcase on the desk. "If we don't show the board something promising soon, we could be in serious trouble."

"I know what's at stake, but working in makeshift prefabs without the proper equipment—"

"*Proper equipment?*" His father's eyes bulged, and his face turned an unhealthy shade of red. "We created the serum in the basement of a strip mall office with the help of three assistants. You and your lab full of employees should be able to do *something* of value without forcing us to haemorrhage more money."

Where was this coming from? Was the company really in that much trouble? "Where would you have me focus our limited resources?"

Dropping onto his chair, his father unloaded the files in

his briefcase. "I want you to identify ways to retroactively stimulate NG-1882."

Retroactive stimulation?

Jasper had been suggesting that very thing for the past two years. They knew how to deactivate the genes, and had been well on their way to discovering the correct balance of adrenaline and hormones required to activate young genes before most of their research was lost in the fire. But until now, they hadn't dealt with activating genes left dormant. "That's an entirely new direction."

"Is that a problem?" he barked.

Jasper shook his head. Eliza and Steve would be thrilled for the reprieve from their current assignments. His father grumbled something unintelligible that sounded like a dismissal and went back to sorting through his briefcase.

Jasper closed the door to the office behind him. When he turned around, he caught sight of one of his employees reading a motivational poster at the end of the hall. "What're you doing out of the lab, Steve?"

The new geneticist smiled and waved at him. He looked so young, with a mop of blond hair and a barely-there mustache. "Lauren and Betty have been bickering over the CRISPR-Chip since you left," Steve said with a friendly smile, "and it's driving me insane. So I took a walk."

Those two women were going to be the death of him. "How'd you get in this building? Did someone let you in?"

"No. I used this." Steve handed him a keycard from his lab coat pocket.

It looked like one of the restricted-level access cards. "Where'd you get this?" Jasper asked, turning the card over in his hand.

Steve shrugged. "It's the one the lady from HR gave me."

"I'll have to get you a new one." Jasper put the card into his own pocket. The only people who had those cards were himself, his brother , and his father. "You'll be happy to hear that I'm changing your assignment."

"Do I still have to work with Eliza?"

"I thought you liked working with her."

"I suppose she's the lesser of many evils," Steve said, scratching the back of his neck. "Man, this place is a lot bigger than it looks from the outside." He nodded toward the ominous padlock still in place on the door to the storage room. "What's in there?"

"Old research."

"Are they afraid the files are going to escape or something?"

Jasper frowned at a new CCTV camera aimed at the black door. "Looks like it."

"Weird." Steve shrugged and turned toward the exit.

"Very weird." The fact that Jasper, the CEO's brother, the Head of Research—a descendent of The Humanitarian Organization for Order and Knowledge's founder—wasn't allowed access to data that could prove vital in understanding their research made absolutely no sense . . . unless what was concealed within was more horrifying than what he had already uncovered.

FOURTY

"L et's go to your place," Deacon whispered, steering Vivienne toward the stairs.

The rest of the congregation was disappearing through the secret door Peter had opened at the back of the amphitheater.

"But everyone is going to The Wendy Bird." And Vivienne had been stuck in her apartment all week. She wanted to go out.

"That doesn't mean we have to join them."

She twisted out of his hold so she could scowl at him. "Are you embarrassed by me or something?"

"What?" His brows came together and he shook his head. "No. Of course not. How could you even say that?"

"Then why don't you want to bring me to the pub? Every time I suggest it, you give me some lame excuse. I want to celebrate with everyone." Peter had said that going to The Wendy Bird after Leadership meetings had become a tradition, and that going their separate ways afterwards allowed for resentment to settle.

"*Fine,*" Deacon grumbled. "I'll give you one hour. Then you're all mine."

Vivienne certainly wasn't going to argue with that.

The doorway led to a tunnel lit with bronze sconces. Eventually, they reached a pentagon-shaped room lined with more tunnels and doors. The walls extended upward into darkness, making it feel like they were at the bottom of a well. She could hear people talking and shuffling down one of the other tunnels, but the sound echoed, so she wasn't sure which one they had gone down. Deacon brought her to one to her right, and they followed it around corner after corner to a—

"What is that?" Someone had painted cherubic fairies dancing in a nightscape around a tiny house with a young girl locked inside.

"All the tunnels have some sort of mural," Deacon explained from behind her. "I think this one's Slightly's."

She had a hard time envisioning the irritable man painting anything, much less a masterpiece that belonged in a museum. "Why? It's not like anyone's ever going to see it."

"To distract intruders." Deacon pointed to a blinking red light in the ceiling. "Gives the security team a chance to catch up."

A beautiful distraction.

They continued until they came to a set of stone stairs, worn smooth and dipping in the middle. Ahead, she heard a door slam shut. When she tried to move forward, Deacon's grip tightened.

"Just so you know, there's a blind spot right"—he shifted so that her back pressed against the wall—"*here.*"

"Isn't that convenient?" She yanked him by the collar until his body was firm against hers and kissed him.

Deacon gripped her hips, lifting her so that her legs could

clamp around his waist. Her skirt slipped up her thighs as his hands made their way beneath. His tongue grew more insistent, stealing her breath and her heart, and the way his hips ground against her made her adrenaline zing and pulse skyrocket and—

"How would you feel about being late to the party?" he murmured against her neck.

"Someone might see us."

"I already told you, there's a blind—"

The slam of a door echoed through the hollow hallway, dousing the fire within her.

"*Dammit.* One hour," Deacon said after giving her a hard kiss. "That's it."

She nodded, trying to catch her breath. "Make it forty-five minutes."

"You drive me mad. You know that, right?" he said with a laugh, setting her down and adjusting his jeans.

"Yeah, well, I don't exactly feel sane around you either," Vivienne giggled, smoothing her skirt back in place. But she figured that was love. Heat and fire and insanity.

The entrance to the tunnel looked like an abandoned wooden shack. Gnarled branches bent over the roof like something out of a nightmare. A worn dirt path led to a whitewashed pub with a thatched roof and a sky-blue door.

Inside, the paneling on the walls was painted the same color as Wendy's dress in the cartoon Vivienne had loved as a kid. A carved wooden sign hanging above the shelves of liquor had been cut into the shape of a girl flying with outstretched arms.

"Here." Ethan appeared beside them, shoving two pints of amber liquid into their hands. "You're gonna need these."

Vivienne wasn't sure what that meant, but she thanked him and took a sip. Whatever was inside smelled like applesauce that had gone off, but it tasted amazing.

369

"It's cider," Deacon told her after taking a drink from his own glass.

Cider. Vivienne liked it. Really liked it.

"Aoibheann is circling like a shark," Ethan said, nodding his chin toward Deacon, "and I'm pretty sure Gwen is looking for you too."

Deacon muttered and drank . . . and drank . . . and drank. When he put his glass down, it was nearly empty. "Wanna hide in the corner and make out?" he murmured against her neck before pointing to a chair beside a stone fireplace.

"Sounds good to me. I'm not letting your exes ruin my night."

"It's not just *his* exes," Ethan told her with a smirk. "Alex is looking for you too."

Deacon cursed. "I knew we should have gone straight home."

Vivienne told him not to be such a coward even as her own stomach sank.

"Don't worry, I'll run interference," Ethan promised, grabbing his own pint and following them to a couch across from the fireplace.

Deacon threw himself onto the chair and pulled her onto his lap, then buried his face in her neck, his hands trailing up her knees to the hem of her—

"Deacon!" she squirmed and swatted his hand away.

"What?" His crooked grin oozed false innocence.

"People can see us." No one seemed to be paying them any attention, but still.

"*And?*"

"And I don't feel comfortable with your mom or your grandfather watching you feel me up in the middle of a freaking bar."

"Can I feel you up when we get back to your flat in"—he checked his watch—"thirty-six minutes?"

"I guess so."

"Actually, it's thirty-five minutes."

"Are you going to count down the whole time?"

"Thirty-four and a half . . . "

He was ridiculous, but she loved him anyway.

From the corner of her eye, Vivienne saw Aoibheann searching the crowd. At the other end of the bar, Gwen waited by a door marked STORAGE, talking to the guy who had been sitting next to Deacon at the meeting.

And Nicola was coming toward them carrying a tray of shots. "Celebratory drinks, anyone?" She sat next to Ethan and offered one to him as well. His mouth pressed into a thin line, but he took it and knocked it back.

It was the same nasty licorice stuff from earlier. Vivienne choked it down, and Deacon cursed when he finished his.

The PAN were all drinking and laughing—even Lee Somerfield and Slightly seemed to be engaging in a civil conversation at the bar. Peter was sitting on the edge of a chair, staring at a soccer game on the television, shouting and cursing every so often with Nibs and Curly hunched over their pints beside him.

Vivienne studied the static hands on a sunburst-shaped clock hanging behind Peter. Frozen in time, like Vivienne and the rest of the patrons in the bar.

"Are you *sooo* glad we came tonight?" Deacon whined, gathering her hair and moving it aside so he could brush his lips across her pulse. "Drinking here is *sooo* much better than anything we could be doing without an audience."

"Shut up, you big baby. I'm having fun."

"You know what else would be fun?" Deacon said, leaning closer and suggesting something that made her face burn and definitely sounded a lot more fun than being in a room full of people.

By the time Vivienne finished her drink, Deacon had her heart racing with his scandalous whispers, and she desperately had to pee.

"I'll be right back," she announced, standing and steadying herself against the back of the chair.

"You're leaving me on my own?" Deacon asked, looking genuinely worried.

Ethan snorted and buried his laugh inside his glass.

"You're the idiot who thought it was a good idea to sleep with half of Neverland," Vivienne laughed, locating the bathroom across the bar. Nicola stood and followed her.

"Well done, baby bird. You've managed to convince Dash to make a commitment."

Vivienne turned to find Aoibheann glaring at her, a glass of wine in her hand. "Oh, *heeey*, Aoibheann." She gave the stiff Mermaid a hug and managed to keep a straight face when she pulled away. "*So* good to see you again."

Aoibheann's mouth gaped open, and her eyes widened. "W-what?"

"Sorry, I *really* have to pee. But we can totally continue this after I'm done in the bathroom. *Byeee.*"

"What the hell was that?" Nicola asked when they got to the door.

Vivienne shrugged. "I've decided to kill everyone with kindness tonight." It seemed like a better alternative to slapping members of Leadership.

"You have more restraint than I would," Nicola muttered, disappearing into one of the three stalls.

When Vivienne was finished, she met Nicola by the sink. The soap smelled like roses, and the water in the faucet was like ice.

"I never told you congratulations on your engagement," Nicola said, glancing at Vivienne as she washed her hands.

"Yeah, I noticed."

"I'm really happy for you two."

"*Really?*" Nicola's pinched expression certainly didn't look very happy. "Because at the beach, you said there were other guys out there."

"I know what I said. Dash has always been up-front about the casual nature of his relationships so that girls know what to expect—or *not* to expect—from him. I thought you were taking things too seriously. You wouldn't be the first." A sigh. "Turns out, I was wrong."

"If you're happy for us, then why do you look so sad?"

"Not everything is about you," Nicola grumbled, rolling her eyes. "Ethan and I broke up the same night you and Dash got engaged."

"*What?*"

"Don't tell anyone, okay? We were waiting until all this shit was over to let people know."

Vivienne nodded and followed her out of the bathroom. Nicola and Ethan had broken up? They had seemed so happy together on the island. Had something happened?

Before she could ask, Deacon appeared, his arms crossed and eyes narrowed. "We need to talk."

Her stomach dropped. "Why? What's wrong?"

Lacing his fingers with hers, Deacon tugged Vivienne toward the exit. She hurried along behind him, confused and worried and—why were they going toward the tunnels?

"Deacon? Is everything okay?"

"You've had your hour." His grin flashed in the darkness. "Now I get mine."

Vivienne's apartment felt as cold as the tunnels, and she slipped her hands beneath Deacon's shirt to warm them up.

"Your hands are bloody freezing!" he hissed. Goosebumps rose over his skin, and the muscles in his stomach tightened, but he didn't try to escape her frigid fingers.

"It doesn't help that the stupid heating is still broken."

"I can think of a good heater that'll have you warmed up in no time," he said with a wink.

"Was that supposed to be a pickup line?"

"Everything I say to you is meant to be a pickup line."

"In that case," Vivienne giggled into his neck, peeling off his waistcoat, "I'd kill for a working heater." Shivering, she popped the button on his jeans. "Does it take long to warm up?"

He removed her top with a single jerk. "Depends on how cold you are."

"S-so cold."

"Then I'd better hurry up." He caught her by the waist and hauled her to the bedroom.

She shimmied out of her skirt and tossed it onto the floor. "I'm *f-freeeezing*."

Struggling with the buttons on his shirt, he cursed when he got halfway down and pulled it over his head. She threw herself into his unsuspecting arms, sending him bobbling backward into the armoire.

There was a sharp, shattering crash, and the scent of lilacs wafted from the floor.

Deacon swore and told her not to move before carrying her to the bed and flicking on the lamp. When he pulled off his socks, there were cuts oozing on the bottom of his feet. "There's broken glass everywhere. I don't know what broke, but—"

"It was my mother's perfume." She forced back the tears welling in her eyes. It was just perfume.

"Shit, Vivienne. I'm so sorry." Deacon stooped and swept rainbow shards into his palm. "I didn't mean to break it."

"It's my fault. I pushed you."

"Do you have something to put this in?" The wet, fragrant glass sparkled in his palm.

"In the kitchen. I'll go—"

"Stay put. I don't want you cutting yourself." He disappeared, only to return a moment later with a broom and a dustpan. The muscles in his back stretched taut as he reached for more glass, and his unbuttoned jeans slipped lower, and every bit of Vivienne's concern for her mother's perfume vanished.

When he stood and asked if she had a hoover, she pulled him onto the bed with her. "You're sexy when you clean up."

"Is that so?" He slipped one of her bra straps off her shoulder and replaced it with his mouth. "I wash dishes as well," he murmured against her burning skin.

"But do you do laundry?"

The other strap met the same fate as the first. "I wash, dry, *and* iron."

Who knew cleaning could sound so sexy? "I love—"

Light from the lamp reflected off something beneath the armoire.

"What is it?" Deacon pulled back onto his haunches. "What's wrong?"

"*Move.*" She pushed him off her and escaped to the edge of the room. Behind her, Deacon collapsed onto the duvet with a groan.

As she kneeled on the damp floorboards, a shard of glass sliced her knee. She pulled it out and stuck her hand beneath the armoire, but her arms were too short to reach the object at the back.

"I'm *really* enjoying the view," Deacon drawled from the bed, "but would you mind telling me what you're doing?"

"Get over here and help me move this thing."

He rolled off the mattress and gingerly stepped closer. With one jerk, the armoire came away from the wall. She skirted around him and picked up a glass vial, still damp with lilac perfume. When she stood and held it to the light, the yellow liquid inside sloshed from one side to the other.

"Is that what I think it is?" Deacon whispered.

Vivienne's entire body ignited when her gaze locked with Deacon's. "It's HOOK's poison."

ACKNOWLEDGMENTS

The first people I'd like to thank are the readers across the globe whose support and love for The PAN has been nothing short of overwhelming. I feel like your love for these characters rivals my own, and getting to share them with you for another book has been a dream come true.

The only way I've been able to finish this book is because I married the most supportive man in the world. Jimmy, all those hours I spent holed up in the office, hunched over "my precious" wouldn't have been possible without you.

Colin and Lilly, you are my greatest joy and my greatest accomplishment.

Mom, I apologize in advance for the "racy" nature of this book. But, let's be honest, you did introduce me to romance novels. I love you. You're the strongest woman I know.

Dad, I'm looking up and moving forward.

My sister Dani has encouraged me to keep my momentum throughout this process. And without my sister Megan constantly bugging me for more "stuff" to read, I wouldn't have hit this deadline.

To my in-laws, Phyllis and Shay: thanks for all your support and for helping out with the kids.

To Mila, who designed yet another stunning cover. You were on-point with this vision, and the result is brilliant.

To Elle and all my fellow Midnight Tide authors: thank you for being a perfect home for this story and such an amazing support system. And Candace, thank you for being my go-to in this author journey.

And finally, to my editor Meg Dailey. Working with you has been a delight. Will we do it again for book 3?

ABOUT THE AUTHOR

 Jenny grew up in Oakland, Maryland and currently lives in County Tipperary, Ireland with her lilting husband and two tyrannical children. Her love of reading blossomed the summer after graduating high school, when she borrowed a paperback romance from her mother during the annual family beach vacation.

You can find Jenny across social media @authorjenny-hickman or follow her author journey via her newsletter at www.jennyhickman.com

ALSO BY JENNY

The PAN Trilogy
The P.A.N.
The H.O.O.K.

MORE BOOKS YOU'LL LOVE

If you enjoyed this story, please consider leaving a review!
Then check out more books from Midnight Tide
Publishing!

Music & Mirrors by Candace Robinson

Before Ridley became the Mirror Keeper, he was just a guy in love who'd had a tough life before meeting Leni. Through Leni, he thought he'd found a way to truly live in the music they loved. But in the Mirror Dimension, everything can easily be broken—even their bond.

Leni has been haunted by shadows her whole life. She had kept the burden a secret from everyone—except for Ridley and her brother—and turned to music as a distraction. But those shadows are what led her to become the Piper, whether she wanted it or not. The only reason she continued on her destructive path is the secret she must protect at all costs.

Now back in the Mirror Dimension, Ridley and Leni must face punishment by the royals in charge of the curse. Music alone won't be enough to help them this time. In order for Ridley and Leni to save themselves, they must seek help from the two people they almost killed. If they can't band together to defeat the royals, Leni will end up dead and Ridley will become something he truly hates.

Available
3.17.21

Magic Mutant Nightmare Girl by Erin Grammar

Holly Roads uses Harajuku fashion to distract herself from tragedy. Her magical girl aesthetic makes her feel beautiful-and it keeps the world at arm's length. She's an island of one, until advice from an amateur psychic expands her universe. A midnight detour ends with her vs. exploding mutants in the heart of San Francisco.

Brush with destiny? Check. Waking up with blue blood, emotions gone haywire, and terrifying strength that starts ripping her wardrobe to shreds? Totally not cute. Hunting monsters with a hot new partner and his unlikely family of mad scientists?

Way more than she bargained for.

Available
3.10.21